PROXY WAR

AEGIS
BOOK 1

S.W. MICHAELS

Copyright © 2025 S.W. Michaels

SWMichaels.com

Cover Design © Josh Smith

JoshSmithCreative.com

All rights reserved.

ISBN: 978-1-958800-17-1 (Paperback)

ISBN: 978-1-958800-18-8 (eBook)

This book or parts thereof may not be reproduced in any form, stored in any retrieval system, or transmitted in any form by any means—electronic, mechanical, photocopy, recording, or otherwise—without prior written permission of the publisher, except as provided by United States of America copyright law.

This is a work of fiction. Any references to historical events, real people, or real places are used fictitiously. Other names, characters, places and events are products of the author's imagination, and any resemblances to actual events or places or persons, living or dead, is entirely coincidental.

CONTENTS

Welcome to Proxy War — v

1. The Gift — 1
2. Bloodied Knuckles and Keyboards — 6
3. The Hydra's Den — 23
4. Bits, Bytes and Betrayal — 30
5. Jasmine and Gunpowder — 47
6. A Family Affair — 52
7. Blockchain and Sinker — 75
8. Legacy Code — 85
9. The Unreliable Narrator — 103
10. Down the Rabbit Hole — 108
11. Buried Truths — 132
12. Digital Crossroads — 138
13. Bureau 121 — 156
14. Red Star Rising — 163
15. Out of Place — 175
16. Trojan Tactics — 180
17. Raspbian Riddle — 189
18. When the Bell Tolls — 193
19. Kernel Panic — 202
20. Black Box — 210
21. Singing Bluebird — 217
22. Overflow — 247
23. Need-to-Know Basis — 263
24. Secrets in the Pi — 279
25. Trust Fall — 284
26. Social Engineering — 301
27. Seoul Searching — 305
28. Crossing the Threshold — 322
29. A Deadly Vow — 330

30.	Machinations of a Madman	340
31.	Paranoia Pursued	343
32.	Cornered	348
33.	Desperate Measures	350
34.	Contingencies and Consequences	361
35.	The Bleeding Edge	365
36.	The Best Laid Plans	374
37.	The Art of Deception	378
38.	The Twisted Mirror	383
39.	Wayfaring Stranger	388
40.	The Awakening	392
	Epilogue	401
	Author's Note	404
	Thank you for reading!	407
	Also by S.W. Michaels	408
	About the Author	409
	Acknowledgments	411

WELCOME TO PROXY WAR

Thank you for diving into this thrilling tale!

Intrigued by the intersection of technology and humanity, from cyber warfare to AI and the dark recesses of the human psyche? Subscribe to my newsletter for exclusive access to techno-thrillers, psychological suspense, **free short stories**, and the latest in cutting-edge innovation. Let's explore the complexities of our digital age and unravel the mysteries of human mind.

swmichaels.com/subscribe

Books by S.W. Michaels

The Aegis Series
Proxy War (This book)
Prompt Execution

More coming soon...

1 / THE GIFT
CIPHER

The knife wavered in Cipher's hand, a rare flicker of emotion betraying his steely facade. The dimly lit Las Vegas hotel room closed in around him, a stark contrast to the garish city lights below. Before him sat a fellow trade show attendee, bound to a chair, eyes wide with terror, mouth gagged to stifle his desperate pleas.

This wasn't part of the plan. The virus should have remained hidden, buried within thousands of flashy URLs, poised to spread like wildfire across the globe. But this man—this insignificant, curious nobody—had unwittingly stumbled upon the truth.

Earlier that week, during their initial tests, Cipher's team had compromised the man's machine. It was a routine infection, one of many intended to lay the groundwork for the larger attack. The man, however, was more observant than most. He'd noticed subtle changes in the behavior of his device, sparking a curiosity that would prove fatal.

Hours ago, on the trade show floor, he'd witnessed Cipher's team discreetly replacing URLs at various booths. To most, it would have seemed innocuous; perhaps just last-minute updates to marketing materials. But for this man, it was the missing piece of a puzzle he'd been unconsciously assembling all week.

In that split second, Cipher had seen the shift in the man's eyes—first realization, then fear. He'd watched as panic set in, the man's gaze darting between Cipher's team and his own compromised device. He'd figured out how the virus was being released. And that meant he had to be silenced.

Cipher leaned in, the blade hovering inches from the man's throat. Beads of sweat formed on his captive's brow, his heart pounding audibly in the tense silence. There was no turning back. The mission demanded sacrifice, and Cipher had never shied away from necessity.

The Reconnaissance General Bureau had handpicked him for his unwavering loyalty and ability to operate unencumbered by conscience. North Korea's elite intelligence agency boasted many assets, but few matched his blend of technical prowess and moral flexibility. This virus, his *gift* to the world, was as much a test of his allegiance as a weapon against the West.

He pressed the blade against the man's skin, feeling the resistance before flesh yielded to steel. The man's eyes bulged in terror, muffled screams filling the room as blood seeped from the wound. Cipher watched dispassionately, his mind already calculating the next steps: The cleanup, the disposal.

Emotion had no place here. This was just another task to be completed, another obstacle to be removed.

As the life drained from the man's body, Cipher wiped the blade clean, his movements methodical, almost ritualistic. The room fell silent, save for the faint hum of the city outside. He stepped back, surveying his work.

The man slumped lifeless in the chair, his once-vibrant spark of realization now extinguished. Cipher felt nothing, no guilt, no remorse, only the cold satisfaction of a job well done.

Turning away, he pocketed the knife and retrieved his smartphone. With a few quick taps, he sent an encrypted message to the cleaners:

CIPHER

Package ready. Room 1309.

Satisfied with the immediate confirmation, he slipped the phone back into his pocket. Downstairs, the trade show buzzed with excitement, innovation, and excess, oblivious to the darkness unfolding mere floors above.

A quick glance at the time told him he only had a few minutes before he needed to rejoin the crowd below. His handlers would be waiting near the elevator in the lobby. The virus was already in motion, its impact imminent. With this task complete, there was no longer a rush. He'd silenced the one person who might have slowed them.

As he left the room, he wiped down the door handle, allowing himself a moment of reflection. This day had been fermenting for decades, since American forces brought neocolonialism to his home. To Bosnia.

The scent of soot still haunted him, a poignant reminder of his family home turned pyre. Inside, his parents had perished in the flames, sacrificed in the name of geopolitical maneuvering. He could still hear their screams; terror and agony piercing the night as special forces arrived after the artillery stopped.

Though he never saw an American flag or a NATO star, their movements betrayed them. Their precision and pristine weaponry pointed to one conclusion: Only a professional military could operate with such deadly efficiency.

The memory was seared into his mind, an indelible scar that would never fade. He recalled his mother's eyes widening in fear, how his father shielded them as soldiers stormed in, their weapons trained on helpless civilians. Smoke, heat, gunfire. It all blended together in a nightmarish cacophony which haunted his every waking moment.

The covert American war machine had used humanitarian aid and UN pawns to progress their agenda. They spent years erasing his people's culture, exploiting their economy, their resources, and supporting rebel groups in efforts to destabilize the region. All in the name of enforcing a global order that benefited the few at the expense of the many. It just so happened that the few were never from the Balkans, they were always from these United States of America.

As he stepped into the elevator, Cipher pushed the button for the lobby and stared at himself in the mirror. The face that gazed back was a mask of calm, belying the tempest of emotions churning beneath the surface.

In his reflection, he saw not just himself, but the ghosts of his past—his parents, his homeland, all the lives shattered by American imperialism. Their silent screams echoed in the confines of his mind, fueling a rage that burned hotter than the flames that had consumed his childhood home.

He adjusted his suit, his fingers brushing against the hidden pocket where his knife rested, a grim reminder of the lengths to which he would go to see his mission through. The weight of it anchored him to his purpose, each movement a silent vow to the memory of those he had lost.

This was no longer about personal vengeance; it had evolved into a crusade against a system that had robbed him of everything.

This was just the beginning. His *gift*, a digital plague born from the ashes of his past, would spread far beyond this gaudy city, far beyond US borders. The Reconnaissance General Bureau would see to that; their resources ensuring his vengeance would know no bounds.

And when the world finally grasped what had happened,

it would be too late. The systems they trusted, the institutions they believed in; they would all crumble, leaving only fear and uncertainty in their wake. In that chaos, Cipher would find his justice, and perhaps, finally, silence the echoes of his past.

2 / BLOODIED KNUCKLES AND KEYBOARDS
ALEX

A clenched fist sailed toward her head in a slow-motion arc, each moment stretched and magnified, as if time itself had paused.

Perfectly manicured fingers and sparkling jelly bracelets blurred together as the blonde girl's hand cracked against Alex's cheek, sending her reeling sideways in a sudden whirl of pain and surprise.

The cold, hard concrete rose upward, greeting her with a firm smack to the side of the head that resounded like a gong.

Ringing filled her ears, and pain exploded in her shoulder as the blonde twat pounced on top of her. The girl's hands closed in an iron-like grip around Alex's neck.

Her tiny trembling fingers squeezed tight as blood dripped from her nose. Alex could still hear the crunch of her backpack smashing into the girl's face, flattening her nose only moments earlier. The full water bottle at the bottom made the perfect weapon.

She should've anticipated this response, but no words had been spoken since she silenced the ethnic jeers of the two girls, one blonde and one redhead—or at least, that's how she thought of them.

With the first cheerleader down, her assault continued with a kick to the gut of the redhead, followed by a physics book against the cow's face.

The equal but opposite reaction of the girl tumbling down for the count would've made even Sir Isaac Newton proud. She never got up after that.

The thought of the rain cascading down on the motionless redhead made her smile, even as the blonde witch squeezed her throat, dripping blood all over Alex's face.

With one hand pushing upward against her attacker, Alex reached out with the other, sliding it along the edge of the damp sidewalk, searching for something, anything that could help.

And then she found it, buried in the grass.

The blare of a horn ripped her out of the memory, yanking her back to the cold, wet present—a yellow cab swerved around her, spraying filthy brown water over her already grubby jeans.

She gasped, staring down at the puddle and chunks of what she hoped was road debris clinging to her legs. That was the second time in the last hour that her life had flashed before her eyes.

The fight lingered in her thoughts as she clenched her bloody fingers and winced. They still stung from hitting that racist cheerleader bitch.

Swallowing down a mouthful of blood, she replayed the events of the past hour, or at least the story she planned to tell her parents.

The last thing they wanted to hear was how she'd gotten into another fight. Good girls didn't use fists. They ignored naysayers and problems, like her taekwondo sessions had drilled into her.

What her dojo neglected to teach her, however, was how deep bullying stung. Challenging someone's identity without understanding their situation didn't sit well with even the most rigid follower of nonviolence, especially when they attacked the ones she loved.

As the faint glow of her building came into view through the mist, her heart rate quickened. Lying had never come easy for her. It wasn't in her nature. She always preferred brutal honesty to sugarcoated bullshit.

Maybe it stemmed from her days as an orphan, or the simple fact that she'd finally found a family to take her in. She'd been with the Mercers for as long as she could remember, though anything before the age of eight was hazy. Everything except for her first adoptive family —those she recalled vividly. She just never told anyone about them.

Her mom blamed the orphanage for her memory gaps, but Alex wasn't so sure. Sister Gene's smiling face remained a persistent comfort from those early days. Picturing it still brought her solace, even today.

Ever since the Mercers had taken her in, they'd treated her as their own. She called them Eomma and Appa almost instantly, and unlike her neighbor friends, she never sassed her parents.

People thought she behaved out of fear of being sent back to the nuns, but she knew better. The Mercers were good people. She didn't behave out of fear; she did it out of respect.

Well, maybe a little fear. Sister Gene would often take her dessert if she got lippy. It was amazing what you could make a kid do by taking away their pudding a few times.

About the only way you could tell she wasn't the Mercers' biological child was that they were both Asian, and she wasn't. In fact, they'd even changed their name from Myung when they immigrated, hoping to help their future children fit into American life. Not that it mattered to Alex—she already looked like she'd fallen off a tractor in rural Idaho.

Blonde hair, mismatched eyes, and ruddy cheeks that

blazed crimson whenever she lied. That, and when she'd been crying—whether from sadness or, like today, when the tears came out while she was kicking people's asses.

She paused at the bottom of the rusty stairwell leading to the second floor. She bent over, brushing at her jeans. A bit of mud flaked off, but plenty clung stubbornly. Even worse, it reeked. Either that, or someone had spilled something on the stairs.

Her faded blue jeans hadn't seen a proper wash in what felt like ages. With the building's laundry machines out of commission and her parents juggling two jobs, it fell to her to lug their baskets of dirty clothes ten blocks to the laundromat.

But not today. They were out of detergent, and she'd been too preoccupied with planning her future to worry about laundry.

Not that anyone in her house would have noticed.

When she stood up straight, she caught the faint hint of two voices screaming from the second floor. It was like hearing the crack of distant thunder over the rush of water in the nearby downspout. The voice with the harsh edge was unmistakably her mother's.

The woman could shatter glass and peel paint when her anger reached a crescendo. And judging from the feud revving up in apartment twenty-three, Alex was walking into quite a storm. There was still hope she could slip past undetected.

"I have homework," she muttered. That should be enough. Studies were always important, especially to her parents.

Uttering the words, her voice croaked, and saying them aloud hurt. She cringed as she rubbed her throat, pulling her collar higher to hide the shadowy remnants of Leslie's fingers. The sensation of being choked still lingered on her skin, taunting her.

Leslie had been on top of her long enough for the edges of

Alex's vision to blur. She'd frantically clawed at the grass until her fingertips brushed against something buried within. If she hadn't dug that rock out of the tiny patch of turf, there's no telling if she would have survived.

Why do people have so much hate in their hearts?

She asked herself that question all the time. Far too often for someone her age. At least that's what her AP English teacher told her after she read her admissions essay a few weeks earlier.

While the teacher hadn't made her read it aloud in front of the class like everyone else, she still had Alex read it to the other teachers.

The words had come out softly at first, but as she progressed through the paper, they grew in strength and conviction. By the last passage, her voice had risen to a crescendo, her final words practically a scream.

But now, at the foot of the stairs, she merely whispered to herself.

"Hate exists not as a permanent scar upon the heart, but as a challenge, a call to action for each of us. It is an invitation to embark on the most noble of journeys: To reach out with an open heart, to listen with a compassionate ear, and to build, with the bricks of our shared humanity, a world where love triumphs over hate, understanding overcomes fear, and unity replaces division. This is the path to a brighter, kinder future —a world not of hate, but of hope."

Alex took a deep breath and exhaled, her heart still pounding against her ribcage. But not because of her tussle with the cheer captains. This was something more profound.

As she'd given that speech to the teachers, a sense of clarity had washed over her. She'd realized her life's purpose. It began with escaping Fremont. California was the last place on the planet she wanted to be, but more than that, she yearned for a fresh start. To change the world. To leave her mark.

And if that meant bashing some bullying heads and scalping a few bleach blonde bimbos for hurling ethnic slurs at her parents, well, then she'd do it a million times over. While some might call her actions a form of hate, she saw them as a necessary stand for justice.

In her mind, her acts were not of aggression, but of protection; a way to shield not just her family, but the very values she held dear. She was fighting against the hatred that sought to divide, using her strength to uphold respect and dignity for all, regardless of background.

To her, this was more than retaliation; it was a commitment to the ideals of empathy and unity, a personal battle against the forces of ignorance and intolerance.

"Aren't you going up, Lexy dear?" Mrs. Myeong gently brushed her arm, pulling her out of her reverie. She hadn't even heard the fragile old lady shuffle up beside her. But that wasn't unusual given her slow pace and the hum of the rain growing louder by the second.

"I... just wanted to..." Alex's gaze drifted upward as her mom's voice crashed through the pause like a thunderbolt, louder than ever before.

She cringed at the verbal assault playing out above, her mind surfacing memories long ago suppressed. A past she dared not relive.

"Why don't you come in for some cookies?" Mrs. Myeong shuffled toward her unit a few feet away, drawing Alex's attention.

She shook her head and bowed slightly. "Thank you, Mrs. Myeong. Maybe next time. I have homework to do."

The old lady bobbed her head and slowly slid her key in the lock, glancing back. "Be sure to put a cold compress on that neck." Her eyes lingered on Alex's collar. "I usually find that wrapping frozen peas in paper towel works best. It'll decrease the blood flow and should help reduce the bruising too. Plus, it just feels good." She winked and disappeared through the doorway.

Alex inhaled sharply, reaching up to tug her jacket higher, ensuring the zipper was fully closed.

How had Mrs. Myeong even noticed? My chair reached my shoulders? Either she'd watched her cover it up, or somehow, she'd seen her down the road. Near the alley.

Alex had lingered in the dark corridor behind the building longer than prudence dictated, but she had to be certain she'd left no traces.

Wiping the photographic evidence from the girls' phones had been child's play, especially since they were too stupid to set passwords. She never figured out why the girls were filming her while hurling racial insults on camera. But she didn't care. They'd paid for their actions.

While deleting the incriminating material should've been enough to send a message, she had an ace up her sleeve. Before erasing the video, she'd forwarded it to her burner email. That would be her ultimate leverage. If it ever got out, the press and the teachers at school would have a field day with it, particularly the Asian ones.

But she wasn't done. She planned to forward the audio track to the girls later. It would be the icing on the cake. Once they realized they couldn't point the finger at her without implicating themselves, they'd be pissing their pants.

"Mrs. Myeong?" Alex quickly stepped toward the closing door, lowering her gaze respectfully. "You didn't... by any chance—"

"See anything," Mrs. Myeong interrupted, flicking on her lights and casting a glow into the darkened hall. The aroma of ginger and garlic wafted out, enveloping Alex in the warm, comforting embrace of a home-cooked meal. "I didn't see nuthin but courage. But if your mom asks"—she started into her apartment—"just tell her you got elbowed in class or something like that. You kids still play basketball at school, don't you?"

The old lady's gaze flitted between Alex's mismatched eyes —one blue, one green. Despite knowing her neighbor well, Alex couldn't help but feel self-conscious. That genetic quirk had been fodder for teasing her entire life.

She swallowed hard, shrugging off the discomfort. "We... haven't started basketball yet this term."

Mrs. Myeong shrugged. "Well, as I see it, your mom won't know any better than I do. Besides, from where I was standing, you made one hell of a slam dunk. Or maybe I should call it a swing dunk?" She smirked and turned, closing her door slowly.

"Have a good evening," Alex said, tipping her head as she watched the door click shut.

"Basketball," she muttered, turning toward the stairs with newfound energy. "Why didn't I think of that?"

When she finally reached the top of the stairs, she paused, every muscle in her body screaming in agony. She fought hard to hold back tears, and while she did, one thing became clear: Tomorrow was going to be a painful day.

After catching her breath, she started toward her apartment. The shouting had ceased for the past few minutes, but that didn't mean her parents were done.

Far from it.

They could hurl verbal barbs for hours. While they never resorted to physical violence like her first family, their words could cut just as deep.

The few friends she had often joked that her real parents must've been lawyers. It was the only explanation, they'd say, for her quick wit and perfectly timed snarky comments. But Alex knew better. She'd learned it from her adoptive parents. When they got going, they were relentless.

As she approached her door, she reached out to turn the

knob and froze. Faint hints of weeping drifted through the door, muffled cries echoing in the now silent hallway. The sound made the hair on her arms stand on end.

Alex knew her parents' pattern well. Their verbal sparring matches often ended by crying and hugging it out. It was their marital dance, a vocal waltz of emotions and frustration that somehow helped them navigate the hard times.

And lately, those times had grown more frequent. Making ends meet had become a Herculean task the past few months, especially since her father leased a shiny sedan for his new gig job driving people around town.

Her dad always preached that physical violence was for the weak of mind and heart. But the stifled sobs seeping through the door gave Alex pause. Something about them sounded different this time. Familiar, yet ominous, as if hinting at a more sinister turn of events.

She couldn't shake the feeling that the mood in the apartment was dire. A nagging fear crept up her spine. *Had my father finally snapped?*

Maybe it was her own recent bout of rage coloring her perception, but Alex's skin crawled as she eased the door open, cautiously peeking inside.

The room's atmosphere hit her immediately. A tense, unsettling scent hung in the air. Not unpleasant, but noticeably off-kilter. As if the very molecules had absorbed the bitterness of the argument, leaving behind a faint, electric trace of stress and raw emotion.

Her gaze fell on her mom. She was lying on the far couch, still in her maid's uniform from her second job at the nearby hotel.

From the looks of it, she'd collapsed into a limp pile after coming home from work. She was whimpering softly, blotting her eyes with tissues. Her jet-black hair, normally pristine in its bun, had come undone, stray strands veiling her face.

Had Alex not heard the earlier commotion, she might have assumed her mom was simply exhausted from a hard day's work.

What scared her was that she couldn't see her mom's eyes. It was almost like she was hiding them.

The feeling of fear wasn't new, but it was an emotion she'd never experienced under their roof before.

On the other side of the room, her father paced anxiously, weathered hands running through his thinning salt-and-pepper hair. His cheap shirt and slacks, a uniform of respectability on a budget, hung loosely on his frame. The clearance rack clothes were a necessity, a facade of success for his job as a driver.

In his tired eyes, Alex saw the weight of their struggles, the burden of providing for his family amid mounting financial challenges.

"Appa? Eomma? What's going on?" She eased into the living room, sliding off her shoes before gently closing the door.

Just before the latch clicked shut, she caught the blinds in the apartments across the way snap back into place.

Nosy ass neighbors needed to mind their own business.

Turning around, she realized the room was barely lit, which wasn't all bad considering her wounds. She swept her bangs over her right eye, hoping it would help divert attention elsewhere. But she had to force herself not to wince at the sudden motion.

"Lex!" Dad spun toward her, his back to her mother. "You need to go to your room." He gestured toward the hallway.

She swallowed hard, fear rising in her chest. The words of her paper echoing in her mind.

She wouldn't let panic take over. Not today. Even if it meant standing up for her mom.

"No," she muttered, tossing her bag down beside the end table.

"Excuse me, young lady." Dad recoiled, scowling, spittle on his lip. "You heard me. Go. To. Your. Room!" His arm shot to the side again.

"No." She slid quickly toward her mom and knelt down. "Not until I check on Eomma."

With her father to her right, his gaze locked on hers, she glanced sideways at her mother. She couldn't see any bruises on her face, and if anything, her mom seemed as shocked by her actions as her father.

"Please, Lex. Just do as you're told." Mom's voice was hoarser than usual. She tried to clear her throat, only to lean forward, hands clutching her head as she swayed in place.

Alex reached out to steady her.

"I'm... fine," she snipped, knocking her hand away.

Ever since starting new anti-dementia meds, her mom had been having regular bouts of dizziness. They'd even occurred at work, but fortunately, nothing bad had happened. Not yet, anyway.

"Listen..." Mom glanced at Alex's neck and went to reach out, but Dad stepped closer.

"Please, Lexy." He gently rested his hand on her shoulder, making her flinch. "I'm not hurting your mother. You know I wouldn't do that. We're just... talking."

"That's an understatement," Alex whispered. "The entire neighborhood could hear you."

Mom snapped her finger. "Don't sass your father. He may be a screwup, but he's still your dad."

She lowered her head. "I'm sor—"

"What the hell does that mean?" Dad interrupted, his voice shifting from comforting to a scream in a split second.

Alex was about to get up when Mom snipped back. "Well, maybe if you stopped browsing pornography, we wouldn't have to move out."

He raised his hands and growled. "I told you I wasn't browsing porn! I haven't done that in—"

"Is she kidding?" Alex shot upright, glancing between them. "Why would we have to move? What the heck happened?"

"I..." He spun around, heading toward the kitchen. "This is between me and your mother. Why don't you—"

"Tell her!" Mom snapped, her sharp tone catching Alex off guard and igniting a flicker of fear. "She's affected by this, too."

Alex glared at her dad and crossed her arms. She couldn't imagine what he'd done to get them evicted. Even if Mr. Andrews was a scraggly old sod, it wasn't like him to kick someone out without cause.

Her father's back was to her, and she half expected him to turn around and scream. Instead, he collapsed into the wobbly chair at the kitchen table, its cheap plastic creaking eerily in the tense silence.

He sniffled, wiped his face with his shirt, then cracked open the lid of their chunky old laptop. "Fine! Take a look if you must. While you're at it, you can humiliate me like your mother does. She's got plenty of insults, you probably do too."

"Come on, Appa." She slowly stepped into the kitchen and took the chair opposite him, spinning the laptop toward her.

It was a Dell, an '04 model. He'd picked it up cheap from an estate sale a few years back. She was amazed it still worked.

Her father only used it for banking and reading news from back home in South Korea. She'd installed all the latest antivirus software on it, but keeping up with updates was like trying to catch rain in a sieve; they were endless.

She tried to unlock the machine with the usual Control+Alt+Delete key sequence, but instead of seeing Windows, a frightening message appeared:

Homeland Security - *National Cyber Security Division*: THIS COMPUTER HAS BEEN LOCKED. THE WORK OF YOUR COMPUTER HAS BEEN SUSPENDED ON THE GROUNDS OF THE VIOLATION OF THE LAW OF THE UNITED STATES OF AMERICA.

It went on to list some official-looking charges:

Article 184. Pornography Involving children. Imprisonment for the term of up to 10-15 years.

Article 171. Copyright. Imprisonment for the term of up to 2-5 years.

Article 113. The use of unlicensed software. Imprisonment for the term of up to 2 years.

Stranger still was the message at the bottom:

To unlock the computer you are obliged to pay a fine of $200. You must pay the fine through MoneyPak.

"Why would they ask for money?" she muttered to herself.

Her father mistook her question as directed at him. "I don't know. I just did what it asked me to do. The last thing we need is the government threatening to deport us."

"You didn't?!" Her gaze shot up, locking on his. She'd told him countless times never to give away his bank information online. Never.

She glanced at the screen, then back at him. "How many times did you do it?"

"I... I don't know." He ran his fingers through his hair. "Three... four, maybe. It kept coming up, so I kept paying!"

"No, Dad! No!" She leaned forward, hiding her face in her hands. This wasn't happening.

"See!" Mom reached over her shoulder, pointing at the screen. "It says it right there. I knew it. Pornography! And children of all things!" She stepped backward, covering her mouth with her hand. "Oh, Jin-woo. Tell me it isn't so."

Dad shot to his feet. "Damn it, woman! I told you the truth! I didn't do nuthin. Just dialed up that modem thingy like Lexy showed us, checked my email to see if there were any clients waiting, and when I clicked on a message, BAM! Up pops this."

"Wait!" Alex squinted at the official-looking government images. There was no back button, and he didn't appear to be in a browser. "You opened an attachment? I told you never to—"

"No!" Dad shook his hands violently, then noticed her recoil in her chair.

Instead of screaming, he calmed himself and slid down onto his seat, resting his palms flat on the table. "I just clicked a link from Chad, my dispatcher at the limo service. The screen flashed a few times and—"

"Wait," Mom cut in. "I thought you said you were driving for Uber today?"

"I... did." He bit his lip, holding back a bellow. "But as

usual, you never listen." His gaze snapped to her mom, eyes blazing. "Like I told you already, their software was on the fritz again. And rather than sit around and wait, I came home to check if Chad had anything for me. Maybe a few airport runs or something. If I could access email from the car, I would've. A few more rides and I could've bought a newer phone."

Alex sighed. She needed to separate them if she was going to make progress on this.

"Eomma," she began, standing and facing her mom. Her mother's eyes were a turbulent mix of outrage and sadness, as if she couldn't trust her husband. As far as Alex knew, he hadn't given her reason not to, but anger was clouding any hope for rational discourse. "Why don't you go take a shower? You had a long day, and you're probably tired. I'll talk to Appa, see if I can help fix this." As she gently touched Mom's arm, her gaze snapped from Dad to her Mom. "Please."

Her mother closed her eyes and took a deep breath. "Fine," she exhaled, her body visibly surrendering.

"Thank you." Alex bowed as her mom left the room, making her way into the tiny bathroom they all shared. "I'll put some tea on!"

"Chamomile, please!" Mom called out.

"Absolutely," Alex replied, turning back to the laptop. "Appa, would you start the water? I need to look at this thing."

Dad didn't argue, he simply pushed up and headed to the counter. "Do you think you can do anything? Can you get our money back?"

"Not likely," she whispered. Their rent money was probably halfway around the world by now.

She held the power button down, waiting for the familiar hard beep signaling the device was rebooting.

When the Windows screen flashed up, she repeated the sequence twice more until Windows Recovery mode appeared. After finding the restart into safe mode option, a few minutes later she had a neutered version of Windows with simple networking support.

"How'd you get in?" Dad asked, stepping behind her.

She groaned. "I showed you how to reboot like this before. It's safe mode, Dad."

"I barely know how to use this thing as it is." He pointed at her hands. "What happened to your fingers? They're all... scratched up. Wait," he leaned forward, "is that blood?"

"Dad!" She shook her head. "Please! Give me some space."

"Fine." He raised his hands, stepping away. "The tea's prepped. When the water starts to boil, go ahead and pour it in the pot."

He headed for the door.

She spun around just in time to see him pulling it closed. "Where are you going?"

He paused, peeking his head back inside. "To make some cash. If you can't get our money back, rent ain't gonna pay itself."

"Dad!" she shouted, pointing toward the bathroom where the shower was hopefully drowning out her voice. "What about Mom?"

Dad lowered his gaze, head shaking slightly. "I just... I can't fight anymore. I'm sorry. If I go now, maybe I can pick up some high rollers at the airport. Sometimes they fly home late from Vegas." He slid backward. "Love you, Lex. Tell your mother I..." His voice faded as the door clicked shut.

"Damn it!" she muttered, slamming her hand against the table.

Never in all her years as his daughter had he left them like this. He knew his wife was fragile and getting worse daily. Sure, the dementia meds helped, but if she were even a tenth of her regular self, she wouldn't have accused him of watching child pornography. Not after all he'd done for them.

And then there was the laptop. She'd never debugged a

virus before. Hacking applications, that was something she could handle. A virus was another matter entirely.

Alex slumped into the chair, her body aching with every movement. The earlier fight had taken its toll, leaving her bruised and battered. She'd barely made it up the stairs, and now she had to take on this monumental task alone.

She stared at the computer screen, the desktop full of files blurring before her eyes. The weight of responsibility pressed down, suffocating in its intensity.

How am I supposed to fix this? How can I protect my family from financial ruin when I can't even save myself from a back-alley brawl?

Tears of frustration and despair pricked at her eyes, but she blinked them away. Crying never solved anything. It wouldn't heal her wounds, and it certainly wouldn't recover the stolen money.

No, she had to be strong. She needed to push through the pain and doubt and find a way to make this right.

Because if she failed...

She couldn't bear to think about living on the street.

With a shaky breath, Alex reached for the keyboard, fingers hovering over the keys. She may not have all the answers, but she had to try. For her mother, for her father, for the life they'd built together.

She wouldn't let this virus, this faceless enemy, destroy everything they held dear.

Even if it meant sacrificing comfort and peace of mind.

She would find a way.

She had to.

3 / THE HYDRA'S DEN
CIPHER

Passing through the security gates, Cipher felt the icy tendrils of the dawn wind penetrate his jacket. Seconds later, the rusty barrier clanged shut, sending the barbed wire atop the fence into a tizzy. Its razor-sharp edges shimmered in the morning sun, a stark reminder that even in the embrace of the new day, shadows of the past lingered, ever ready to ensnare the unwary.

Once through, his two handlers peeled off, disappearing into a hidden alcove. But he continued onward.

Deep down, he knew watchful eyes and cameras lurked around every corner. He wasn't sure why, but their presence reassured his superiors he was under their control.

The fools were blissfully unaware of the serpent in their midst, and he planned to keep it that way until his venom left them paralyzed and defenseless.

Unless he was waving a gun or shouting anti-establishment propaganda, he wasn't of much concern. At least to these outer guards. The inner security teams were far more challenging.

He stepped over a muddy pothole, making his way past row upon row of dilapidated flower beds, avoiding the cloud of flies swarming a nearby dumpster. From the looks of it, the corpse was still in there from two weeks earlier.

The message from above was clear: Don't fuck with the wrong people, or you'll end up forgotten, discarded like yesterday's trash. In this place, even flies claimed more respect than the memory of a traitor.

A few feet past the dumpster, the wind picked up, the resulting stench confirming his theory about the body.

He fought to keep down his rising breakfast. Smells were his weakness, particularly those entwined with death's embrace.

He dabbed his lips, eyes narrowing at passersby. In his hand was an aged linen handkerchief, its intricate fabric worn from years of use. Each precise fold was a silent, menacing ritual, a reminder of the love that had once filled his life, cut off too suddenly, too harshly.

As he distanced himself from the makeshift grave, he spotted two of his programmers passing by. They avoided making eye contact, and he swore they flinched as he pocketed his handkerchief.

Fear was an exquisite tool, a masterstroke when wielded with precision. It was an art his father had imparted to him in youth, teaching him to sculpt dread into a motivator more powerful than any promise of reward. Though he didn't realize it at the time, his parents' death had changed his appreciation for their unorthodox life lessons.

The pair of second-rate programmers should be downstairs, not dawdling outdoors. Their day was just beginning. They should be busy spreading the virus, making their people and supreme leader proud. Anything to make their government appear stronger than it was, especially to the outside world.

He made a mental note to check their schedules later.

Around the next corner, he stumbled upon another dilapidated water fountain. Beside it lay two recently deceased dog carcasses. It must have happened last evening; the telltale swarm of flies hadn't yet descended.

He shuddered, quickening his pace. The sooner he reached his facility, the better. This place was too grim, even for his liking.

They only cleaned up when the upper brass visited. Before they arrived, they'd parade garbage trucks and an army of forced laborers through the complex.

They'd spread thousands of roses, petunias, and fake grass as far as the eye could see. And after the brass left, it'd all be dead within a week.

Passing under another set of electronic eyes, he reflected on how this slice of North Korean hell was really no different from America. Both were filled with a false sense of happiness and security.

Whether in their airports, on their streets, or in their substandard train stations, a closer look revealed near-identical scenes. People in the US lived out their lives thinking they were free, when in fact their every whim was choreographed. Manipulated from afar.

American citizens, influenced by their mass media and large corporations, bear a striking resemblance to North Koreans when observed up close. The only difference was the method of control: One employed barbed wire, while the other wielded social economics and brash consumerism.

The deeper the United States entrench themselves in their supposed democratic worldview, the worse they felt about themselves and the rest of the world.

And the results spoke for themselves: Internal conflict among the people, poor health of their population, and mountains of debt that took their citizens a lifetime to pay off.

If that wasn't as bad as a gun to the head or razor wire to the arm, he didn't know what was.

Entering his building through the security checkpoint, he surveyed the drab, peeling industrial facade. He had to hand it to the US, though, at least they tried making it feel livable. A mocha latte sounded great right about now.

His assistant emerged from a concealed nook just inside the door. "Good morning, sir."

Caught off guard, he recoiled, instinctively raising his fists. She immediately shrank back, fear evident in her eyes. Dropping to her knees, she bowed her head to the cold marble floor.

"I'm... sorry, sir." She peered up briefly before returning her gaze downward. "Forgive me, please." She tentatively reached out before withdrawing her hand, not daring to touch him. But judging by her trembling, she would've licked his shoes if he asked her to.

He smirked. Apparently, word had spread after his last verbal chastising for being startled. The event happened a few months prior, and that guy disappeared soon after. He heard that General Tau shipped him off to work in a mining camp.

This time, however, Cipher controlled himself, slowly lowering his arms to his sides. He didn't want this new assistant to disappear. He'd actually grown quite fond of her. She wasn't only pleasing to look at; she was oblivious to most of what he did. A fact which made it a heck of a lot easier for him to skim off the top.

"Get... up," he growled, glaring at the woman. She scrambled to her feet, her gaze never leaving his shoes.

When he glanced down the hall, he saw a crowd of people lingering about, staring at them. "Don't you have somewhere to be?" he shouted, his voice echoing through the corridor.

The gathered audience scattered like cockroaches exposed to light, skittering back to their desks.

Once he was happy they were alone, he returned his attention to his assistant, her eyes still firmly fixed on the floor.

As he contemplated her punishment, he noticed her figure

seemed more curvaceous today than usual. For the first time in a long time, a wave of arousal passed over him.

He couldn't explain it, but seeing her like this with her pouty lip and the tear stains on her ample bosom made him want to rip her clothes off and make her do his bidding. It also helped that her white blouse and jet-black pencil skirt were practically painted on.

Either she'd always been hiding that perfect body under her clothes, or he'd been too busy to notice. Perhaps visiting America had ruined his sense of proper dress.

The stark contrast of her stunning beauty against her usual conservative attire seemed less like camouflage and more like a deliberate tease. A challenge to uncover the depths of her allure he'd previously overlooked.

And then he saw this for what it was. Another test.

He could almost feel the cameras zooming in, willing him to make a mistake. To show that visiting America had weakened him.

If he reacted inappropriately, they'd make his life hell. And yet, if he didn't, they might punish her. While the latter hardly concerned him, he wondered what she looked like beneath those layers of form-fitting fabric. It seemed like such a waste to send her away to a mining camp.

"The next time you come to meet me, you'll be standing in plain sight. Is that clear, Ms. Choe?" He reached out and forced her chin up, meeting her eyes.

She nodded sharply. "Yes... yes, sir."

"Good." He held her gaze, waiting to see if she'd look away. If her attention drifted to the camera over his shoulder, it would confirm his theory about his superiors testing him. But if she held her ground, then...

Her emerald gaze flickered up and to the right, then back to him. It was only for a split second, but it happened.

As soon as her eyes shifted, she realized her mistake. The subtle quiver of her lips betrayed her feelings.

She'd failed her mission by meeting the ever-present eye of the CCTV camera positioned behind him.

In that moment of weakness, he smiled. She may not have known it then, but she belonged to him now.

Cipher's fingers danced over the keyboard in a blur of celebration and relief. He wasn't sure why he had doubts. He'd perfected the hydra on countless machines over the past few years, just not on a scale like this.

He checked the balances of their encrypted currency dumps, covering his tracks as he hopped between machines. There were hundreds of thousands of dollars in every file he found.

It was more money than he'd ever seen in his entire life, more than anyone from his obliterated hometown had ever laid eyes on.

He shook away the bloody memory, refusing to let the void in his chest drag him down like it usually did. Instead, he allowed it to propel him forward, launching him headlong into his destiny.

The virus's victims were being taught a lesson, as he had been. The hard way.

Their governments didn't protect them. They sought to control them, to manipulate their perceptions and actions, ensuring obedience at any cost. Even if that took their last dollar.

Through the chaos he'd unleashed, he'd expose the illusions of safety and the steep price of blind trust. His code was a wake-up call, a digital revolt against the invisible chains of those in power.

While he knew they wouldn't see it at first, enlightenment would come with time. Just as his parents' lessons became clearer the longer they were gone.

Staring at the piles of money streaming past on his monitor, one thing was clear: It would take months for their money mules to move this kind of cash. Even with all the college recruiting his digital soldiers were doing, it wouldn't be enough.

As he contemplated alternative ways to transfer large sums of money through their network of fake companies, his computer chimed, yanking him out of his fiscal reverie.

He usually shut off sound effects on his machines, preferring visual indicators over audible intrusions to his flow. But for this situation, he'd programmed a special alert to cut through the silence—a sonic beacon designed to highlight the urgency.

The alert meant only one thing: Someone was talking about his virus online. Someone he loathed with every fiber of his being.

"Fucking Ninja," he muttered, flipping open the streams to the internet relay chats he frequented.

4 / BITS, BYTES AND BETRAYAL
ALEX

With her father out of her hair and the computer under control, Alex kicked off the virus scanner update and started poking around the file system, searching for the offending program.

She'd read about malware and computer viruses online, but never imagined she'd have to deal with them on her own computer. Her father knew better than to click on just any link. She'd shown him how to inspect URLs countless times, but he was always in too much of a hurry.

She shook her head, knowing it wasn't his fault. It was the bad actors online. Hell, for all she knew, it could be some script kiddie down the street.

The thought of stealing someone's hard-earned money using a virus made her skin crawl. People had a hard enough time making ends meet nowadays.

They feared their neighbors, teachers, the government, and now even being online. Evil was everywhere in the world, seeping into their lives in ways both big and small, leaving no place where they could feel completely safe.

Maybe that was why she preferred the solitude of computers. Ever since her first adoptive family let her use their computer, she felt in control behind the keyboard.

She met her online tribe in those early chat rooms, the people who stuck with her throughout her childhood journey through multiple homes. Unlike her fleeting connections with adoptive families, her bond with the digital world, and its faceless people, remained steadfast.

Plus, it was a place where she could make a difference. Online, her stronger self emerged naturally, whereas offline it only surfaced during moments of anger.

Computers weren't inherently scary to her. They were simply machines, following their programming. The humans behind them, however, they were capable of true evil.

After about twenty minutes of hunting and pecking through the laptop's file system, she came up empty-handed. Everything seemed in place.

If the antivirus didn't uncover the problem, the only way she could find the attack vector was by comparing the entire hard drive to a backup. And the most recent copy she had was from the clean install she performed a year ago. While not ideal, it was better than nothing.

She checked the status of the virus scanner update. Her heart sank. The progress bar showed only five percent.

"You're kidding me," she muttered.

"What is it?" Mom asked, walking up behind her while drying her hair.

Alex glanced up. "What's... what?"

Her mom pointed at the screen, still rubbing her long black hair with the towel. She looked refreshed. "You were frustrated about something on that... that blasted thing. What was it?"

"Our internet." Alex lowered her head, running hands through her tangled hair. "It's friggin awful."

"Did you finish your work?" Mom raised her eyebrows. "You know. On that... thing."

"It's a laptop, Mom." Alex squinted at her screen, sinking deeper into her chair as her mom passed into the kitchen.

She knew the word; she just hated electronic devices. Always had. She claimed they rotted kids' brains staring at them all the time.

"Sweetie!" Mom squealed, reaching across the stove. She yanked her hand back before trying again to tweak the dial to the off position. It took a few attempts before she reached it.

"Shit!" Alex bolted upright. "I forgot!" She hopped toward her mom but was too late.

With her head buried in the screen, she'd somehow missed the hiss and splutter of boiling tea water. It usually whistled when it was done, but not this time.

By the time she reached her mom's side, she understood why.

"The lid wasn't seated properly." Her mother slipped on an oven mitt and carefully adjusted the kettle's lid. Once secure, she poured the boiling liquid into the waiting pot with the infuser.

Steaming water cascaded over the perforated metal ball, releasing a dance of golden chamomile petals. They swirled and unfurled, infusing the liquid with their delicate, soothing essence.

"That smells wonderful," Alex whispered, leaning forward to inhale deeply. Her body ached all over. Plus, she was still chilled from the rain. A cup of warm tea sounded perfect right about now.

"Want some?" Mom smiled, glancing back at her. "Say..." She leaned forward, peering into the living room. "Is your father home yet?"

A sudden chill raced down Alex's spine, fear and surprise knotting within. At first, she thought her mother was joking, but the seriousness of her expression said otherwise.

The heated argument from minutes earlier seemed worlds away in her mother's forgotten gaze.

Alex wrestled with telling her, debating whether resurrecting the fiery quarrel would serve any purpose for her mother's clouded memory, or if it would simply reopen fresh wounds.

The weight of decision pressed heavily on her mind, a silent plea for guidance screaming through the fog of dementia shrouding her mother's awareness.

Fortunately, the loss of memories left room for new realities.

"Oh, that's right." Mom nodded and turned, opening a cabinet. "He's driving with Uber tonight. He told me this morning."

She studied the mugs on the counter, as if seeing them for the first time. "I still can't believe people pay so much just to get from point A to point B in a nice car. It's crazy! What's wrong with a cab? I mean, I like cabs."

She pulled out two cups, picked up the teapot, and made her way to the living room.

As her mother disappeared around the corner, Alex stared at the glowing laptop screen.

Part of her wanted to delve deeper into the mysterious mess ensnaring her father, to understand the shadow looming over their family.

Yet she also yearned to share her joy—the university acceptance letter hidden in her schoolbag. A dream nurtured through countless nights of study and determination.

Even as this triumph beckoned, she knew the woman before her, the one who would share in her joy, wasn't quite her mother anymore. She'd become a silhouette of her former self, reshaped by the encroaching shadows of dementia.

At this bittersweet crossroads, Alex longed not just for celebration, but for a connection increasingly out of reach.

"Lex! Come sit with me!" Mom called out. "You can study later. Besides, Jeopardy's on. It's only a few minutes in. We haven't missed much."

Alex closed her eyes, resigned to letting her mom lapse into her false reality. She sounded so happy, as if she truly wanted to spend time together. That was a gift in itself, given her recent tendency to sleep when she got home from work.

"Small wins," she muttered as she reached over and grabbed the sugar bowl.

"What did you say, sweetie?" Mom looked away from the TV as she came into view.

Alex smiled, holding up the oddly shaped dish she'd made in sixth grade pottery. "Sugar?"

"Oh yes!" Her mom extended her cup, eyes aglow in the television's light. "One cube, please."

HOURS LATER, Alex found herself staring at her acceptance letter, eyes glazing over. The logo from the University of Michigan was a haze of maize and blue.

She'd longed to share her achievement with her mom, to see pride and joy in her eyes. But the moment had passed, overshadowed by her mother's declining mental state and their looming homelessness.

After her mom went to bed, Alex stayed up, multitasking between restoring her father's laptop from a clean image and forwarding last night's altercation audio to Riley and her friend. The recording should send a reminder that actions have consequences.

While Alex was the one that physically lashed out, their

despicable behavior provoked the confrontation. They needed to learn that bullying had repercussions.

After she finished restoring the laptop, she double-checked her backup of the virus that upended her life. With the evidence secured, she could begin unraveling the tangled web ensnaring her family, one thread at a time.

Behind the acceptance letter, the command line streamed output into a terminal window. With the restore complete, she moved on, downloading the Cygwin Unix tools and starting her analysis of the backup. Cygwin offered a more straightforward path than Windows' limited shell to understand the virus's changes, at least to her. She wasn't a fan of Windows.

Scrolling up, she double-checked the command line she was running:

```
> diff -r --brief "C:/" "E:/"
```

The command was correct. The problem was, there'd been nothing meaningful in the results. She'd hoped to find something by now, but it was still running.

In the morning, after she'd gotten some sleep, she'd review everything in more detail. But without a smoking gun like a *.dll* or *.exe*, hope was fading.

She'd been flipping between the acceptance letter and the terminal for nearly an hour. It was excruciating, and she didn't know why she was torturing herself like this.

Maybe it was the realization that her dreams had been so close she could taste them, only to have them tossed away like yesterday's trash.

Between her mom's mental spiral and her family's possible homelessness, leaving seemed an impossibility.

Plus, there was the small matter of the tuition. Forty thousand dollars per year. That was a shit ton of Benjamins, certainly more than she'd ever seen. Paying for out-of-state college was no joke. Even with potential financial aid, there was no way she was getting out of college without a mountain of debt.

But that's what dreams were for, right? Aim high and... she squinted, failing to recall the rest of the phrase. Twenty-four hours without sleep did that to a person.

Setting down the letter, she stared at the screen of scrolling text and stretched her sore fingers. She couldn't stand not knowing what her father had gotten roped into. When the antivirus turned up empty, she knew sleep was out of the question.

The first thing she did was submit a ticket with a photo of the laptop screen to the makers of the shitty excuse for a virus defense app. If they couldn't protect against a simple email link attack, what was the point?

"Greed," she muttered.

As if on cue, her terminal command got a hit.

```
Only in E:/Windows/System32: wpbt0.dll
Only in E:/Windows/System32: 0tbpw.pad
Only in E:/Windows/System32: 0tbpw.js
```

"Holy shit!" She leaned forward, rubbing her eyes, reading each letter of the *dll*. w—p—b—t—0... the letters were as meaningless as the company they paid to protect their machine. It was like paying the mob for protection while the city you lived in was kicking you in the gut. Except in this case, it was antivirus companies and Microsoft.

Dynamic Link Libraries, or d-l-l's as they're called, were stored chunks of executable code that could be loaded into memory when needed. For hackers, they and their *exe* counterparts were the keys to the digital kingdom. Gateways to infiltrate any Windows system and extract valuable data without a trace.

At least if they went undetected. But not this time. She'd found them, damn it, and she intended to crack the virus open. To track them back to their creators.

Maybe it was the residual adrenaline from earlier, or the verbal battle she'd walked in on, but she craved revenge. If she was destined for a shelter, she wanted a name to curse under her breath, and it sure as hell wouldn't be her father's.

"Who made you?" she whispered, copying the files from the backup drive to her MacBook.

Her aging 2006 Mac was barely held together by stickers from video games and app developers, but it served her needs well. The image of the glowing Apple logo being pulled from a magician's hat still made her smile.

With the copy complete, she pointed the *xxd* tool at the file and piped the results to the *less* command.

Though she'd only started learning Unix a few years ago, it quickly became invaluable to her learning. It was as if the handcuffs of the computer's user interface had disappeared, replaced by a toolbox.

This time, however, she wasn't sure what she was looking for. That's where the *xxd* hex dump tool came in handy. It let her peek inside the raw contents of the *dll*.

While not exactly a virus writer, she still recognized some familiar text when scanning the output. The same words she'd read on her father's computer last night. Reading them now made her heart race.

```
00000810: 4943 412e 0a48 6f6d 656c 616e
ICA..Homelan
0000081c: 6420 5365 6375 7269 7479 202d
d Security -
00000828: 204e 6174 696f 6e61 6c20 4379
 National Cy
```

```
00000834: 6265 7220 5365 6375 7269 7479 ber
Security
00000840: 2044 6976 6973 696f 6e3a 2054
Division: T
```

To the untrained eye, the numbers and random letters meant nothing. But Alex knew better. If this text was in the executable, it was likely the source of her rage.

With a smoking gun in hand, there was only one place she could turn to find out who made it. At least until she had the time and energy to uncover any calling cards in the virus itself.

That place was IRC: Internet Relay Chat. One of the last bastions of hacker culture left on the open internet, a shadowy realm where the digital elite convened in the obscurity and comfort of their simple text interface.

There, amidst the strangely named hashtag channels and cryptic nicknames, she could probe for whispers and rumors, sifting through the chatter for clues that might lead her to the creator of the malicious code. The question was where to start. EFnet, Rizon, or Undernet were just three of the dozen IRC networks she'd need to explore.

Glancing at her display, she saw it was almost three AM. There was no way in hell she could sleep now. Not with the quest for truth in reach.

The digital trail was a labyrinth promising answers just beyond the next turn.

But before embarking on her next adventure, she needed coffee.

ALEX SIPPED THE BITTER, steaming liquid, her thoughts drifting back to the first time she'd joined the IRC network. It was a distant memory from a challenging period of her childhood, one she preferred not to dwell on.

Back then, the letters I-R-C had stirred a flicker of recognition, their significance lost in her hazy past. Yet their impact remained undeniable. On that fateful night, when the weight of her troubles felt overwhelming, those letters had sparked a curiosity that compelled her to seek their meaning.

Joining the network had been serendipitous, setting her on a path that would shape her future in ways she could never have imagined. It opened a door to a realm where she found solace, kinship, and the power to confront life's challenges.

A scratching sound from the living room interrupted her thoughts. It sounded like someone fumbling with the lock on the front door, but as suddenly as it started, it stopped.

Emerging from her bleary-eyed zone of text, she squinted at the time.

"Seven AM," she whispered, her eyes still coming into focus on her room.

Too many hours of scrolling through tiny print, combined with a lack of sleep, had left her already battered body screaming for reprieve.

She'd been juggling several private chat threads and fast-moving public conversations for hours now. While she'd learned much about the virus from her dark web friends, details about the attackers themselves remained elusive.

The IRC denizens called it FBI Ransomware, much to the chagrin of supporters of the US government. Everyone knew the FBI wasn't behind the attack, but that didn't prevent the agency from being associated with stealing people's money.

Foreign members on the channel reveled in the name, which wasn't surprising given the growing anti-US sentiment around the world. While she'd always been oblivious to the news, the residents of the chat networks weren't.

The notion that the world hated her country shocked her,

and she freaked out when the fringe members on one channel got wind of her being in the US. Had she not masked her IP address through multiple VPNs, her cheapo home router would've been melted to slag.

After the unexpected assault, she reconnected through a different VPN and then Tor, using an alternate username on IRC itself. One she hadn't used in a while.

Once she rejoined the channel using her recovery password, the room exploded. Script kiddies and lurkers lashed out, flooding the chat with barbs and conspiracy theories about the virus's origin.

Theories ranged from the NSA to North Korea, Russia, and Eastern European crime groups. She noted these for later investigation, especially the puzzling Eastern Europe connection.

She focused on listening to people who'd shared legitimate code or hacking techniques in the past. The rest, well, they were blowhards looking to pick a fight. Or, as she knew it, just another night on IRC.

When a direct message from N3tN1nja popped up on her screen, she nearly logged out. Their handle had driven many a flame war since she'd joined this private hacker channel a few years back. But in all that time, they'd never once messaged her.

N3tN1nja was an OG on the server. A member of the Old Guard who claimed to have hacked before computers were a thing. Whenever they got nostalgic, they'd reference red boxes and blue boxes. The names amused her.

You always knew someone was old when they mentioned using coin-operated phones.

The OG's message flashed up, demanding a response:

> **N3TN1NJA**
> You know these people are just tossing out misinformation, right? Most of them work for foreign governments.

She rubbed her eye and winced. Her fingers still stung from earlier that night. Foreign governments seemed unlikely, and for some reason, she felt compelled to challenge their theory.

> **L3X1C0N**
> If you say so. And being a script kiddie is the peak of cyber artistry.

Her handle in this session was L3x1c0n. She rarely used it on this server. It was a wordplay on her real-life nickname and the word 'lexicon.' A fitting tribute to her drive to master both the terminology and art of hacking.

The OG's response was uncharacteristically lengthy.

> **N3TN1NJA**
> I'm serious. This isn't about throwing shade. This goes deeper. Far deeper. Their agenda on this server isn't just about hacking for the thrill or the challenge; it's about manipulation and control. These people aren't acting in good faith. They're here to recruit, to propagate their narratives, and to weaponize information. We're talking about state-sponsored activities, psyops that aim to destabilize and distort.

She stared at the words, doubt flooding her mind. *Who is this person? And why the hell are they telling me this?*

> **L3X1C0N**
> And why am I supposed to trust you?

While waiting for their response, she half-heartedly

scrolled through the conversations she'd missed on the private channel. The second N3tN1nja's reply appeared, her eyes snapped to the direct message.

> **N3TN1NJA**
>
> I know you've seen their techniques and the precision of their misinformation campaigns. You've questioned it before. They have a ready-made narrative at their disposal, even if it sounds like it's coming from a fellow hacker. You think that's by accident?
>
> They're acting on a whole different level of cyber warfare. I'm telling you the truth. They're using chat rooms like this as their training grounds to spread their propaganda. You need to be critical of the information being shared, question the sources, and understand the motives behind them.
>
> This isn't just about being a skilled hacker; it's about recognizing when your abilities are being aimed at someone else's target. Trust me, I've probably been at this longer than you've been alive.
>
> Stay sharp, Byt3Linguist. Question everything, and don't let these people exploit you for their nefarious ends.

Her eyes widened as she took in the name they'd called her. Byt3Linguist. It was the handle she'd been using earlier. Before they attacked her for being from America.

The only way N3tN1nja could've figured out it was her was if they'd infiltrated the server. Their knowledge of her name sent a chill down her spine. But it was worse than that.

The one-time password recovery system she used was

supposed to be encrypted and anonymous. She'd seen the source code. At least, what was purported to be the code.

Now she wondered if anything she'd said today was truly secret. They could be tracking her location even now.

As she weighed her options, N3tN1nja unleashed a torrent of messages on the channel. They claimed to have intel on this newest attack vector.

From the looks of it, they'd figured out how the virus worked. The exploit started by injecting code into every web browser on the user's machine. The key was the *JavaScript* snippet she'd found earlier that night—the one with the *.js* extension. Apparently, the hackers used it to run the executable.

She opened the file in a text editor after a quick scan with *xxd*. Even now, studying the short snippet of code, she marveled at how something so simple could trigger such a devastating attack. That it could wreak so much havoc and change so many lives.

With web browsers buried in the bowels of Windows, it was no wonder it rendered a user's machine useless. If only her father hadn't revolted at using Linux, he wouldn't have gotten into this mess.

A few minutes later, N3tN1nja dropped another bombshell. The virus wasn't a simple one-and-done thing. It was a programmable shell—or ransomware-as-a-service, as they called it.

They weren't just making the attack look like an FBI warning; the virus could be weaponized for anything. And likely already was.

This revelation ignited a firestorm of accusations and spam on the channel, followed by a wave of bans and kicks unlike anything Alex had seen since the last permanent server split.

Her screen suddenly flashed another message from the OG:

> **N3TN1NJA**
>
> Use your whois logs to follow the addresses of the people I booted. The truth will set you free from doubt.

She read the words repeatedly, their implication sinking in.

While automatically running a *whois* command on a new user to the channel wasn't uncommon, N3tN1nja knowing she did this confirmed her suspicion: The server was under their control.

The question was, what would the logs reveal?

Before she could look, the latch on the front door clicked, followed by the squeak of its hinges. The sound snapped her back to reality, and she reflexively locked her screen. Her fingers danced over the keys so fast she didn't register the action until the login prompt appeared.

Her father didn't need to know how far she was taking her research. Plus, if he learned she'd hit a dead end recovering his money, he'd insist she stop.

As a foreigner, her father lived in constant fear of deportation. Most of their neighbors shared this anxiety.

That life of constant fear was why people like the cheerleaders got away with their taunts. Her community made easy targets, and no one dared complain.

Thoughts of the earlier confrontation made Alex's neck tingle. She instinctively reached up, rubbing her skin and pulling her nightshirt higher. Even with concealer, too much rubbing would reveal the bruises.

"Hello?" her father called out.

Alex jolted upright, wincing as a sharp pain in her side reminded her she'd hit the pavement. The memory of the rough concrete scraping her skin raw as she desperately searched for that rock was overwhelming.

Even now, she wondered if she'd gone too far. She hoped the girls were okay.

Alex swallowed down the thought. She needed to stretch and tell her father the good news. Well, not good news, exactly, but at least she knew it wasn't entirely his fault they might be homeless soon.

Sliding out of bed, she tucked her laptop away on the bottom shelf of her nightstand, leaving the lid slightly ajar. She couldn't afford to miss any messages from the still-buzzing channels.

As she stepped into the hall, she glanced down, carefully avoiding the creaky floorboard, fearing it might wake her mother. But her caution proved unnecessary.

"Lex!" a woman's voice pierced the apartment and likely echoed through the entire building.

When Alex looked up, her jaw dropped as her gaze landed on an impossible sight—Aunt Min, in the flesh.

She'd only known her aunt through late-night video calls and overseas birthday cards. She'd been a presence in her life that was both familiar and utterly alien.

And now she stood in front of her, arms outstretched, larger than life. A stranger suddenly less strange.

Her mind raced to reconcile her aunt's presence here instead of halfway around the world in South Korea.

It was only when her father appeared behind her aunt, lugging two giant suitcases through the front door, that the pieces clicked into place.

"How'd... you... I don't understand!" Alex stammered, her voice betraying surprise and fatigue.

Her aunt didn't bother with a reply. She merely rushed forward, enveloping Alex in a boa constrictor-like embrace.

"I can't believe I can finally hug you." Aunt Min beamed,

showing every tooth in her mouth. When she let go, she reached up and pinched Alex's cheeks like a toddler.

"Ouch!" she winced, the nip and hug aggravating her side.

"Oh sorry, dear." Aunt Min gently rubbed her cheek. "I get carried away sometimes. I just…" She covered her mouth. "Never thought…" Tears welled in her eyes as she trailed off, staring at Alex.

Alex smiled back and leaned in, her own emotions bubbling up. Despite exhaustion and pain clinging to her, a warmth spread through her chest. The initial shock and weariness melted away as the gravity of this moment settled in.

This was the first person she'd ever met from her parents' extended family. She wanted to savor every second.

"It's okay," Alex whispered, hugging her tight. "I'm just… happy you're here. I can't believe it's…" She squeezed harder, communicating what words couldn't.

This physical connection bridged the gap created by years of distance and screens.

As they stood in quiet embrace, Alex heard her parents' bedroom door creak open.

"Is that you, Jin?" her mother asked groggily.

Alex glanced over her shoulder, her arms still around her aunt.

Mom rubbed her eyes as she came into view. "I… thought I heard—" She drew in her breath, and before Alex could speak, a screech of excitement and disbelief filled the apartment.

The next thing she knew, Alex was a sister sandwich.

5 / JASMINE AND GUNPOWDER
CIPHER

When Cipher typed in his server recovery password, the screen flashed white, instantly closing his connection.

> Connection denied

"What the hell?" he muttered, trying again. Same result. His jaw clenched, a storm brewing in his eyes.

With each failed attempt, his urge for retribution grew, every keystroke a vow of vengeance.

This time, he tried reconnecting through an emergency VPN from a more mainstream provider. It wasn't guaranteed to be secure from prying eyes, but the risk was necessary.

Maybe the chat server was blocking inbound IP addresses. He'd seen this defense used during the notable IRC netsplits of the 90s and early 2000s. The latter of which resulted in permanent network forks like Rizon, one of his preferred chat networks.

The public VPN connected just fine, but his attempt was still met with failure.

"Damn it!" He shoved away from his desk, spinning his chair, struggling to control his temper.

His anger rose every second he was in the dark. Not knowing what was being said about them was maddening.

N3tN1nja had revealed nearly all their secrets on the channel. Finding the virus was a layup for any skilled hacker, but N3tN1nja had turned over the entire blueprint, explaining its utilitarian design and how it could be used for any purpose, not just scamming money. The term "ransomware-as-a-service" wasn't without cause.

Spinning in his chair, Cipher suddenly remembered the camera watching from over his shoulder. It had caught not only his outburst but the same eruption from the entire pen of programmers beyond the glass partition.

He stopped spinning and flipped open the chat logs. Judging by the number of kicks he'd captured before being booted, most of his team had been cut off.

If he had any hope of getting ahead of this, he needed to get out there and direct his people. Seconds mattered at a time like this. They had to rotate their electronic cash dumps or risk losing everything.

While N3tN1nja may have cracked the virus' shell, they hadn't detailed how its backchannel worked. Cipher hoped they hadn't figured out how the cash was proxied to their data stores. If they had, his life might be as short as the lifespan of his virus.

He sprang from his chair, yanking open the door in a split second.

Beyond lay his troops, his pool of programmers, heads down, submerged in the glow of their screens. Many of them were staring at the same failed connection message he'd seen seconds earlier.

"Rotate the proxies!" he barked. "Move the cash dumps, now!"

The urgency in his voice sliced through the room's silence like a zero-day exploit breaching a firewall. What he didn't expect was dissension.

"We can't," a programmer replied, eyes fixed on his keyboard. "It's too soon. Our next proxy rotation isn't scheduled until..." He paused as if to look for the time.

Cipher didn't wait for the man to finish. He drew his Makarov PM, thumbed off the safety, aimed at the man's head, and pulled the trigger.

The handgun felt like an extension of his resolve, a silent ally whispering promises of retribution meant for N3tN1nja, now directed at this challenge to his authority.

The recoil surged through the pistol, transferring into him, a violent yet controlled dance of Russian engineering thrusting back into his hand with surprising, comforting force.

A sharp crack sliced the silence. A split second later, the man's head exploded outward, spraying his low cubicle walls and that of his neighbor with cerebral fluid.

The scene was gruesome.

Bloody chunks rained over the woman opposite him, coating her in a blanket of red from her once-talented comrade. Her bloodcurdling scream echoed through the space, but the moment her eyes met Cipher's, she quelled her emotions, lowering her ear-piercing shriek to a dull whimper.

She knew who was in command, even if fear had a stranglehold on her instincts.

"Rotate the goddamn proxies and grab the cash!" He lowered the Makarov, its slight weight belying its destructive power. "Unless someone else has a problem with that?"

No one said a word. Even the whimpering woman held her tongue. Instead, the room transformed into the familiar clatter of keyboards, a symphony of digital ambition he'd long associated with power.

The Makarov, now silent in his hand, had done its job by asserting his resolve. In this world of shadows and screens, it was the power of command that ruled supreme, not just gunpowder.

And if he hoped to maintain the trust of General Tau and his superiors, he had to rule with the iron fist his father had hammered into him as a child.

As he surveyed the room, the familiar scent of jasmine wafted past, signaling Choe's arrival. His body instinctively relaxed, but he stiffened his posture as he holstered his gun. He refused to let his superiors see him in a moment of weakness.

"I want the secondary team working on a DDoS attack," he said, knowing Choe was already taking notes behind him. She was always taking notes.

"Who should we target?" she asked, her voice soothing. It made the hairs on his neck stand on end.

"I want that IRC server down," he demanded, turning to face her.

Her emerald eyes briefly thawed his anger, a change imperceptible to others. He'd be sure to take out some of his frustrations on her tonight when she visited his apartment. She still had a debt to repay.

"And while you're at it," he continued, eyes narrowing on his monitors, "I want a team working on finding N3tN1nja and that Byt3Linguist character. They're too new to that room. Something tells me they're a part of this retaliation."

Choe tilted her head skeptically. "We've already tried tracking down N3tN1nja. Every attempt came up empty. Remember? It's like they're not only hiding, they don't exist. They're digital ghosts."

His gaze locked on hers. "Then try harder! Put a dozen fucking people on it if you need to. I don't care what you do or how you do it, just find them!"

Choe didn't say a word. She knew better. She simply

bowed and turned on her toes, double-timing it to the neighboring building where their second team operated.

He didn't watch her go. He bit his lip, staring at his machine. There was something about Byt3Linguist's persistent questions around reverse engineering the virus. They seemed almost too deliberate, too leading. Like they were designed to stir up a hornet's nest.

If his soldiers hadn't lashed out when they admitted being from the US, there was no telling what they would've uncovered.

Cipher turned and drummed his fingers on the railing, a silent countdown to his next move. He had to track these hackers down, following their digital footprint back through the chaos they'd sown. Once he did, the reckoning would be swift.

6 / A FAMILY AFFAIR
ALEX

"I still can't believe you're here," Alex's mother said, staring at her sister. "It's surreal." She turned to her husband, smiling from ear to ear. "How did you hide this from me for so long?"

Dad looked up from his phone and swallowed hard, glancing uneasily between Alex and Min-Seo, his sister-in-law. He'd already told the story once, but repeated it to avoid embarrassing his wife.

"After your parents passed last year, Min-Seo and I started planning her move here to the states." He glanced over at Min. "She couldn't bear being alone in Seoul anymore."

"We wanted to surprise you." Aunt Min reached over and squeezed her sister's hand, fighting back tears for reasons Alex suspected were different from earlier.

She'd tried warning her aunt about her mom's dementia during video chats, but she wasn't sure her aunt understood how bad she was getting. While medications had slowed the decline, memory gaps made interactions like this uncomfortable.

Aunt Min looked over and winked at Alex. "We would've told you both sooner, but mountains of paperwork delayed us." She chuckled. "I didn't even tell your father I was coming today. My visa was just approved yesterday." She smirked at Alex's father. "I phoned his driver service after my plane touched down, hoping he'd be working."

He nodded. "She was just lucky I was between Uber runs. I checked out of the app after Donny called and headed straight to the airport. Almost got a ticket en route as well. Donny said it was an emergency." He ran his hand over the back of his neck. "I should've known who it was when he said the name was Max."

Her mother snorted, squeezing Aunt Min's hand. Alex recalled her mom explaining that Min used the name "Max" whenever she wanted to hide her identity, partly as a joke, being the opposite of her nickname, and partly to flip American stereotypes on their head. The only thing "Max" about her tiny form was the vibrant, eclectic mix of clothing she wore. She was like a walking rainbow.

Alex yawned for the third time in a minute, and then quickly downed her coffee.

"That's your fourth cup since I got here," Aunt Min said, wide-eyed. "You're gonna be up all day."

Alex shrugged and stood up, heading to the kitchen for another round. Caffeine was her best bet at staying awake, especially going on twenty-six hours without sleep.

"Sometimes I think Lex's blood is seventy-five percent coffee." Her father winked, getting up for a refill himself.

"I learned from the best," she retorted, filling his mug with a smile.

"Sure, now you admit you have a problem," he said, nudging her while spooning a heap of sugar into his mug. "Last week you said we were imagining things."

Alex smirked. "I only admit to problems that come with coffee-based solutions. Now pass me the cream, please."

Her aunt shook her head at their banter. "So, tell me, Lex—"

Alex's phone rang, cutting through her aunt's question.

She darted across the room, digging frantically through her school bag for the phone. The interruption was curious; everyone who'd want to reach her was already here, especially on a Saturday.

After she found the ancient clamshell, she flipped it open and froze when she saw the name.

RILEY SANCHEZ

Her heart hammered in her chest, disbelief coursing through her veins.

How did Riley get my number? And why the hell would she call after last night's confrontation?

The questions swirled in her mind, a storm of confusion and apprehension.

With her thumb hovering over the answer button, she hesitated, torn between the urge to confront the girl and the instinct to protect herself from whatever this call might bring.

The phone rang again, and she glanced at her family, doing her best to shove down her feelings. "I should... take this in my room." She ducked down the hall without waiting for a response.

After she gently closed her bedroom door, she pressed the button to connect.

"What the hell do *you* want?" she snapped, being sure to keep her voice low enough so as not to be heard in the other room.

"It's good of you to answer," Riley said. "I hope I woke you."

"Bitch," Alex whispered, preparing to hang up.

"Thank you," Riley replied sarcastically. "Actually, I'm

calling to thank you for last night's makeover. Black and blue really suits me."

Alex narrowed her gaze, uncertain where this was going. She wasn't about to admit anything to this witch over an open line.

"I'll take your silence as a confirmation of your deed," Riley continued. "Not that we need it with the evidence we have against you."

"What do you want, Riley?" She reached up and rubbed her neck, suddenly feeling phantom fingers around her throat.

Riley must have covered her phone with her hand because she could hear her speaking to someone else. She just couldn't make out what they were saying.

A few seconds later, she came back on. "I want to talk. One hour, in the parking lot across from last night's... altercation."

"What makes you think I'm interested in talking?" Alex asked, leaning against the door.

Riley snickered. "Because if you don't, I'll show the police footage of you brutally attacking me and Janice."

Alex's heart plummeted. Panic pulsed through her veins as she replayed every moment of the previous night in her mind. She was certain she'd left no evidence behind. *Was Riley bluffing?* She couldn't risk it.

"Fine." She glanced at her watch. "I'll see you at eleven at—"

The call disconnected, and she glared at the phone, wishing she could strangle Riley through it.

A sharp rap on her door made Alex screech, jarring her from vengeful thoughts.

When she opened it, her Aunt Min was smiling back on the other side. "I was just checking to see if you were okay."

She wondered if her aunt overheard any part of the conversation. The doors in their apartment were paper thin.

"I'm... good." She forced a smile. "I just need to... meet my study buddy downtown. I forgot all about it."

She pocketed her phone, letting the silence hang between them for a few seconds. "Well... I should get going. It's a long walk, and I need to gather my things."

"That sounds like fun!" Aunt Min beamed. "I could check out some shops while you meet your friend." She turned and snatched her purse off the end table without waiting for a reply.

"I..." Alex scurried out of her room, searching for an excuse to dissuade her aunt from going. "I don't know how long I'll be."

"That's okay." Aunt Min checked her wallet. "It's better than sitting around here by myself. Plus, I've never shopped in an American clothes store before."

"Wait... what?" Alex squinted toward the empty kitchen. Both her parents were gone.

"They had to work," Aunt Min explained. "Your father got a page about some high-roller client asking for him, and your mother forgot she had a cleaning shift at that hotel she works at. What's it called again?"

"Belvoir," Alex muttered.

"That's right." Aunt Min snapped her fingers and opened the door.

Alex shook her head. She couldn't believe this was happening. Her aunt couldn't be there when she met Riley.

As she started toward the door, Aunt Min stopped her. "Aren't you forgetting something, young lady?" She glanced past Alex.

She spun around to where her aunt indicated; her school bag was on the footstool.

"Right," she said, slinging it over her shoulder.

As she stepped out the door, Aunt Min cleared her throat.

Alex tilted her head and shrugged. "Now what?"

"In Seoul, we usually lock our doors when we leave." Aunt Min eyed the open atrium between the buildings, her gaze lingering on the apartment with the black-papered windows. "I don't know about Fremont, but I'd guess it works similarly."

Alex sighed, fishing her keys out of her backpack. Her aunt was as snarky as her mother. "Sorry. My mind's somewhere else."

She quickly locked the door and spun around, heading toward the stairwell.

Aunt Min jogged up beside her, and they walked down the stairs side by side. "Are you sure you're okay, dear?"

She nodded, fighting down a tumultuous mix of concern, fear, and reluctance. "I'm peachy. Jusssst... peachy."

ALEX HAD difficulty scanning the cars in the small parking lot. Most of them had tinted windows, which made it nearly impossible to tell if anyone was inside.

One of the many discomforts of living near people with money was the struggle to keep up with the Joneses, especially when every new car in the driveway was a silent battle for supremacy. These lemmings needed SUVs like a fish needs a bicycle, yet each model was more extravagant than the last.

She managed to ditch her aunt at a boutique clothing store a few blocks away. Mom said her sister could spend hours window shopping, only to buy cheap knockoffs online later. While her mother thought it was strange, Alex saw it as a clever way to maintain appearances without breaking the bank.

During their walk, Aunt Min kept eyeing her neck, repeatedly asking if she was okay. At one point, she even tried to adjust the collar on Alex's jacket. While she claimed to be straightening it, Alex swore she was trying to rub off the makeup covering her bruises.

With her mind elsewhere, she missed Riley's approach.

"Nice try with the coverup," Riley scoffed, eyeing her with amused contempt. "It's like, totally off from your skin tone. Seriously, did you grab that at the dollar store? So generic."

Alex turned and gasped, trying hard not to stare at Riley's swollen purple eye or her black and blue nose wrapped in tape. She looked like she'd been smacked in the face with something heavy; probably because she had.

Alex drew a circle in the air around Riley's face. "You might wanna try some concealer yourself."

"Fuck off, Annoy-Lex." Riley rolled her eyes, voice dripping with disdain. "Clearly, you're just desperate."

Alex suppressed a laugh, suddenly less bothered by her bruised neck. "What the hell do you want, Riley?"

"I'll tell you what we want," a man said from behind her.

Alex flinched, spinning around. When she saw who it was, she inadvertently turned her back against the building, boxing herself in.

Not her best move.

"What I want," the man continued, "is to know why you assaulted my daughter and her friend last night."

"Stupid," she muttered. She should've known Riley wouldn't come alone. Judging by the man's bad dye job and noticeable use of bronzer, he was clearly her father. He looked oddly familiar, but she couldn't pinpoint from where.

Riley inhaled sharply. "Excuse me, what did you call my dad?"

"Nothing." Alex swallowed hard, glancing between them. "I was just clearing my throat."

"How about you act your age?" Riley's father reached out and nudged Alex's shoulder.

She recoiled, rubbing the spot. People didn't touch her. Not without permission.

"Touch me again, asshole, and you'll regret it." She pointed at Riley. "You can ask your offspring what happened last time someone pissed me off."

He stepped back, hands raised in a placating gesture. "Now, now. There's no need for threats. We're all civilized here."

She smirked. "If you're threatened by a high school girl, maybe you should think twice about your manhood."

He scoffed. "Exactly what I expected from the likes of you. And just look at yourself." His gaze dropped to her hands. "My daughter ends up looking like she's been through a tornado, while you come out of it merely needing a manicure, not that you could afford one."

Alex shrugged, examining her nails. "I don't know. I think they're feisty. But maybe you should teach your offspring how to fight? Either that, or shut their trap."

"You've got a sharp tongue on you." He curled his nose. "Someone oughta wash your mouth out with soap."

She sighed. She didn't need to deal with this shit right now. If she wanted to have a useless adult insult her, she'd rather be in gym class listening to her obese teacher tell her how lazy she was.

"Did you coerce your daughter into luring me here for a reason, or do you just enjoy belittling teenagers? Though, it has been insightful. At least now I know where Riley gets her charming personality from."

Riley's father narrowed his gaze, clearly confused. But instead of asking her what she meant, he lashed out, dropping his act.

He leaned forward, his face dangerously close to hers. "I'm going to love ruining you and your shovel-headed parents. They'll be deported by tomorrow if I have anything to say about it. You done screwed with the wrong family, you trailer park trash. Insulting me is one thing, but hurting my innocent daughter was the biggest mistake you ever made."

Riley snickered behind her hand.

"Innocent my ass," Alex muttered, wiping spittle off her shirt. "And next time, say it, don't spray it, Daddy-O."

Riley's father lunged toward her, jamming his finger into her chest. "Don't fucking talk to me like—"

"Get your goddamn hands off my niece!" Her aunt sprinted up beside Alex and snatched at the man's wrist, twisting it to the side.

He winced and tried to pull away, but instead of wrestling himself free, he dropped to his knees, wincing. "Shit! That bloody hurts!"

"I suspect it does." Aunt Min peered sideways at her. "Are you alright?" she mouthed.

Alex nodded, still rubbing her chest. "He's got pokey ass fingers," she whispered.

Aunt Min snorted, a brief but genuine display of amusement. It was moments like these that reminded Alex why her aunt was her favorite. Even if they'd only talked from afar.

"Let him go!" Riley demanded. She reached for her father, but thought better of it and pulled back. "Or... or I swear, I'll call the cops."

"Go ahead," Aunt Min challenged. "I'll be more than happy to show them the video of your dad assaulting my niece."

"That's nothing," Riley's father grimaced, his hand still in her aunt's vicelike hold. "I've got a video showing your precious little niece brutally attacking my daughter and her best friend. According to her school records, she's eighteen, which makes her liable to be tried as an adult under California law." His attempted smirk became a whimper as her aunt twisted further.

Aunt Min glanced at Alex. "Is that true? Did you do that to her face?"

She bit her lip, momentarily torn between lying and the truth. Before she could decide, Riley held up her smartphone, a jittery video playing on the screen.

Alex cringed, watching herself swing her backpack at Riley's head. It donged louder than she remembered, sending Riley down to the ground like a sack of potatoes, her phone clattering beside her. The device ended up pointing skyward at the girls from below.

The new angle captured Alex fighting with another girl, kicking her, then swinging something heavy, knocking her down with a thud.

During the scuffle, Riley clambered up and flew at Alex, landing a decent cross for a frail girl.

Alex rubbed her cheek, watching the video. Echoes of the sting still lingered, and she suddenly wondered why it never bruised.

But a judge wouldn't care. No amount of bruising would matter. This video made her look like the aggressor, especially with what came next.

Aunt Min gasped, releasing the man's wrist as she watched Alex grab at the grass. It was like she knew what was coming.

Seconds later, Alex came out swinging with a rock, bashing it repeatedly against Riley's face.

Blood sprayed everywhere on Riley, yet somehow, missed Alex entirely, as if she had an invisible force field or something.

Again, not a good look. Given the girls' injuries, it was hard to see the fight as anything but an unprovoked assault.

Glancing at Aunt Min, Alex saw tears and disbelief in her eyes. Her aunt stared back with disgust, just like Riley's dad.

And then a wave of fear passed over her as she realized who Riley's father was; his face had been plastered all over town. He was running for the friggin mayor of Fremont.

"Shit," she muttered.

"That's right," her father sneered. "The little skank saw her life flash before her eyes, didn't you?" He grinned. "I can see those bars slamming in your face even now."

But Alex was ignoring him, staring instead at her aunt's hurt and confused expression. The idealized image of her niece had shattered in mere moments, and all from a single recording.

"The video," she muttered. That was it. She'd forgotten about her copy.

"It was captured on Harper's phone," Riley snipped, arms crossed. "Right before you attacked. I was so scared." She shuddered dramatically, as if rehearsing for court. "It was awful. I didn't know what to do."

When their eyes met, Alex offered a wry smile. She swore she'd wiped their phones clean. The two girls shared an unusual relationship, their phones adorned with each other's pictures as wallpapers, making it challenging to distinguish one phone from the other.

Harper was likely using Snapchat or something. The footage was probably in the cloud when Alex grabbed it. What her version of the video neglected to show were the taunts and jeers leading up to that pivotal moment of anger. She must've started recording just as Alex lunged toward them.

Aunt Min reached over and gently tugged her arm, pulling her away. "We should go."

"No!" She yanked her hand back, eyes locked on Riley. "What about your phone? Where's *your* video?"

"I don't..." Riley cast a fleeting glance at her father. "I don't know what you're talking about."

"Alex!" Aunt Min pleaded.

Alex ignored her, focusing on Riley. "Surely you checked your school email this morning, right?"

Riley's nose scrunched up. "Why on earth would I do that? It's the weekend."

"What's she talking about?" Her father stepped up beside her, a glint of fear in his eyes.

"Damn!" Alex covered her mouth, her confidence swelling with each passing second. "You really should check it. There might be a missing assignment to finish."

"What the hell is she going on about?" Riley's father tilted his head, staring at his daughter. His gaze spoke volumes about the lies between them.

Little did he know, this was probably the tip of the iceberg.

"I'm confused too," Aunt Min said, returning to Alex's side and sliding her arm through her elbow. "Why are you talking about school?"

Her aunt squeezed her arm gently. Not a "let's get the hell out of here" squeeze like earlier, but an "I've got your back, just be careful" gesture. It was all Alex needed to plow forward.

"I... don't have a video," Riley said, straightening her flowery dress. "Harper was the only one who caught it. And we're lucky too." She scowled at Alex. "Otherwise, you'd have gotten away with this."

Alex glared back. "Maybe you oughta check before you say anything else."

"Her school email?" Riley's father asked, confused. "Why would she—" And then realization struck.

He snatched Riley's purse off her shoulder, tore it open, and retrieved her phone, tossing the overpriced handbag aside. With practiced precision, he flipped the device on, brought up the mail app, and swiped down to retrieve new messages.

His body deflated when the device dinged with new mail, and he saw the sender's name. "Are you—"

"LexBear01?" Alex interrupted. "Yep. That's me. My

father used to call me Lex Bear when I was little." She smiled. "Why don't you hit play? Maybe then you'll see the whole picture."

Without waiting, Alex reached out and tapped play on the attachment.

The video began, except this time it started from several minutes earlier.

Aunt Min leaned closer, trying to watch over the man's shoulder.

Alex didn't bother. The events were etched into her memory, having endured them in excruciating detail the previous evening.

The searing image formed in her mind's eye as the audio played back. Ethnic jeers and taunts from the two girls, every disgusting slur in the book and a few she'd never heard before last night. Each word made Alex cringe, fighting the urge to slam the girl's face into the pavement. Consequences be damned.

As if that weren't enough to bear, they started insulting the entire immigrant community in Fremont. And that's where Riley really tripped up. You could almost claim the girls weren't themselves, as their faces hadn't appeared on camera. But always the performers, Riley panned the phone toward Harper, who broke out in laughter.

And then, it got worse.

"When my father gets elected mayor," Riley's voice spoke from behind the camera, "he's going to slip in some laws to rid this town of those shovel-heads. He told me last week. He's tired of dealing with their kind always asking for higher pay. It's sickening."

Alex looked from the shocked face of Riley's father to her aunt. It was only then that she realized Aunt Min wasn't watching the video anymore. She was staring at Alex.

"I had to." Alex's lip quivered, her hand clenching into a fist. "I couldn't... take it anymore."

"This... this doesn't prove anything." Riley's father tapped delete on the message just as the carnage began. "It's... your word against ours. I never saw the full video. I'll say as much under oath." He slid the phone into his pocket, a smug smile forming. "You see, there's something that makes you and me different, Ms. Mercer. I'm a powerful man, and your parents are nobodies. I think we both know who the courts will side with."

Aunt Min gasped. "We'll just see about that. I'll be happy to take the stand myself."

Riley's father broke into a belly laugh. "And who the hell are you?" He waved his hand up and down, appraising her. "Are you even a citizen?"

"No," she muttered, "not yet. But that—"

"Means everything." He eased forward, lowering his voice. "Your word carries no weight here. If you're not a citizen, you're useless. I'll make certain of that, right after I get you deported."

He circled them like a predator, stopping behind Aunt Min. "You know what truly disgusts me?" His voice dropped to a venomous whisper. "My family—we fought and clawed our way up from nothing in this country. Three generations of proud Mexican-Americans who earned our place here."

He reached out and flicked Aunt Min's jacket collar, making her flinch. "We adapted. Assimilated. Became real Americans." His face contorted with revulsion as he moved back into their line of sight. "But your people? You huddle in your little enclaves, bowing and scraping, chattering in your gibberish. Always the same—whether it's your trashy convenience stores or your discount nail salons." He gestured dismissively toward the neighboring salon. "At least we had the dignity to leave our old world behind."

Alex's hands curled into fists, her nails biting into her palms. Every muscle in her body screamed to lash out, to make him pay for every poisonous word. "So that makes you better?" she spat. "Betraying your own immigrant roots to punch down at others?"

"Better?" He barked out a harsh laugh, straightening his designer jacket. "Look around you, little girl. I'm running for mayor while your parents clean toilets and drive strangers around town." He tapped his chest. "The proof's in the pudding, as they say."

Aunt Min stepped forward, placing herself between Alex and Sanchez. Despite being a head shorter, she somehow seemed to look down at him, her voice carrying the weight of generations of endured prejudice. "And yet here you are, threatening a teenage girl and her family. Such dignity." Her lips curved in a cold smile. "Such... American values."

Mr. Sanchez's face darkened, and he stepped closer until he was inches from Aunt Min's face. "Values?" He reached into his jacket pocket, pulling out his phone. "Let me show you some American values. One call to my friends at ICE, and you'll see exactly how this country treats mouthy immigrants who don't know their place." His fingers hovered over the keypad. "I hear the detention centers are particularly lovely this time of year."

Aunt Min's earlier bravado crumbled as the reality of her precarious situation hit home. She stepped back, fear filling her eyes. She'd only just arrived, and already the system was working against her. All because a poor excuse for a human refused to admit his mistakes or his daughter's. It wasn't fair.

Well, Alex wasn't having any of it. She reached into her pocket and pulled out her cheap-ass clamshell phone, held it in front of them for a split second, and hit the end button.

"What's... that?" Riley's father asked, reaching for the tiny device.

She gripped it in her fist before swinging her other hand forward, purposely missing his face. "Back off!"

He yipped like a dog and flinched away.

"It's insurance." She smiled at her aunt. "Let's just say I covered my bases in more ways than one."

Aunt Min took her hand again and squeezed it tight.

"The audio won't hold up," he snapped, eyes darting. "It could be anyone saying those things."

"Maybe." Alex shrugged. "But between the school's permanent copies of student emails, and my online backup..." She turned to Riley. "I'm pretty sure we're covered. I'll be certain to send a copy to the press this afternoon."

"What... copy?" Riley's father sputtered. "This is Riley's phone." He pulled her smartphone out of his pocket. It was still on.

Alex tugged Aunt Min's hand and tilted her head down the street. They were done here.

As they turned to go, Riley's father called after them. "You're lying! You have nothing!"

She shook her head as Aunt Min pulled her closer, walking away side by side.

"Check the *Sent Mail*, Mr. Sanchez!" Alex shouted. "And remember..." She craned her neck backward at the two of them staring at the device. "There's always a trail, especially if you're too stupid to cover your ass."

She watched him fumble with the device before finding the *Sent Mail* folder. He tapped the screen and staggered sideways, sliding down against the glass window to the ground.

He'd seen the copy of the message Alex sent out to multiple emails. While he might be powerful in this small town, he couldn't escape the reach of the internet.

They walked in silence to Dino's Diner. Alex had been there a few times with her parents, but they rarely ate out nowadays. When they did, her father always chose all-you-can-eat places, preferring to get as much as possible for the money.

After the hostess seated them in a booth, a waitress approached. They were still staring at each other in silence, neither sure what to say to the other. They hadn't even looked at their menus yet.

The waitress smiled, holding her pad at the ready. "What can I get you both to drink?"

Aunt Min flipped the menu over, searching for beverages, so Alex spoke first. "Coffee please, cream and sugar."

"Do you want a latte? A mocha? Or maybe a chi—" the waitress began, reaching to point at the drink list.

"Just a coffee," Alex interrupted. "Plain old coffee." She attempted a smile, but it came off forced, and the waitress sensed it.

The woman's smile cooled as she turned to her aunt. "And you, dear?"

"I'll have a mimosa." Aunt Min smiled. "Actually, make that two."

The waitress glanced at Alex, their eyes locking briefly. "We don't serve minors here."

"And neither do I!" Aunt Min retorted. "They're for me, and I'm offended you'd even insinuate otherwise. If I had half a mind, I'd ask to talk to your—"

"I'm sorry," the waitress said, flushing with embarrassment. "I just... I assumed."

"You know what happens when you assume?" Aunt Min asked, cocking her head slightly.

The waitress nodded. "I make an ass out of you and me." She lowered her pad and stared. "My grandmom used to say that all the time."

"Well, it's been a long morning... for both of us." Aunt

Min reached out and took Alex's hand, giving it a squeeze. "And unlike her, I need more than one drink."

"I'll get right on that," the waitress said, tapping her pen nervously. "And the drinks... they'll be on the house. Again, I'm sorry. While I'm getting your beverages, the specials are here." She pointed at the paper clipped to the menu. "I recommend the chicken and waffles. It's never been on the menu before, but we have a new chef joining us from Georgia. I had them the other day. They're delicious"—she rubbed her stomach—"and if you're already having a rough morning, it could be just the right sweet and savory you need to get back on track."

Aunt Min grinned. "That sounds wonderful."

When the woman left, her aunt glanced at Alex, eyes glimmering with exhaustion.

Alex just stared back. Her aunt always spoke with such power and confidence, never taking shit from anyone. She wasn't at all like her mother, at least not her mom of the past few years. There was a time when her mother was like her aunt. Strong. Confident. Focused. But her mom never liked confrontation, preferring the path of least resistance. But not Aunt Min. She lived life to a different drumbeat, commanding a room when she wanted to, or blending into the background. And she did it so smoothly, you could hardly notice.

"What is it?" her aunt asked, rubbing her chin. "Do I have something on my face?"

Alex shook her head. "No. I was just... marveling at how you carry yourself. Even when people treat you like shit, you always seem to recover. To rise up. Mom used to tell me stories about the things you got out of as a kid. You're amazing."

Her aunt chuckled.

"What?" Alex asked.

"I wouldn't call how I dealt with your Sanchez friend 'rising above' anything."

"Well..." Alex's voice faded as the waitress set down their drinks. "Thank you."

"Did you two decide on breakfast?" the waitress asked.

"We'll both have chicken and waffles," Aunt Min said, handing the menus back with a smile.

Alex tilted her head, studying her aunt. Ordering for her felt weird, especially since she wasn't a kid anymore. Though somehow she'd known exactly what she wanted.

They'd been pretty close online for years, spending hours talking on countless voice chats. It was no wonder her aunt knew she was a breakfast lover who'd jump at the chance to try something new, like chicken and waffles.

Not that Alex dined out enough to call herself a foodie, but she loved browsing food porn online. Part of her couldn't imagine making the kind of money where you bought whatever you wanted to eat. She usually only ate well at school, when the cafeteria let kids like her eat for free. They called it 'The no child goes hungry' program, or something like that. She called it her culinary lifeline.

When the waitress left, Alex pulled her coffee close and tore open a few sugar packets, shrugging off the faux pas. Maybe it was a Korean thing. Her aunt was just being nice; there was no need to get food ragey.

She stirred in the sweetener and eyed her aunt. "As I was saying. You handled yourself with the Sanchezes with grace. There's a time and place to stand up, but there's no sense in arguing with crazy."

"I hear that," Aunt Min said, raising her mimosa for a toast.

Alex poured a dab of milk into her mug and stirred quickly. She clinked her cup against her aunt's. "To rising above."

Aunt Min smiled. "To rising above."

Seconds later, she lowered an empty glass. She wasn't kidding about needing a drink.

Suddenly, Alex's phone chimed. It was sitting on the bench beside her. The message was from an unknown caller, but she knew right away who it was from.

She stared at the phone briefly, then slid it across the table.

Aunt Min pulled it closer, squinting at the tiny text screen.

UNKNOWN CALLER
Tell me what you want?

It took her aunt a few seconds to realize who it was from, but when she did, she raised her second glass in the air and offered a toast. "To college!"

"College?" Alex coughed, swallowing hard as she lowered her mug. "What... what are you talking about?"

Aunt Min glanced at Alex's bag, then back up. "Let me see that fancy letter you're hiding. The one with the embossed seal."

"Letter?" Alex narrowed her gaze. "What letter?"

Then it hit her. The college admission letter in her bag. She'd been staring at it since it arrived.

"Go on." Aunt Min gestured toward the bag. "Take it out."

Alex slowly flipped open the messenger flap and pulled out the pristine white envelope, carefully passing it to her aunt.

She snatched it out of her hand and held it up. "The University of Michigan," she read aloud, squinting at the intricate text. "Is that the state that's shaped like a mitten?"

Alex giggled and took a long swig of coffee. "It is."

"It's gotta be as cold as hell up there," Aunt Min said as she unfolded the paper.

Alex watched her read the letter, mouthing the words one by one.

For some reason, she found herself getting anxious. She didn't know why, but sharing her dream with someone else put her nerves on edge. That was probably why she never told anyone she'd applied in the first place. It was a dream that felt too far out of reach.

Lately, her parents had been too involved in their own lives to ask about hers. They hadn't brought up college in months. Not that they were bad people, just preoccupied. From keeping a roof over their head to food on their plate, life was hard. Especially as immigrants.

When Aunt Min glanced up, she was grinning ear to ear.

Before she could say anything, Alex lowered her gaze to her mug. "It doesn't matter. I can't afford it. Forty grand a year, it's... too much. Plus, I need to take care of Mom."

She swooshed the remains of the coffee around and downed the rest.

As her aunt stared back, the waitress paused at their table. Without a word, she topped off Alex's mug and disappeared, moving on to the next diner.

Alex smiled at her cup. Bottomless coffee was wonderful.

"It's funny how fast things go from empty to full, isn't it?" Aunt Min slid the letter across the table, face up. "It says you have until February first to decide. That's only a few more days away."

She stared down at the maize and blue embossing, running her fingers over the delicate letters. "It must cost a fortune to print these things."

Aunt Min smirked. "That's why they have to charge an arm and a leg for that tuition."

A cold reality suddenly overcame Alex, one far more stark than not having the funds to attend a dream school.

"Did Dad tell you?" She peered up at Aunt Min, squeezing the mug handle. "We're gonna get kicked out. He lost the rent money to a virus. A computer virus."

Aunt Min nodded, unflinching. "He did. Jin-woo mentioned it this morning when he picked me up at the airport. He told me everything. About his mistake, his huge fight with Soo-yeon, about you walking in last night with those marks on your neck."

Her aunt reached out, pausing short of touching her neck. Her fingers trembled briefly before she pulled away. "He shared all the gory details, and then he asked me to turn around and get back on that plane."

Alex rubbed her eyes, wiping at the tears she hadn't realized were coming. Her father knew about her fight last night, and he didn't say anything. Not a word.

She thought she'd seen the recognition in his eyes, but he chose not to cause her more pain. Not after their argument. Instead, he focused on taking care of them. Both of them. Despite having messed up.

Aunt Min slid her hand across the table and rested it on Alex's. "But I'm here. I didn't leave." She smiled, rubbing her fingers. "Don't worry about your mom and dad. We'll be fine. Besides, I've got enough rent money for a few years. Even at California's insane rates. That tuition, though." She rapped a knuckle on the acceptance letter. "That's too rich for my blood."

She tilted back her drink, emptying the remains of her mimosa. "For that..." She lowered her glass. "For that, we'll have to ask your friend, Mr. Sanchez."

Alex let her words sink in for a second, not quite understanding what she was insinuating. Not until comprehension struck.

Her gaze shot up from the page, locking on her aunt's deep brown, jeweled eyes. "Can... can I do that?" She glanced around, scanning the diner before leaning forward. "Is that... legal?" she whispered.

"Probably not." Aunt Min waved at the waitress and then

toward her. "I think it's called extortion. Or maybe bribery. I don't know. Either way, I'm pretty sure it's not legal. Not even in the greatest country on earth."

Alex's heart sank. Even if she got away with it, she wasn't sure she could live with herself. She wasn't wired that way. She'd worked too hard to let her dream be tarnished like that. Taking hush money had never occurred to her.

"But—" Aunt Min began.

The waitress arrived with their plates of waffles and chicken, along with two more mimosas for her aunt.

After she set the delicious-smelling dishes in front of them, she disappeared.

Aunt Min took out her silverware and started cutting the chicken. Her eyes fixed on the crunchy breakfast delicacy as she used the knife to butter each nook and cranny, following it up with a healthy dose of maple syrup. She then poured the sugary brown liquid over the plate like a candy maker perfecting an intricate design.

"But what?" Alex asked, leaning forward, staring into her eyes. "You said 'but' and never finished."

Aunt Min forked a piece of waffle and chicken and popped it into her mouth, moaning as she enjoyed the breakfast treat.

Alex's stomach growled as she watched her chew, clearly savoring every second of the taste explosion. She swallowed, dabbing the edge of her mouth with her napkin.

Only then did she meet Alex's gaze.

"But... it's not illegal for us if we get someone else to do it." She grinned and winked, glancing at Alex's untouched plate. "Now go on and eat. Before your food gets cold."

7 / BLOCKCHAIN AND SINKER
CIPHER

He confirmed the name and number in the mule database and quickly scanned the bio one last time.

Exchange student, check.

Graduated from secondary school middle of his class, check.

Comes from a poor family, check.

Taking out huge amounts of student loans, double check.

"A goddamn master's degree," he whispered, shaking his head as he hit connect. His computer did the rest, connecting the call from halfway around the world.

The North Korean government paid the Chinese handsomely for an anonymous internet connection that let them reach anywhere on the globe, even under the nose of the Americans.

In this case, he was making an internet phone call routed from Pyongyang, to Beijing, and then ultimately through a PBX in New York City, the financial capital of the Western world. Receiving a call from there was proof enough of the legitimacy of their venture, at least to a rube.

Which was precisely what he was looking for.

After a few seconds of silence, the phone rang and Cipher adjusted his earpiece, clearing his throat.

It was go time.

On the second ring, a man picked up. "Hell... o?"

"Is this Rajesh Gupta?" Cipher asked, his voice crisp and clear, with a hint of Eastern European accent.

"It... is," the voice said, grogginess evident. "May I... ask who's calling?"

Cipher shifted his attention to the notes on his screen. Staying on script was key to landing this student.

"I'm reaching out from Huanjing Bank," he began. "I see here you submitted an application for an internship in one of our remote financial analyst roles."

He paused, letting the words sink in.

Rajesh had applied for an opening in the fake company nearly a month ago, but between his secondary school in India and the college he attended in the States, it took that long to get his records.

While bribing people in India was trivial, in the United States, they were a bit less unscrupulous. And for some reason, his university in Florida had been surprisingly costly to crack.

He'd never paid a thousand dollars for a transcript before, but then again, he'd never had a master's degree candidate apply to be an intern. And from the looks of his records, he was under water with his student loans.

"I... think so," Rajesh muttered, confusion lacing his words. "But that... was a while ago. Over a month. Your company never called me back, so I assumed you'd already filled the role."

"Not at all," Cipher said, taking notes as they went. "While we move slower than most, once we know what we want, we strike. And I hate to admit it out loud, but we rarely miss."

He let the sheer ego of the statement hang in the air before continuing. "In fact, after our conversation, assuming it goes well, I can make you an offer over the phone. Which brings me back to your application, Mr. Gupta. Are you still looking for a summer program?"

Silence stretched from the other end of the line, as if Gupta was weighing his response. That usually meant only one thing.

"I assume, then, that you already have a pending offer?" Cipher probed, hoping Gupta hadn't accepted one already. If he had, he didn't tell his school. It would've been in his transcripts.

"I... was actually planning on accepting an offer today. I have a few, one from Redmond, another from New York, and several from the Bay Area." A faint squeal echoed over the line as Rajesh sat down in what Cipher assumed was a squeaky chair. Muffled key clacking followed, suggesting he was looking up something online. "To whom am I speaking?" he asked.

Cipher grinned and pulled up the webpage for their dummy corp, scanning the details. His image, or at least one that resembled him, was there on the 'About Us' page. "This is Vladimir Wenxian, I'm the—"

"CEO," Rajesh stammered. "Wh-why would you be calling me about an internship?"

"Like I said earlier, once we know what we want, we move fast." Cipher brought up the young man's grades.

Middle of the road in his class and not particularly excellent at anything. Based on his late application to grad school, he was doubling down with this master's degree nonsense, hoping something would take. Probably because he couldn't find a job.

The Western world had snared the poor lad in its deceptive traps. They'd sold their people on the necessity of college long ago. Governments were persuasive that way, especially when they controlled the economic purse strings.

Besides, how else would they lure the populace into lifelong debt? After that, there was always homeownership and kids.

A vicious loop.

"I see you've got high marks from one of your professors," Cipher said, injecting a hint of approval into his voice. Even if it was a lie.

"Uh... that... that must be from Professor Sanders," Rajesh said.

Cipher shook his head. Wrong, but he'd go with it.

"Indeed." He scanned the transcripts for the name. "He's your Econ professor."

"She," Rajesh corrected.

"Sorry, she." Cipher made a note. "That'll come in handy if you make it into our intern program."

He marveled at how people in the West could be so ignorant about the real world. Professors didn't mark up transcripts. They wrote letters of recommendation. And given his grades, this kid couldn't pay for one. Especially being nearly three hundred thousand American dollars in the hole.

"How about we turn it up a notch, Rajesh?"

"Alright, sir."

Cipher smiled, selecting the first question from his database. "Imagine you're valuing a mid-sized tech company planning to go public next year. They have stable revenue and are making sizable R&D investments. Talk me through your valuation approach. Given the company's diverse activities and future prospects, which methods of assessing worth would you prioritize and why?"

A textbook question. Even though their job was a front for washing stolen money into crypto, they still needed to look legit if audited. With the ridiculous number of hedge funds in the world, everyone was always analyzing everyone else.

"Well," Rajesh began, "given the company's growth potential and industry, I'd use both the Discounted Cash Flow method for revenue projections and comparative analysis to benchmark against similar companies. The DCF would help capture the value of future innovations, while comparables provide a market realism check."

Cipher nodded, jotting down observations. The kid wasn't half bad. His answer was spot on.

"Interesting choice," he said, ticking 'yes' on the mule recruiting form and waiting for the next question to pop up. "Could you elaborate on how you'd project the free cash flows in your DCF model?"

He had no idea what he was asking most of the time, but whoever wrote these questions did. All they wanted from him was a solid European voice to deliver them. That, and the ability to close the deal.

Rajesh paused. At first, Cipher thought he was considering his answer. Then he caught the faint click of keys when he turned up his volume. The little fucker was cheating.

After a few more seconds of typing, Rajesh finally answered. "I'd... forecast the cash flows by... factoring in a growth rate, maybe ten percent for existing products. Oh yeah, and an increased rate post new product launches."

Cipher jotted a note. Rajesh fell silent again, probably scrolling through whatever webpage he'd found.

"Is that it?" Cipher prodded, wondering if he should chance it with this one.

"No," Rajesh faltered. "I'm missing something. I think... Yeah, I'd also need to adjust for the company's reinvestment in R&D."

"And then?" Cipher scanned through the lengthy answer on his screen. The kid had missed a lot.

"Can you give me a hint?" Rajesh asked. "I'll be honest, sir... I'm a bit rusty on valuations. We're working on mergers and acquisitions strategies right now."

"I appreciate the honesty." Cipher nodded. Admitting weakness wasn't all bad.

He skimmed his script, picking out the next keyword. "What about the terminal value?"

"Oh, shit! The t-value." Rajesh groaned.

He could almost see the young man kicking himself.

"For the terminal value, I'd likely use a... perpetuity growth model? Right?" Rajesh asked, his confidence waning.

"Go on," Cipher said.

"That's assuming a conservative growth rate, of course. One slightly below the industry average. To account for market saturation risks."

Cipher nodded, fighting a yawn as boredom threatened to overwhelm him. He loathed this part of his job. Still, he continued peppering the man with textbook questions for another thirty minutes.

The clock in his screen's corner ticked down the ideal time before he should end the call, leaving the candidate convinced they'd been properly challenged. At this rate, he'd finish about a dozen questions.

Beyond testing their knowledge, the key to success with any money mule candidate was ensuring they knew next to nothing about their real task: money laundering.

By the time he finished his script, he realized the kid was quite talented. He may have started by cribbing notes, but Cipher hadn't heard typing since. Maybe that master's degree wasn't a waste after all.

The software in their interview app flagged Rajesh as a low to medium risk mule. He might get wise to their deal, or he might not. Only time would tell.

Given the kid's situation, Cipher decided to give him a

shot. Worst case, he'd cut him loose early if he got too smart for his own good.

He switched to the closing section of his report. "I have one last question for you, Mr. Gupta."

He scanned Rajesh's financials, doing some quick math. With only a few months left in school, the harsh reality of repaying student loans loomed. Helping him halve his bills should be excellent motivation to keep quiet. Especially considering the amount of money he'd be moving for them.

Rajesh cleared his throat. "What's that, sir?"

Cipher smirked. Time to go in for the kill. "How would you like to make a hundred grand this summer?"

He swore he heard a gasp over the line, but it was quickly silenced. The line fell eerily silent, and for a split second, he wondered if they'd been disconnected.

"Rajesh, are you there?" He tilted his head, checking his PBX connection and waiting for a reply.

"I... am," Rajesh finally said, voice trembling with disbelief. "I just... I thought you said a hundred thousand. As in... US dollars?"

Cipher chuckled, savoring the thrill of the hunt. "Well, if we paid you in yen, that wouldn't get you very far, would it?"

"No, sir." Rajesh laughed. "That wouldn't even cover rent."

"So, what do you say, Rajesh? Come work with us." Cipher gazed out the glass partition into the bullpen of programmers.

"What would you have me doing, sir?" Rajesh probed. "You haven't said anything about the job yet."

While normally a red flag after dropping the paycheck, he couldn't fault the kid for not wanting to waste his time. A summer without experience wouldn't please his Western overlords.

"As I mentioned earlier," Cipher said, "you'd be coming

on as a remote financial analyst. That means you get to work from the comfort of your dorm, helping us do some company valuations."

"Is it an M&A role?" Rajesh asked.

"Not exactly." Cipher flipped through the post-offer playbook Choe usually walked the mule through. "Besides valuations, you'll learn a lot about crypto and tearing apart financial statements."

Throwing out cryptocurrencies would either scare him off or reel him in. He was about to find out which.

"Bitcoin?" Rajesh asked, keyboard clacking faintly. "Isn't that up nearly three hundred percent this year?"

And there it was.

"That's right." Cipher smirked, typing out the offer email and hitting send. "You'll have a front-row seat to the evolution of a new financial paradigm using blockchain. What do you think? Will you join my team?"

The line went quiet. You could practically hear the gears turning in Rajesh's head.

Nearly a minute passed before he replied.

"I'll accept it on one condition," Rajesh said.

Cipher raised an eyebrow. "What's that?"

"I report directly to you and only you," Rajesh said confidently. "Like you said, Mr. Wenxian, when you know what you want, you strike."

He squinted, almost asking who Mr. Wenxian was before remembering his fake last name.

This kid was a go-getter. He liked that.

"I'm a busy man, Mr. Gupta. I can't promise you hands-on time every day."

"Fair enough," Rajesh said. "But I learn fast. I'm a hard worker. What do you think? Do you need a new assistant this summer?"

Cipher smirked as Choe approached his office door, eyeing him through the glass.

He held up a finger, pointing to his earpiece.

"I tell you what..." He stood, adjusting his uniform. "You sign the NDA and agree to the terms in your inbox, and you have yourself a deal. Okay?"

"Done!" Rajesh shot back, his voice brimming with excitement.

Cipher motioned Choe in.

"That's wonderful, Mr. Gupta." He tapped the verbal acceptance button on the mule application and closed the window. "Looking forward to working with you this summer. My assistant will contact you later this week with your start date. Until then, good luck with your classes."

"Thank you so much, Mr. Wenxian," Rajesh said. "I promise you won't regret it."

"I hope not. Now you have a wonderful day, Rajesh."

"You too, sir."

He clicked disconnect and unhooked his earpiece.

Choe sauntered in, a mischievous glint in her eye. "Another mule in the bag?"

"Indeed," he said, striding around the desk. "This one was a hard sell, but I think he'll be useful."

He eyed the tally on the far wall screen, calculating the time to clear that much cash. His virus was raking in some serious numbers, making it increasingly difficult to move the funds in secret. Foreign banks were becoming more vigilant about money laundering. They'd need twice the mules to cover their transactions. Either that, or go bigger.

As Cipher gazed upon the fruits of his labors, he contemplated his next move, his mind whirring with cold, ruthless efficiency.

The mules were naïve, eager recruits, but a necessary evil in his grand design. They were the sacrificial lambs bearing the brunt of the risk while he reaped the rewards. For in the end, it was only his legacy that mattered, his name would endure long after their souls, or those of his overseers, faded into oblivion.

8 / LEGACY CODE
ALEX

The past few months vanished in a blink. Alex swallowed down the rising lump in her throat as she neatly packed her suitcase. Unlike the rest of her college peers, she wasn't arriving with a carload of possessions.

There would be no dressers crammed with outfits, secret microwaves, or entertainment systems for her dorm room. Her life fit in these two suitcases. Excess had never been part of her upbringing, and she was fine with that. About the only room accessories she was taking were the University of Michigan flag her father bought online, and photocopies from her sketchbooks.

She flipped through the crisp white pages, wondering if her roommate would even want the odd caricatures and alien-like symbols on their walls. While the art held meaning for her, telling stories of her past life experiences and feelings, she wasn't sure Michelle would appreciate them.

That was the name of her new college roommate. They'd only video chatted a few times, but hit it off instantly. They messaged and emailed every day. And while Alex couldn't afford to attend the on-campus orientation like most students, she attended what she could remotely.

Michelle relayed her angst-and-joke-filled synopsis of the boring in-person events via instant message. It made Alex feel included, even if she missed the fun parts.

Like Alex, Michelle had grown up in California, so the Midwest's bitter cold would be new to both of them. They shared a love for anime and computers, but Michelle had only discovered her passion for programming in her senior year, lagging behind Alex's expertise.

From what she said, Michelle had built a website and a few simple apps. Though her work paled compared to Alex's, the university didn't seem to care. Michelle had packed her first three years of high school with college prep classes, making her major a mere technicality.

Alex stopped flipping the sheets, pausing on her newest piece, a black and white phoenix sketch. It was her favorite drawing to date, having taken ages to perfect the proportions and shading. Dozens of failed attempts preceded this final rendition. When she glanced up, a copy of the same image hung on the wall of her room.

The mythical bird rose from a burning building, sketched to appear slightly blurred, almost pixelated. If you looked closely, the house melded her current apartment with her first adoptive home, except in the picture everything was falling apart.

And then there was the phoenix in the center. Instead of feathers, the bird had intricate wings, and a beak made of microchips. The composition was meant to depict a biological transformation within a physical one, a rebirth amidst collapse.

She'd created this image earlier in the spring, after accepting her admission to university. At the time, she was neck deep into deciphering the virus and honing her programming skills. Though progress was slow, the picture symbolized her emergence into her true self, rising from the ashes of her past.

The idea of attending college still perplexed her. Even that morning, she'd pinched her arm when she woke up, waiting for the dream to end yet not wanting it to.

She was about to undertake a life change, the likes of which she hadn't faced in nearly a decade. Not since that fateful day she met her parents for the first time.

The chatter of two women pulled her from her memories, returning her to the task at hand. She carefully stacked the pages, sliding them into a folder inside an inner pocket of her new luggage.

As she returned to her drawer to grab another handful of clothes, her mom and aunt entered, their hands overflowing with dishes and drinks.

"What's this?" Alex tossed her shirts into the case and reached over to help. Steaming pizza slices and crispy breadsticks teetered precariously on the plates.

"We're not gonna leave you in here to pack all alone. Not on your last night." Mom leaned in and pecked Alex's cheek, making her way to her aunt's bed.

Alex and Aunt Min had been sharing this bedroom for the past five months, ever since her aunt moved to the US. It was tight with two twin beds and a tiny desk doubling as an end table, but they managed.

'The closer the family, the better,' her dad always said.

To Alex, having her aunt as a roommate was like a long-lost sister moving in. They spent hours talking into the night about everything from boys to basketball.

Though they'd video chatted for years, in-person interactions were an unfamiliar experience. It was scary, yet eye-opening at the same time, having someone to relate to and confide in. Someone who knew what it was like to live alone, travel the world, and didn't just dream of paying rent. Despite being a year older than her mom, her aunt was definitely young at heart.

One thing she'd learned about her aunt after she moved in was her obsession with sports. We're talking over the top insane. She never missed her favorite teams when they played, no matter where they were. The television in their tiny apartment had never seen so much use until she arrived.

Her aunt was devastated to learn Alex had never watched any sort of sport, but was excited to fix it. She refused to let her niece attend a university like Michigan without knowing a thing or two about their basketball and football programs. Apparently, she was quite the sports nerd, whereas Alex couldn't distinguish a three-point shot from a field goal. All she knew was they both gave the same result.

The women laid out the plates in the center of her aunt's bed and sat on opposite sides as the delicious aroma of the cheesy, tomatoey pizza wafted through the room. Alex took the middle, pulling out the chair from the tiny desk and flipping it sideways.

"I've never done this before." Alex smirked, carefully taking a plate and a slice of thick pizza to avoid dripping grease on the comforter.

It was Chicago style, her aunt's favorite. They'd eaten it every other week since she moved in. She called it the one true pizza, and everything else paled in comparison. Alex agreed, though pizza was a rarity before her aunt's arrival. Her parents usually cooked traditional Korean food when they ate at home, which was most meals.

Aunt Min's arrival had changed a lot.

"I've been trying to get you to pack all week," Mom said, winking. "You should get a good night's sleep. It might be your last for a while."

Alex stared down at her plate. Sleep was the furthest thing from her mind. She wasn't even sure she could.

Aunt Min thwacked her sister's arm. "Leave the girl alone. Can't you see she's nervous?"

Mom rubbed her biceps. "No, she's not! She's excited. I can tell."

Alex took another bite and swallowed it down in silence. Her emotions swirled like a vast cauldron filled with every random thought and feeling she'd ever had.

Excitement, fear, sadness, hope. All there, in varying proportions, each ready to overtake her thoughts.

"It's actually a little of both, and..." She paused and sipped her soda, glancing between them. "I don't know how to explain it. It's like all my feelings are fighting for attention, but only one's on the surface right now."

Her mom lowered her slice, peering into Alex's eyes. "Which one's that?"

Alex swallowed hard, nibbling the crunchy dough. She let the yeasty goodness settle before answering.

"Love," she finally said, smiling at both of them.

The honesty overwhelmed the sisters. They tossed their food aside and practically bowled Alex over, their faces awash with tears and smiles. It felt wonderful.

Deep in their cocoon of feminine bonding, they hadn't heard her father come home. Not until he stepped into the room.

"What's all this crying?" he asked, surveying the tangle of bodies. "Did someone die?"

"No..." Aunt Min reached back, pulling him into the pile.

He didn't resist. He simply wrapped his arms around the three of them.

"We're just saying goodbye," Aunt Min whispered. "Tomorrow, your daughter leaves this house a young lady. Next time you see her, she'll be a collegiate woman."

He leaned back, eyeing her. "Not too much like a woman, I hope. We don't need no babies yet."

Mom socked him in the stomach. "Says you. Whenever she's ready, Grandma Mercer is here."

Alex shook her head, her face warming. "You won't have to worry about that for a long while." She smirked. "I've got things to do, places to visit, and experiences to have. I need to... find myself. Find my calling."

"That's what I like to hear." He kissed her forehead, then quickly turned his attention to the pizza. "Now, let's eat! I'm starved."

Mom shook her head, tsking as she slid back to the bed. "You've got the emotional range of a gnat, you insensitive clod." Her words were sharp, but the softness in her eyes belied a love that had weathered countless storms.

He glanced at his watch and shrugged. "What? I have a pickup in an hour, and I'm not about to stink up the car with fast food. I just had her detailed."

"Cut it out, you two. Tonight isn't about you." Aunt Min made Dad a plate and eyed Alex. "It's about her." She handed him the overflowing dish, then took a bite of her own, talking between chews.

"So tell me something," her aunt began. "Why computers? What makes you so certain it's your calling?"

Alex recoiled, tendrils of fear splashing to the surface of her emotional cauldron. The question caught her off guard, and she wasn't sure how to dodge it. Honestly, she was shocked it hadn't come up in their late-night gabbing, or any time before that day. Her parents had never really asked her why. They just followed her lead, never questioning it.

Mom tilted her head, eyeing Alex quizzically, probably wondering about the answer herself. Or maybe she was trying to think back to when Alex first mentioned computers. She'd always waited for Alex to come to her before prying into things. It was both her charm and her flaw as a parent.

What she failed to grasp was that American teens could bottle up far more emotions than their parents realized. Ever since entering high school, Alex felt like a teakettle on the verge of boiling over.

"It's because she's good at it," her father answered, eyeing the half-eaten slice of pizza in his hand, clearly oblivious to the women's mental states.

It wasn't until no one replied that he looked up and saw the two women staring at Alex.

The second his eyes met hers, it was too much. She couldn't hold back the onrush of emotions and broke down in tears.

"I'm sorry..." Aunt Min leapt to her side. "I didn't mean to—"

"No!" Alex interrupted, shaking her head. "It's fine. Really." She swallowed hard and set down her food, fighting the urge to curl up. "Like I said, I'm an emotional roller coaster right now."

Her aunt rubbed her hand and Alex smiled weakly, reaching for her soda. Her throat was suddenly parched.

When she slurped the last drop through her straw, her stomach settled and she took a deep breath.

"You remember how the social workers told you I came up through some rough homes?" She paused, eyeing her parents.

Mom nodded. "Yeah..." she said, her voice trailing off.

Dad lowered his plate, looking at Alex. "We met with your caseworker dozens of times before we actually met you. They told us everything, I think."

"I'm not sure they did," Alex said, her voice barely above a whisper. She stared at her hands, the weight of her past pressing down, threatening to crush her under the burden. "Most court papers involving minors are sealed, even from adopting parents. And except for telling you that my homes were unstable, they couldn't really say much more."

The faint scars on her knuckles seemed to throb in unison, each one a painful reminder of families that had cast her aside. Her first foster family, however, they'd been the cruelest, leaving wounds that still ached.

As she traced the marks on her hand, memories of abuse churned in her mind, threatening to drag her into the darkness. She closed her eyes, taking a deep breath, trying to decide where to begin.

After a moment of heavy silence, she spoke, her lip quivering. "My first adoptive parents... they fought a lot. Like, a lot lot."

"The young couple from Colorado?" Mom asked.

Aunt Min snapped her head around, glaring at her sister. "Let. The. Girl. Talk, Soo-yeon." She lingered for a second before turning back. When their eyes met, her face softened as she squeezed Alex's leg. "Go on, sweetie. You were saying..."

Alex nodded, clenching and unclenching her fists, trying to stop the shaking and to muster the resolve to just spit it all out. The entire story. But the longer she waited, the harder it was to form words.

"It's okay," Dad said, his voice unusually soft. "You don't have to talk about it if you're not ready. It doesn't matter anymore."

Alex closed her eyes. "It does, though, and I do want to tell you. You've earned the right to know. It's just... I haven't thought about this in a long time."

She opened her eyes, meeting his loving gaze. It was a refuge where she could lay bare the deepest parts of herself without fear of judgment or rejection.

The brown flecks in his irises reminded her of fall leaves. Like those on the maple tree outside her bedroom window at the younger couple's house.

"I don't think they knew what they were getting into," she said, fidgeting with the hole in her jeans. "They were really young, and they'd just found out they couldn't have kids. For some reason, they thought they were failures if they didn't have children running around. And apparently, adopting me was their solution."

She tugged at the frayed edges. "What they failed to realize, though, was that their relationship was barely holding on. The IVF had taken its toll. The bills, the self-judgment... it was too much." She slid her finger into the gap in the fabric, feeling the scar on her leg. "The first time he hit me... I was running to help her. My adoptive mom."

She instinctively rubbed her cheek, where remnants of the strike still lingered.

Her father broke down into silent sobs, raising a hand to cover his mouth.

But Alex couldn't look at him. If she did, she wouldn't be able to continue. Whenever he cried, she fell apart. There was something about a man being emotional that made her melt.

Instead, she just pretended this was another therapy session at the orphanage.

"He didn't mean it," she continued. "I know that now. He was winding up to hit her, and I... I walked into his path." She lowered her hand back into her lap. "After that night, they only fought behind closed doors. But it happened more and more often."

Her father whimpered, and she grasped his free hand, still not risking eye contact.

"It's going to sound weird, but... that was the first time I used a computer." She withdrew her hand. "It was all I could do to pass the time when they locked me in his office."

She shuddered, recalling the cold of the room. "I spent hours in that tiny room, staring at the screen. I tried using headphones to drown out their screams, but nothing helped. No amount of music could silence the crack of a hand across a face, or the thud of a body hitting a wall."

Alex shifted in the chair, trying hard to hold back the waves of toxic memories from those days. The metallic scent of blood surfaced in her mind, a pungent reminder of her painful past as it fought for control.

It was so long ago. She'd been so young. So innocent.

It always amazed her how vividly she could remember her darkest memories, but the good ones, they seemed to fade in an instant.

"On one of the nights I was locked up, I stumbled onto an IRC server. I found the weird icon on his machine and accidentally clicked it." She smirked at the thought of finding the mIRC icon. The one with the smiling face. "He buried it in a folder with his porn."

She shook her head. "His wife probably didn't even know he downloaded it. Anyway... I wandered the server all night, watching people argue and talk. It was a strange new world to me. The anonymity of the channels stripped away the pretenses and facades that people usually hid behind. The yelling in all caps, the honest and candid discussions... it was eye-opening. There I was, barely eight, and these strangers thought I was one of them. I could ask them almost anything and they'd answer me. I could share my opinion, and they wouldn't dismiss it. For the first time in my life, I felt like I belonged. In that corner of the net, I could shed my troubled reality and reinvent myself. I could become who I wanted to be."

A moment of silence passed between them as she remembered that feeling. The freedom, the acceptance, the sense of belonging; it intoxicated her childish mind, a glimpse of a world where she could be more than the sum of her scars. But like all happiness, it was destined to be shattered.

"And then I slipped up." She glanced at Aunt Min, whose eyes were transfixed on her words.

Unlike her parents, Aunt Min wasn't crying. Her gaze radiated strength, a quiet resilience speaking of battles fought and won. Battles similar to Alex's.

"What... what happened?" Aunt Min asked. "How'd you

slip up?"

"I shared too much," Alex said softly, guilt and resignation in her voice. "Those first weeks online, I carelessly exposed more and more minutiae about myself. Maybe my subconscious was dropping clues on purpose, but my new friends pieced everything together—what I was going through, where I lived, that I was just a kid." She shook her head, staring down at her jeans again. "I was clueless back then."

"I don't..." Mom paused, catching her words and glancing at her sister.

"Go ahead." Alex picked at the loose threads on her jeans before looking up. "It's fine. You can ask."

Mom swallowed hard. "I don't understand. How was it bad that your friends figured out what you were going through?"

"It wasn't, I guess." Alex rubbed her palms down her legs. "When the police came, the husband acted shocked. He asked me to strip down and show the officer my body. To prove I had no bruises." Her hands started shaking.

"He didn't!" Dad exclaimed.

"He did," she whispered. "And I... I did as I was told. The officer actually made me stop. I'm pretty sure he was as uncomfortable as I was. He stepped outside after that, and his partner..." She swallowed hard. "A female officer checked me over. It was humiliating, especially since my father wouldn't leave. She tried to get me to signal if I was okay, but at the time, I had no idea what she was doing. I was so stupid."

"No, you weren't." Mom slid onto the floor in front of her. "You were just scared. You were a child."

Alex nodded. "After they left... he..." Tears broke loose, cascading down her cheeks.

She drew in a shuddering breath, her voice hoarse. "He beat me... over and over again. The pain, it was unbearable. I thought I was going to die. But he kept demanding that I tell him who I'd been talking to."

Her lips trembled as tears traced paths down her face, stinging long-healed cuts. "I made up a story... about a school friend. How they must've told their parents. I was terrified he'd find out about my online friends and take them away. They were all I had. They were my true family."

She stared down at the threads on her knee. They'd bunched together again, like twisted, mangled knots—a reflection of her tangled past. A reminder that truth, no matter how painful, could never be fully buried. That it would always find a way to surface, like a festering wound that refused to heal.

"It wasn't until the next day that he finally left me alone." She separated the threads again, this time slowly braiding them together. "When he left my room, he went across the hall and started fighting with his wife. As soon as I knew he wasn't coming back, I got online to ask my friends why they turned me in. Why they hurt me."

She sniffled, wiping her eyes. "That was when I first felt it."

"Felt what?" Aunt Min whispered.

"Love," Alex muttered. "The outpouring of affection, it was..." She shook her head. "I'd never seen it before. Not from strangers, and never from my adoptive families. At least not until I met you."

She glanced between them, lingering on each face, memorizing their expressions. She wanted to remember this moment, this feeling.

"That was how I knew you loved me." She bit her lip and nodded. "You were real... and you accepted me, scars and all. But more importantly, you accepted each other, for better or worse. I wasn't your last choice for a family when all else failed. I was your first choice." She shook her head, wiping at her tears. "I don't know why you picked me, but I'm happy you did."

Her parents and aunt all slid forward, wrapping their arms around her. In that embrace, she could literally feel their love flowing through her. The burden of her secrets lifted, replaced by a sense of peace.

They sat like that for what seemed an eternity.

Aunt Min was the first to let go, her voice quivering. "What happened to them? To your... first family?"

Alex met her aunt's eyes, a sudden calm passing over her. She didn't know why, but digging up the memory didn't hurt as much this time.

"The next day after work, he started beating his wife again. I don't know what came over me, but I... I cracked. I fought back."

Dad peered up, confused. "You fought back? But you were only... eight."

Alex straightened her back. "I couldn't take it anymore, hearing him yell at her like that, knowing it should've been me. It was too much. I..." Her voice trembled, her frame shaking as memories flooded back. "I told my online friends what I was planning, begged them to call the police again. I was too scared to call nine-one-one myself, afraid he might hear me or pick up the phone."

She glanced down one last time at her knee. The braided threads around the hole formed a uniform pattern, a metaphor for her life, once tangled and frayed, now woven together into a cohesive whole.

In the harmony of the threadbare pattern, she found purpose, a newfound clarity, a path forward through the darkness.

"I know it sounds weird, but that computer was my lifeline." She ran her fingers over the threads. "It gave me hope in my darkest hours. That feeling of control, of power, that's why I want to go into computers. Not for the geeky electronics or games. I know you don't get it, but the internet is my generation's great unifier. It's our megaphone, our voice in this crazy world we live in. It's our way of ensuring we're heard. And you know what, Dad's right. I am good at it."

When she looked up, he was smiling, but she could tell he was still confused. She hadn't finished her story.

"After I hit enter on that message," she continued, "I said goodbye to my friends. Then I logged off and wiped his entire drive."

She snickered quietly, feeling the rush of adrenaline even now, just like all those years ago.

"I'd never done anything like that before. I knew there was no going back when I hit go. But you know what?" She shook her head. "I didn't care. It felt liberating knowing the pain it would cause him. His entire digital existence was on there. Hell, his business was on that thing, and I deleted it in a single click. One. Powerful. Click, and his life changed forever."

She smiled, remembering the moment vividly. "His problem was that he loved that goddamn job more than anything. Certainly more than his wife... or me."

She sensed her father relax with a slight sigh. He thought her story had ended.

But her aunt knew better.

Maybe she'd read Alex's body language, or perhaps she hoped there was more to her fight than wiping a computer. Either way, her posture remained tense.

And rightfully so.

Alex stared into her eyes. An intense understanding passed between them, a quiet acceptance of Alex's pain and the lengths to which she'd gone to survive.

"After I destroyed his illusion of power," she said, "I knew I needed to do more. At the time, I didn't understand why, but looking back, I think it was because of what he'd done to his wife. She wasn't particularly strong, and she'd never been very affectionate with me.

"But that's not the real reason." She shook her head slowly. "No. It was the way he knocked her out in front of me that first time. I was so scared that night, I... I peed myself. Seeing her lying there, motionless, face covered in blood, I kept wondering why she never fought back. That's when I realized that if *she* didn't fight for herself, then *I* needed to fight for her."

Alex paused, recalling the woman's glassy gaze that evening. The life in her eyes long ago extinguished.

She shuddered, remembering the sickening sound of flesh against flesh, the muffled whimpers of pain echoing through their paper-thin walls.

Pushing past the memory, she continued. "That dull thump of her collapsing, it was all I could see and hear every time I heard a noise from the other room. Day after day, night after night, for months on end, that moment replayed in my mind. He'd hurt her again and again, and she just lay there, letting him do it. But that night was different. That night, the pain she felt was my fault. He was taking out his anger on her, anger meant for me, and that... *that* was unacceptable."

She clenched her fist, focusing on the drawing of the circuit board phoenix taped to the wall of her room. She could practically feel herself rising from those pixelated ashes.

"Unlike her," she continued, "I stopped cowering and fought back. I grabbed the only thing I could find in his office —a strange brass obelisk on his desk. Some award, I think. To be honest, I always thought it looked like a penis. But I'll tell you what, it made the perfect weapon. I held it upside down with both hands and waited by the door until I heard sirens approaching."

She swallowed hard, remembering that moment behind the door, about to face her tormentor. The fear was almost overpowering, but something deeper propelled her forward.

"As soon as I heard the distant whine, I yanked open the

door." She lowered her gaze from the phoenix to her father. "I didn't know where he'd be in the room, but when the door swung wide, I saw him. He was standing with his back to me, staring out between the blinds in the front window. I didn't pause to question what I was about to do. I simply lunged forward, swinging the heavy ass obelisk at his head. I whacked him with everything I had. Every ounce of strength my tiny body could muster."

Her hands trembled so violently, she could practically feel the vibration of the weapon hitting him in the head even now. The smell of the blood; it was intoxicating.

As her words faded, Aunt Min broke the silence. "Did you..." Her voice trailed off.

"Kill him?" Alex asked, glancing over.

She noticed a mix of concern and excitement in her aunt's eyes, a chill-inducing blend of fear and anticipation.

At that moment, Alex realized her aunt understood the depths of her pain, the primal urge to lash out against those who had hurt her so deeply.

She shook her head. "No. I didn't kill him. I could have, though. The police didn't burst in for another five minutes. No, his wife ended up stopping me."

"Wait a minute," Mom waved a hand. "She doesn't defend herself, but she stops you from hurting *him*? That... that makes no sense. What the hell was wrong with her?"

"She was protecting Alex," Aunt Min whispered. "She didn't want her to have to live with the pain of having killed someone."

Alex and her mother both turned to face her.

"What?" She shrugged, looking between them. "It's what I would've done."

Alex nodded, acknowledging the unspoken bond between them. "That's actually what she told the police. That, and that I saved her life."

The room fell silent.

Alex felt them watching her. Everyone except her father. For some reason, he was looking down.

"What is it, Appa?" She reached over, taking his hands in hers. "What's the matter?"

He shook his head. "I'm so sorry," he muttered. "I didn't know."

"Didn't know what?" she asked, confused.

He glanced up, sorrow and regret etched into his face. "I didn't know what I've been putting you through. When your mom and I fight, I... I'm so sorry, hon. I should've—"

"No, no," she interrupted, sliding down on the floor beside him. "You couldn't have known because I never told you. Either of you. Besides, your fights with Mom are nothing like theirs. Trust me. Yes, I get scared when you argue. Hell, I think the entire neighborhood does. But I know you wouldn't hurt her. Deep down, I know."

He lowered his head in shame, tears streaming down his face. "That's no excuse," he muttered. "I still should've known. I'm your father, for crying out loud. The signs were all there. How uncomfortable our fights made you. How you always checked on your mother." He sniffled, wiping his eyes. "It's so obvious now. I failed you."

She squeezed his hand. "Appa, please don't beat yourself up. This is on me, not you. I should've told you about my past years ago. You and Eomma have been nothing but amazing parents." She wiped her eyes. "You gave me a home. You made me feel loved every day, and most of all"—she glanced at her aunt and mom—"you gave me a family. A real one. Not an Instagram family like the phonies around here. You gave me the real deal. The kind that accepts you for who you are, flaws and all. One that never lets you forget how much you matter, how much you're loved."

Alex looked between them. "I love you. All of you. I'm

going to miss you guys at school. More than you can imagine."

For the third time in an hour, they piled together on the floor, eyes filled with tears.

In the knot of bodies, the love binding them was palpable, a force that could weather any storm. Their tears were not just of sorrow or pain, but of gratitude, joy, and hope for a brighter future.

A future filled with the unbreakable ties of family.

9 / THE UNRELIABLE NARRATOR
CIPHER

The results from his tool dared him to click and see the details. He'd written a simple script to review traffic and media logs from his programmers in the bullpens. They probably didn't realize their every move was being tracked, but they should've known better.

This monitoring capability was one of the few advantages of the Red Star OS he'd helped develop. It was the only operating system used throughout North Korea. They didn't simply have control over their internal governmental systems, they could see into their citizens' as well. Every email they opened, like button they clicked, or video they watched; the Central Committee knew and could use it against them. No one was safe. Except him.

His superiors didn't realize he could circumvent his own creation. In fact, he was doing it right now. If the security team were asked what he was working on, they'd swear it was programming new countermeasures for their virus. What he was really doing, however, was tracking down their failure.

A few months back, after N3tN1nja and Byt3Linguist outed his virus and its attack vector, he knew something was off. No way they'd cracked his code that fast. Not without inside help. Hell, even he couldn't have reverse engineered it so quickly, and he wrote the damned thing.

But for some reason, that wasn't important. When he approached his superiors about a possible mole in their midst, they were adamant he was wrong.

They claimed their security checks and surveillance protocols were impossible to circumvent. No matter how vigorously he contested, they fought him. General Tau even went so far as to order him not to pursue it further. And as Cipher was in his charge, he couldn't question the man. At least not publicly.

Instead, he continued his search in secret. He couldn't trust anyone incapable of admitting their faults, especially the self-serving nomenklatura, the privileged elite within the Workers' Party of North Korea. These high-ranking officials sat pretty on the piles of cash his virus raked in. With nearly a hundred million US dollars a month, no one was keen on rocking this gravy boat.

If it were up to him, he'd have shut down their assault and retooled to focus on tracking down the mole and adjusting the virus's signature. It was the only way to throw off the white hats and antivirus companies. But the nomenklatura wanted none of it, and the general was their bulldog.

He ordered Cipher to start work on new permutations of the virus's lock screens, to create unique variants for each country, building on his ransomware-as-a-service platform. But the general made it clear: until the virus stopped printing money, Cipher was to leave it be.

Even if it was a waste of his time and talent, he had little choice. For now, he'd play along. If the Pyongyang elite could help him root out N3tN1nja and Byt3Linguist, he'd begrudgingly cooperate. With the hackers out of the picture, his future plans would be a hell of a lot easier.

It was only a matter of time before the current variant of the virus was neutered. After that, he was gone. His hydra would lose one head, but it still had a second, at least as long as he remained under the radar.

The mole was another problem entirely, and they needed dealing with. Even if the nomenklatura didn't see it, he did.

If they wanted to keep milking their cash cow, the mole had to be rooted out and silenced. His team may have failed to bring down the IRC network, but he wasn't failing at this.

He tapped on his monitoring tool's output and studied the results. There were several unusually large uploads from the programmers' workstations. But given how many attack vectors were embedded in pornography and gaming mods, the transfers weren't out of the ordinary.

The result wasn't as damning as he'd hoped, but hints of something more lingered: unusual traffic patterns to new machines. Ones outside the agreed-upon networks.

And then he saw it. An unmistakable digital footprint.

His cursor hovered over a particular address that made his pulse race. A machine he knew well. Too well. One he often used to mask his jumps to the second head of his hydra.

If these logs were right, then someone in the bullpen or security was following his trail through the network.

He needed to cover his tracks. And fast.

"Shit," he muttered, frantically searching through the other data from his tool.

From the looks of it, they hadn't reached out to any of the other machines he'd used. At least not yet.

Every part of him wanted to stand up and look around, to slam his fists on the table. But he refrained from showing emotion. It was the surest signal to his overseers that they needed to pay attention to him. If they tried to figure out what he was doing, his fake application usage and traffic would show he was programming. And right now, his body blocked his screen, so he didn't dare move.

He took a deep breath and did the first thing he could

think of. He wiped his tracks. The advantage of being a programmer of a government-mandated operating system wasn't just having access to the data, it was being able to change it.

When he considered where to place blame, his mind flashed back to events months prior. He thought of the members of his team who'd provoked N3tN1nja and Byt3Linguist on that IRC channel. The most glaring culprit was the woman who lashed out at Byt3Linguist when they inadvertently revealed their location was in the US.

With an event in mind, he quickly searched the full logs of that fateful day. His fingers flew over the keyboard as he entered the search parameters, a bead of sweat streaking down his face. But he didn't dare wipe at it. They couldn't see it from behind.

A half dozen names sprang up on his screen. As he mouthed their chat handles, he envisioned the faces: Icy Goliath, Sweaty One, Mr. Smiles, the Mousy Shrew, and Crier.

Oh yeah, Crier. Her name was Nari. He'd almost forgotten about her.

He could still hear her guttural cries as her cube mate's brains exploded across her face. She was the one who instigated the attack, who made the first strike on Byt3Linguist.

She was the perfect scapegoat to implicate with the traffic patterns from his hydra. Even if they hadn't discovered it yet, if they were following his tracks, they must suspect something was amiss.

He hastily adjusted the logs, burying traffic to Crier's machine over the past year. Subtle changes, planted in ancillary systems on her work and personal computers. Changes that might not show up on their initial searches. Not until they found a smoking gun.

"A gun," he whispered. He needed something to nudge

them her way. Something obvious that wouldn't have come up on their first scans.

As he racked his brain over what he could use, his mind drifted to N3tN1nja and how they might have infiltrated his people. What they could have done or agreed to, a deal or offer that would cause a patriot of the North Korean Workers' Party to flip sides.

And then it hit him, a smirk easing into the corner of his pursed lips. The solution was elegant yet disarmingly straightforward. He could leverage their reliance on antiquated IRC networks for communication.

For starters, he'd insert fabricated digital breadcrumbs, strategically placed, encoded conversations on random channels. Then he'd hide a cipher on her home machine, somewhere deep in a recently deleted email.

When security reviewed her next weekly backup, her messages would incriminate her. They'd find her sharing sensitive information only someone like her knew. Someone with intimate details of his virus. Their findings would paint a damning picture of espionage, subtle enough to evade their initial scans but incriminating once discovered.

As he executed his plan, a sinister grin flickered across his face. With a few keystrokes, he set the wheels in motion, ensuring chaos would soon reign from the shadows.

Yet, amidst the brewing storm, his ultimate goal remained clear: to see the world burn, being careful not to be consumed by the flames himself.

10 / DOWN THE RABBIT HOLE
ALEX

She was light years from Fremont, from being cooped up with her laptop in their tiny two-bedroom apartment. Alex kept expecting to wake up in a shelter, dressed in tattered clothes, and ready for another day on the street. And if her aunt hadn't shown up, that's exactly what would've happened. Add to that her little Sanchez family situation, and her life felt like reality TV.

With her roommate Michelle still asleep, Alex quietly packed, sliding her new laptop into its sleeve. She'd left her old, dependable computer with her family. That way, they had a reliable way to talk to her at school. Plus, it was a useful safety net for her extracurricular activities.

She'd already infiltrated most of her neighbors' networks before leaving for college, giving her a series of safe routers to hop through. Those hacked machines were her digital smokescreen, providing multiple layers of protection against anyone tracing her online. Drawing attention to herself at school was the last thing she needed.

As she threw her bag over her shoulder, she stepped around her roommate's colorful model on the floor. It was a miniature-scale oak tree filled with hanging computer displays.

The university had accepted her art proposal, along with dozens of other student projects, and was already well underway constructing the exhibit across the street, in the arboretum.

Easing open the door to her dorm room, she slipped out and pulled it closed. It squeaked at the last second, sending her roommate into a moaning tizzy. When the lock clicked shut, Alex spun around, dashing down the stairs. She had to make the next bus transfer to North Campus. Otherwise, she'd be late for her appointment with Professor Newtown.

It'd taken just a few lectures to get on good terms with the professor in the only programming class they let her take as a freshman. She couldn't go another term without a more advanced course. One she could actually learn something from. Hell, half the time she was in the computing lab, she ended up teaching the students from her Intro to Programing class.

Her counselor called the intro classes weeder courses, but she saw them for what they really were. Cash cows, and an excuse for the university to make you pay for an extra year.

Well, she wasn't about to throw away her money so easily, even if it was extorted. It was still her time, and she'd rather spend it learning something useful.

She sprinted out the front door of the dorm just as the north commuter bus sped off.

"Shit," she muttered, glancing down the road as a blast of icy wind buffeted the nearby snowbank, cutting through her unbuttoned coat.

She shuddered and zipped up, wrapping her scarf tighter around her ears and neck. Michigan weather sucked. Every time she blinked, it changed. The weatherman predicted temperatures in the sixties tomorrow, which was hard to imagine right then with all the layers she had on.

"The Bursley-Baits will be here in a minute," a voice said behind her.

When she spun around, an older man was walking toward her, making his way along the sand-covered sidewalk the university used instead of salt to combat the icy conditions.

The man wore a tweed overcoat and matching hat, his silver-streaked hair just visible on the sides. Even though he wasn't wearing glasses, he had a scholarly look about him, as if they'd be a natural accessory.

She swore she'd seen him around North Campus before, but couldn't place where.

"Thanks." She nodded, stepping into the covered enclosure for protection from the wind.

The man followed her inside, taking up post in the opposite corner. His battered messenger bag was slung over his shoulder, and judging by the patches adorning the exterior, he was into computers.

"Is that the BSD Daemon?" She pointed at the tattered red devil toting a golden pitchfork on his bag flap.

The man smiled and glanced down at the patch. "That it is. I got it at DEF CON in '93."

"The inaugural year," she muttered, easing closer to see other patches.

He chuckled, studying her. "How'd you know that?"

"Who doesn't?" She gestured to his bag. "That's Tux the Linux penguin, started in '91 by Linus Torvalds. And that"—she squinted and tilted her head—"is a hashtag, I think. Either you like IRC, or you're into other Unix special characters. Throw it next to an exclamation point and you can shebang something." She smirked.

He let out a half-suppressed laugh. "Have we met? Not many students know their way around a command line nowadays, and you look familiar."

Alex shook her head. "No. Can't say we have."

She looked away, feeling his eyes scan her up and down. Encounters like this were why she avoided jogging through neighborhoods or in gyms. The park was different; with fewer people overall, especially men, she felt safer. Besides, she was too fast for most of them anyway, and the thought of them trying and failing to catch her brought a wry smile to her face.

That morning, her jog was cut short by the art exhibits being built in the arboretum. While she was excited to see her roommate's masterpiece in the show, she was pissed she had to run through the Quad, flaunting her sweaty self across campus.

"I'm certain I've seen you before," he insisted, studying her.

"I don't think so," she said, avoiding eye contact. "This is my first semester."

Talking to new people was hard, even about things she loved. Computers, those were easy; humans, they were a whole different ball game.

She peered down the street. The next bus was rounding the corner, and based on the glowing yellow sign, it was the one they needed.

Glancing at her watch, she drew a sharp breath. "Shit." There was no way she'd make her appointment on time. Not the best first impression if she wanted to get into this class. She'd need to come up with an excuse.

"Are you a TA?" he asked, refusing to give up.

Alex shook her head. "Nope." She eased up to the curb as the bus approached. "You've probably seen me in the computer labs, though. I'm usually in there helping my classmates when I get bored with my normal coursework." She glanced over her shoulder at the dorm. "I'm not into the party scene. I prefer to stare at an LCD over chugging MGD any day."

He smirked and stepped up beside her. Neither seemed

comfortable saying the next word, which suited her fine. Small talk was hard enough on its own, especially with her mind spinning as she tried to figure out how to smooth things over with the professor. She only hoped he wasn't a stickler for promptness. If he was, she'd be done for.

Once she boarded the bus, she was taken aback. People were crammed in like sardines, with hardly a place to stand. She squeezed her way toward the back, navigating the tightly packed crowd. About halfway there, she found an empty spot beside an elderly Asian gentleman, easily in his seventies. A Hangul puzzle book rested on his lap, its distinctive characters unmistakable after years of watching her parents solve similar ones at the kitchen table.

"Please…" He stood up, wobbling as he did. "Take my seat."

"No, no." She shook her head, gently touching his arm. "It's fine. I can stand." She motioned to the vacated seat. "Anjajuseyo." She smiled. "Please sit. The ride can get bumpy."

He smiled back, clearly surprised she knew Korean. After a brief pause, he eased down, sliding his cane between his legs.

Once she was sure he was sitting, she grabbed the overhead bar next to him. There were no other places to stand, and she wasn't about to shove deeper into the crowd.

When she turned around, she noticed the man from her bus stop standing in front of her, still eyeing her uncomfortably. His gaze shifted between her and the elderly man.

She shuddered at the idea of being scrutinized by a stranger. It made her skin crawl. Despite her efforts to avoid looking at him, she couldn't shake the discomfort settling in her stomach. The close quarters of the bus offered no escape, and she suddenly wished for the journey to end.

The next few minutes were unpleasant, filled with his frequent glances in her direction. It was as if he were trying to recall where he'd seen her before, or worse, undressing her with his eyes. She couldn't tell which.

As the bus pulled up in front of the North Campus Commons, the hiss of the air brakes signaled their arrival. The crowds started piling off almost immediately, and she disappeared into the throng, escaping the stranger's gaze and heading to her appointment. Even though he had some cool patches, he stared too much. Nerds always had their quirks.

Knowing the Commons would slow her, she leaned into a full-on sprint, navigating around the short, squat building and heading toward Engineering across the Quad.

Each step on the sandy pavement echoed through the crisp air, her thoughts drifting to Aunt Min. She pictured her aunt going about her daily routine, and a smile tugged at her lips. Without her help, college would've been impossible.

After their run-in with the Sanchez family, her aunt sought help from a friend in South Korea. He agreed to act as a middleman, but demanded a ten percent cut.

Alex had wanted to ask her aunt about her friend's profession but decided against it. She didn't want to look a gift horse in the mouth. After several tense back-and-forth negotiations, she sent the video recordings to Mr. Sanchez along with her demands. He agreed to pay her yearly, as long as the video stayed hidden. The rest went off without a hitch.

The money flowed through her aunt's friend, who then made Alex's tuition payments through a shell corporation he'd set up. It was simpler that way, leaving no trace back to her or her family. As far as the university was concerned, she simply had a wealthy benefactor. After taking his cut, her aunt's friend sent the rest to Alex on an untraceable visa, which she used to buy herself a new computer and a few airplane tickets to visit her family during the holidays.

With the thought of seeing her parents at Christmas lingering in her mind, she barely realized she'd entered the

Engineering building. If it weren't for the squeak of her wet shoes, she might still be in her zone.

She hurried to the elevator, hitting three—Professor Newton's floor. While she'd only ever talked with him via email, she got the impression he rarely made exceptions for undergrads. It was a miracle she'd even managed an appointment, but if there was anything she'd learned from her aunt, it was to fight for what you wanted. And instead of risking an email rejection, she aimed to meet him face to face, hoping it would be easier to secure a yes in person.

The elevator doors dinged open and she quickly stepped out, following the signs to his office. Once there, she took a deep breath and knocked. Seconds ticked by, but silence was the only reply.

She knocked again, louder this time. More silence, leaving her puzzled and even more anxious than before.

Sliding out her laptop, she double-checked the time. "Nine AM," she muttered, stealing a quick glance at her watch. Ten after nine. Her heart sank.

Though she was late, she still expected him to be there. He had class downstairs at nine thirty. Maybe this was his way of giving her an answer.

Just as she was about to leave, footsteps echoed down the hall. She turned and did a double take. The man from the bus was walking toward her.

He froze when he looked up from his smartphone. "We meet again," he said, eyes locking on hers. "Can I... help you?"

She glanced between him and the door. "Are you... Professor Newton?"

"I am." He flipped aside the BSD Daemon patch and pulled out his keys. "And you are?" He unlocked the door and stepped inside.

She cleared her throat, hesitating at the threshold of his office, unsure if she should enter without being asked. "I'm

Alex... Alex Mercer." She wrung her hands. "I emailed you about getting an exception for your course. EECS 489."

"Computer Networks." He eyed her curiously. "Do you have all the prerequisites taken care of?"

Alex straightened. "No, but I'm pretty tech-savvy."

He shook his head. "Being a fangirl and knowing dates of conferences doesn't make you a good programmer, Ms. Mercer. Understanding data structures, algorithms, and the foundations of computer systems are the skills you need. That's why we have required courses."

She forced a smile, frustration simmering. She hated being underestimated. "I can code a linked-list, a hash table, or work through any Unix problem you come up with. I know I'll succeed in your—"

"Alright, design me an algorithm," he interrupted, his gaze piercing straight through her. "I want you to ensure reliable data transmission over an unreliable network, something similar to how TCP operates on top of IP." He checked his watch and then motioned toward the chair opposite his desk. "You have fifteen minutes, Ms. Mercer. Amaze me!"

She stared at him, unsure how to solve his riddle on the spot. She needed some time to think.

"Fourteen minutes." He raised an eyebrow. "I've got places to be. Do you want in, or don't you?"

Without a word, she leapt across the threshold, collapsing into his guest chair. In one swift motion, her bag was open, and her laptop was on his desk.

A few keystrokes later, she had a terminal up with *vim*, her editor of choice, and began typing out her assumptions.

Assumption: Packet loss, out-of-order delivery, and varying transmission delays.

Problem: Write an algorithm to solve for the above and ensure reliable data transmission over an unreliable network.

She studied the problem statement, her mind a swirling mess of hypotheses.

Professor Newton gestured at her laptop. "That looks cool. What is it?"

She tilted the lid down, staring at the sticker he was pointing at. "Oh, that... that's supposed to be a virus," she muttered. "A computer virus. See the robot's legs and head? It's shaped like a hexagonal prism." Her fingers traced the outline of the sticker. "It represents the geometric structure of some viruses."

Her cheeks warmed, suddenly self-conscious about her niche interest. "I'm into hunting down computer viruses and seeing how they work," she added, her voice trailing off.

He looked at her with a mixture of curiosity and skepticism as he stepped around his desk and moved to her side.

She cracked open her computer and he leaned in, reading what she'd written.

He grunted in approval and checked the time. "Pseudocode is fine. You only have twelve minutes left. Show me you know your head from */dev/null*, Ms. Mercer."

She chuckled at the analogy and got to work. To begin, she jotted comments outlining her approach and outcomes, a roadmap for the code she was about to write.

Step by step, she filled in blanks with pseudocode, slowly forming her algorithm's base. While not as clean as she'd like, she could only hope it was enough to impress him. Timeliness was more important than elegance.

He watched her fly through the editor and *man* pages, having long ago mastered *vim* and her way around a terminal.

She even managed to get a few grunts from her macros for fast compilation and syntax checks.

When his watch beeped, she sighed. She hadn't finished the second fork in the logic, but the base of the outer algorithm was in place.

He didn't say a word, he just grabbed his bag and headed for the door.

"What about... the course?" she asked, swallowing hard as he paused with his back to her.

Silence filled the room, electric with tension. Seconds passed before Professor Newton slowly turned, leaning against the door with a contemplative look.

He wasn't happy. She could see it. She'd blown it.

"You've shown promise, Ms. Mercer," he finally said, his voice measured.

Her heart skipped a beat.

"Your algorithm isn't complete," he continued, "but you obviously have a keen understanding of the foundational concepts. I tell you what." His face never wavered from her eyes, just like on the bus. "Finish the algorithm while I'm teaching my next class. If it's done to my satisfaction, you're in. If not, well, you'll have to complete those prereqs like everyone else and queue up in a few terms. What do you say?"

His challenge hung between them. An opportunity, a sliver of hope. This was a test not just of her coding skills, but of her determination and resolve.

She smiled, excitement rushing through her. "I'm in!"

As he turned to leave, he paused. "I expect you won't plagiarize any code, Ms. Mercer."

"Never," she rebutted. The thought wouldn't occur to her.

"I'll know if you did," he said.

And with that, he left her alone with her thoughts, the blinking cursor, and a challenge that could change everything.

ONE MONTH LATER

Alex tore her gaze from the display, eyes widening at the bustling computer lab. Rows of state-of-the-art workstations stretched before her, each worth a fortune. She blinked, astonished that every single one was occupied. The room was abuzz with the clatter of keyboards and the hum of processors.

Mechanical, industrial, and computer engineering students crowded around the high-end desktops, burning the midnight oil on midterm assignments. Everyone except her. She'd finished weeks ago. Procrastination wasn't her thing, not with her time-consuming hacker hobby.

There was also the small wager she made with Professor Newton for a spot in his next class. She probably hadn't needed to nudge him after acing his test, but she figured it couldn't hurt. Sometimes, for people to break rules, they needed a stake in the game. She bet him she'd get an A in his class, and if she didn't, she'd grade his assignments for an entire year.

What he didn't know, however, was that she had no intention of being his assistant. The bet was just to secure her spot in his lecture. The A was already hers. She just needed him to believe it was on the line.

She glanced back to her computer screen and continued reading a news article about her family's nemesis, the Reveton virus.

Reveton was the revised name for the 'FBI Ransomware' virus that stole her father's money. A few months after N3tN1nja outed it as a reusable shell on IRC, hundreds of unrelated ransomware threads converged from other online attacks. Most people thought these were new viruses, but it was the same one dressed up in different disguises.

The Reveton virus exploded overnight. Its makers had translated it into nearly every European Union language and country, plus several international variants. It was the United Nations of viruses, indiscriminate in its attacks.

Money was money. The question was: where were the funds going?

Alex flipped from the article back to the IRC channels she'd been watching. After N3tN1nja told her to look at her IRC client logs that fateful night, she dug in.

At first, she saw nothing, struggling instead to decipher the various logs she'd enabled. But after a few days of fruitless scrolling through hundreds of megabytes of transcripts, she broke down and wrote a script.

The result was a mess of python code to parse the connection details of every user on every channel she'd encountered. It was a lot of noise, but once she'd figured out the data, she massaged it into a format she could mine. After that, the toughest part was aligning the IRC logs with her network traffic dumps. And once she wrangled those, the data points leapt out like jackrabbits from the brush.

When she further refined her analysis to differentiate the virtual private networks (VPNs) from the other traffic, the patterns emerged with startling clarity. The evidence was undeniable, and color-coding users N3tN1nja had kicked that night only highlighted the relationships.

Correlating user handles would've been nearly impossible in IRC's heyday. Back then, over ten million people were online, but nowadays, the old-school social networks were afterthoughts. With applications like Facebook, Twitter, and Tumblr, the backwoods hashtags and text interface of IRC were antiquated and rarely used by the average netizen.

She'd connected hundreds of IRC handles to the same cluster of network addresses. Even more than she'd seen banned from that channel. These were the bad actors

N3tN1nja had warned her about, and they weren't just on the channels talking about hacking.

These users spread propaganda and false information across dozens of channels on various networks. To what end, she couldn't fathom. But she didn't stop there.

Alex dissected the virus command by command, breaking it into slices to identify how and where it sent the money it collected. It was painstaking work, but that wasn't the toughest part. The real challenge was getting in the middle so she could watch the cash change virtual hands. Figuring that out had consumed her for the past few months.

Ever since Professor Newton gave her the nod, he asked her to sit in on his networking class a semester early. He claimed it was to prevent her failing next term, but she knew better. She was the only student asking questions and keeping lectures lively. Plus, attending his class kept her sane, especially given the sluggish pace of her current programming course. She absorbed new concepts almost daily, soaring high while most students struggled to stay afloat. And in her spare time, she taught herself to reverse engineer virus executables.

Sucking at the teat of computer science was her drug, and she was happy to OD whenever possible. In fact, during this week's lecture, she learned about reverse proxies. Or, as she dubbed them, middle men.

They were like her aunt's friend who facilitated her college payments to the university, but she couldn't say that out loud. Instead, she explained the concept to her roommate using a different real-world analogy. She asked her to imagine she'd ordered groceries online, but instead of delivering them directly to her house, she had them sent to a friend's house.

The friend would check the delivery for mistakes, repackage the groceries in new bags, then bring the order over. In this scenario, the friend acted as a reverse proxy, handling and checking the shipment before it reached its final destination. Best of all, the grocery store never received her roommate's actual address. It remained a secret.

Once she'd learned that golden nugget, Alex could put herself in the shoes of these bad actors. As a virus, she'd want to ensure her traffic wasn't sniffed, at least not the final destination. It'd be foolish if the authorities knew where the money was going. Then they'd just try to get it back.

The virus maker's workaround was ingenious. They hacked well-known websites and data centers, installing reverse proxies. This not only obscured the smoking gun, it also slowed down the authorities. Law enforcement couldn't possibly obtain and act on search warrants for hundreds of data centers simultaneously.

To further complicate tracking, the reverse proxies were stealthy. Most of the time, they silently relayed regular traffic, invisible to even the most diligent of admins. But every once in a while, they'd wake up when Reveton reached out, routing stolen money to the bad actors without drawing attention.

No logs and no records of the connection. Add to that a little self-destruct code, and you had an automated reverse proxy that erased itself without a trace.

Reveton likely had hundreds, if not thousands, of these compromised servers scattered across the globe, constantly routing their money.

She pulled up her hacked binary just as a message from an old friend arrived.

> **N3TN1NJA**
>
> You still racking your brain on our little viral friend?

Her fingers hovered over the keyboard, debating if she should tell them how far she'd gotten. The funny thing was, she still had no clue if N3tN1nja was a man or a woman. Not that it mattered, but it felt odd not knowing how to address them.

> **L3X1C0N**
> I wouldn't call it racking so much as cracking.

Their reply came swiftly.

> **N3TN1NJA**
> So, you made progress then?

She smiled, eyeing her friend's IP address. It was offshore, in Switzerland, just like always. Impossible to trace without far more skills than she had. She typed out a reply.

> **L3X1C0N**
> Slowly. School's been crazy this term, but I've picked up some new tricks between the erratic weather.

As she hit return, she wondered if she'd overshared. It was an ongoing battle she'd waged her entire life. Staying anonymous was tough nowadays, especially if you wanted to form lasting friendships. Virtual or not, being alone sucked.

Just as she was about to launch her newest creation, they replied.

> **N3TN1NJA**
> Don't miss your bus home. You'll be trapped in a lab all night.

She gasped, spinning in her seat, scanning the computer lab. No one was paying her any attention. Anyone stuck on North Campus this late was focused on their screens, not each other.

Most were burning the last of their wicks after too much

procrastination. Either that, or they were like her and had no life.

Does N3tN1nja know who I am, or are they just guessing?

Sure, every college had buses, but the specificity of the comment chilled her to her core, especially the part about being stuck at the lab. When the buses stopped running, the walk home would take hours in the snow.

She shook her head, drawing in a deep breath. She was going crazy, reading too many conspiracy theory channels online. It made her wary of everything she saw and read, even strangers on the bus.

Without another thought, she switched to the terminal window where her program was waiting for her. The code wasn't elegant, but after much trial and error, she'd uncovered the virus's mechanisms for transferring the money.

The process took weeks of painstaking work, stepping through the executable using *gdb*, a Unix debugger. The low-level application let her view and manipulate memory addresses, then observe the consequences. Sort of like adjusting pieces of a complex jigsaw, where each piece could fit perfectly or collapse the entire structure. Usually, it ended in her starting over, but sometimes, lightning struck.

It was in these serendipitous moments that she watched the virus at work. The executable decrypted a chunk of its own memory, which, from what she could tell, resulted in a convoluted lookup table. While the table itself was a black box, the output wasn't. She'd isolated the lookup logic, making it callable via a script.

Each time she called the script, it spat out a new IP address, the street addresses used to map out every machine on the internet. From there, the virus followed one of a dozen known URL paths, looking for a way to talk to a reverse proxy on that box.

That's where her coursework ended and her hobby kicked in.

Now that she knew the address of a virus's remote proxy, she needed to hack in. Otherwise, she couldn't insert a man-in-the-middle program between it and the hackers.

After a few hits of *nmap* and *wget*, her go-to networking tools, she realized this machine wasn't running a web server. At least not at the moment. Even if she could access through an alternate route, *http* attack vectors were more common and easier to execute.

Since that IP address would take too long to hack, she ran the script again and again until it spit out an easier target. It didn't take many tries.

With a new address in hand, she ran another simple tool she'd cobbled together. It interrogated the remote machine for unpatched holes. Luckily, the idiots were running an outdated *java* web server instance called *tomcat*.

Alex chuckled as she quickly located and launched another brute force attack, except this was one she'd downloaded. It was one of hundreds of cracks she'd collected over the years.

She never understood why network administrators weren't better at their jobs. This machine was easily four years out of date. It was no wonder this virus was ravaging the internet with such easy targets lying around.

Bing, bam, boom, she was in with root privileges in under five minutes. After covering her tracks by deleting access logs from both the *java* process and the system itself, she hunted down the virus's reverse proxy.

While she wasn't sure what to look for, now that she knew what was running on the machine, it shouldn't take long to find something hanging out and listening to...

And there it was. A lone child process embedded in the web server. Despite not knowing which of the twelve paths triggered this particular proxy, it didn't matter. She simply tried each in sequence until she got a bite.

On the second try, she hit pay dirt. From there, it was child's play. She installed a custom jar file of her own making on the web server's class path, slipping her code between the server and the awaiting proxy. All that remained was restarting the process to pick up her change.

Though she'd only learned *java* in the past month during the Intro to Programming course, the antiquated language favored by big enterprises came in handy. The terminology was crazy at times, but given how many machines ran it online, it was a useful tool in her belt.

The executable she'd thrown together was simple enough. It captured a list of all outbound network connections before, during, and after the proxy was called. As an added precaution, her patch even allowed her to manipulate the payload sent to the proxy, an insurance policy she wasn't sure she'd need but felt safer having.

With everything set, she swiftly exited the machine and the five hops she'd taken to get there.

One could never be too careful.

AFTER A FEW MORE HOURS OF repeating the same processes, she'd installed a dozen proxy hacks and called it a night.

While she wasn't sure when it would trigger, once her patch paid off and she found the upstream server, she had a good idea what came next. She'd need to hack into a bank.

They couldn't move this kind of money without access to a financial institution of some sort. But hacking a bank was out of her league, even if it was overseas. She'd heard some of those were as easy to crack as a rusty old padlock, challenging without the right tools, but far from impossible with some know-how.

The thought of the illegal act reminded her of that fateful evening earlier that year. The night she'd nearly lost everything.

She opened her web browser, this time clicking the bookmark at the top of her list. A page she visited at least weekly.

The headlines sprang up:

Fremont Teen Saves Classmates from Violent Attack

Two honor roll students from John F. Kennedy High School were assaulted near Central Park Library last week. The attackers, described as large tattooed men, allegedly followed the teens for several blocks before jumping out of a caravan of cars. The victims' identities have been withheld due to their minor status.

According to reports, the teens were saved by the quick actions of fellow senior, Alex Mercer, who was nearby. Mercer, who's been practicing taekwondo since age eight, successfully fought off the assailants. The attackers fled the scene, and no footage of the incident has been recovered.

Mercer declined to be interviewed for this story. Classmates describe her as a loner who prefers computers over football. Mrs. Myeong, Mercer's downstairs neighbor, spoke highly of the young woman: "She's the perfect student and friend, with one heck of a right hook. She takes care of her family and community, and doesn't take crap from anyone."

Sources confirm Mercer will attend the University of Michigan this fall to study Software Engineering.

> The Fremont Times respects Mercer's privacy and wishes her luck in her future endeavors.

She blushed reading the story even now. Riley and Harper had lied to the police and the press to save the Sanchez reputation. They couldn't explain their wounds any other way than spinning their tale, but at least she came out looking good.

Alex wondered if the two families ever considered telling the truth, but people like them were so used to fabricating lies, it was second nature. It was all about maintaining their image and social standing, no matter the cost.

Either way, she was better off with this story than the alternative. For all she knew, she could've done time for assault. Even with her evidence against them, there was no telling what a judge would do nowadays.

Most people thought California was progressive, but follow the money and you quickly realize the truth. Money moves mountains and shuts mouths.

And in her case, bribing them for her tuition was both gratifying and disgusting. She wondered if she'd become as bad as they were. Her only hope was staying grounded and not losing her moral compass.

She closed the browser and flipped over to IRC to see what she'd missed the past few hours. Only then did she notice several unread messages in her dock.

Hoping to hear from her aunt, she switched to the Messages app. Unexpectedly, she found several new private messages from Riley Sanchez.

She sighed, fighting down the bile rising in her throat. Her finger hovered over *Delete*, willing her resolve to harden.

But curiosity won. She tapped Riley's icon, revealing the string of messages.

RILEY SANCHEZ

19:30 : Hey Alex, you there?

19:32 : We need you. Well, actually, it's my dad. He needs your help. Super important, so hit me back ASAP.

20:01 : Hope you're not ghosting me. This is serious business. It's about our "little deal."

Alex looked up, scanning the lab to ensure no one was standing behind her. Not that it mattered. The messages were already tagged to her account.

Riley was an idiot for reaching out like this. There was nothing worse than dealing with stupid people, or in this case, stupid criminals.

She returned to the thread. Judging by the timestamps, the halfwit had been spamming her for hours.

RILEY SANCHEZ

20:45 : Look, if you wanna keep going to that overpriced school, I suggest you stop whatever you're doing and text me back.

21:10 : Sorry if I came off harsh before. Things are a fucking mess, and we seriously need your help.

21:11 : To be more precise, it's my dad who needs you.

22:51 : This isn't a joke anymore. I'm expecting an answer in the next hour, or there will be consequences.

> 23:30 : You're not giving me much choice here. If I don't hear from you tonight, I'll be reaching out to your aunt first thing tomorrow. How about you ditch the kegger early and hit me up? Shit's getting real over here.

The rapid-fire messages were ridiculous. Why Princess Riley didn't just call was beyond her. It would've been hella easier than typing these out, and faster too.

All she could think was that Riley's father wanted an electronic trail of their communication, but she wasn't born yesterday. She'd read enough Reddit threads on entrapment to see his game from a mile away.

Alex gathered her things and quickly logged off her workstation. She then darted out of the lab, heading upstairs to the Commons main floor. It was only twenty degrees outside, but she couldn't risk anyone overhearing her conversation.

Just before stepping out, she reached into her bag, pulling out her flip phone and voice modulator from the inner pocket. In seconds, she'd swapped the SIM card for her burner, and plugged in the modulator. The cheap novelty gadget served one, and only one, purpose: disguising her voice.

After testing the connection and confirming it wasn't her regular number, she zipped up and stepped into the frigid Midwestern night.

The icy wind slapped her face, making her gasp and shiver. She quickly pulled up her hood, concealing her headset from passersby.

Taking a few steps toward the clock tower, she tapped Riley's name and hit connect. She glanced down at her phone, expecting the familiar ring, but it never came. Riley must've been waiting; she answered instantly.

"Hello," Riley said hesitantly.

Alex stood with her back against the frozen brick of the

clock tower, facing the Engineering building. "If you say my name or anyone else's, I hang up. If you so much as hint at who I am, I'm done, and I won't call back. Is. That. Clear?"

Her voice sounded like a cartoon robot, and she fought not to laugh at herself. She sounded hilarious.

"I don't..." Riley paused. Judging by the muffled voices in the background, she'd covered the receiver. Just as Alex was about to hang up, she returned. "How can I be certain who I'm talking to?"

"You have two minutes." Alex bit her lip. "I know you're recording this. What the hell do you want?"

She checked her watch. She didn't know how long it'd take to trace a cellular call, but she didn't care. Two minutes was plenty of time for her to get to the point.

The next thing she heard were faint rustling sounds. Then Mr. Sanchez came online. "I need you to hack a computer for me."

She drew in her breath. *He had to be kidding, right?*

"Not happening," she muttered, her voice remodulated to a low-fidelity DJ.

"Then our deal is off," he said.

The line fell silent for several seconds, his threat hanging between them, despite the thousands of miles. He was waiting for her to say something, anything, to his remark.

She reached up and blew warm air into her numbing hand.

He knew she couldn't afford tuition herself, at least not legally. And she wasn't even certain she was still eligible for financial aid next year, considering she'd already declined it this past year.

Without his money, she might have to take a semester or two off, or worse, drop out.

"I know the bind you're in," Riley's father said, his ego swelling. "It seems you need me as much as I need you."

His voice made her skin crawl, and she wanted to hang up. Either that, or reach through the phone and strangle the fucker.

She took a deep breath, exhaling to clear her head. "Where is this computer?"

"It doesn't matter," he said, lowering his voice as if concealing his request from his daughter. "Just get in, install something, and get out. It's a simple job. Okay?"

She sighed. "Do I have a choice?"

"You could come home," he said, voice dripping with condescension.

"Fine." She fought back a surge of anger rising in her chest. "I'll send Riley an email. You can reply with the details."

"That's great!" he said. "I'll make it worth your while. I promise. Let me get you Riley's—"

"That won't be necessary," she interrupted. "I've already got it."

She cut the line and screamed at the top of her lungs, her piercing howl echoing across the frozen quad.

If she didn't know better, she'd have chucked her phone into the darkness. But she knew it wouldn't help. Destroying things never did.

In the distance, she made out two figures spinning around. They glanced her way before quickly ducking into the building.

"Shit," she muttered. She needed to get back inside the Commons. The last thing she wanted to deal with was the campus police.

11 / BURIED TRUTHS
CIPHER

The decrepit elevator screeched to a halt and dinged. After an unusually long pause, the doors finally parted, shuddering open.

Beyond lay a dimly lit passageway. As Cipher eased forward to look around, a sharp cry echoed down the corridor.

The moment he passed into the tunnel, the hairs on his arms stood on end as a blast of blood, sweat, and mildew assaulted his senses.

He fought to suppress the overwhelming churning in his stomach. The urge to vomit.

The general's cryptic summons left him uncertain of what lay ahead. It merely stated that they'd uncovered the mole and needed his help in breaking them.

For all he knew, they were about to torture him, and he was walking into a trap. But not showing up was practically admitting his involvement in planting the evidence, even if they couldn't prove it.

Without further hesitation, he pushed the thought aside and pressed on.

The stories of what happened down here in the bowels of

this facility were ghastly, even for someone like him, comfortable with the murky waters of morality.

The darkest echelons of the Korean military used this place to torture their people, citizens and soldiers alike.

He cautiously made his way down the dank, narrow passage. Lights flickered on overhead, casting eerie shadows. The air was heavy with mold and decay, each step echoing in oppressive silence. As he moved forward, the dim lights behind him flickered and gradually faded, plunging his path into darkness.

Each wavering light cast fleeting glimpses of the horror within each cell—barred doors, either rusted shut or hanging ajar, standing as silent witnesses to time's relentless march. The cells appeared to have been abandoned for decades, their secrets entombed within crumbling walls.

Leaning into a cell as he passed, a putrid stench assaulted him, unmistakably rotting flesh. He grimaced, covering his mouth and nose with his hand in a futile attempt to block the nauseating smell.

The cramped space was cluttered with debris and mildewy objects resembling human remains, though the dim light made certainty difficult. Bone-like fragments heaped in a corner suggested a body which had been contorted in its final moments.

The sight of the skeleton stirred a deep, simmering anger within him, dragging painful memories to the surface. It echoed the tragedy of his town. Fires from American shelling and guerrilla attacks had left their homes decimated, reduced to ashes and charred remnants.

He could still feel the heat of the inferno that swept their shanty town, the acrid smoke burning his lungs as he watched everything he knew crumble before his eyes. They'd been defenseless, powerless against the onslaught of destruction raining down upon them.

While he might be overreacting to the mangled remains, he knew torture was second nature to these people—to governments in general. Leaving someone to decay in a shadowy dungeon, abandoned to their own filth, was a cornerstone fear tactic the nomenklatura employed to maintain strict control over the populace.

This brutal approach silently testified to their iron grip on North Korea. It mirrored American tactics, except they didn't defecate where they lived. They preferred doing it overseas, all in the name of protecting their foreign interests.

He stared at the maggot-laced skull as a giant centipede crawled through its eye sockets. As it spiraled out of the mouth, another chorus of screams echoed down the corridor. He gripped the rusty cell bars, knuckles white with tension.

"I was wondering where you'd gone," Choe said, stepping out of the darkness.

He flinched and spun around. A faint patch of blood spray was just visible on her blouse, easily mistaken as part of the design, except that it was fresh and still glistening in the overhead light.

Once again, her sudden appearance caught him off guard, but he concealed his surprise, hoping she hadn't noticed his momentary weakness.

As he stared at his assistant, it dawned on him that she'd somehow passed down the hall without triggering the lights. It was at that moment that he realized his mistake. He'd misread his little mouse from the very beginning.

Where he thought he'd broken her, forcing her to do his bidding, she'd played him. Leading him on, playing his anger and rage like a fiddle.

The revelation was brief, but it was there. She saw the twinkle in his eyes as realization sank in. Without a word, their once palpable sexual tension evaporated, replaced by a cold, wary distance.

She was no longer puppet nor ally in his battle; she was the enemy. Maybe not as formidable as the Americans, but certainly not someone he could trust.

"Where are they?" He lowered his hand, clasping it behind his back while rubbing the moist orangish rust between his fingers; all the while, imagining it was his enemies' blood. The ones who'd ruined his virus.

"They're just ahead," Choe said, turning and gesturing down the corridor. The lights flashed on, illuminating the path forward.

Screams echoed from farther down. Bloodcurdling screams.

Only then did he realize it wasn't a single shriek but two voices intertwined. Two people feeling pain beyond imagination.

Without another word, he strode out of the cell, nearly knocking Choe aside in his haste. He blazed toward the cries of those who'd crushed his dream, the executioners of his virus, hastening its demise far before its time.

With each passing moment, he envisioned himself delivering their punishment, coaxing out confessions through gritted teeth. As each lash ripped through their bloody red skin, as every shock scorched their very being, he'd use their pain to channel his fury, mourning his creation's untimely death but relishing the rise of his hydra's second head. Of his vengeance.

HE WIPED his hands of the deep red fluid, using the remains of the once-white shirt to clean off the traitors' sticky residue. They folded soon after he arrived, turning each other in and admitting to helping N3tN1nja. In exchange for virus details, the hacker had offered them passage out of Pyongyang. But not for themselves, for their families.

What was strange, however, was that no matter how hard he pushed, he couldn't get them to talk about Byt3Linguist. The name seemed like a ghost in the night. Either that or a shadow of N3tN1nja themself.

But that didn't matter. Not yet. They'd gotten details of how to contact N3tN1nja's network. Now they needed to set a trap. One that could flash a light on the hacker's whereabouts. To expose them, leaving them vulnerable to a targeted strike.

He lifted the phone and typed in the code to reach the bullpen. To reach his army of programmers.

Choe's peer picked up. The guy was her opposite in every way. Where she was limber and sexy, he was stiff and vile. Where she was alluring, he was repulsive by any definition.

"Rotate the proxies," Cipher said, voice crisp and unemotional.

"But it's too soon," the man said. "It's only been a week."

Cipher growled, fighting the impulse to rip the phone from its mounting. The last idiot who'd challenged him had died for it. "Question me again, Hyun-Soo, and I'll have you down here alongside the maggots and these other traitors. I don't care if you're General Tau's nephew. Rotate the fucking proxies. Is that understood?"

His lip quivered as he waited for a reply, willing the man to say something other than yes. But his wish never came.

"Yessir! Right away, sir." The line cut a second later.

He didn't have time to deal with the backlash of rotating proxies too soon. They risked detection with each passing hour, and he couldn't risk losing the virus. His hydra was too valuable, and from what the traitors said, N3tN1nja was hot on their trail.

"Shall we return topside?" Choe eased up beside him.

"No!" he barked. "I'm not done here. Not yet."

In one swift motion, he turned on his heels, lifting a scalpel from the tray perched on the rusted metal cart. He held it up, turning it over and over, watching the mirrored surface of the deadly blade catch and shimmer in the light.

And then, without question or hesitation, he lunged forward, toward the still whimpering form of the bound prisoners.

12 / DIGITAL CROSSROADS
ALEX

The second she clicked open the email, her heart sank. Not because of the text, she hadn't even read that yet. It was the image that caught her off guard.

There, center screen, was a picture of Riley's father and her mother. He was leaning close, arms seemingly around her, posing for a selfie. From the looks of it, her mom was still in the uniform for her second job at the hotel. He must've run into her there. It was the only explanation that made sense.

If he thought sending this picture would convince her to help him, he was sorely mistaken. It was a low blow, even for a prick like him. If money weren't so tight, she'd be on the next flight to Cali, ready to show the Sanchez family exactly what happens when they cross the line.

She'd sent Riley a message from one of her many burner email accounts. They were easy to create, and since Tutanota came on the scene, secure emails were guaranteed. Privacy was crucial in situations like this, and even with Tor and multiple VPN hops, she still felt exposed using email. Search warrants made even the best companies' privacy claims evaporate in an instant.

Next time she talked to N3tN1nja, she needed to ask their advice on doing transfers like this. Which reminded her.

She flipped over and started up her IRC application. She'd been in such a hurry to check her email that she hadn't even logged in for the morning.

With her chat sessions starting, she flipped back to the email and grabbed the IP address Mr. Sanchez had sent. While the body of the message clamored for attention, she just needed to get started. Else she'd give up and tell the asshole off.

She started up some network mapping commands using *nmap* and a few other tools. Before going deep, she needed to know what she was working with.

After multiple failed attempts, she determined the machine was running Debian Linux, a pared-down open-source operating system. Most were, if their owner dared hook them up to the internet.

While Debian was normally very secure, she knew better than to assume it was unhackable.

Switching to IRC, she brought up a direct message to one of the Rizon bots. This crude automation functioned as a search frontend to an online exploits database, except these exploits weren't yet public. They were private treasures, closely guarded security secrets shared only among a tight-knit hacker community.

After greeting the bot, it prompted her for credentials.

She immediately flipped to another terminal and typed her extra-long password, retrieving a time-sensitive public verification key that she then gave the bot to authenticate herself.

Once in, she entered her search string and hit go.

```
> Search: Debian Linux 5.0.4, Remote
Exploit
```

Only those who'd earned the trust of the darknet admins

on this server had access to this bot. For her, that meant N3tN1nja.

As she waited for the results, she brought up the email again and read Mr. Sanchez's message. Her stomach churned with every word.

To: Alex Mercer
From: Mr. Sanchez
Subject: Honor the Deal, or Else

I know you'll honor our agreement, but just in case, I wanted to share something. I didn't even know it at the time, but I ran into your mother the other day. Riley pointed her out in the hotel lobby during a fundraiser. She looks so happy in this picture, doesn't she? Our meeting was actually quite fortuitous. She thanked me profusely for everything I've done to help the Korean people. It was truly heartwarming, and I have to say, if I ever had to tell her the truth about her daughter, it would be a shame. But I won't have to do that, right?

She didn't know why she'd even read it, but knowing this man had talked to her mother gave her chills.

Glancing at the image, her mother's happiness struck her. It was hard to tell which version of her mom she'd been that day, her normal, happy self or a medicated imitation. Regardless, he'd overstepped more than one line by talking to her mom and taking the picture.

She'd make him pay, eventually. She might not know how today, but she'd make sure he regretted ever threatening her.

With her thoughts on the image, the ding of her chat

terminal brought her back to the moment. She flipped over to see who it was, but she knew before she got there.

The familiar chirp of the blue jay had been assigned to only one person.

> N3TN1NJA
>
> What ya up to, Little Bird?

The question lingered on the screen for over a minute.

At first, she hesitated, unsure how to respond. But then, the image of her mother resurfaced, and she realized she needed advice. *Who better to turn to than an anonymous hacker I met online?*

This wasn't something she could confide to her college roommate, Michelle. Despite how close they'd become, Michelle had no idea of the lengths Alex had gone to in order to pay for her education.

> L3X1C0N
>
> Debating whether to accept this gig. I need to infiltrate a system to square a debt.

> N3TN1NJA
>
> Interesting. What machine?

> L3X1C0N
>
> Uncertain. I've only got an IP, some code to install, and a stack of cash. Enough to clear debts for the next year.

She'd already told them she was in school a few months back. It just slipped out one night. But she never said where.

While she knew it was dumb, those were the types of mistakes that coding at three AM did to the mind. Bad decisions were made in the middle of the night for a reason. She just happened to make hers in front of a computer, not a bar.

> **N3TN1NJA**
>
> Need any help?

She hesitated, fingers lingering over the N and O keys. Getting help would be nice. Besides, she could probably learn a thing or two from them. They'd been at this for more years than she'd been alive. At least if she believed their story.

With her resolve wavering, she sighed and typed a reply.

> **L3X1C0N**
>
> Sure. But only if you don't mind me being slow.

> **N3TN1NJA**
>
> No worries. I always love to put on my professor's hat. Have you ever used tmux?

She shook her head, sounding out the word t-mux. She'd never heard of the app before, but after a quick search of the Unix man page, she saw it was a terminal multiplexer. In layman's terms, it meant two people could type in the same window and both see the output. It was the old-school way to message between computers in real time.

She could immediately appreciate the utility if you wanted to teach someone.

> **N3TN1NJA**
>
> I take your silence as a no. Use the following commands to attach to my session.

After a short pause, N3tN1nja shared the connection details.

Racking her brain, she couldn't think of a reason why this would be insecure. But she wasn't taking chances they could track her down.

Her fingers danced over the keyboard as she quickly

opened a new terminal, using a secure shell to hop through a half dozen machines. It required copying and pasting multiple credentials from her password manager, until finally, she landed on N3tN1nja's IP address. The secure connections should help cover her tracks, at least for a while.

When she entered the *tmux* command and joined the session, she noticed her window was split into three. Two terminals and one middle section, where a message waited:

> **N3TN1NJA**
>
> We can work together from here. The top terminal is mine, the bottom is for you, and the middle is to chat in private. Let me give you a quick tutorial.

They rapid-fired their explanation of the keyboard incantations to navigate up and down the screen and attach to her own window. It was confusing at first, but Alex was a fast learner. She ran a few simple commands to see what type of machine she'd connected to.

After playing around for a few minutes, she was ready.

> **L3X1C0N**
>
> Alright. I'm GTG.

> **N3TN1NJA**
>
> Good. Why don't you show me what we're working with, and then we can go from there?

This was the point of no return. Up until now, it was a simple hacker peer showing her some new tricks. As soon as she typed the IP address into their chat, there was no going back.

They must have sensed her hesitation.

N3TN1NJA

> I understand your trepidation. You don't need to tell me what you're installing. I'm sure you already know what you're dealing with. I'm just here to help you figure out how to get into a machine. Right?

She swallowed hard, mind racing. The truth was, she had no idea what she was dealing with, neither the target machine nor Sanchez's payload. It was a double whammy of uncertainty that left her feeling completely out of her depth. But she couldn't let N3tN1nja know that. The longer she waited to reply, the more obvious it would be that she was in over her head.

Without wasting another second, she typed the same commands she'd run earlier, executing *nmap* on the target address. After a brief pause, the familiar results flashed up.

N3TN1NJA

> Interesting.

The message appeared instantly, but the silence that followed was excruciating.

"What's interesting?" she muttered to herself.

And then, as if on cue, they replied.

N3TN1NJA

> Almost everything about this machine is locked down. Everything except the telnet port. It's too convenient. Something feels off. It's like whoever paid you, they want us to attack it there.

She looked back at the scan. While she'd run the script countless times, the idea that it could be a trap had never occurred to her.

She'd read about these types of setups before.

> **L3X1C0N**
> You think it's a honeypot?

A chill ran through her. Honeypots. They were admin traps, making hackers think they'd found an easy network to crack. She could picture some smug sysadmin watching right now, tracking her every keystroke while the real system sat safe and untouched. All while they traced her location, drawing closer with each command she typed.

> **N3TN1NJA**
> I do. Let's try some other tricks before we enter the front door, shall we?

She chuckled, but before she could reply, N3tN1nja leapt into action. They split their screen on top into two terminals. In the first, they ran another command. One she'd seen before, but never run herself. It was *openvassd*, a newer security scanner evangelized by white hats, ethical security hackers.

Maybe N3tN1nja wasn't a bad guy like she imagined.

FIVE HOURS and a six-pack of Faygo Rock & Rye later, Alex rested her head in her hands, coming off a sugar high. She knew damn well she'd asked more questions than she'd answered during this paired hacking session. N3tN1nja didn't seem to mind, though. In fact, they were downright teacherly, and good at it too.

She tilted back the last of her favorite Midwestern soft drink, only to lower it and find a pair of eyes glaring at her from the next row.

"Can I help you?" Alex asked, lining up the empty can with the others.

The delightful scent of the sweet beverage overpowered

the industrial air pumped into the lab, making it easier for her to focus and stay awake.

"You know you're not supposed to drink in here." The frat boy tilted his chin at her contraband sodas.

She shook her head and returned her attention to her screen, ignoring the prick. The last thing she needed was shit from a hormone-laden Greek wannabe.

The guy reached forward and rapped his knuckles on her table. "I'm talking to you, Miss Farm Girl."

His words sank in, anger rising. *Farm girl? Who the hell does he think he is?* Sure, she hadn't showered in days, her hair a tangled mess atop her head, but that didn't give him the right to label her. She was far from some country bumpkin, and his audacity only fueled her growing resentment.

Alex clenched her jaw, biting back the scathing retort dancing on her tongue. Instead of sniping back, she slowly turned, glaring at the guy.

At first he didn't react, but he recoiled as she stared him down. "I'm going to find a lab monitor," he said, standing and glancing toward the entrance.

"You do that." She grinned, eyes burning through him. "I'll make sure to tell them about the porn you've been watching all night. Even the stuff you saved on your thumb drive. What're ya doing, whacking off to it in your frat room?"

The guy spun around, fear and embarrassment etched across his face. He probably thought he was being sneaky choosing the machine near the wall.

Little did he know she had eyes in the back of her head. And while she had no proof of his indiscretions, the threat alone was enough. His shocked expression said it all.

"Fuck you too," he muttered, grabbing his shit and storming out.

She knew she wouldn't hear from him again, but just in case, she picked up the cans and walked to the recycling bin.

Bending over, she stashed the empties under the reams of wasted printer paper near the bottom. The only way anyone would find them was if they really wanted to.

Back at her laptop, she unlocked the screen and glanced at her notes. She had dozens of pages of high-quality learnings from the prior night. Tricks she'd never seen online about how to bang on a machine, check it for backdoors, and weasel her way in.

But even with all she'd learned, each attempt had ended in failure. One after another, they hit a wall, coming away empty-handed and no closer to getting inside.

Just as Alex was about to call it a night, she glanced at her second monitor. Her regular IRC channels were open, filled with thousands of unread messages. All but one.

In that private message, staring her in the face all night, was the way inside they'd been looking for.

L3X1C0N

> We can always try the front door?

N3TN1NJA

> You mean a brute force password dictionary attack?

Alex smiled, glancing at her query from earlier. The remote exploit search she'd run against the Rizon hacker bot.

She didn't waste another second. She typed the exploit identifier into the message window to N3tN1nja.

L3X1C0N

> CVE-2011-4862

There was no need to share more than that. CVE stood for Common Vulnerabilities and Exposures, or as hackers knew them, former zero-day exploits.

They were the high-valued passageways black and gray

hats used to get inside networks. And at the same time, they were the shields that, when exposed, white hats and security researchers used to defend their electronic fortresses from intrusion.

N3tN1nja knew as well as she did that the target machine was running an older version of Debian Linux. One that, for some reason, the admins of this particular network hadn't bothered to patch in over two years.

Not long after she entered the cryptic CVE string, she smiled as her self-doubt faded and a rush of confidence washed over her.

> N3TN1NJA
>
> Front door it is. Nice find, Little Bird. Before we bash our way inside, we should mask our route, though.

She had no idea why they kept calling her that, but she didn't mind. To her, it was endearing, the kind of thing a friend might say. Especially an older friend.

Maybe it was N3tN1nja's mentor-like nature, but ever since they'd confronted her after her brutal attack on chat, she'd seen them as an adviser. Someone to look up to. And tonight was no different.

She watched as they weaved through machine after machine, setting up an untraceable pathway through dozens of hops. They carefully chose the perfect host from which to knock down that front door.

When she saw the address of where they finally landed, she did a double take.

She'd seen the leading three octets of the IP address before, but just to be certain, in the other window she ran a *whois* command.

It spit out the details of their jump point:

```
refer: whois.dotgov.gov
domain: GOV
organization: Department of Homeland
Security
```

When she saw the organization name, she froze, her stomach knotting. They were using a government machine to knock down this front door. If that didn't underscore N3tN1nja's reach, she didn't know what did. Either that, or they were a three-letter agent of some kind, which meant she was screwed.

There was only one way to find out.

L3X1C0N

> Are you a government agent? By law, you have to tell me if I ask.

Their response was swift.

N3TN1NJA

> You're kidding, right? You've been watching too many late-night TV shows if you think that's how it works. If I were, which I'm not, I wouldn't have to tell you. Especially if it put my investigation at risk. I assume you're asking due to your little whois check below.

She'd forgotten their commands were visible to each other. But that didn't change the pang of fear in her gut.

L3X1C0N

> Maybe. It's not every day someone hacks into a government machine. There's a line some people cross, and that's one I've never so much as tapped a toe over.

> N3TN1NJA

> Don't worry. I'm not a government suit. I just stumbled upon this machine when they were setting it up a few years ago. I'm not even sure they know it's outside their firewall. It used to serve up images, but now it sits here unused.

While still not convinced, their story piqued her curiosity. Plus, she needed to get in and install the patch, whatever the hell it did.

The more Alex thought about it, the more she realized there was no ideal machine to do it from, so why not a government one? It should throw any admin watching them off their trail.

> L3X1C0N

> Alright then. Let's do this. I assume you have a way to trigger the telnet encrypt overflow? I don't have that trick up my sleeve and would need time to figure it out.

She was sort of hoping they'd call it a night. Not only was she tired, she was starting to think she should look at the payload before they uploaded it. But then again, ignorance was bliss.

Before she could second-guess herself, N3tN1nja uploaded some type of binary named after the vulnerability, *cve_2011_4862*. Once in place, they executed it.

She wondered again who they were, and how the hell they had so many exploits sitting around. A few seconds later, their *tmux* terminal connected, flashing a prompt on the other side.

```
> fremont-vt1: ▮
```

The square cursor flashed on her screen, waiting for their

next command. The name was eerily familiar, especially since Fremont was where both she and the Sanchezes' were from.

N3TN1NJA

Shit! We're in.

Her pulse raced, and her palms began to sweat. She wasn't sure why, though. This wasn't her first hack. She'd compromised hundreds of systems over the years.

But this, this was different. It was the first time she felt like she was doing it under pressure, not for the sheer joy of learning. As if she weren't leading this hack, and that felt strange.

N3TN1NJA

You're up, Little Bird.

Alex swallowed hard, staring at the suffix of the machine. *What the hell could vt1 mean?*

L3X1C0N

Should we maybe poke around first?

N3TN1NJA

We could. But the longer we're sitting here, the more likely they catch us.

She took a deep breath, willing herself to upload the patch Mr. Sanchez sent her. But before she could do it, she typed out the command to see everything that was running.

```
> ps auxwww
```

Her screen filled from top to bottom and then some, and she slowly scrolled up, scanning the executables and the youngest processes. The ones that had been running since the machine last rebooted. A certain process caught her eye.

```
USER PID %CPU %MEM STARTED COMMAND
vtuser 35 0.1 5.2 21Feb12 /usr/bin/voting-
terminal 8088
```

It didn't take N3tN1nja long to see the same thing she had, and based on their message, they were as surprised as she was.

> **N3TN1NJA**
>
> It's a goddamn voting terminal!

She didn't wait for them to say anything else. She needed to know for herself. The only way she could think to do it from the inside was to telnet to the same machine.

```
> telnet localhost 80
Trying 192.168.1.1...
Connected
Escape character is '^]'.
```

Before N3tN1nja could jump in, she typed the follow-up command to load whatever web page was on the machine.

```
GET / HTTP/1.0
HTTP/1.0 200 OK
Content-Type: text/html; charset=utf-8
...
```

What followed made her blood run cold. This wasn't simply a voting machine, it was one of the voting terminals used in the Fremont elections. The same election that Mr. Sanchez was up for reelection in.

As she stared dumbfounded at the output, her mind turned over the implications of what she was about to do. Her friend, however, took the words out of her mouth.

> N3TN1NJA
>
> I'm done! No way. I won't do this. Not for you, not for anyone. Like you said, there are lines, and we just crossed one of mine.

And with that, her connection dropped. Not only from the voting machine. It cut all the way out, through every single hop, including their *tmux* session. They were all gone.

All she saw was her own terminal staring back at her, screaming out in stark, silent accusation.

```
Connection lost
```

It took her a second to catch up to what was happening, to what her friend, her mentor, was saying.

She'd pushed them past their breaking point. And not because she was egging them on. Hell, they'd done most of the driving.

In her ignorance, she hadn't even considered what Mr. Sanchez might be asking her to do. Not that she'd guess how low he'd go.

But there was something more. Something deeper was eating at her. Rather than let it simmer, she grabbed hold of it and cracked it open.

She started a new terminal and quickly changed to where she'd downloaded the patched code from the Sanchez email. Then she did what she should've done the second the message arrived.

```
> xxd patch-vt1
```

Even the name of the patch shouted at her, and when she hit return, her life flashed before her eyes.

```
000008e8:  4672 6565 6d6f 6e74 2045 6c65   Freemont Ele
000008f4:  6374 696f 6e20 436f 6d6d 6973   ction Commis
00000900:  7369 6f6e 2e20 566f 7469 6e67   sion. Voting
0000090c:  2054 616c 6c79 2e20 5361 6e63    Tally. Sanc
00000918:  6865 7a20 3234 3537 2c20 4e65   hez 2457, Ne
00000924:  7774 6f6e 2032 3130 342c 2055   wton 2104, U
00000930:  6e64 6563 6c61 7265 6420 3230   ndeclared 20
```

She'd come seconds away from fucking up her life forever. From turning into not just a black hat, but enemy number one in the eyes of the government.

The bastard Sanchez was setting her up to rig the election. He was so worried about his competition that he was forcing her to hack a voting terminal.

As she stared at the screen, she found herself needing to get away. To get out of the lab.

She slammed her laptop shut, unplugged the external monitor cables, and tossed it into her bag. Within a minute, she had her coat on and was halfway up the stairs.

She couldn't breathe. Everything around her suddenly swirled in an unfamiliar mass of colors and shapes.

It was only when the bitter cold of the outside air hit her face that she gasped and fell to her knees in a snowdrift. The icy wet mound offered a shocking contrast, grounding her back to reality.

"Are you okay?" a man called out, rushing to her side to help. "Do you need—"

"Get away!" she screamed, waving her arms and sending him reeling backward. "Don't fucking touch me!"

Alex stumbled to her feet and ran, her mind blank with panic. She didn't know her destination, but she needed to escape, to put as much distance as possible between herself and her mistake.

13 / BUREAU 121
CIPHER

Choe stood beside Cipher, her face an expressionless mask. Her sleek, form-fitting black attire spoke volumes, hinting at a seductive allure and an underlying danger that was impossible to ignore.

After his awakening in the torture chambers, he had dug deeper into Choe's background online. It took several wads of well-placed cash and calling in multiple old debts, but the results were eye-opening. She wasn't just a masterful chameleon; she was a trained assassin. A killer, nurtured from birth by the nomenklatura to execute their will.

From what his contact said, Choe was part of something called Bureau 121 within the Reconnaissance General Bureau, North Korea's intelligence and clandestine operations division. It was a cyberwarfare unit formed after the Iraq war and quickly elevated to top priority by the nomenklatura.

And in Cipher's case, Choe wasn't simply an online soldier, she was trained to seduce the enemy to keep him under their control.

"Our people have tracked down the hackers to America. One of them is in their Great Lakes region, and the other is on the West Coast." Choe highlighted the regions on the map.

He shook his head in frustration and stared down, kicking at the ground. "I think we'll need a bit more precision than that to catch them."

She shot him a sideward glare, a hint of smugness playing at her lips. "You'll be given more details once we arrive. We can't risk you reaching out to your associates and slipping away, now can we?"

Her words hung in the air, a not-so-subtle reminder of the power she held over him. Especially since the general gave her control of their program after the virus leak.

"I never told you this," she began, her finger tracing the outline on the map, "but before you arrived in the interrogation chamber the other day, I managed to get our little canaries to sing a few notes myself." She glanced over at him. "I didn't give it much thought at first, but after you finished breaking them, the pieces fell into place."

She paused, smirking as she savored the moment. "We followed the moles' breadcrumbs to track down our hacker friends. And the best part? We used the very network they thought was so secure against them. IRC."

A chill ran down his spine as the implications sank in. If infiltrating the hackers' communications was so easy, what secrets of his own might they uncover?

He'd always hated IRC, preferring mainstream social networks to infiltrate the Western populace.

"Impressive, isn't it?" she continued, rapidly scrolling through what looked like years of chat logs.

He couldn't read much with how fast the text moved, but he caught stray highlights. Random personal details dropped in different IRC channels, the sort people let slip without realizing how they contribute to a larger mosaic. Each tidbit seemed insignificant on its own, but woven together, they formed a tapestry that revealed far more than the individual threads.

Choe relished his discomfort, watching him squirm to pluck out details. "You've spent years discounting our programmers, but they're not as bad as you let the general and I believe. They analyzed every conversation the mules had saved, and some that only recently surfaced. That last detail was peculiar." She glanced at him, a knowing glint in her eye. "It's funny how sometimes the most revealing information comes from unexpected places, wouldn't you agree? Almost as if someone wanted us to find it, someone with intimate knowledge of our systems and protocols."

She let the question linger, locking her gaze with his, leaving him on edge. The silence stretched between them, thick with unspoken accusations.

Finally, she continued, her voice slicing through the tension. "We combined the moles' personal chats with N3tN1nja, along with years of their archived messages. That's when the picture really took shape. We found the clues we needed, the pieces falling into place like a well-crafted puzzle. And now, we have them exactly where we want them."

Cipher clenched his jaw, masking his unease. She knew. Somehow, she'd discovered he'd rewritten the logs on the moles' machines, even if he'd inadvertently pinned it on the right person. The twinkle in her eye left no doubt. She had him cornered, and they both knew it.

The fire in her eyes was both intoxicating and terrifying. He'd seen it in bed countless times before, mistaking it for seductive allure.

But now, now he saw it for what it truly was. A fierce determination to manipulate and control, a killer's resolve hiding behind each sultry glance.

He'd underestimated her for the last time. Going forward, he needed to bide his time, playing along with her little game, until he found a way to protect his own interests. To escape from the grasp of his overseers.

"Just sit back and enjoy the trip," she said, stepping up beside him. "We'll have our hackers in hand soon enough."

Cipher raised an eyebrow and returned his attention to the US map. "Why even take me then? Certainly the general has operatives on the ground. People capable of dealing with these..."—he gestured dismissively toward the screen—"these nuisances."

He fought to appear indifferent, despite yearning to deal with these irritants himself, to subject them to pain befitting their crimes, like he'd done to the traitors.

It was crucial he maintain a facade of disinterest. His eagerness mustn't show through.

Choe narrowed her gaze, her hazel eyes piercing his thinly veiled act. She knew how he felt about Byt3Linguist, and especially N3tN1nja. He'd taken out his frustrations over them on her body many nights.

"We're not fools, Cipher." She locked her arms across her chest. "You're going because we need you on the ground in Florida when this is over. Your private mule down there has clammed up, and according to his last email, he'll only deal with you, and in person at that. I'll strangle the little fucker when we're done with this." She eyed him suspiciously. "But before I do, we need you to get a substantial transfer from him. Our little virus has been busy, very busy." She winked, sending a shiver up his spine. "Besides, N3tN1nja's had a hard-on for you for years. There's no telling what traps they might set for us, and maybe we'll get lucky having you there to corner one of them."

She paused, letting her words sink in. He hadn't known she'd been talking to his intern, but it wouldn't surprise him if Rajesh had figured out the bitcoin transfers. That kid was too smart for his own good. More importantly, though, he wanted to know what she meant by getting lucky having him there.

He couldn't shake the feeling she intended to use him as a human shield.

"The question is..." she continued, studying the map intensely. "Which location should be yours?"

He tilted his head, unsure what she was leading him into. She was talking in riddles. *If I'm going with them, what's the issue? They'll obviously send me with her, won't they?* She knew more about him than anyone. Unless...

"Who else is joining us?" he asked, trying his best to keep his eyes on the highlighted map of the United States.

There were easily ten to fifteen states in the selected regions, in several of which he had contacts. New York and Chicago were high on his list, as were most of the major cities in California. Anywhere technology bloomed, he knew people.

Money broke down even the staunchest proponents of democracy, and in the United States he'd smashed many a moral compass. Still, that meant nothing if his wardens were talented. Bullets always trumped cash if you were fast enough.

He briefly glanced at her and then back at the map.

No. That wasn't it. Her pause was far more telling than she realized. She was honestly torn. He could tell by how she was biting the inside of her cheek, a habit he'd noticed whenever their sensual conversations turned personal.

He was beginning to wonder if their information on the hackers was really as extensive as they'd led him to believe. This wouldn't be the first time the nomenklatura had stretched the truth to fit their needs. The question was, how to use this detail against them?

Without waiting for a reply, he blurted out, "I'll take the cold." He pointed at the Great Lakes region highlighted in green, his fingers trembling slightly. "I've never been there in the fall, but I always meant to visit. I heard the colors are spectacular this time of year."

When he peered at her, she was studying him intently. Probably questioning whether his offer was self-serving or a ruse. He could almost hear the gears turning in her mind.

A moment later, she emitted a silent sigh and reached forward, shutting off the display. "No! You'll take the western target. Tae-Woo and his brother will be your shadows. We leave within the hour."

With that, she spun on her heels and headed toward the door.

As she disappeared around the corner, he crossed his arms, relishing the conviction of her decision.

He tried his hardest not to smile, but if there'd been a camera on this side of the room, it would've caught the smirk creeping onto his face.

Guiding her decision was almost effortless. For someone who prided herself on her cunning, she was surprisingly easy to steer.

A few carefully chosen questions, a subtle shift in his body language, and she'd made the call he'd wanted all along. She was out of his league in games of the mind.

Even as he savored this minor victory, his thoughts raced ahead, plotting his next move.

Returning here wasn't an option. They'd kill him as soon as he stepped foot on North Korean soil. He'd served his purpose with the nomenklatura, and he'd be nothing but a liability after the transfer.

No, he needed to find a way out, a path to freedom that didn't end with a bullet to the head. He'd have to be smart, leveraging every asset and advantage at his disposal. But if anyone could pull it off, it was him. He'd spent his entire life outsmarting those who sought to control him, and this would be no different.

The gears in his head began turning, pieces of a plan falling into place. Time was of the essence; he had to act while they were still off balance. It wouldn't be easy, but then again, nothing worth doing ever was.

14 / RED STAR RISING
ALEX

The triple ring of her phone jarred her out of a fitful sleep. The annoying device had already rung twice in as many hours, but she'd ignored the first two. Judging by the ringtone, she knew who it was, and if she didn't answer, the rings would only become more frequent.

Reaching out, she slapped her hand on the relentless device and lifted it to her ear, activating it.

"Hello, Aunt Min." She rolled onto her back and winced as a beam of light from the window struck her eyes.

"It's about time!" her aunt said. "I was starting to think you were ignoring me."

She sat up and swung her legs over the side of the bed, her own stench hitting her seconds later. "Don't be silly." She yawned. "I've just been... busy. Studying."

Lying had never been her strong suit, especially to family. But white lies weren't the worst thing she'd done this weekend. Over the past day and a half, she hadn't left her bed except to see if N3tN1nja replied to her questions.

They hadn't.

She eased upright and stepped toward her desk as Aunt Min chattered in her ear. When she tapped the space bar on her laptop, she quickly typed her password and the screen came to life.

But instead of seeing a reply, all she saw was the message she'd sent early Saturday morning after trudging through snow from North Campus.

L3X1C0N

> I'm sorry for roping you into that. I feel so dumb. As you can tell, I was way out of my depth. I had no idea what I was being asked to do, I swear. I only now looked at the patch, and it's absolutely terrifying, worse than I imagined. I almost fucked up bad.

While enduring the dull throbbing of her frostbitten fingers, she'd sent N3tN1nja the only message she could think of. The truth.

Staring at the nearly empty IRC window, she groaned every few seconds as her aunt talked her ear off. She was going on about everything from noisy neighbors to her mother's split personalities, to dealing with her father's crazy hours. It was a machine gun rat-a-tat-tat of conversation with no end in sight.

As her aunt's stories droned on, Alex's gaze drifted to the colorful artwork adorning her roommate Michelle's side of the dorm. The vibrant hues and abstract patterns reminded her of the outfits her aunt always wore, the memory tugging at her heartstrings.

Part of her wanted to make Aunt Min stop talking, to tell her everything that happened last night and seek her guidance. The confession danced on the tip of her tongue, desperate to be heard. She longed for the comfort of her aunt's reassuring words, the promise that everything would be all right.

But she couldn't. She'd already relied on her aunt too much, burdening her with the weight of her prior mistakes.

Hell, she wouldn't even be at college if it weren't for her unwavering support. No, this time, she needed to take responsibility for her fuckups.

She closed her eyes, fighting to wall off her emotions. Despite craving her aunt's advice, involving her would only put her at risk. She couldn't bear incriminating the one person who'd always been there, who'd sacrificed so much to help her succeed.

With a deep breath, she steeled herself. She had to handle this mess alone, without dragging her aunt down.

"So, who do you think will win?" her aunt asked.

She shook her head, leaning back in the chair, uncertain how to reply. "Win... what?"

Aunt Min sighed. "Have you been listening to anything I've said the last ten minutes?"

"I have... I just." She covered her face. "I'm sorry."

The words were both apology and admission.

Her aunt didn't pause. "It's okay. Really. Just stop gawking at boys when they walk by, will ya? I was asking who you thought would win the local mayoral election? After I ran into Mayor Sanchez last week at your mother's work, his daughter cornered me. She and I got to talk—"

Alex sat forward, startled. "About what?"

"Oh, now you're all ears." Her aunt snickered. "I see how it is."

"I don't trust those fuckers." Alex blurted it out, realizing too late she'd sworn. It was the first time she'd sworn in front of her aunt. "I'm sorr—"

"Don't be," her aunt consoled. "I don't trust them either. It was actually quite sad. The girl asked if I knew anyone in local politics. Said she needed help with her father's campaign." She clicked her tongue in disapproval. "I can only imagine what, but judging by his early polling, I could hazard a guess."

That detail would've been invaluable days earlier. Maybe she should've stayed in touch more. "Sorry I haven't called much," she said, guilt in her voice.

"Would you stop!" her aunt shot back. "You're in college. You've got studying to do, and a future to make for yourself. Don't worry about what's happening back here. But do me a favor, would you?"

She nodded, rubbing her face with her hands. "Anything?"

"Just let us know you're all right sometimes," her aunt said, worry lacing her voice. "Even if it's through those blasted messages. I'd rather get a quick text in the middle of the night than be left in the dark. Can you do that for me?"

"I can, and I will." She swallowed the lump in her throat. "I promise."

"Good," her aunt's voice brightened. "Now tell me, have you kissed anyone yet? Boy? Girl? I don't care which."

Alex burst out laughing as a weight lifted off her shoulders. One she hadn't realized was there since tearing out of the computer lab.

In that moment, she knew what she had to do. Sanchez could go fuck himself, and she'd tell him as much. She'd find a way to pay for college on her own terms, even if it meant drowning in debt.

"No, I haven't kissed anyone." She stood and walked to the window. "But there was this frat guy in the lab the other night. I about made him piss himself."

Her aunt snorted. "Tell me more."

AFTER NEARLY AN HOUR on the phone, Alex desperately needed a shower, having marinated in her own stench for too long.

With clean clothes and a smile in her heart, she checked her laptop again.

There was a message waiting for her from her roommate, Michelle, who wanted to meet up in the labs on North Campus, in the Electrical Engineering and Computer Science (EECS) building. Alex quickly replied, saying she'd be there in an hour after she grabbed something to eat.

Flipping back to IRC, there was still nothing from N3tN1nja, but a few private messages from her other netizen friends had popped up. People she chatted with on her Byt3Linguist handle from the #anime, #politics, and #conspiracy channels she frequented.

She only used the Byt3Linguist account for fun nowadays, leaving L3x1c0n for all things hacking. It was easier that way, especially after the attacks a few months back when people learned she was American. She laid low with her old handle, avoiding the edgier channels. Besides, tons of her friends only knew her by that name, and she wasn't about to bridge them to her alt.

What was strange about these messages, however, wasn't that they were wondering where she'd been. It was what they were warning her about.

> **MYSTICMOON**
>
> Yo. Some dawg named HilaraFruit been sniffing around on #anime, asking questions about you. Be careful. They's offering serious crypto for your digits.

> **ALI3NATTAK**
>
> Watch your six LinguisT. Some n00b with the handle D3thToClownS was inquiring about you on #conspiracy... 1,000 bitcoin for your personal deets. I had the bot ban 'em, but they're making the rounds.

Similar messages had come in from other friends she'd

made over the years, all referencing different IRC handles asking about her. It was nice knowing people had her back and didn't sell her out. Not that they could have. She hadn't shared much about her real life with many of them.

Being online was dangerous enough, and breaking anonymity was a newbie mistake. Her first rule was never to mix physical reality with the virtual one. It was a surefire way to invite trouble into your life.

When she looked up the price of bitcoin, she did a double take. Five thousand dollars for some random girl was a lot of cash. Whoever they were, they wanted her badly.

Just as she was about to log off, her connection dropped. At first, she wasn't sure what was up, but when she switched to her logs, she saw what happened.

Someone had gained access to one of her jump points masking her real IP. They'd triggered her safeguards by pinging a machine she'd previously logged through. One she'd compromised a lot deeper. Though they hadn't pinged her laptop, based on her *ssh* jump history, they were getting dangerously close to tracking her down.

She leaned back, drawing in her breath, a shiver reverberating up her spine.

The stark realization of what was happening suddenly sank in.

She was the target of a literal manhunt.

Chilling moments like this underscored the risks of hacking, but also ignited a fiercer determination.

She'd come to college to master computers and help people like her father—people who'd been taken advantage of online. The scumbags looking for her right now were no different from the ones who'd exploited him. She just had to figure out who they were before they tracked her down. Maybe then she could stop them.

And that gave her an idea.

She flipped through her file explorer and found her IRC logs from earlier in the year. Back when she'd first talked to N3tN1nja about the mass channel ban, she'd spent countless hours scrounging through those logs, trying to pinpoint a pattern within the madness.

With the log files open, she quickly searched up the chat handles her friends had given her. The ones asking about her.

The search didn't take long. Both HilaraFruit and D3thToClownS were instant hits, and when she checked the logs for the other names, most were there too.

Now she needed to know who these people were. Maybe they'd given hints of where they were from on the channels. In their conversations.

She went back to searching her logs, trying to see what her stalkers talked to people about. While she didn't have logs for every channel on the server, she did have transcripts from channels she was on.

One by one, she scrolled through their messages. The only commonality her stalkers seemed to have was their love of arguing. Whether the topic was world politics, abortion rights, or the age-old *emacs* vs. *vim* debate, these idiots were intent on stirring up trouble. She hated trolls.

But one thing was missing from all their chats. Personal details. No hobbies, restaurants, favorite shows, or anything linking them back to being human. Besides several heated days fighting about Asian politics, they were ghosts. As far as she could tell, they could've been bots.

Her heart raced with the implications. N3tN1nja had said these people worked for foreign governments. If true, and they were still trying to track her down six months later, she must've been onto something. But what?

At the time, she'd been a newbie with viruses and hadn't gotten far cracking Reveton apart. But N3tN1nja had. They were the one who'd flipped over that rock in public, not her.

"Shit," she muttered, glancing at the anime nagas poster on her wall. "The proxies." She'd forgotten all about them.

If they were after her, maybe her proxy hack had found something she could work with.

She hurriedly opened multiple terminals, hopping through secure shell after secure shell.

Once she'd masked her route, she accessed the first of the dozen or so reverse proxy machines. As soon as she did, she gasped.

Her hidden logs were overflowing with traffic. The virus had been busy stealing money, and from what the logs were showing, the hackers had raised the stakes.

The transactions weren't for hundreds of dollars, like with her father. People were being taken for thousands at a time. That wasn't just life-changing money, that was *life-ending* money to most people.

She ran a quick *awk* command against the logs, summing up the total cash they'd stolen since she'd started her script. When the final tally scrolled by, she nearly fell out of her chair.

"Two hundred thousand dollars," she muttered, running her hand through her damp hair. "Holy shit!"

Part of her wanted to wipe the file, but another longed to download it and transfer the funds to one of her accounts.

Maybe the hackers wouldn't move it right away. She'd read they did that sometimes to avoid the Feds. That kind of cash would change her life. Hell, it would change her entire family's life.

As she stared at the glowing green-on-black digits of her terminal, her mind raced through how that money could affect her future. But no matter how excited she got, reality quickly settled in. Unless she could return the cash to the rightful owners, there was no way she could take it for herself. She wasn't wired like that.

No. She had to stop these people, and fast. As she stewed on how, a new idea began to form in her mind.

She quickly searched the proxy logs, extracting all the upstream addresses where the money was being uploaded. From there, she ran each of them through her network mapping application, looking for commonalities in the destination machines.

Within minutes, a pattern emerged. She just had no idea what the hell it meant. The addresses from IRC matched the ones from her proxy, but stranger still was where they led.

"What's *Red Star OS*?" She squinted at her screen and opened a web browser, searching for the name.

She gasped as she scanned the articles that came up.

It *was* the goddamn North Koreans, which eerily aligned with the fringe conspiracy theories circulating after the virus was unmasked. While they'd gotten little else right, the implications were staggering.

She could have an enemy government searching for her. If that didn't freak a person out, she didn't know what would.

With her heart pounding, her attention returned to the piles of cash waiting in her terminal. Across the dozen machines she'd infiltrated last week, she'd collected over two point six million dollars.

That was a hell of a lot of Benjamins. Enough to make anyone weak in the knees, even someone as morally grounded as she felt.

"No!" She clenched and unclenched her fists on the desk, knuckles turning white. She took a deep breath, holding it before gradually releasing. In and out. In and out.

She focused on the sensation of air filling her lungs, resisting the urge threatening to consume her.

"They're bad people, Lex." She tapped her fingers nervously on her keyboard. "And we aren't like them. But maybe..."

She flipped back to IRC and opened a direct message to the exploits bot on Rizon. After entering her password, she typed out a new search.

```
Search: CentOS or Fedora or Red Star OS
2.0, VIM or Emacs Exploit
```

The articles she scanned earlier said that Red Star OS was actually a fork of CentOS and Fedora. Apparently, the North Koreans couldn't risk democracies influencing their people, so they created their own operating system for civilian and government use.

While the North Korean regime likely managed the OS with an iron fist, they probably weren't on top of fixing vulnerabilities. It was pretty much a universal truth that governments were never speedy when it came to technology, and she couldn't see how they'd be different.

As she scanned more articles about Red Star OS, the search results from the bot popped up, filling her chat window. Her excitement rose with every exploit that scrolled past.

There were numerous attack vectors she could try, but one in particular stood out. A Mack Truck sized exploit in *vim* between versions three and seven.

It was mind-blowing that something so invasive had been in the wild for so long. Apparently, this attack allowed arbitrary code execution simply by encountering certain character sequences in a file. And according to the IRC logs she'd read earlier, *vim* was the preferred editor of her stalkers.

Her gamble was whether these people even opened the files in *vim*. If they didn't, they'd probably assume the file was corrupted when they loaded it into another application. Either that, or they'd be able to read the script she tried to embed.

"Unless..." She ran her hand along her chin, the image of a

Trojan horse forming in her mind. The key was disguising the horse to look like its surroundings.

She hurriedly grabbed a few lines from one of the remote files and disconnected from all the proxies. Staying connected too long might alert an admin to her presence, and she needed time to write the hack.

With her target in mind, she began piecing together a script to turn the tables on her attackers. Or in this case, make her horse blend in with the rest of the data.

As she typed out her idea, she jumped at a sharp knock on the door to her dorm. She leapt from her chair, backing toward the window. Her heart thumped in her chest.

They'd found her. How the hell did they find her?

Just as she started searching for the small knife her roommate used to carve her models, a voice called out from the other side.

"Lex!" a girl's voice shouted, repeating the thump. "It's Sue from down the hall. Michelle's trying to reach you. Are you in there?"

"Shit," Alex groaned. She'd forgotten about Michelle.

"Hey, Sue!" she shouted. "Yeah, I'm here. I... I just fell asleep. I'll call Michelle. Thanks for waking me."

"You alright?" Sue asked, concern lacing her voice.

"Yeah... I'm fine." She stepped toward the door, checking the peephole before cracking it open, feigning sleep. "I'm exhausted. I was up late studying." She yawned. "Thanks for the wake-up. I could've slept all day. I owe you one."

Sue squinted at her before shifting to a smile. "I hear ya. I could pass out myself. Good luck on midterms."

"You too." Alex smiled back, closing the door as Sue walked away.

When the latch clicked shut, she drew in a deep breath and exhaled, her racing heart still struggling to recover. She needed to chill the hell out. She'd covered her tracks. There was no way they could track her down. Not here.

As her pulse slowed, she hopped back to her laptop and opened Messages. She didn't even remember quitting it, but when it stopped bouncing in the dock, it popped up with dozens of unread messages from Michelle.

After scanning the wall of frantic messages, she typed a reply.

ALEX

> Sorry, lost track of time. ⏰ I'm heading up now! 🚌 Be there in 20 minutes. I'll grab snacks on the way.

Her response was quick.

MICHELLE

> I was getting worried. Glad you're ok. Grab my power 🔌 brick, would you? I totally forgot it.

Alex glanced at her roommate's desk. The charger sat there, waiting.

ALEX

> Charger, check! See you soon 😃

With charger in hand, she quickly packed her bag and bolted out the door.

The sooner she got to North Campus, the sooner she could hack together this Trojan.

15 / OUT OF PLACE
CIPHER

The frigid afternoon wind off the ocean cut through Cipher's sweater like gauze. He shivered, cursing the Pyongyang idiots who thought a lightweight cotton weave would suffice in this weather.

Sure, no one expected the temperatures to drop so suddenly, but it was fall in Fremont, California. With climate change, anything was possible.

Arms crossed and body trembling, he leaned against a telephone pole in an attempt to block the wind. A half-torn campaign poster of a mayoral candidate named Sanchez was stapled over his shoulder. Someone had vandalized the picture, adding black horns and orange fire bursting from the man's mouth. The artwork was surprisingly well-done, and it was clear Sanchez wasn't popular in these parts.

"The pinnacle of democracy," he muttered, returning his attention to their target: An apartment in a low-end affordable housing complex.

After greasing the right palms at the local internet provider, they'd narrowed down the IP address's physical location. Each ISP had its own network address block, and once they'd tracked down the hacker's machine, they just needed an employee willing to take a bribe. With most of the company's operations outsourced to contractors, it wasn't much of a challenge. Corporate loyalty was a quaint notion from a bygone era of America's past, before shareholder profits trumped fair pay.

In the overcast daylight, the building looked shabby and in need of several coats of paint. Empty planters lined the railings and flipped over lawn chairs awaited warmer weather.

Even so, it looked more inviting than his North Korean accommodations. That wasn't saying much, though. A cave would have more appeal at the right temperature.

He couldn't help but see this neighborhood for what it was. The perfect place for a hacker to disappear. Everyone who lived here was down and out and probably kept to themselves. It was the ideal cover for someone looking to fade into the background and chip away at society.

After several days of sneaking past border guards and hiding in the cellars of South Korean operatives, they arrived at the airport in Seoul. Only then did Tae-Woo finally reveal their destination.

Cipher held back his excitement, and after passing through security, he quickly ran some searches to familiarize himself with the area before their arrival.

Apparently, this part of Fremont boasted a sizable Korean community. While it shouldn't have been surprising, it made him wonder if Byt3Linguist or N3tN1nja were defectors. The irony wouldn't be lost on him, or the nomenklatura for that matter. Heads would roll if they turned out to be a family member of the Workers' Party.

They'd landed at San Francisco International a few hours earlier. After an unexpected stop in Oakland for firepower and additional muscle, they drove straight to Fremont. Though they only gave him a knife, his guardians were armed to the teeth. And they should be. If either of their targets was home, there was no telling what they might face.

While he stood out in the open pretending to fit in, his handlers were out of sight, doing what shadows did. He couldn't pinpoint their locations, but he knew they'd be there the moment he needed them.

Reaching up, he tapped his earpiece, activating his connection to Tae-Woo and his brother. "Coast is clear. I'm going in." He started toward the apartment.

"Negative!" Tae-Woo shouted, halting Cipher's brisk walk and catapulting his heart into a frantic pace.

"What is it?" He spun around, half expecting CIA or FBI agents to be swarming him on all sides. But there was only the sound of children playing in the distance.

"They're online," Tae-Woo said.

Cipher pulled out his phone and forced a smile as he circled back to the pole, pretending to receive a call. The truth was, his handlers had refused to give him a SIM card until they were done here and on the next plane to Florida.

"Who is?" he whispered, activating his Wi-Fi with a swipe of his thumb.

"We don't know," Jin-Soo, Tae-Woo's brother, replied. "But their access point is hot. Whatever it's running, your people can't seem to bypass the firewall."

"Idiots," he muttered.

"What's that?" Tae-Woo asked, their connection crackling.

"Nothing." He faked a laugh. "It's probably a special hardware build. I doubt our people can get past N3tN1nja's handiwork. Not without..."

He never finished the sentence. The others already knew his thoughts. They'd been forced to listen to his rant the entire way there.

Without him leading the assault, they wouldn't make

much progress breaking through. Not unless it was a vanilla install, which N3tN1nja would never use.

Situations like this were why the nomenklatura kept him on such a short leash, and they'd miss him when he was gone. Most of their people were decades behind the rest of the world with computers, but under his tutelage, they'd made leaps and bounds over the past few years. Their problem was figuring out how to not kill their soldiers when they stepped out of line.

He pretended to end his call and scrolled through the Wi-Fi networks on his phone. There were easily fifty networks within range, but when he switched to his war-scanning software, the suspect network flashed up like a beacon in the night.

```
HideYoKidsHideYoWiFi
```

The name screamed "attack me" and "leave me alone" at the same time. With a moniker like that, N3tN1nja could lure in and hack dozens of devices attempting to join the network just for fun. That is, if they were worth their salt.

His phone, however, wasn't a regular smartphone. He had a custom Android build he'd designed for infiltrating networks like this. Even if he wasn't with his team in North Korea, he could still lead his own personal assault from here.

"What are you doing?" Tae-Woo asked in his ear. He must be actively watching him from somewhere.

Cipher grimaced, half wishing the idiot was nearby so he could show him. "Doing what the imbeciles back home couldn't. I'm hacking in."

He tapped his screen furiously with his thumbs, starting his assault on the device's firewall.

Whatever it was running, the router was either taxed or

slow as hell. His attempts to break in were taking longer and longer each time.

16 / TROJAN TACTICS
ALEX

After triple checking her edits, Alex injected the Trojan into this instance of the reverse proxy. Almost immediately, intercepted cash transactions began appearing in her log, and she swallowed down the rising lump in her throat. There was no going back now.

That was the last of the proxies she'd infiltrated. Her proxy war was in full swing, and all she had left to do was wait.

While testing her script, she realized there was more to the virus than met the eye. Half the executable never seemed to load into memory, which meant it never ran. The more she tinkered, the more it felt like an onion, each layer revealing new complexities and hidden secrets.

That fact didn't help her frayed nerves. She was already well past scared at this point, her mind racing with second guesses.

What if I make a mistake? What if they traced it back to me? Even if they are the North Korean government, they couldn't just openly attack someone on US soil. Right?

She shook her head, pushing the doubts aside. She was in too deep to back out now. All she could do was trust her skills and hope her plan would work.

If she hadn't screwed up her exploit, then as soon as one of the North Korean hackers viewed the cash dumps in *vim*, they'd trigger her Trojan. The script itself was simple and to the point, and she was actually thrilled with how it turned out.

Her Trojan installed a tiny fragment of code in the user's local shell file, then deleted itself. That way, they never knew how they'd gotten compromised. At most, they'd find the loader script. But by then it was too late. They'd have no idea how it got there.

The shell edit was nearly undetectable, and she leaned into the fact that most people never looked at their startup scripts after setting them up. Hell, she hadn't checked hers in over a year until today, when trying out her hack.

Her loader was where the magic happened. It executed a simple set of background commands any time a user opened a new terminal window. It was only three lines of code, but the results allowed her to do almost anything on the hacker's machine. For now, it simply loaded a URL. One fitting for these attackers.

With her plan in place, she exited all the machines and switched to IRC. Her last message to N3tN1nja still sat unanswered, but she needed to send another. Her fingers trembled as she typed it out.

> L3X1C0N
>
> I found them. It took a while, but I did it. I followed the Reveton money trail and laid a trap. Ping me when you're on. I'd like to share the d33ts.

She hit enter without considering the consequences. For all she knew, N3tN1nja was from North Korea, and had been grooming her for the past year.

But her gut said they weren't. Even though she still hadn't figured out if they were male or female, she considered herself a decent judge of character. Plus, after the Sanchez voting debacle, she felt she owed them some good news.

Her last message had been sitting unanswered for nearly two days without reply, which was crazy considering how often N3tN1nja was usually online.

At one point, people on IRC accused the handle of being a bot or a *daemon*, like the book by the same name. But she knew better. Their private messages over the past year convinced her they were human, not some glorified automated cron job.

At the moment, however, they'd fallen off the net, and she couldn't help but feel it was her fault.

"Is everything alright?" Michelle asked from the computer to her right. The normally chipper voice of her Italian roommate was only a fraction of its usual volume and intonation.

"Everything's fine," Alex muttered, looking up. "Why?"

They'd only been roomies for a few months, but got along great, even with Michelle's makeup fetish and colorful outfits. Today's pairing practically burned Alex's retinas.

"Because you look frazzled." Michelle squinted. "Are you sure you're okay?" She leaned forward, but Alex quickly locked her desktop.

"You're not even working on the project, are you?" Michelle nudged her shoulder.

Alex smirked and started packing up. "I finished that a while ago."

She slid her laptop into its padded sleeve, its surface adorned with school-themed stickers, a departure from her usual anime and tech decorations.

With her bag packed, she stood, tossing it over her shoulder. "Ready for some grub?"

Michelle groaned and stared at her screen, her eyes glazing over the wall of red compiler errors. From the looks of it, they'd be coming back later, which was fine with her. She'd spent many nights on North Campus this year, preferring the computer lab to dorm life on Central Campus.

"I really should finish this." Michelle ran her hands through her perfectly combed hair, adjusting her scrunchies to wrangle a few stray strands drifting into her eyes.

"Tell you what..." Alex leaned closer, her gaze darting around. "I'll bring you back some pepperoni slices and a pop."

Michelle smiled playfully. "Faygo, Rock and Rye?"

Alex lowered her head, snickering quietly. "If they have it."

She glanced at her machine, then at the lab entrance. Several students were already making their way toward her workstation.

Michelle must have read her mind. "Don't worry." She bent down and unplugged the aging Sun Ultra tower, instantly powering it down. She then pulled a colorful 'Out of Order' sign from her bag and draped it over the keyboard before shutting off the display.

They'd printed the fake warning signs their second week of school. It was the only way to hold a spot without making a scene. You just had to be careful a lab monitor didn't catch you setting it out. If they did, you'd lose lab privileges for the rest of the school year.

"I got your back, sister," Michelle whispered, waving her away. "Now get me some grease... oh... and maybe a candy bar."

"Candy bar, check." Alex started toward the exit, maneuvering past the advancing students.

As she reached the entrance, an audible sigh emanated from behind her. She spun around, pressing her butt against the door handle to open it. She watched the two exasperated engineering students walk away from her workstation, while Michelle struggled to suppress a grin, but failed miserably.

With her spot saved, and her trap set, all Alex could think about was quelling her growling stomach. She hadn't eaten since last night, and four or five slices of greasy pizza sounded amazing. She could practically smell the overcooked dough.

Pushing open the door to the stairs, she made her way down three stories to the lobby.

Just as she was about to exit the stairwell, her phone vibrated. It was probably Michelle asking for something else.

She pulled out her aging clamshell from her pocket and flipped it open, drawing in her breath when she read the display.

```
HideYoKidsHideYoWiFi : Connection compro-
mised. Performing system wipe.
```

"What the fuck?" she snipped, her voice echoing in the empty stairwell.

Goosebumps prickled her skin, an icy shiver running down her spine.

She turned sideways, leaning against the wall as the stairs started spinning.

They'd found her Raspberry Pi back home in Fremont.
But how the hell did they track me down?
How long had they been watching me?
And more importantly, had they tracked me here?

The questions kept coming as the implications of the message spiraled through her mind.

She'd been online for hours, so it was impossible to tell what they had or hadn't learned.

Hell, she was only one hop away from that machine. That access point was a regular launching pad in her routine, and she'd used it countless times as a secure gateway to the broader internet.

By now, she had to assume the North Koreans had her real network address and were coming for her. It was entirely possible they were already lurking nearby.

Without warning, the door swung inward, and she screamed, sending the two entering students stumbling backward, eyes wide with shock. They hadn't expected to be greeted with a shriek.

"Sorry. You... you scared me." She peeked her head out the opening and scanned her surroundings. Except for the two of them, the lobby was empty.

With her heart pounding in her chest, she tentatively stepped out of the stairwell and into the open.

Glancing around, she suddenly felt unsure of what to do or where to go.

She couldn't show her face in the Commons, let alone in line at a restaurant. And there was no way in hell she could venture back to her dorm room. Not yet. Not until she knew it was safe.

As she considered her options, the still-shocked students took a wide berth around her, whispering between themselves as they headed up the stairs.

"What?" she screamed, raising her hands. "Haven't you seen someone scared before?"

They flinched at her words, and several others eyed her suspiciously as they passed, like she might lash out and attack them.

She looked back at them the same way, unsure who she could trust; the janitor at the end of the hall, the scholarly gentleman in tweed entering the building, or the elderly woman leaving the restroom. It could be all of them, or none of them.

Her attacker could be any of the people wandering the campus, searching for her. Ready to pull the trigger. Assuming they had a trigger. For all she knew, they'd dispatch her through more stealthy means like poison, or worse, a shiv wielded by a seemingly innocent passerby, the cold steel hidden beneath a benign smile.

Standing there was stupid. Her mind spiraled uncontrollably out in the open. Her best option was to keep moving. At least until she figured things out.

As she shoved open the doors to the Diag, a frigid wind blasted her in the face. But worse than that, a tall, lanky figure in front of the H. H. Dow building spun around, eyeing her sudden arrival.

She'd never seen him before, but for some reason, he looked out of place. Too old to be a student. And judging by the overcoat and lack of a bag or briefcase, not there to teach.

Raising her collar, she turned left, heading straight for the Commons. The bus to Central Campus was just past there. After that, she'd have more options. North Campus was too secluded.

When she felt like she'd gotten a safe distance from the man, she glanced back. Her eyes widened.

He'd started to follow her and was only a few yards back, whispering into his jacket.

She couldn't make out his words, but the crunch of salt under his feet was deafening.

"Crap," she muttered, glancing around.

To the right was the new Walgreen Drama Center. The lights in the lobby glowed like a beacon in the night. She'd never had reason to go inside and didn't know her way around.

That was a hard no.

Left was the Duderstadt Center. A choke point, but public with plenty of people.

She'd probably be safer in there than out here.

As she headed for the building, the wind picked up and the man called out from behind her. "Hey! Are you Alex Mercer?"

In the distance, another person, a woman it seemed, came

out of the Commons, striding toward her and talking into her lapel, just like the man.

"Shitty, shit, shit," Alex mumbled, eyeing the nearby building, adrenaline coursing through her veins.

The rush of emotions reminded her of the night with Riley and her friend, the same acrid taste of panic flooding her senses.

But this was more than a confrontation over ethnic slurs; this was life or death.

Her body tensed as a sense of dread seeped in.

"No!" Alex shook her head. She needed to focus. To find a way out.

She could scream, but no one was around. People didn't exactly linger outdoors in the frigid Michigan fall.

She kicked herself for choosing such a cold ass school.

The building was too far to save her. The man would be on her any second.

If the woman arrived, it'd be two on one. They'd easily overpower her.

Throw a knife or a gun into the fray, and she'd be helpless.

There was only one way out.

She spun around, facing the man just as he reached inside his jacket.

It was now or never. She had to act.

Lunging forward, she drove her palm up and into the man's face, crushing his nose against his skull.

He shrieked and reached up, blood spurting between his fingers as he clutched at his shattered nose.

But she didn't relent. She pivoted, snatching at his arm and rolling forward, gracefully flipping him over her shoulder into a nearby snowdrift.

As his head sank into bloody slush, she slid over and flipped open his jacket, pausing when she noticed a holster inside.

He'd been reaching for a fucking gun.

The situation had escalated from bad to worse in a blink. But she was pot committed now.

Acting on instinct, she unclasped the weapon, taking it in her hand and spinning around.

The cold steel of the pistol pressed against her palms, a weighty reminder of its lethal potential.

She swung the deadly weapon toward the woman rushing at her, causing her to dive to the ground and slide behind a snow-piled trash can.

Alex waited for her to rise and fire, but she never did.

Rather than risking an approach only to be ambushed, she did the only thing any sane person would do.

She ran.

As fast as her legs would carry her, she tore ass back toward engineering, slipping the gun into her coat as she approached the doors.

There was no point running around with a weapon and causing a stampede.

Once through the vestibule, she didn't stop to hide. She dashed straight through and out the rear, heading to the only other spot she knew on campus. A hidden place where she'd studied when she needed to get away.

It wasn't far, but it also wasn't frequented by others.

All she could do was hope they wouldn't look for her there.

17 / RASPBIAN RIDDLE
CIPHER

"Damn it!" He looked up and glared at the distant apartment windows. Hours of hacking attempts had proven fruitless.

The WiFi router's security protocols held his attacks at bay better than he expected. Whoever built it knew what they were doing. Either that, or they got lucky.

A few minutes earlier, he finally got in through their firewall using a complex buffer overflow attack. After checking the OS type, he was surprised to see something called *Raspbian*. A flavor of Unix he'd never heard of.

He would've searched on his phone, but he didn't have a SIM card. Like any good hacker, he did the next best thing: An internet search using the compromised device's WiFi.

The idea should've set off alarms in his head, but it didn't.

Maybe it was jet lag or the thought of guns pointed at him, but he typed the query anyway. Using the pre-installed *lynx* command line browser, he opened Google and the connection just dropped. Bam. Offline.

The fucker must've set up their defenses to shut it down when an unexpected app launched. Purpose-built machines like this weren't uncommon. Some were honeypots, designed to keep hackers busy.

He hadn't fallen for one in years. Until today.

He closed his terminal and pocketed his phone, berating himself for the rookie mistake.

N3tN1nja wasn't a fucking newbie, and if this was any indication of Byt3Linguist's skills, he'd need to up his game.

"Look out," Tae-Woo whispered, his voice sounding like he was on the move. "Gyeongchal!"

Cipher spun to see a police car easing up to the curb beside him.

His first instinct was to run, but he knew better. American cops were well organized, especially in larger cities like this. They'd corner him quickly, and besides, they had guns. Last he checked, he couldn't outrun a bullet.

So, he did the only other thing that came to mind. He stepped toward the car.

"What the *hell* are you doing?" Jin-Soo growled.

"Shut your fucking trap!" He reached up, pretending to brush his hair back, but instead swiped the earpiece out and tucked it under the collar of his sweater.

The police cruiser's window slid down.

"Hello, officer." Cipher squatted by the car door and smiled. "Chilly night out."

"Indeed," the officer said, sizing Cipher up. "We've received a few calls about loitering around the neighborhood." The officer narrowed his gaze, typing something into his computer before returning his attention to him. "That wouldn't be you now, would it?"

"Guilty as charged." Cipher pulled out his phone, waving it in the air. "I've been trying to reach my friend. We were supposed to play snooker."

"Snooker?" The officer looked puzzled.

"Sorry," Cipher chuckled. "You call it pool or billiards, I think." He mimed lining up a shot on a tabletop.

"Ah, billiards! Gotcha." The officer nodded, typing again.

Cipher wasn't sure what to do next. For all he knew, the officer was calling for backup.

Suddenly, Cipher's walkie-talkie vibrated. Thinking fast, he pretended his phone had rung and glanced down. Feigning recognition, he smiled and held the device up.

"That's them! I think he finally got his lazy ass up." He covered the screen. "Mind if I take this?"

"Certainly." The officer nodded, studying Cipher as he turned to take the fake call.

As he raised the phone, he lifted the earpiece with his other hand, keeping it out of the cop's view.

Tae-Woo's voice exploded the second it touched his ear. "What the fuck are you doing? I've got crosshairs on that pig and another one on you."

"Hey, Johnny!" Cipher said, raising his voice for the cop to hear. "Are we still on for billiards, or are you chicken shit?" He shook his head slightly, hoping Tae-Woo wasn't stupid enough to kill a cop. They'd have every officer within fifty miles on their asses if he did.

"What are you on about?" Tae-Woo snapped. "You took your damn earpiece out."

He cupped his hand over his mouth, "Stand. The. Fuck. Down. I don't know if this is your first time out of Pyongyang, asshole, but we need more finesse here in America. Now play along." He glanced back, smiling at the cop.

"It's him!" Cipher shouted. "The idiot fell asleep watching the tube."

The officer smiled back reassuringly. "Glad it's nothing serious. You should try California Billiards. They're new. Opened last year."

Cipher tensed, unsure at first what the officer meant.

Then he realized the man was trying to help them find a place to play snooker. The response was unexpected, and a far cry from how a North Korean officer would have reacted.

"The snooker place," the officer clarified, noting his confusion.

Cipher grinned and tipped his head in thanks. "California Billiards, thank you, sir." He spoke into the phone. "Hear that, Johnny? California Billiards. Now move it! I've been standing out here in the cold waiting for your sorry ass for over an hour. You're buying the first round, buddy."

"Have a good night." The officer waved as the cruiser eased away, disappearing into the distance.

A shudder passed through Cipher's body. Not only was that a close call, he was bloody freezing.

"Nice work, boss," Tae-Woo said.

The irony of being called 'boss' wasn't lost on him, especially seconds after having a goddamn gun aimed at his head.

He knew who really called the shots out here. It was General Tau, his cold-blooded puppet master across the world. And if he had any hopes of staying alive long enough to escape, he needed results.

Without pausing, he turned and eyed the apartment he'd been watching all night. There was only one light on in the place, and it came on just before sunset. The telltale sign of a simple automation. He was starting to wonder if anyone lived there at all.

Resigned to taking control of his situation, he pocketed his phone and started forward.

One way or another, he was getting inside that apartment.

18 / WHEN THE BELL TOLLS
CHOE

The carillon's bells cut through the chilly fall air with a series of haunting notes. Choe shuddered at the somber tune, cinching her hood against the breeze.

The bell tower stood as an architectural eyesore. Had she not been obliged to surveil it for hours, she'd never have given it a second glance. The designers of the structure clearly prioritized function over aesthetics.

But now, she had no choice but to sit still and wait. Her target had taken refuge in the towering building a few hours ago, soon after Tae-Woo's crew botched their hack out west.

Apparently, Cipher had screwed up, and now she had to listen to these infernal bells every half hour.

Though they were unsure if their target had been using that network, the timing was suspect. For now, they were biding their time, waiting to strike when the target was exposed.

They'd tracked the hacker to this Great Lakes town after months of failed attempts to corner them online. It was only after she and Cipher tortured the moles that they turned N3tN1nja in. At least, they claimed it was N3tN1nja. No one seemed to know who Byt3Linguist was.

The memory of that afternoon made her body tingle. She'd never seen Cipher in his element before. For almost a year, she'd played his unassuming assistant in a meticulously crafted ballet of deceit, one her masters had prepared her for since childhood.

However, seeing him with the knife, easing the traitor to her breaking point—it was a masterstroke. Even now, she ached for his assertive hold on her wrists.

She shook off the memory, knowing she needed to focus on the immediate mission. He could never discover her true feelings. Such revelations were forbidden, lest she face General Tau. The levels of pain he would inflict upon her were incomprehensible.

Gazing through the moonlit night, her eyes fixed on the darkened structure. She caught a flicker of orange and yellow light in the distance, like the dance of an open flame.

At first, she thought it was the reflection of the nearby headlights shining toward the red girders holding the bells. But it reappeared, this time accompanying a haze of smoke.

"It's on fire!" Ki-Sung's voice called over her earpiece. She was her twin sister and counterpart on this mission. If Choe was yin, then Ki-Sung was yang, twins, yet opposites in every way. She also happened to be a detail Choe had kept from Cipher, even to this day. Let him believe Eun-kyung was her partner; the nomenklatura's lies served her purpose. Like them, she understood the power of keeping secrets, of letting others see only what you wanted them to see.

"Shit!" Choe leapt forward, sprinting toward the building.

Whoever was inside was either suicidal or creating a diversion. Chaos was the easiest way to disappear, and nothing summoned emergency response like a fire in an old public building. Especially one as old as this bell tower.

She needed to act before the cavalry arrived. While she

preferred a living, breathing body for information extraction, she'd settle for a dead one, given the day's failings.

Sliding to a stop in front of the building, she realized the structure wasn't solid black like she'd imagined. It was tinted glass. Peering through the darkened panes, she could just make out the unmistakable outline of stairs rising upward. Flames flickered near their base.

"What the hell?" She reached out, testing the door handle.

It was unlocked and only slightly warm.

She pulled it open, peering inside. In front of her were two upturned cans, fires burning strong in each one.

Stepping into the tower, she locked the door behind her. Even a few precious seconds could matter if someone tried to come in and stop her.

With the door locked tight, she covered her mouth with her coat, easing past the inferno. She could feel the heat singeing her arm hair.

Only then did she realize they weren't cans, but upturned bells. Their tarnished green and bronze surfaces suggested they were old. Probably from the original construction in 1937.

She craned her neck upward, following the stairs. They wound their way to a red platform where the carillonneur sat and played those god-awful tunes; at least when they weren't automated.

Besides the red girder staircase, there was nowhere else to go. All she could see were scraps of old boxes and cracked paint cans, but apart from that, the place was empty. There was hardly a hiding spot to be found.

Something was off.

She reached into her jacket, pulling out her Glock 19. It was a simple weapon with a reassuring weight and balance. Not her Makarov PM, but acceptable, and more importantly, readily available in the US without paperwork. For the right price, that is.

"It's an empty room," she whispered into her microphone, sweeping her gun upstairs. "I'm heading up."

"Be careful," her sister cautioned. "Something smells off about this."

All she could smell was burning cardboard and paint, but she felt the same way. If this was all there was, then where had their target gone? And why the hell were they drawing people here?

Before climbing, she stepped around the foot of the stairs, keeping her eyes upward in case someone came into view.

There were no other exits on the ground floor, and no one was waiting in hiding.

With the first floor clear, she leapt up the stairs, taking three or four at a time, pausing to aim her gun around each corner.

She'd practiced these maneuvers countless times as a kid, and could do them in her sleep. But this was her first real-world op.

Years of training had honed her into a scalpel, ready to slice out the virus plaguing her homeland.

Step by step, landing by landing, her pulse pounded. The rhythm of her breathing drove her deeper into the belly of the beast. She was a shadow hunter, and her mission was clear: eliminate the threat.

As she climbed, she couldn't help but notice the dilapidated state of the tower. There was peeling paint on the girders and debris was strewn everywhere.

The tower was falling into disrepair, which made sense with the trash piles below.

Reaching the top, she tiptoed into the open air, finally free of the wretched stench. Smoke billowed past her head, arcing sideways as the breeze kicked up.

The carillon's piano-like controls emerged through the tendrils of soot, giving her pause as she drew a silent breath.

There, at the giant levered keyboard, sat a cloaked figure dressed all in black. With the smoke enveloping them, they resembled a specter summoned from the shadows.

Even with their back turned, she sensed their awareness of her. Their posture shifted subtly, acknowledging her arrival without turning.

Suddenly, their fingers danced across the controls, unleashing the bells into a chaotic symphony of dissonance.

She covered one ear with her free hand, struggling to stay steady amidst the clamor while keeping her weapon trained on her target. It took everything she had not to shoot.

"Stop!" she screamed, as a wave of nausea and lightheadedness hit. She sidestepped around the shrouded carillonneur, gripping a railing for support.

All the while, the music continued, melancholy notes filling the night air and sending a ripple of unease into the inky blackness.

Maybe it was the bells, or maybe the adrenaline, but her legs started to weaken and give way. She'd never been sensitive to sound before.

"I said stop!" she screamed again, dropping to one knee, her gun still aimed at her target's heart. It took all her focus to keep her hand steady.

Feeling her strength fading, she sank down even further, her back coming to rest against the wire railing.

Another gust whipped through the tower, sending the smoke spiraling skyward and flipping her target's cloak up, revealing a feminine shape underneath. *They're a woman!*

"What do you want?" the figure asked, their voice robotic, probably through a modulator. They sounded like a frigging robot.

"You... know what we want?" Choe squinted, her vision blurring. *What the hell is happening to me?*

"Why are you... on the ground?" Ki-Sung asked over her

earpiece, her words coming in short gasps as if she'd been running.

Choe glanced over her shoulder into the darkness, narrowing her gaze as she searched for any sign of her sister. For some reason, the distance kept blurring, refusing to come into focus.

When she turned back, her target was on her, grabbing for the pistol.

She tried fighting back, using her free hand to knock the woman away. But she was too fast and Choe's grip too weak.

The next thing she knew, the woman snatched away the gun and turned it on her. Choe drew in a sharp breath, only to cough on a mouthful of noxious fumes.

"The smoke..." She blinked, struggling to focus.

When her vision cleared, the figure came into focus. A woman stood before her, wearing a gas mask straight out of a dystopian nightmare. A canister jutted from each side, blacked-out goggles obscured her eyes, and a dark fabric hood concealed her face completely.

"The smoke, indeed," the robotic voice said.

A gloved hand reached down, but Choe couldn't move or resist. Her body failed her.

She could only watch in silence.

"You're probably wondering why you can't control your muscles," the robotic voice began. "It's because I've drugged you with a special tetrodotoxin. It's still got its quirks. You know, military testing and all. That's also why your eyes are so heavy. But don't worry, they'll stay open."

The woman squatted down, removing Choe's phone and earpiece. She then tapped the speakerphone button, holding it closer to her masked mouth.

"Choe!" Ki-Sung shouted, her cry barely audible over the wind. "I'm almost... out of the building. Have to... climb down. Keep 'em busy."

"I'm fine," the cloaked woman said. But it wasn't the modulated robotic voice this time. It was Choe's voice.

Somehow, she'd recorded it.

And then realization hit. She must've been watching and recording them for hours while they were outside waiting for her. They'd been played like a violin, every move anticipated.

"You're... fine?" Ki-Sung's voice wavered with uncertainty. "Then why were you sitting down?"

Choe could tell her sister had stopped running. Only her breathing was audible now.

She wanted to cry out, to scream for help, to urge her sister onward. But no amount of willpower could counteract the effects of the drugs. Her body wouldn't respond.

"The bastard knocked the wind out of me," the cloaked woman said. "Caught me off guard. But I finished him."

Ki-Sung gasped. "So it's a man, then? Is it... N3tN1nja or Byt3Linguist?"

For the first time, the figure seemed startled. She recoiled, clearly confused. One of those names was unexpected. But which?

"I don't... know," the cloaked woman stuttered. "But I'll meet you at the rendezvous point."

Shit!

They'd really fucked up talking over the radio earlier. But at least they'd never said where they were meeting up. Her sister was still safe.

"Are you sure?" Ki-Sung asked, her voice laced with concern.

The woman pulled something from her pocket, tapping a screen. Suddenly, a faint siren rang out, not from an emergency vehicle, but from the mask.

What kind of maniac has a siren recording at the ready?

It was then that Choe realized who she was staring at.

This wasn't some newbie. This was N3tN1nja, a seasoned black hat with years of experience harassing governments.

"The police are coming," N3tN1nja said.

And with that, she leaned forward, stabbing a knife repeatedly into Choe's side.

Choe tried to scream, but nothing came out. No agonizing wail. No bloodcurdling shriek. Only pain. Uncontrollable pain.

"Go! Run," N3tN1nja whispered into the phone. "I'll catch up with you at..."

She paused. For a split second, Choe wanted to smile, thinking her sister had hung up. But she hadn't.

"The petrol station, right?" Ki-Sung's voice wavered. "Off route... two forty-four."

No!

"Yeah, the petrol station," N3tN1nja said. "Sorry, I just found something interesting that took me by surprise. I'm heading out now."

"What'd you find?" Ki-Sung asked.

N3tN1nja tapped another button on her device. A second later, the sound of someone running played back. It was faint, but convincing. And that was the point. To make her sister think she was on the move.

"It was N3tN1nja," the cloaked woman said, standing upright. "There is no Byt3Linguist. They're the same person."

"The same person!" Ki-Sung gasped. "Then who the hell is Cipher after?"

"His tail," N3tN1nja replied. "Give me a second. I gotta go silent."

She muted the phone before pocketing it, keeping the connection live.

With the device stashed, the masked hacker leaned forward, tapping a canister and bringing her face to Choe's ear.

"Your sister will meet the same fate as you." N3tN1nja's voice was no longer modulated. It was normal now. She sounded... American.

"I'm going to kill her, but don't worry. I'll make sure it's slow next time. Very slow." N3tN1nja pulled away, the darkened goggles fixed on her. "Just like you did to Nari."

Nari? The name was momentarily unfamiliar. Then, in a flash, Choe remembered; Nari was the Crier, the one she and Cipher had tortured back home.

"I can tell you know who I'm talking about. But just in case you forgot..." N3tN1nja reached under the cloak and pulled out the knife again, driving it repeatedly into her other side, each strike a savage punctuation on her quest for vengeance.

Choe could feel the blood pooling under her legs, but the rest of her body was numb.

It was only then that the grim reality of her situation set in.

She was going to die in this tower, at the hands of this beast. This scourge of society.

She'd failed the general, but worst of all, she'd failed her sister. The only family she'd ever known.

Her mistakes meant that Ki-Sung would meet the same fate, and the thought filled her with a bitter rage.

While she hoped her sister would fare better, deep down, she knew Ki-Sung would fail, just as she had.

N3tN1nja was out of their league. No one was prepared for them, not even Cipher.

As Choe's consciousness faded, her last sight was N3tN1nja pulling out a smartphone and typing furiously.

She couldn't read the message, but her trained eyes caught the recipient's name:

Alex

19 / KERNEL PANIC
ALEX

Alex bounced her leg beneath the back row of computer desks, gnawing on her nails. It was a disgusting habit she'd had since childhood, but at this moment, it was the least of her concerns.

A stolen Glock weighed down her pocket. Blood stained her jacket. Two North Korean assassins were hunting her. With everything she had going on, nail-biting seemed inconsequential.

Her mind still reeled from her bloody encounter in the Diag, and she almost missed the faint squeak of a door opening in the distance. She froze, head tilted toward the noise, muscles coiled and ready to spring into action.

Pitch blackness enveloped the room, broken only by the soft glow of LED lights on the computer towers. After a few seconds ticked by, Alex peered out from behind the desk, eyes locked on the lab door. She inched forward, hyper-aware of the motion sensors that could betray her presence.

Just then, lights in the hall flicked on, casting a silhouette on the frosted glass door. A janitor approached, his cart squeaking down the corridor. Alex held her breath when he paused in front of the darkened lab. But he didn't enter. He simply adjusted something on his cart and moved on, resuming his evening routine.

"Phew," she breathed, ducking back down.

She'd discovered this room her first week at school, when she was exploring North Campus. Tucked in the basement of the aerospace engineering building, it was a time capsule of ancient hardware—a computer lab forgotten by time.

The SPARCStation resting against her back was easily fifteen years old, and on any other day, she'd question its purpose down there. But at that moment, she was just thankful for the empty room.

What do I do now?

Her phone vibrated in response. She pulled it out, reading the message:

> UNKNOWN CALLER
>
> Alex, it's N3tN1nja. You need to disappear, like now. The North Koreans are after us. They already butchered Nari, my informant. They came for me next. I barely escaped with my life, and I think you're next. Watch your back, and trust no one. Especially Cipher.

"What the literal fuck?" Alex ran a hand through her hair as the room began to spin.

The implications of the message were clear, even if the warning came too late. It all but confirmed her suspicions about her attacker's identity.

But that wasn't what bothered her.

Reading and re-reading the message, all she could think about was where she'd fucked up. N3tN1nja and the North Koreans had somehow hacked her.

She thought she'd wiped her electronic trail perfectly, just like her friends taught her. Every step, every precaution, taken with meticulous care.

She never attacked from the same machines twice if she could help it. She always covered her tracks, wiping host logs as she went. And she always, always used regular people's home networks on one of her hops. It made it harder for law enforcement to follow her; they needed special warrants. At least that's what she'd read online.

For her, those machines often meant hopping through compromised networks back in Fremont—routers she'd hacked in her apartment complex or nearby businesses. She even bought a few Raspberry Pi units with money from odd jobs and installed them as servers in telco closets around town.

It baffled her how people never questioned finding something foreign plugged into their wall sockets. They'd usually just ignore them, not wanting to break anything.

She'd programmed her Raspberry Pis to randomize their Wi-Fi network names to avoid suspicion. *HideYoKidsHideYo-WiFi* was one of them. She wished she could remember which device had that name in rotation, but couldn't. And the flash drive with the name rotation script was back in her dorm. She had no way to check it now.

Alex groaned, running her fingers through her hair. "Jesus, Alex. One second you're fighting for your life, and now you're fixating on Wi-Fi names? Get it together, girl!"

She quietly bumped her head against the desk's front panel, trying to nudge her mind back on track.

The fact was, if N3tN1nja knew who she was, then the North Koreans and this Cipher character probably did too. And if they had her name, it wouldn't take long to dig up her address.

My family! She needed to see if they were okay.

Flipping back to messages, she tapped out a quick note to her aunt.

ALEX

> Hey Aunt Min! 😊 Hope you're well. How're things at home? Heard there was some commotion in the complex. Sally, from a few units down, texted me. Know what happened?

She read it back. There was no Sally. She was lying through her teeth, but her aunt and parents wouldn't know any better. They never talked to anyone in the building, preferring instead to keep to themselves. Her only goal was getting them to talk.

She sent the message and stared at the device for what felt like an hour. Glancing at the clock, she sighed. Only minutes had ticked by.

Her parents were likely at dinner. Since Aunt Min moved in, Dad had developed a fondness for Sunday night all-you-can-eat restaurants.

That was a relief, though. It meant they probably weren't near one of the compromised routers in the building.

As she slipped her phone back into her pocket, it clanked against the gun she'd snatched earlier. She pulled the weapon out, turning it over in her hands.

It was heavier than she expected, and solid, too. Not at all like the cheap plastic toys she'd held in costume shops. This thing had heft.

She'd browsed countless gun sites online. A few years back, she nearly bought one and even went to the store with her dad to put it on layaway, but it ended up being too expensive. So, technically, this was her second time holding one.

But this was her first time touching a loaded weapon. Her parents had always refused to let her shoot one back home. Not that she could get a license in California at her age.

The idea of target practice had intrigued her since childhood. Sort of like the archery phase she went through when she started reading dystopian fiction. This, though, wasn't an image on a website. This was a legit gun. And for all she knew, it'd killed people.

"What the hell am I doing?"

She clicked the safety on and reached forward, carefully stashing the handgun atop the neighboring workstation. It was safer there than on her person. At least for now.

Staring at the far wall, she pondered her next move. Michelle's texts were blowing up her phone. Her short, panicked messages were piling up, urging her to respond, but Alex dared not reply.

Michelle's last text said police were searching the building for someone. Normally, they only saw rent-a-cops from campus security doing rounds, but she said these were legit police. With guns and everything.

Glancing at the pistol, she suddenly realized how out of her depth she was. First with the vote rigging, and now this. Ever since that fateful night earlier in the year, when her stand against prejudice backfired spectacularly, she'd made one bad decision after another. She never quite read the situations correctly or grasped the consequences of her emotional reactions.

And all for what? Some inner drive to right the internet's wrongs? To avenge her adoptive parents' attackers?

She was one person, not an army of US Cyber Command operators. Taking on a foreign government was beyond her, even with help from online randos like N3tN1nja. And judging by their last message, they were on the run too.

Which brought her back to how her friend had gotten her number in the first place. The sheer improbability of it sent her mind into a tailspin.

In that moment of despair and darkness, she saw her next move. Her stomach churned at the thought. She had to go to the police. Tell them everything.

Without questioning the epiphany, she slid out from under the desk as the overhead lights flickered on.

She was briefly blinded, spots dancing in her vision. Squinting, she reached out to steady herself, trying not to kick anything. The sudden brightness revealed just how dark her hiding spot had been.

Reaching the door, she leaned against the exit bar, unlocking it and slowly swinging it out. Once through, she eased it closed behind her.

Making noise wasn't high on her to-do list. The sooner she was in police custody, the better.

During her sprint into the building, she'd spotted a campus phone near the entrance. She was pretty sure she could reach an actual police officer from there. Not one of those wannabe cops with tasers.

The halls of the Francois-Xavier Building were empty that time of night, especially on a Sunday before midterms. Most aerospace students were either queuing for the wind tunnel or at home, recharging for the week ahead.

As she entered the main lobby, she eyed the yellow phone just inside the door. She thought about using her burner phone to make the call, but realized the police might find a call from Canada suspicious.

She still had no idea how N3tN1nja got her number. The only people with this line were her friends, family, and...

"Shit," she muttered. The school had her mobile on file. N3tN1nja must have infiltrated their network.

Her hand hovered over the bright yellow receiver, trembling in the glow of the strobing blue light. If N3tN1nja had hacked a government computer, then breaking into a college network would've been a cakewalk.

She clenched her fist. "Make the damn call, Lex!"

Snatching up the phone, she held it to her ear and went to

dial 911, but it immediately started ringing. A few seconds later, a soothing voice answered.

"Campus Police, how may I help you?" the female voice asked.

Alex took a deep breath, exhaling to steady herself.

"Hello?" the voice continued. "Are you alright? Do you need help? I see you're in the Francois-Xavier Building lobby. Should I send an officer?"

"Yes," Alex said, clearing her throat, voice hoarser than expected. "My name is Alex Mercer, and I was... I was attacked. I've been..." She swallowed hard, her hand trembling as she steadied herself against the wall. "I've been hiding here. I don't know if... if they're still—"

"Did you say, Alex Mercer?" the woman interrupted.

Alex nodded, brows furrowed. "That's right, I'm a freshman in computer engineering."

A pause stretched over the line as she grappled for words, unsure what to say next.

But out of the corner of her eye, she caught flashing blue and red lights outside. When she looked up, there was a cop car racing toward the front of the building.

"Wow," she muttered, lifting the receiver. "That was fast. You must've—"

Alex gasped, freezing mid-sentence as a second and third car sped into view, screeching to a stop nearby.

The roar of engines and squeal of tires ripped through the night, like a wild animal announcing its presence.

When two officers hopped out of each car, she flinched. That was a lot of cops.

With practiced precision, two officers disappeared around the side of the building, two held a position outside, and the final two sprinted toward the entrance.

Toward her.

She gasped, stepping backward, watching in awe as the doors burst open in slow motion.

The officers rushed in, guns drawn and aimed squarely at her chest.

"What the heck?" she shrieked, raising her hands.

"Down!" the man screamed, tipping his pistol toward the floor. "Get the hell down on the ground. Now!"

Instinctively, Alex dropped to her knees, pressing herself flat against the ground while struggling to keep her hands up. She didn't need to be asked twice.

Her heart thundered against her ribcage, a wild drumbeat in the shocking silence following the cops' sudden entrance.

Everything fell into an eerie calm as the officers advanced, their expressions twisted with menacing warning.

She lay motionless and dumbstruck on the frigid tiles, struggling to process the turn of events.

But one stark truth crystallized amidst the chaos: she was scared out of her mind.

20 / BLACK BOX
CIPHER

He stared at his phone, the weight of the last message squeezing his chest. Choe was dead, and the situation out east was unraveling. Her and her partners had been brutally murdered while attempting to take out their target in a small college town.

Worse still, after all their effort, they still had no idea who'd done it. Byt3Linguist or N3tN1nja.

They'd lost three of their best operatives. Their only clue was a grainy picture of a cloaked figure in a tower, seated before a strange piano-like contraption. Choe's partner, apparently named Eun-kyung, sent the image on before disappearing herself.

He never thought Choe would fall to a second-rate hacker. Maybe she was only good at lying. She'd certainly kept him in the dark about her twin. That knowledge could've made for some interesting extracurricular fun if he'd found out sooner. But alas, her skills in deceit and torture hadn't been enough to keep her alive.

Where others might have felt sadness or remorse at losing someone they knew, his father had taught him better. Friends and loved ones only made a person soft and easy to manipulate. Only misery and solitude made a person stronger.

"Amateurs," Cipher muttered, pocketing his device and returning his attention to the window.

He'd been watching the apartment for most of the afternoon and evening. Whoever lived here either never moved around, or they weren't home. Even if the lights had come on.

Peering in the window one last time, he assessed the situation.

Judging by the remains of the sandwich bags, breadcrumbs, and cutlery on the counter, they'd recently made a meal. If they were spending the afternoon out, they could return any minute. If he wanted the upper hand, he needed to get inside. Now.

He scanned the edges of the window frame with his phone's crude flashlight, checking for electric locks. The windows in the apartments were too old to have built-in sensors.

With the coast clear, he tried the first of three balcony windows. The door had already failed, so these were his last options for a non-forced entry. No luck with the first window—it was sealed shut.

Sliding sideways, he tested the second window. Nada. It budged half an inch, but otherwise was secure.

Only one more to go.

He maneuvered past the small patio table, sliding the chair aside. Once clear, he stepped in front of the window and glanced around, making sure no one was watching him. He then closed his eyes and carefully lifted.

The window glided upward with no resistance.

"Bingo," he whispered, poking his head inside.

There was nothing on the other side blocking his way. It was an easy entry. Without pausing, he ducked low and slid through the opening.

As soon as he passed into the apartment, he knew something felt off. He'd been in thousands of homes throughout his life, and this didn't feel right.

After his family's home was destroyed in Bosnia, he'd hopped from hostels to abandoned buildings, hotels, and halfway houses. He'd drifted until he finally settled somewhere he could call home. Or homelike. North Korea was just another chapter in his journey through life.

The house smelled old. Not aged building materials old, but elderly-resident old.

He couldn't pinpoint it, but the mix of talcum powder, mothballs, and lavender was present wherever he'd encountered senior citizens. It was the universal scent of a person's twilight years. That and diapers.

He eased the window shut and started scoping the place, sweeping through each room in turn.

The apartment was sparsely decorated. What furniture there was looked like it'd come from a thrift store. But then again, this wasn't the wealthiest area of town.

Working down the hall, he peered into the bedroom. More of the same. Pink and white bed coverings, flowery curtains, and neatly folded pastel linens screamed female occupant. And a girly one at that.

It wasn't until he reached the bedside that he realized who lived here. There, next to the phone, was a picture of an elderly couple dressed in a tuxedo and gown. Beside it rested an expensive-looking leather journal begging to be opened.

Gingerly opening the cover, he flipped through page after page of flawless handwritten penmanship. It was a personal diary, and the most recent heartfelt passages were clearly by a woman missing her husband.

This was no hacker's home. The tenant was either being played, or aiding and abetting a criminal. The question was, which?

He set down the journal and approached the dresser. A flatscreen television sat on top. After scanning the jewelry laid out on the doilies, he checked the back of the TV. There was an ethernet cable connected to it from the wall, which meant it had to be entering the apartment from somewhere else.

With that clue, he spun around and marched to the living room, finding the same behind that television.

"Now, where would I stick the internet router?" he muttered, scanning the tiny space. He tried to put himself in the mindset of someone doing a quick install.

In every country he'd lived, installers were lazy. Sure, a rare few took their job seriously, really wanting to make customers happy. But most were paid per installation and were always in a hurry.

Drilling straight through outside walls was common. They didn't care how it looked; they needed to install their equipment. Making it pretty was usually an afterthought or an accident.

Only with that insight did he notice the thin white cable trailing along the baseboard into the kitchen.

"Gotcha," he muttered, tracing the cable into a cabinet on the outside wall of the apartment.

Opening the door revealed his prize: a cable modem, a router, and a nest of wiring. As he traced the coaxial cable into the first box, he paused, staring at the tangle of ethernet wires jutting out the other side. There, nestled in the middle, was a small box. Not much larger than a pack of cigarettes. It almost looked like a power supply.

Whoever set this up was routing all the network traffic through it. Flipping it over, he realized what he was looking at: etched into the plastic on the bottom was a piece of fruit, a raspberry, to be exact. This had to be that strange Wi-Fi device he'd connected to outside—the one running *Raspbian*.

He went to unhook the cables but paused when his phone vibrated in his pocket.

Pulling it out, he did a double take. There was no SIM inside, and he thought he'd been disconnected from the Wi-Fi. But somehow he was still online. Even stranger was the caller. Choe was trying to reach him via Skype.

Maybe she wasn't dead, after all.

He hit answer and lifted the device to his ear, but didn't speak.

"Hello, Cipher," a robotic voice said.

The hair on his neck bristled at hearing his name from a computer. The highly modulated voice seemed to echo in the silent apartment.

"Who the hell is this?" he whispered, glancing through the curtains into the darkened alley. No one was out this late, but he couldn't be too careful.

"I think you've already figured out who this is," the voice said.

He honestly had no idea. If it was either target, he had a fifty-fifty chance, so he took a shot.

"N3tN1nja?" He crouched low, flipping around with his back to the wall, eyes on the front door.

"Your colleagues are dead," the voice began. "And thanks to you, they suffered horribly. I made certain of that. I suggest you get moving, if you know what's good for you. The authorities are already on their way. They won't be long now."

Cipher tilted his head, wondering if they actually knew his location. Choe wasn't dumb enough to write it down, and his minders had burner SIMs in their phones. N3tN1nja had no way to track him.

"That's right," the voice continued. "Your assassins were very helpful. Chatty, even. Well, the first one wasn't. Can't blame her, though. She was paralyzed. The second one, however... She crowed like a rooster at dawn."

He shook his head, weighing the likelihood of the voice's threats. The moles' warnings about N3tN1nja's manipulation echoed in his mind.

While he knew Choe wouldn't give him away, her partner was an unknown. The general had never mentioned who she'd been working with, so he could only assume she wasn't as capable. If so, there was no telling what N3tN1nja might have tortured out of her.

"You're lying!" he shot back, calling their bluff.

Cipher sprang up, darting to the front window. Easing the drapes aside, he peered at the units across the courtyard.

"Am I?" the voice asked. The line went dead.

He stood in doubtful silence for several seconds, staring out the window. There was nobody in sight.

The call abruptly cut off, replaced by a series of beeps. As he lowered his phone to shut it off, the disconnect tones faded, giving way to a new sound—distant sirens echoing in the night.

At first, he didn't believe it. Then a voice screamed through the earpiece tucked under his collar, overpowering even the approaching sirens. His doubt evaporated instantly.

"Son of a..." He swung his arm sideways, toppling a lamp as he bolted to the rear of the apartment. He skidded to a stop beside the open cabinet.

Fury fueled his movements as he thrust his hand inside, snatching the tiny black box and ripping it out. Cables and all.

Adrenaline surged through him.

He didn't care what evidence or destruction he left behind. He just needed to escape. And fast.

His fingerprints wouldn't be in any US databases, or any other government's, for that matter. Not unless they had friends in North Korea.

With device in hand, he hopped out the open window and

bolted down the alley, disappearing into the night. His heart pounded with a mix of fear and resolve.

N3tN1nja was going to pay if it was the last thing he did. And at this point, it probably would be. He had nothing left to lose. Hell, he'd be lucky to make it back to North Korea alive, let alone in one piece.

But he'd be damned if he was going down without a fight.

Whatever secrets that black box held, whatever information N3tN1nja had been so desperate to protect, Cipher was determined to uncover it.

It was his last chance, his only hope of ending this once and for all.

21 / SINGING BLUEBIRD
ALEX

The police read Alex her rights in the lobby of the aerospace engineering building. Screams and frantic shouting, mostly from the cops, blurred together. Confusion clouded her mind as she struggled to grasp what was happening. One second she was calling for help, the next she was handcuffed in the back of a squad car.

Tense silence filled the ride to the police station. Every minute or so, one of the officers would turn and glare at her.

Alex leaned forward at one point, noticing the cop in the passenger seat had his gun in his lap, hand firmly gripping the handle. As if she could try anything from the backseat with her hands contorted behind her back. Clearly, they were pissed about something, but neither would tell her what.

What surprised her most was how she kept it together. From the moment the cops came rushing in, she didn't panic, fight, or turn into a babbling idiot. Sure, she was caught off guard and still playing catch-up, but unlike earlier when she felt helpless, now an unfamiliar calm washed over her. It was almost as if the inevitable had finally come to pass, and her body just peacefully surrendered to it.

As she settled into the cold, uncomfortable chair, she took

a moment to absorb her surroundings. The interrogation room was a far cry from the sleek, modern spaces she'd seen on TV. Instead, it bore the marks of age and neglect, a testament to the countless stories and confessions these walls had witnessed.

The heavy metal table before her was scratched and worn, its surface marred by years of use. Strange stains speckled the once-shiny exterior, a grim reminder of the room's long history.

She couldn't help but wonder about the people who'd sat in this very spot before her, the secrets they'd spilled under the pressure of interrogation.

The stark white walls seemed to close in, their clinical sterility broken only by the faint shadows cast by harsh fluorescent lights overhead. It was a space designed to unnerve, to strip away comfort and leave the occupant exposed and vulnerable.

Mirrored panels stretched in front and behind her, undoubtedly concealing watchful eyes. Even now she felt the weight of their gaze, the unspoken judgment and suspicion hanging heavy in the air. Every movement, every flicker of emotion on her face, was being analyzed and dissected by unseen observers.

Sitting there, alone and confused, her mind drifted off. Somewhere safe and dark, where they couldn't see her. She grappled with her next move. She didn't exactly have an attorney on speed dial, and the events of the past few days still swirled chaotically in her head.

About the only thing she could think to do was call Aunt Min. She'd know what to do, just like with the Sanchez mess. Which was ironic, considering she was new to this country.

Alex smirked at the thought of another one of her aunt's nameless friends helping her, when suddenly, the door swung open.

A tall, lanky man holding a brown manila envelope walked in, shutting the door behind him. He was mid to late thirties, with blond hair, and wearing a gray pinstriped business suit that looked quite expensive; way beyond a police officer's salary.

He looked like a Wall Street banker from the movies, but he seemed out of place, like he was uncomfortable in a college town. Maybe he was a Fed.

When he glanced at her, she grinned back.

"Is there something funny?" he asked.

"Not really," she muttered, holding his gaze.

He paused, puzzled. "So what are you smirking about, then?"

"How you look like an investment banker who took a wrong turn." She shrugged. "But I guess that's what happens when you're a Fed in a small town like this."

She regretted the words the moment they left her lips. It was a snarky reply that would only antagonize him. She didn't even know if he was a Fed, but something about his demeanor rubbed her the wrong way.

His jaw clenched, a flash of annoyance in his eyes. Her little joke had struck a nerve, and she felt a twinge of satisfaction at getting under his skin.

If they were going to make her uncomfortable, then turnabout was fair play.

"So, Alex," he began, "do you often find yourself cuffed in interrogation rooms, mocking those trying to help you?" His voice dripped with condescension.

Alex remained silent, her gaze steady.

"I've seen your type." He leaned in, hands planted on the table. "Young, arrogant, thinking you're untouchable. That you're above the law. It's your whole generation. How does it feel, Alex? Being on that side of this table? Knowing your actions have consequences?"

She fought the urge to flinch, her aunt's face flashing through her mind.

He shook his head. "Nothing? Is this all just a big misunderstanding?" He pushed off the table, smirking. "A bright, beautiful young woman like yourself, caught up in something she doesn't grasp. Is that it? Did you bite off more than you could chew?"

She clenched her jaw, refusing to rise to his bait. He was trying to make her doubt herself, to question her actions and motives.

She wasn't falling for it.

He studied her intently, his eyes undressing her. "You know, I've been doing this job for a long time," he said, his tone patronizing. "I've seen people like you make all sorts of excuses: 'It was a harmless prank' or 'I didn't mean to do it'. But the truth is, Alex, there's always a choice. And you chose to break the law."

He paused, letting his words sink in. "So, I'll ask you again. Do you understand the gravity of your situation? The trouble you're in?"

"I don't know what you're talking about," Alex said, her voice cool and calm. "Why don't you enlighten me, Mr. Wall Street? You seem to have all the answers, yet here I am." She glanced around. "Five minutes in, and I still have no idea why I'm here."

She smirked, but her satisfaction was short-lived. He held up an envelope, his gaze boring into her. "Do you know what's in here?" he asked, his voice cold and measured.

Her eyes locked onto the envelope.

Other than a case number written in neat black marker, there were no other markings on the outside. It was one of those odd envelopes with the round buttony things and the thin red string you used to fasten it closed. She always found those off-putting.

She shrugged, her handcuffs attached to the table jingling. "I have no idea. I left my X-ray glasses in the dorm."

"Smart ass!" He tossed the envelope down, glaring.

The air crackled with tension, yet her calm persisted. Maybe it was shock or denial, but deep down, she knew she'd been fighting for what was right. Her methods may have been unconventional, and getting caught up with the Sanchezes was definitely a misstep, but at her core, it was about making a difference and standing up against injustice.

She tilted her chin toward the envelope. "Are we gonna stare at each other all day, or are you planning on opening that? I'm starting to wonder why I'm here."

"You're playing dumb, then?" he scoffed. "A skilled hacker with a right hook like that, I'd have thought you'd play this differently."

A right hook? He must've meant her defensive moves in the Diag.

She clasped her hands, eyes still on him. "It was a palm strike and a throw, not an uppercut. Big difference."

He pulled his chair away from the table and sat. "So you admit to hitting that officer? What about stealing his weapon?"

The revelation hit like a tidal wave. She slid back, shoulders slouching.

He wasn't a North Korean assassin. He was a cop.

Shit. I really fucked up.

Without even realizing it, she found her thumb pressing against the knuckle of her index finger, applying just enough pressure until she felt the familiar pop. It was a nervous habit she'd picked up after countless hours spent hunched over her computer, her fingers dancing across the keys.

In her current situation, it probably wasn't a wise move, but the urge was almost subconscious—a reflexive response to the stress of the moment.

None of that mattered, though. She'd hit that man out of fear and self-defense. Nothing more.

"Well..."—she straightened up—"I didn't know they were an officer. They never identified themselves as one." She paused, studying his reaction. "Last I remembered from school, the police had to do that. You know, the law and stuff. You should check the tapes."

She clung to that cop bit, hoping it was true. It's what felons always said in movies, anyway.

"Tapes?" he asked, his attention shifting to something over her shoulder.

There it was. The tell. He knew the Diag was under surveillance. It was the busiest open space on North Campus.

"Yeah, the Diag tapes." She flattened her hands on the table, fighting the urge to crack another knuckle. "If you know about me hitting the officer, I'm sure you already checked 'em. I'd bet the entire Diag is being recorded. At least if you believe the student paper."

He ignored her. "Where's the sidearm, Alex?"

She'd forgotten about the gun and was surprised they hadn't asked about it sooner. That would explain the knee in her back during the pat-down, though.

They'd smashed her face against the tile for what felt like an hour. She could still feel the chilling imprint of the university logo against her cheek.

The officer who lost it must be pissed and embarrassed. Better to tell them where it was now.

"It's in the basement computer lab of the Francois-Xavier Building." She glanced at the glass behind him. "I stashed it on top of a computer while I was down there hiding from my attackers."

She paused, biting her lip, unsure what else to say. "Don't worry, the safety's on. I would've taken the clip out but," she shrugged, "I didn't know how."

The officer reached up to his ear, gaze drifting to the ceiling behind her. Glancing over her shoulder, she spotted a small camera tucked in the corner.

She'd been so caught up, she hadn't noticed the camera before now.

Looking back, the man lowered his hand. "Well, let's hope no one found it and uses it to kill someone. That would be unfortunate." His tone carried a smugness, as if he relished the possibility of pinning another crime on her.

Fuck this and fuck them.

"So that's it?" She looked up. "You're ignoring what I said about the officers not identifying themselves?"

She met his gaze, his dirty brown eyes boring into her. Something about him reminded her of Mr. Sanchez. Same smug superiority, same way of making her feel small and stupid. He was cut from the same cloth as that asshole.

He leaned forward, his brow furrowing in a show of practiced concern. "You seem confused, Alex. Are you sure you're remembering things correctly? Sometimes stress can play tricks on our minds."

"My memory is fine," she said sharply. "I was acting in self-defense." She crossed her arms, leaning back. "And before I say anything else, I'll be needing a lawyer."

"That won't be necessary," he said, his hand suddenly trembling. He was either new at this or realized he'd fucked up and pushed her too hard.

"You know, you remind me of them," she said, attention returning to her cuffs. She wasn't sure if he'd take the bait. But he did.

"How's that?"

She smirked. "Because, like those other officers, I don't know your name. You walked in here, started demanding answers, and didn't bother introducing yourself. For all I know, you could be from any one of the three-letter agencies.

Or hell, you could be a North Korean spy like your friends in the Diag."

"A what?" He contorted his face, confused.

Before she could reply, his attention shifted to the corner again. Except this time, his face slackened. He must've screwed up worse than she thought. Squawks from his earpiece suggested someone was tearing into him.

Seconds later, he shot to his feet and bolted out without a word.

She wasn't sure what she'd said, but something set them off.

"I want my call!" She spun around, glaring at the camera. "I know my goddamn rights. I want my call!"

THE DOOR SLAMMING shut jolted Alex upright. Groggy, she pulled her arms back, but the chains binding her wrists clanged, slamming her arms against the table. Panic surged through her still-waking mind.

She stared at the restraints, struggling to remember why they were there. Her mind was foggy, eyes blinking to dispel the disorientation. Then, realization struck. Memories of last night—the encounter with the police—flooded back, vivid fragments of a terrifying picture. Her heart pounded, each beat a stark reminder of her situation.

She was still in the interrogation room. She must have dozed off waiting for the unnamed agent to return. At least, she assumed he was an agent. He never denied it.

Glancing around the room in search of a clock, she noticed there wasn't one, and more importantly, she had a visitor.

A man stood patiently near the door, staring at her in silence, his brow furrowed. This new arrival was dressed down compared to the last guy, wearing only a wrinkled white shirt and slacks. He looked like she felt. Like shit.

She hadn't slept in at least a day, and while the catnap helped, it wasn't enough. The stress of the moment was too much. But that was the point. They were trying to wear her out.

"Are you going to let me place my call?" she asked as he began pacing along the far wall.

He glanced at her curiously, then looked away, staring at the ground as he continued walking.

After several minutes of tense silence, he finally spoke. "I'm Agent Reed from the Federal Bureau of Investigation." He feigned a smile, stopping in front of her. "I believe you already met my partner, Agent Gregor."

Shit. She clasped her hands together, fighting not to fidget. She'd guessed right. Her situation had escalated from local to federal in a blink.

He narrowed his gaze, as if studying her face. "Do you know why you're here, Ms. Mercer?"

She shook her head, squeezing her left hand to still it.

"How is it that a broke teenager on food stamps pays for an out-of-state university like Michigan? And in cash, nonetheless?" He stared at her, his gaze unyielding.

She didn't say a word. She simply stared back, silent and determined.

"Nothing?" He waved his hand expectantly.

She wasn't saying shit.

"Huh." He flipped the chair around and sat, resting his arms on the back.

She was struck by how clichéd this moment felt; everything from the room and the clothes to the tactics.

"Bad cop, good cop," she muttered.

He leaned closer. "Excuse me?"

She forced a smile. "I said, I want my call."

"We'll get to that." He reached for the envelope still resting on the table.

She'd been staring at it before dozing off, wondering what was inside. It was just out of reach and strategically placed to fuck with her. But now, given his line of questions, she was piecing it together.

He opened the manilla flap, tipping it sideways. A pile of photos and papers spilled out across the table.

She studied the contents. ATM photos. Snapshots of her and Sanchez talking. Some papers that sort of looked like bank printouts.

There was also a small tape recorder that clunked out, sliding well within reach.

"Go ahead." Agent Reed nodded. "Hit play."

She didn't reach for it. Instead, she pushed her chair back, pulling her hands as far as they'd go. "I want my call."

"I tell you what." He slid closer, picking up the recorder, holding his thumb over *Play*. "We listen to this, then, assuming you still have nothing to say, I'll get you that call. Deal?" He raised an eyebrow.

She didn't react, didn't even exhale. Just stared with steely resolve, willing the asshole to get on with it.

He hit play.

"What do you want?" a woman's voice said. The sound of a car whizzed past in the background.

"We need to talk," a man replied. He sounded Spanish.

It took Alex a few seconds to recognize the voices, but then it hit her. Aunt Min and Mr. Sanchez.

The fucker called her family.

Alex leaned forward, staring wide-eyed at the tiny recorder. She pictured the tap on that idiot's phone.

"Last I checked, we *were* talking," her aunt continued. "You've got sixty seconds, then we're done. Mention my name or my family's, I hang up. Now, get to your point, Mr. Sanchez. The clock's ticking."

Agent Reed hit *Stop* and the click made Alex flinch. Her gaze shot up, meeting his smug smile.

He knew he had the upper hand when she leaned forward, desperate to hear more.

Every part of her wanted him to hit *Play* again. But she slid back, silent except for her chains clanking.

He tilted his head. "Still want that call?"

She nodded.

"Good." He stood and moved toward the door. Just before reaching the handle, he turned and made his way back to the table.

She braced for more questions, but instead, he picked up the recorder.

"Tell you what." He raised a finger. "I'll hit play and—"

"My call," she interrupted.

He nodded, waving her off. "Like I was saying, I'll hit play and get you that phone. But... when I return, maybe we can talk. See if there's something in this for you."

"Doubtful," she muttered, inching closer to the table.

The tape recorder and papers were well within reach.

"We'll see," he smirked, pressing *Play* before confidently marching out.

As the door clicked shut, her eyes shot to the recorder as the voices resumed.

"I need your help, and your..." Sanchez hesitated, almost blurting out her name. "*Our* mutual friend isn't answering their phone."

"Nor should they!" her aunt snipped. "Fifty seconds."

"If they're expecting me to honor our agreement for another year, then..." Sanchez paused, whispering to someone.

Alex leaned closer, straining to hear. She could almost make out what he was saying.

"...lex called. She sounded like a shitty computer." It was Riley. She was talking to her father.

"What did... say?" he asked.

The asshole barely covered his mouth. What an idiot.

Her aunt must've noticed too.

"I'm hanging up!" Aunt Min shouted.

"No!" Sanchez pulled his hand from the microphone.

"You're an awful spy, Mr. Sanchez. I'm done."

"Not if you know—" he began, but her aunt slammed the phone down.

Alex sat in silence, dumbstruck.

Was that enough? Could they nail me on only part of my name? And why the hell did she call him a spy?

The tape kept playing a dial tone as her mind churned through the questions.

Then, Sanchez started talking again. The fool hadn't hung up.

"What did she say?" he asked.

"Idiot," Alex whispered, raising her hand to her mouth. She realized what she'd done after she'd done it, but ignored her slip-up.

"She said she'd do it," Riley began, her voice much clearer now. "She said she'd hack into the voting machine."

Alex's heart raced, and she inhaled sharply as the line went silent. The bitch hadn't said her name, but she might as well have.

If they knew who her aunt was, and Riley mentioned hacking, then that was as good as gold in her mind.

But the question was if they had proof it was her. There was only one way to find out.

She reached forward and started rifling through the paperwork on the table.

Photos of her talking to Riley from the ATM. *Not enough.*

Photocopies of bank receipts. Money from Sanchez's

campaign and into another account. Somewhere in the Cayman Islands. *Still not enough.*

Sheet after sheet, picture after picture. *Nothing.*

No mention of her aunt, and only circumstantial evidence against her.

They don't have shit.

The door clicked open. Agent Reed walked in along with Agent Gregor.

At first, she thought they'd come in empty-handed, but then she saw an old-school touch phone in Reed's hand. That, and her backpack draped over his shoulder.

Agent Gregor was staring down at something much smaller in his palm. Her cell phone.

Fuuuuck.

She'd forgotten about her burner.

"I need you to unlock this." Agent Gregor held out the device.

She inhaled sharply. There was a missed SMS on the tiny screen.

```
New Message: NoKorLex
```

For a second, she thought they'd already accessed it, but she distinctly remembered locking it down. They could only see the sender.

"Please unlock this." He waved the phone in her face.

She smiled, leaning back. "Fuck off. I know my rights, asshole. I'm not unlocking shit. Now give me my goddamn call."

"I told you she wouldn't help." Agent Gregor curled his lip, tossing her phone just out of reach. "This generation of college kids are spoiled ass brats. They need to learn shit the hard way. Throw her behind some steel bars, then we'll see if she talks. Or better yet"—he leaned in, placing his hands on the table—"let her rot on assault charges. That'll keep her busy for five to ten. You and I have to catch a plane to Cali."

Agent Reed groaned, his gaze darting between her and Gregor. Realization dawned as he finally understood his partner's ploy.

Without warning, he grabbed Gregor's arm, yanking him toward the exit.

"Get out!" He shoved his partner through the door, slamming it shut.

When he turned around, she was staring at him.

"Sorry." He sighed and walked back to the table, sitting down across from her. "Now... where were we?"

She shook her head. "I'm tired of this game of dumb and dumber you two have going on. For the love of God, just give me my call."

Agent Reed studied her briefly, then glanced down at the spread documents in front of her.

"He's not my partner," he said, still eyeing the papers.

"I don't care," she spat.

"My regular partner got stuck in California. She's throwing the book at former Mayor Sanchez." He crossed his arms, leaning back, his attention back to her. "From what I hear, he's been doing a lot of talking. Implicating others to secure a better deal for himself and his family. Apparently, he's lobbing some wild accusations."

He tipped his head toward her, hinting at more, but waiting for her to bite.

So that was it. Sanchez was selling her out to the Feds. Probably accusing her of crimes she hadn't committed.

She wondered about the election. If Sanchez lost by wider margins than that one voting machine, he might not even realize she hadn't acted. Unless he'd enlisted others. For all she knew, she was his scapegoat.

The question was, what did they know, and what were they expecting from her?

Either way, she wasn't stepping into his trap. It was best to keep playing dumb.

"Sorry, I'm confused." She waved her hand over the documents. "What does all this have to do with me?"

"Do you know anything about voter manipulation, Ms. Mercer?" He paused, leaning closer.

She didn't budge. Her face was the pinnacle of calm. She already knew what he was about to say.

And then he cast his final line. "I think you do. I think you know exactly what I'm talking about, and I think we need each other."

Caution urged silence, but necessity pushed her forward. "How's that?" she asked.

Agent Reed smiled. "As I see it, you've got yourself into a bit of a pickle here in Ann Arbor." He reached into the envelope she thought was already empty, pulling out several more sheets of paper.

A police report, to be exact. A very long police report.

He shook his head, flipping the pages. "Assault on a Law Enforcement Officer, Theft of Law Enforcement Equipment, Robbery, Possession of a Stolen Firearm, Resisting Arrest, Disarming a Peace Officer..." He glanced up. "Should I go on?"

Alex sat there, glassy-eyed and silent as he read the charges, each one more severe than the last.

She'd really fucked up hitting that cop.

Even if he hadn't identified himself, she knew any number of those charges could stick. She was facing expulsion and some serious time behind bars. It didn't take a lawyer to see that.

"What do you want?" She went to cross her arms, but the

chains clanged, yanking her hands down, pain shooting through her forearms.

He sighed and shot up, hopping around the table.

She flinched, expecting he was about to get in her face, or worse.

But he didn't. And before she could say anything, the cuffs fell away, swinging freely off the edge of the table.

"That should be better." He smiled, stepping back.

She slid away, rubbing her wrists. Her right palm had been throbbing since she struck the cop last night, and now both hands screamed in protest.

"Thanks," she muttered.

"No problem." He stared at her for a few seconds, watching in silence as she fidgeted in her chair.

Then, he cut to the chase. "We need you to testify against former Mayor Sanchez."

She squinted. "Testify? And say what?"

He moved back to his seat, pulling another paper from the envelope as he sat down. It was like a goddamn bottomless pit in there. Either that, or this guy was a bloody magician.

"You'll tell the judge the truth," he said solemnly, staring at the paper. "Tell them what Sanchez and his daughter hired you to do. What she and her friend fought with you about in that alley. You'll put those assholes away for as long as the law allows."

He slid the paper forward, then reached into his pocket and retrieved a pen.

She tilted her head, studying him from a different perspective.

He was calm and collected. A cool operator, and a far cry from Agent Gregor.

To her, he seemed like a model agent. Someone meticulously balancing the line between legality and moral ambiguity. And all in the name of justice.

When she looked down at the document, her stomach dropped. It was a detailed confession, and from her quick scan, they had everything.

Every excruciating detail of what Sanchez and Riley had done. She didn't know how the Feds knew, or if they had proof, but the list was long.

Riley's hate speech followed by her attack, Alex stealing the evidence, their meeting, even her and her aunt blackmailing him. It was all there, including Sanchez hiring her to hack the voting system.

Her pulse pounded in her ears. Each beat a countdown to her destruction.

There was no way out of this.

Refuse the offer, and she'd do time for sure.

They'd deport her aunt. Her parents would be sent back home. Life as she knew it would be over.

And if Sanchez was negotiating his own plea, and he offered something bigger, they might not even honor her deal.

Staring at the document, she realized how deep she'd gotten into this legal quagmire.

She'd screwed up everything.

It wasn't the agent's fault. He was just doing his job. But if he really could make her problems disappear, maybe it was worth it.

Alex leaned forward. "I'm not saying I know anything. But..."

She studied the photo of her with Riley and Mr. Sanchez. From the angle of in the picture, it looked like someone had taken it just as they'd gotten out of their car that night. You could actually see the surprise on her face.

"If I *were* to testify against them, what could you do for me?"

When she glanced up, he was nodding, clearly happy to be getting somewhere.

After a few seconds of silence, he picked up her pending police charges from the table, placing them on top of the pile.

"I don't know, that's a lot of charges." He stared at the sheet. "Ann Arbor PD is pretty pissed about what you did to their officer."

He ran his hand over his neck, glancing between the paper and her.

Only then did she notice how disheveled he looked. She'd seen hints of it earlier, but up close, he was barely holding on. Just like her.

Finally, he lowered his hand, slowly shaking his head. "It depends on a lot of things, but I could probably get this reduced to... simple assault, maybe. Possibly even probation with community service. I can't control what the university will do, though."

"Come on..." She shrank back, the wind knocked out of her. The memories of that day came flooding back. The terror of that moment threatened to overwhelm her once more.

Walking out of the computer lab. Seeing the message from her Raspberry Pi at home.

It was as if the hackers had reached through the screen and strangled her. The thought of them finding her or her family had pushed her over the edge, sending her into a blind panic.

Even now, the fear mounted. The same sickening dread that consumed her in the Diag.

She'd been so convinced the man outside was after her. That he was connected to the hackers.

In her moment of terror, she lashed out. She never meant to hurt him. She was desperate to escape her nightmare turned reality.

"I told 'em where the gun was," she said, her voice cracking. "That's good for something, right? I mean, I thought they were North Korean spies, for crying out loud."

Agent Reed leaned back, brows furrowed. "That's the

second time you've mentioned North Koreans. What exactly did you think was happening in that Diag?"

It was only then that she remembered her burner still resting on the table. Depending on what it contained, she could either have something useful, or nothing at all.

The answer lay in her phone.

She cleared her throat, nodding toward it. "What if I could hand you the creators of Reveton?"

He screwed up his face. "Rev what?"

Alex chuckled, grabbing his pen. She scrawled some names across the back of the plea deal, along with a few other details.

Reveton
aka FBI Ransomware
North Koreans and Cipher

While the name Cipher meant nothing to her, she gambled it did to the Feds. Especially if N3tN1nja feared them.

When she slid the sheet toward Agent Reed, his eyes widened as he looked down.

She could actually see the shock register.

"I want full immunity," she began, glancing at her phone. "Nothing touches me or my family. Nothing. And the same goes for college. You fix this with the university. I don't care how, but you make it go away." She looked up, meeting his still-surprised gaze.

"Now go... go talk to your superiors." She swallowed hard, her mind drifting to her Trojan. "But do it fast. If what I think is happening actually is, we need to act quickly."

ALEX STARED at the ATM photo. It showed her aunt smiling beside her as they walked away from the Sanchezes that morning. Taken out of context, they could've been any two people on a friendly weekend stroll.

Why didn't Aunt Min mentioned the Sanchez call yesterday when we spoke? She'd brought up running into him at her mom's work, but said nothing about talking on the phone.

Maybe she feared their conversation was being recorded. That would explain the weird line of questions about the campaign and early polling results.

The signs were there. Alex's weary mind had just failed to recognize them.

When the door to the interrogation room clicked open, she glanced at her phone. She could barely make out the clock.

Four hours. Agent Reed had been gone for four damn hours.

"So much for moving fast," she muttered, looking up.

Agent Reed entered, followed closely by a tall, lanky woman in a moisture-dotted overcoat. Her damp hair suggested it was either snowing or raining outside; in Michigan, any weather was possible this time of year.

"This is her?" the woman scoffed, gesturing toward Alex. "This is your hacker insider?" She glanced at Agent Reed, then back to Alex. "I thought you said she could help us. She doesn't even look old enough to drive."

"Screw you," Alex shot back. "I could code circles around you and your analyst plebes any day of the week."

The woman's eyebrow arched. "My, my. She's got a mouth on her, too."

Agent Reed pushed the door shut and stepped up beside the table. "This is Director Williams from our Chicago office." His eyes widened at Alex, clearly signaling her to chill out. "She leads our task force on Reveton and other viruses. I told her what you said about North Korea and Cipher, and sent her the details on your Sanchez situation. Needless to say, she jumped on the next plane here. That's what took so long."

"Let's hope Agent Reed's confidence in you isn't misplaced." Director Williams eased into the empty chair, reaching for one of the photos. Her coat sleeves dripped water onto the table and papers.

"Too bad about Mayor Sanchez," she began. "He got trounced in the Fremont election. Something like twenty points, right?"

"Twenty-five," Agent Reed corrected.

Alex leaned back, arms crossed. "He's a racist bigot, and so is his daughter."

Director Williams glanced up. "Is that why you didn't help him?"

Alex smirked. "Maybe." She bit her lip. "That and the asshole didn't tell me any details about what he wanted. Once I found out, I fucking dipped. I'm not big on breaking the law, and I sure as hell don't rig elections."

The director pursed her lips and set the photo down, studying Alex.

"Do you have something to say to me?" Alex slid her chair forward, gesturing at the director's face. "Your mouth just twitched. You think I'm lying, don't you?"

"Well," Director Williams began, "if the shoe fits. From where I'm sitting," she picked up the police report, flipping through pages, "you look like a petty criminal trying to run."

Alex glared, heart pounding. She'd known this moment was coming and had been mulling it over since Agent Reed left. They wouldn't just hand her a golden deal on a platter; they'd test her first, make her prove her worth.

But this? This was bullshit. She wasn't about to let this Windy City suit insult her.

"Fuck you!" Alex shot to her feet, snatching her burner off the table.

The director flinched as Alex squeezed the phone, poised to reset it. Five presses of the power button would wipe it clean. After that, not even the FBI could retrieve anything from it.

"I could turn over a goddamn goldmine of intel on this virus." Alex waved the phone toward her, pressing the button twice. "And wrap it in a Pyongyang-shaped bow. But you and your Chicago-sized ego probably wouldn't give a shit, let alone recognize it."

"Come on, Alex." Agent Reed eased closer. "Why don't you calm down and take a seat? Director Williams came here because I—"

"No!" Director Williams interrupted, halting Reed with an outstretched hand. "Let her speak. She obviously has a lot to say. Go on, little girl. Wow me!" She pushed away from the table, crossing her legs and fixing Alex with a skeptical stare.

Alex pressed the button twice more. One more press, and it was gone.

She bristled at being called a little girl. She was a goddamn adult. Half of her wanted to hurl the fucking phone at the witch's face.

But she thought better of it. This could be her only chance to tell her story. If she was going to do this, she'd do it her way.

"Give me my machine!" She glanced from Agent Reed to her bag on his shoulder.

Reed looked at Director Williams, who nodded. Apparently, she kept her agents on short leashes.

Alex didn't wait for him to hand her the bag. She reached in, pulled out her laptop, and set it down next to the director before repositioning her chair.

Settling into her seat, she took a deep breath and fell silent, her mind racing to find a starting point. There was a web of interconnected details to cover, each crucial to filling in the entire picture.

"Why don't you just cut to the chase?" Agent Reed interrupted her thoughts. "Tell us what you know about the virus."

She shook her head. "No. I need to connect the dots. Otherwise, you won't... understand."

With the agents staring at each other, she cracked her knuckles, a plan taking shape in her mind. The shortest route from start to finish. One that would make her case as clearly as possible.

She glanced at Director Williams. "If I show you how Reveton connects to the North Koreans... if I give you a way inside, then—"

"We'll talk a deal," Director Williams interrupted, uncrossing her legs and sliding up beside her.

"Full immunity," Alex said. "For my entire family. Including Aunt Min."

Director Williams and Alex both looked to Agent Reed.

He shrugged. "Her aunt isn't an American citizen."

"Then let her stay here on a permanent visa," Alex countered, facing the director again. "I mean it. I'll even hand you Byt3Linguist."

The director's pupils dilated—a flicker of recognition.

Director Williams slowly tilted her head, hesitating. "You can hand me Byt3Linguist?"

"I can," Alex said firmly. "But only on my terms."

Director Williams leaned back, eyes narrowing. "And how will I know you're not just feeding me some bullshit story? That you're actually telling the truth?"

Alex met her gaze head-on. "Because I've got everything on this machine." She tapped her laptop. "I know more about Byt3Linguist than anyone, and I have proof about the North Korean connection. Solid proof. But I need assurances before I share it."

The director drummed her fingers on the table, silence stretching between them. Even Agent Reed shifted uneasily.

In that moment, Alex wondered if she'd said too much. Revealing what was on her laptop could've been a huge mistake. They could simply seize it as evidence. She'd never gotten around to securing the data on this new machine.

"No." Director Williams stopped drumming, her expression hardening. "You aren't going to sit there and make demands. Not on my watch."

Alex's heart sank.

"Director?" Agent Reed stepped to her side. "Can we discuss this?"

"I've made up my—" she began.

"Director Williams!" He glared at her, tension crackling between them. "If I may ask you to step into the hall. Please. I'd like a word."

Her mouth fell open, and even Alex flinched in shock.

"A word indeed," Director Williams muttered, shooting to her feet and storming out.

Agent Reed nodded toward Alex. "We'll only be a second."

As the door closed, Alex leaned closer, straining to hear.

The moment the latch clicked, shouts erupted from the hall. At first, it sounded like Agent Reed was getting chewed out, but suddenly his voice rose above the director's. Alex caught only fragments, but he was clearly furious.

He was saying something about putting his career on the line and Alex's prior run-ins with the law. She wondered if they had access to her adoption records, because before today, she'd never so much as spoken to a cop. But her records were supposed to be sealed since she'd been a minor. Then again, they were the FBI. They could do anything they wanted. She couldn't decide if her past would help or hurt her now.

Just as the voices faded, Alex leaned toward the door. Suddenly, it flew open with a bang. The director burst in, her face a storm of fury, with Agent Reed trailing behind. Alex jerked back, hands clasped tightly in her lap, heart pounding.

The director marched straight to her, slamming both hands on the table and leaning in menacingly. "Listen here," she snarled, barely containing her rage. "You want a deal? Fine. If you give me Byt3Linguist and their path to Pyongyang, you've got it. But I swear..." She jabbed a finger at Alex's face. "If this turns out to be bullshit, if you're just covering your ass, I'll personally see to it that you and your aunt are locked up so fast and so deep, you'll think Pyongyang is a vacation spot. Do I make myself clear?"

"I want it in writing," Alex said without hesitation, a lump forming in her throat.

Director Williams stared at her, and for a split second, Alex thought she might back out. But then the director glanced over at Agent Reed. "You heard the young lady. Get her an offer. Wake up Assistant US Attorney Smithe in Chicago. He heads up the Midwest Criminal Division. Tell him I'm calling in a favor. Now go." She waved him away. "Ms. Mercer has a lot of ground to cover."

Agent Reed didn't hesitate; he spun on his heels and marched out of the interrogation room.

Once he was gone, the director gestured at Alex's laptop. "Alright, you've got my attention. Get to the wowing."

Alex smiled and turned back to her machine. Opening her files, she prepared to tell her tale. Wowing her, she could handle. She just hoped the director could keep up.

THREE HOURS and four cups of coffee later, the director stared at Alex, stunned. Smudged network diagrams covered the two-way glass.

Alex didn't wait for verbal acknowledgment. She knew

she'd fulfilled their agreement in spades. She quickly stepped to the table and signed the document, then snapped a photo with her phone for safekeeping. With a few taps, the image was forwarded to a burner email at Tutanota.

Director Williams watched her send the message, still wearing that look of reverent awe from when Alex revealed she was Byt3Linguist. And the funny part was, she had the proof: her local chat logs, along with the keys to authenticate with the Rizon chatbots.

Agent Reed leaned against the table, staring at the glass. "So you were the one who kicked off this firestorm with N3tN1nja?"

"If by 'kicked off' you mean simply asking for help cracking the virus, then yeah." She flipped through her mental notes, making sure she'd covered everything. Everything except the parts where she knew N3tN1nja.

It was a dangerous but necessary omission.

While they hadn't questioned her ability to crack into the machines she used, there were a few tense moments where she had to riff and make shit up. But that she could deal with. She'd learned to bullshit her way through most of her life, especially in hacker circles. Plus, given the details she'd provided about the Trojan and her program running inside the North Korean hacker nest, the director hadn't caught on to the gaps. At least, not yet.

"This is huge." The director stood abruptly, eyes transfixed on Alex's crude Trojan drawing explaining her reverse proxy hack. "Were you serious when you said you could run any program you wanted on their machines?"

Alex nodded, flipping open her phone. She brought up the messages app, then turned both her phone and laptop toward the director. Her program was designed to report every time someone uploaded a new Reveton payload, and on her phone was the grand total.

```
NoKorStat: Uploaded 256 files
```

Her stomach churned at the scale of the North Korean operation. If each file contained almost a million dollars, she was staring at nearly a quarter of a billion, give or take a few million.

The amount of human suffering behind these stolen monies was staggering. Her mind flashed to her parents' fight when her father lost their rent. She hoped her family was safe, especially after that message from N3tN1nja.

Alex glanced over at Agent Reed. "Is there any way we can return this money, you know, to the affected people?"

"Maybe," Agent Reed said, "but it would be hard to figure out all the—"

"How long?" Director Williams blurted out, pointing at the whiteboard.

"How long till what?" Alex asked, stepping up beside her. "To track down where the money came from?"

"No! How long until they find your Trojan or move the funds?" Director Williams drew a question mark next to the crude North Korean flag Alex had sketched.

Alex shook her head. "I honestly don't know. I only put the Trojan in there in case."

"In case of what?" Agent Reed asked.

Her mind blanked. She hadn't really thought this through when she'd started her little side project.

That was how most of her hacks played out. They were random acts of learning. But this was more about revenge than anything. Just like when she'd covered for N3tN1nja, she'd been riffing with these hacks. So, rather than lie, she said the first thing that came to mind.

"In case I needed to strike back at the assholes." She sat down, letting the gravity of her words sink in.

"Get me Executive Assistant Director Sinclair of Cyber Command," Director Williams said.

Alex spun around. The director stood in the corner, talking into her cell phone. Alex hadn't even realized she'd walked away. Whoever this Sinclair was, they had a long-ass title that sounded important. She'd never met anyone from US Cyber Command before.

"Good morning, Director Sinclair," Williams began, spinning around and locking her gaze on Alex. "I apologize for the early wake-up call, sir. I've come across a bluebird that's fallen from its nest, and I need your help to bring it in. We're keeping it warm in our Ann Arbor field kitchen."

She nodded. "Yes, sir. Michigan, sir. No, I wasn't aware you were a Wolverine, sir. That *is* a coincidence." She sighed, turning away. "That's correct, my bluebird, sir. It's vital that we act quickly. You'll find the specifics in your inbox within the hour." She picked up Alex's sketch explaining the Reveton virus.

Alex caught the muffled voice on the other end of the line when the director nodded.

"Yes, sir." Director Williams drew a deep breath. "But given the delicacy and potential impact of this recipe, plus the time sensitivity of the cook... I'm requesting your emergency authorization, sir. I need to call in this favor. We have to deviate from our usual... recipe. It's imperative that we act fast and trim this bird's feathers before it flies. Time is literally of the essence, sir."

In the ensuing silence, Alex glanced at Agent Reed, who seemed equally stunned by the coded exchange.

While she didn't know the exact lingo, she could deduce the nature of the director's ask. She was seeking approval to use Alex's Trojan for a state-sanctioned attack. The prospect both thrilled and terrified her.

Her actions could spark a war. An honest-to-goodness cyberwar.

And the carnage would be on her hands.

While the impact might not be measured in bodies, the effects could be no less devastating. Economies could crumble, infrastructure could collapse, and lives could be irrevocably shattered in the digital fallout.

As visions of an electronic battlefield raced through her mind, her hands began trembling, the weight of the consequences crushing down on her.

All of this stemmed from her choices. Her mistakes.

Her breath came in short, sharp gasps.

The only saving grace was her signed immunity deal. The decision on how to proceed with her hack was now entirely up to them, not her.

Agent Reed stepped up beside Alex, lowering his voice. "US Cyber Command may be new, but they have analysts actively monitoring social media and the dark web globally. They're no different from other foreign agencies. Unlike them, though, we've got a lot more red tape to deal with. This back door of yours is bigger than you realize. Just getting something like this in place would've taken months, if not years, of planning and oversight. And you just dropped it in her lap."

She glanced at him, catching his raised eyebrows. Perhaps she hadn't asked for enough. At the time, she'd focused on covering her ass, not coming out ahead. If Aunt Min were here, she wouldn't have made that mistake.

With her mind churning through lost opportunities, she almost missed her phone vibrating in her pocket.

She pulled it out and gasped at the message.

```
NoKorStat: Proxy 12 compromised.
         Cleaning house.
```

"Shit," she muttered, holding the burner up for Agent Reed to see.

He read it, mouthing the words. "What does it mean?"

She eyed the director. "It means your bosses better get the lead out of their ass. They need to figure out what we're doing because our bluebird pie is burning in the fucking oven."

She hopped back to the table, sat down, and began typing furiously, bringing up her notes with the reverse proxy IP addresses. "They may have figured out that I hacked their network."

"What happens if they did?" Director Williams asked, holding her hand over the mic on her phone.

"It could be nothing." Alex glanced up, noting the urgency etched on the woman's face.

Given the gravity of their mission, she decided not to sugarcoat it. "But if it were me," she began, "I'd be shutting everything down, making sure the rest of the operation wasn't compromised. Sorta like what they're doing now."

"Fuck," the director snipped, holding the phone away.

It was her first curse all night, even after the Byt3Linguist revelation. If that didn't underscore her worry, Alex didn't know what did.

The director finally found her nerve, bringing the phone back to her mouth. "The bluebird is burning in the oven, sir. We only have a few minutes left to bring it home. What are your orders?"

22 / OVERFLOW
CIPHER

Fourteen hours into the road trip, Cipher was ready to rip out Tae-Woo's vocal cords. If he had to listen to the man butcher one more whiny country jingle on the car's useless radio, he might just do it.

After their group barely made it out of Fremont, they headed to Oakland and picked up another car. One capable of making a cross-country trek. There was no way in hell they were flying, not after what happened to their team in New York.

Their contacts assured them the ride wasn't hot, but they weren't taking chances. For Tae-Woo, that meant never exceeding the speed limit, following every rule of the road, and avoiding expressways at all costs. He didn't want to risk being seen by any more cameras than necessary.

The problem was, there were only so many routes through the desert—that blistering chunk of useless real estate surrounding nearly every viable route out of California.

His mind kept drifting back to the Raspberry Pi he'd snagged from the apartment—the one piece of evidence that could unravel their enemies' identities. But Tae-Woo had been quick to snatch it from him after his reckless behavior in Fremont.

Now, as they sped down the highway, Cipher couldn't shake the nagging feeling that he needed to get his hands on the device, to see what secrets it might hold.

They were coming up on Albuquerque, New Mexico, and he had to piss. Florida was a long way off, and there was no point in adding to his discomfort.

The backseat of the deathtrap they were in had no cush. All he had for padding was a smelly blanket they'd found at the chop shop. It was like riding in a goddamn horse and buggy, every bump in the road a sucker punch to his bladder.

"I need to take a leak," he said, pointing at a gas station in the distance. "Let's stop there."

Tae-Woo shook his head. "No. We'll stop when we get to Santa Rosa."

"Fine by me." He leaned back. "If you're okay with a backseat full of piss, then I am, too." He faked a relaxed sigh. "The smell can't get any worse in this car. Plus, my ears are bleeding from this shit you keep playing. Maybe the urine stench will be a nice distraction."

Tae-Woo glared at him in the rearview mirror.

He stared back, rolling his eyes and pretending to relieve himself.

"Fine! We'll stop." Tae-Woo flipped on the turn signal. "But no messing around. We're in and out."

Jin-Soo leaned closer to his brother. "We pick up a SIM, yes?" He cast a wary eye over his shoulder at Cipher. "We no checked in since yesterday's near miss with the cops."

Tae-Woo grunted, his knuckles whitening on the wheel. After a few seconds, he sighed and turned into the station. "Screw it. I might as well top us off then." He glanced back in the mirror at Cipher. "After this, we're not stopping again until this tank is bone fucking dry. Got it?"

Cipher shrugged. "Whatever you say, boss. I'm just the brains."

Ever since his outburst and storming of the apartment in Fremont, Tae-Woo had kept him on a short leash. He didn't trust Cipher not to get them into another pickle with the police. Or worse.

He couldn't really blame Tae-Woo. After Choe's epic screwup in New York, Pyongyang was livid. Their concerns were the main reason the three of them were on this grueling ass road trip in the first place. They couldn't risk flying; security was too tight. Plus, they needed to ensure the safe retrieval of their money from Cipher's mule in Florida. After that, they'd be taking a freighter home from Miami. A voyage he dreaded.

With that little detail out in the open, he couldn't help but see his days on this planet being numbered. They'd end him after he'd served his purpose. Hell, he'd probably already be dead if he'd been back home. Only his money mule's demand for a personal handoff was saving him. He had no idea why they wanted it, but he wasn't looking a gift horse in the mouth.

All of that led him to this disgusting gas station restroom outside Albuquerque.

He sidled up to the urinal, careful not to touch anything. The place reeked of piss and cheap American tobacco. He could only imagine the germs lurking here.

The place was so wretched, his handler, Jin-Soo, wouldn't even come in. He waited outside.

Cipher sighed with relief as he emptied his bladder, the pressure lessening with every second.

Suddenly, a loud, flatulent eruption reverberated from the stall to his left. It echoed like the roar of a foghorn, but the noxious stench that followed was even worse.

He drew in his breath and winced, fighting back his gag

reflex. He found himself wishing he had a free hand to pinch his nose. But he couldn't, lest he piss all over himself.

Glancing at the stall, he spotted a pair of giant pants on the ground. They were easily big enough for three men, and were hanging out of the stall near a man's feet.

But that wasn't what caught his eye. There, attached to the enormous belt, was a mobile phone.

He eyed the tantalizing device. From here, it looked like a cheap Android smartphone, probably from one of the massive chain stores nearby. More importantly, it likely had internet access. Something he desperately needed if he was going to survive this mess.

The man's size was a problem though. Even if Cipher could snatch the phone, the giant would be on him in seconds. He needed a diversion—something to keep the man occupied while he made his escape.

After he finished his deed, he tiptoed away from the urinal without flushing and surveyed the restroom.

There was another stall on the other side of the man, and it looked like it was empty. The question was, how to use it to his advantage?

As he took in the revolting space, it hit him. A plan befitting the surroundings slowly took shape in his mind.

Without wasting a second, he slipped into the open stall, locked the door, and started yanking out reams of toilet paper. He balled it up and shoved it into the bowl. Foot after stark white foot.

After about a minute of pulling out the endless reel, the rumbling paper holder caught his neighbor's attention.

"Everything okay over there?" the man asked, his voice deep with bass.

"Yeah," Cipher groaned. "I just... got the runs."

He stifled a laugh and topped off the bowl with one last

tug. The damp white cloth was layered so thick, no amount of flushing would force water past.

"I hear ya," the man said. "Goddamn wife's bean salad is brutal." He followed his declaration with another teeth-chattering blast.

Cipher retched, then hit the lever to flush, jamming one final wad of paper in between the handle and the tank to hold it in place. The more water, the better.

It wasn't elegant, but was good enough for this literal shit show.

With the bowl filling rapidly, he unlocked the stall and stepped out, making his way back to the urinal.

It didn't take long until he heard the telltale rush of water overflowing the toilet and splashing onto the floor.

Seconds later, the guy in the stall scrambled to his feet, backing against the makeshift wall. The shoddy barrier creaked under his sudden girth.

"What the fuck, dude?" the man yelled, water flowing between his legs onto his pants.

The shout was music to Cipher's ears. Without hesitation, he reached down and snatched the phone from the man's belt.

He powered off the phone as he made for the door.

Once the screen went dark, he shoved the palm-sized device down his pants and yanked the door open, bursting out into fresh air.

Jin-Soo waited outside, staring at his watch. "What part 'take fast piss' you no understand, aye?"

"Sorry," Cipher muttered, backing toward the car. "I had to pinch a loaf." He pointed to the bathroom. "I'd be careful in there. That guy fucking stinks."

As if on cue, a scream and crash erupted from behind the door. "What the fuck?"

Jin-Soo grumbled and sprinted up beside Cipher, glancing

back. "You no better do something stupid." He eyed him cautiously.

Cipher faked a laugh. "If you mean take a shit next to a giant who smelled like the Pyongyang slums, then yeah. I did something stupid. But when a guy's gotta go..."

They reached the car and Cipher slid inside, smirking.

He fought not to wince as the cheap plastic phone jabbed his junk, but Jin-Soo wasn't watching. He was staring at the giant of a man waddling from the restroom.

Not only was his face as red as a tomato, his overalls were half done and soaked in water.

Jin-Soo ducked into the front seat. "Oi, that guy's a big one."

The man rounded the corner, nearly bowling Tae-Woo over.

"What the hell?" Tae-Woo screamed, clutching his bag. He almost shoved the guy until he noticed the man's size and sodden state.

Thinking better of it, he stepped back, giving the guy a wide berth. "Watch where you're going, buddy!"

The man growled, scanning the lot as if searching for someone.

With Jin-Soo chuckling up front, Cipher slipped the phone from his pants and slid it under the driver's seat. He didn't dare get caught with the device. At least if they found it down there, he could blame the guys who sold them the ride.

When Tae-Woo reached the car, he tossed the bag onto the front seat, and left the door open as he stepped to the pump.

"Fucking guy almost knocked me on my ass." He unlatched the pump handle and shoved the spigot into the tank, glancing at his brother. "There's a burner with a SIM in the bag. Call the general, but make it quick. I don't know how much time we'll get calling home on that thing. The prices are outrageous here."

"I'm on it." Jin-Soo was already ripping into the bag.

He grabbed the cheap plastic device, ripped through the packaging, and powered it up after sliding in the SIM.

Two minutes later, after keying in a long sequence of numbers, he held the phone to his ear. "I'm checking in about the book I ordered."

"The red book," Tae-Woo hissed through the window. "Damn it, man."

Jin-Soo cleared his throat. "I mean, the red book. I'm checking on the red book I ordered."

A few loud clicks followed, then a barrage of furious shouts erupted from the receiver. Cipher heard the screaming plain as day from the backseat. General Tau was tearing Jin-Soo a new asshole.

Jin-Soo's face turned pale, his eyes widening in sheer terror. He gripped the phone tighter, then turned, eyeing his brother outside with a fear Cipher had never seen before. Not even when they were running for their lives back in California.

Whatever was happening back home wasn't good.

CIPHER WATCHED with mounting exasperation as Jin-Soo finished pairing the laptop with their newest phone. They'd picked it up from one of those massive red, white, and blue American retail stores. This phone could tether to a computer and had a modem that wasn't absolute trash. It cost a few hundred dollars, but that was the price of wireless freedom in a first-world country.

The midday sun beat down as they sat in the parking lot, trying to get online. It was so hot, he could see the heat radiating off their hood and the sea of asphalt surrounding them on all sides.

A bead of sweat ran down his forehead as he groaned, frustration mounting.

He hadn't watched someone navigate a computer this clumsily in years. Jin-Soo's snail-paced movements, his insistence on using the mouse for everything, and his hunt-and-peck typing were maddening.

"Give me that damn thing!" He snatched the machine from Jin-Soo's lap. "By the time you get us through the VPN hops, it'll be nightfall."

Jin-Soo growled, sliding his pistol out from under the blanket and resting his finger on the trigger.

Cipher didn't flinch. Let the asshole shoot him. He was already dead—it was just a matter of when.

He yanked out the useless mouse cable and sighed in relief, quickly navigating through menus using only the keyboard. He initiated hops through various VPN networks to reach their machine in North Korea. After several minutes and a half dozen freezes, the terminal updated with the details of their situation.

Leaning forward, he scanned the screen. Pyongyang was in full-blown panic mode, ordering a stop on all virus operations. They were shutting down the entire array of reverse proxies and going dark.

"Why are they shutting down?" He glanced at Jin-Soo.

"They no take chances. No fingers pointing at them." Jin-Soo waved the gun. "Now, fix it."

Cipher stared, trying to piece together what he'd missed. Based on his cursory scan, he could see they'd failed to wipe several machines, but that didn't require his expertise. If they'd resorted to a full-scale shutdown, then this wasn't just about the virus.

"They don't actually think a shooting changes anything for the virus, do they?" He shook his head. "The authorities here aren't that adept, or fast. Unless..."

Cipher paused, looking at Tae-Woo leaning against the car. He was talking quietly on his phone, occasionally glancing back at them.

When their eyes met, a chill passed through Cipher.

Whatever happened in New York must've been worse than he thought. Or they weren't telling him something.

Jin-Soo nudged him with the gun. "Help! Now!"

"Touch me again with that thing, and I'll—"

Jin-Soo reached up and whipped him in the back of the head with the barrel of the gun.

Metal connected with a sickening crack, and his vision went glassy as he slumped forward, struggling to stay conscious through the pain.

Rage surged within him. He clenched the keyboard, summoning every ounce of restraint not to retaliate. Not yet.

"I say, help!" Jin-Soo cocked the hammer of the gun with a decisive click. "If no, then you die."

"Asshole," he muttered, rubbing his head.

The bump wasn't bad, but it hurt like hell. He needed to focus and get this shit done so they could get out of here. The sooner they left, the sooner he could reach out to his friends.

Gathering his willpower, he returned his focus to the laptop and grabbed the first failing host from the list. He started the login procedure to wipe the proxy.

But an error greeted him.

```
Operation timed out
```

While not an uncommon message for remote connections, these routes were working a few weeks ago.

The error likely meant the administrators of the machine had done an update. But for every hole patched, a dozen undocumented ones typically remained. Such was the nature of the cat-and-mouse game with poorly managed systems.

He swiftly ran *nmap* and a few other tools, confirming they'd updated the machine. Fortunately, the new OS version still had known vulnerabilities. He only hoped they hadn't hired a new admin who was worth their salt.

Once he identified the machine's OS and version, finding the optimal attack vector in their database was straightforward. Even the most meticulously crafted defenses could crumble in the face of well-organized hackers.

After a few queries, he settled on his approach and downloaded the necessary tools. Things were always easier when you had a web server loaded with ready-made hacks.

With everything in place, he launched the attack. He didn't need much—just a vector to remotely execute their code. To pop open the back door, as it were.

He watched the output scroll past as the script targeted specific URLs. It probed for one of several hundred remote code execution vulnerabilities in this version of Linux.

While he'd usually spin up another terminal, there was no way this cell phone tether could handle the load. But that was fine. It gave him time to scroll back and check the output from earlier.

As he scanned the list of machines to hack, a pattern emerged.

He reached out the window and slapped his palm on the roof of the car, causing Tae-Woo to spin around.

He glared at Cipher, covering the phone's receiver with his hand. "What?"

Cipher waved him over.

The muscular man snarled and strolled around the car.

Instead of letting him talk, Cipher jumped in. "Did our bosses say anything about the proxies? The ones that were stuck?"

Tae-Woo screwed up his face. "What are you talking about?"

He kept forgetting he was talking to the muscle, not the brains. The only way to get a straight answer was to go to the source. And sometimes that meant drastic action.

Cipher didn't pause to consider the consequences of what he was about to do. He simply acted, safety be damned.

Without warning, he tossed the laptop toward Jin-Soo and shoved the car door open.

The sudden motion caught both men off guard.

Jin-Soo dropped his gun and Tae-Woo took the door to the face, giving Cipher ample time to snatch the phone from his hand.

Just because he was usually a desk jockey didn't mean he wasn't fit or agile.

With the phone in hand and Tae-Woo still reeling, he raised it to his ear and circled to the far side of the car.

"General Tau," he began in English, "it seems you're in a bit of a bind. Several hundred million dollars' worth of trouble, if my estimates are right."

He wasn't certain of the general's exact plan, but it looked like he was skimming cash off the books during the chaos in the States.

His bosses in Pyongyang had cut most of the reverse proxies hours ago, and the general was now cleaning up the scraps for himself. When it was all said and done, the general would probably pin the loss on him. But if the higher-ups found out, they'd both end up as dead as Choe and her friends.

"I don't know what you're talking about," the general said in Korean, his voice tinged with agitation.

"Oh, fuck off. You know exactly what's going on. I'm the only one capable of cleaning up this hornets' nest you're stirring." He smiled, watching Tae-Woo sprint around the car with Jin-Soo close behind.

"We wouldn't want Pyongyang to find out about your little late-night raid on the piggy bank, now would we?"

He ducked around an oversized SUV and slid across the hood of an old Corvette, narrowly evading Tae-Woo's lunge.

The metal button on his pants left a deep gash in the cherry-red hood, mirroring the angry Asian man's face.

"Can you fix it?" the general asked.

He grunted, slipping between two sedans and ducking behind a pair of tank-like trucks.

"Not if these knuckleheads kill me first." He peered through a window but saw no sign of them. "Get me back to North Korea alive, and without being bruised and bloodied, and you've got yourself a deal."

He spun around, searching for his captors. "What do you say?"

His eyes widened as Jin-Soo stepped out from behind a van, gun raised. The man's eyes blazed with rage as he aimed the deadly weapon straight at Cipher's head.

"Judging by the bloodlust in your muscle's eyes"—he swallowed hard—"they're about to end me."

Cipher didn't wait for the general's reply.

He thrust the phone toward Tae-Woo's charging form with one hand while signaling him to stop with the other.

"It's for you." He winced.

Tae-Woo skidded to a halt, fists clenched. In one fluid motion, he snatched the device with his left hand while his right arm shot out, pinning Cipher against the nearby car by the throat.

He gasped, clawing desperately at Tae-Woo's unyielding grip. His lungs burned for air, but the pressure was relentless.

Oblivious to Cipher's struggle, Tae-Woo brought the phone to his ear.

"Janggun-nim," he whispered. The Korean word for general fell from his lips like ice.

THE MINUTES that followed were surreal. Cipher could hear the screaming through the phone in Tae-Woo's hand. The sheer number of threats coming from the other end made the hairs on his arm stand on end.

To say the general was unhappy would be an understatement. He wouldn't accept failure in recovering his money, even if he was stealing from his bosses.

After the call, his captors' demeanors transformed from egotistical muscle heads to concerned caretakers. They went overboard ensuring his comfort.

Tae-Woo helped him back to the car, turned on the AC, and he even sent Jin-Soo into the store to get them some food and drinks.

It was a bizarre turn he knew wouldn't last. Once they got to Florida and secured the money, he was done for. His only hope lay in surviving past the handoff.

His first order of business was recovering the stolen cash. Then he'd tackle the crypto side of the transaction. They couldn't leave this parking lot until he finished. The hacks required a stable connection, and driving would only complicate things. Better to sit here, burning daylight, than risk losing internet mid-attack.

Cipher stared at the laptop, taking a long drag on the cherry slushy Jin-Soo had given him. The sugary explosion lit up his tastebuds.

His earlier attack on the machine had worked. According to the logs, the backdoor was open.

"Can you recover it?" Tae-Woo asked, eyeing the screen.

Though out of sight, Cipher knew the weapon was just a foot away; a fact he was trying hard to ignore.

He had a dozen machines to hack, and the clock was already ticking. They were due in Florida in three days, and had a lot of road between here and there, especially bypassing the highways.

Tae-Woo waved his hand in front of Cipher's face. "Everything alright?"

He nodded, puckering his lips around the straw. "This shit is sweet." That was a lie. He actually liked it. But he wasn't about to admit to zoning out.

Tae-Woo chuckled, sipping his lime drink. "Americans love their sugar."

Cipher smirked and checked the machine he was on, ensuring no one else had logged in since his hack. Then he ran the other script he'd downloaded.

It executed in under a second, restoring the remote secure shell access they'd gotten months earlier. Unless the administrator had reset to a baseline image, they likely wouldn't have checked for changes in their install.

"Bam!" He slammed the car seat in front of him when the shell command connected. "We're in."

He quickly checked the machine to ensure everything was in order.

```
> lsof -i
...
COMMAND PID USER NODE NAME
sshd 5471 root TCP redwood2.local:ssh->192.168.45.67:22 (ESTABLISHED)
sshd 5476 root TCP redwood2.local:ssh->172.16.84.29:22 (ESTABLISHED)
...
```

His fingers lingered over the keyboard as he studied the output. Each line showed an open file handle or connection. Multiple processes were running, which was expected for a web server.

But there should only be one *sshd* process running. His.

He furrowed his brow, unease creeping up his spine. Something wasn't right.

"What?" Tae-Woo asked, leaning closer to see the screen. He must've seen the look on Cipher's face.

"There's someone on the machine." He studied the unfamiliar IP. A quick query confirmed it wasn't one of theirs.

This was someone else.

Tae-Woo looked from the screen to him and back. "Is it... one of our people?"

Cipher shook his head, his mind turning over what he should do. The process number was close to his own, which meant they'd logged in a few minutes after him.

He could simply *kill* the process and finish the cleanup, but then he wouldn't know who it was or what they were doing.

"What should we do?" Tae-Woo spun around, voice cracking. He scanned the parking lot, as if someone was watching them.

Cipher, however, was in the zone, hardly noticing his guards' bizarre behavior.

He knew what he should do, what the safe move was.

But deep down, he also knew who was likely on the machine. Only two people could've found this proxy, and one had killed his people.

For the second time in the past hour, he made an erratic, irrational decision. He opened a chat session with the other user.

```
> write root
I see you're busy mucking around where you
don't belong, N3tN1nja. Wasn't there enough
bloodshed in New York for one night? -
Cipher o
```

As he hit enter, Tae-Woo's eyes went wide. "What the fuck are you doing?" He snatched his gun from the seat pocket, aiming it at Cipher's head.

Cipher didn't so much as flinch at the muzzle leveled at him. He simply grinned, waiting for a reply. "I'm saying hello to our friend. The one who killed your colleagues in New York."

"He's doing what?" Jin-Soo asked from the front, struggling to see the screen.

"Why the fuck would you do that?" Tae-Woo growled, spittle flying onto Cipher's face.

He reached up and slowly wiped the flecks of saliva away, glaring at the two men. "Because I can."

23 / NEED-TO-KNOW BASIS
ALEX

Alex didn't wait for the director to get her answer about the bluebird pie—or whatever cryptic codeword she'd used. Instead, she swiftly prepared a dozen terminal windows, executing the necessary hops through her web of machines to cover her tracks.

"Next time, I'm building in a self-destruct sequence," she muttered, eyes darting across the collection of windows.

Focused on her screen, she barely registered the soft click of the door closing behind her. By the time she spun around, Agent Reed was already sliding up beside her, hefting a machine of his own.

It was massive—at least four times the size of her laptop, more portable workstation than mobile computer.

As he flipped open the lid, Agent Reed studied the ports on her machine before extracting a retractable cable from his behemoth. "FireWire 800, right?"

She froze, eyeing the offering. "What's this for?" She took it, examining the connector. It was FireWire alright.

"I'll need to copy something to your machine." His gaze returned to his screen. "We don't do wireless, which makes this the safest way to do the transfer."

His fingers flew across the full-sized keyboard, easily matching her speed.

And then it hit her. He'd been playing her the entire time. "You're not FBI," she breathed. "You're a goddamn Cyber Command Analyst... aren't you?"

He twisted his hand in the air. "Sorta. I'm a field agent who dabbles in computers. Let's just say I know enough to be dangerous and bridge the two agencies."

She pulled over the cable, hesitating near her FireWire port. She'd made too many mistakes in the past day, and she didn't need them hijacking her machine. Besides, her laptop was a minefield of illegal rootkits, backdoor scripts, and hacker tools—enough to add up to years behind bars if they wanted out of her deal.

As if reading her mind, Reed bent down, glancing at the director in the corner. "Don't worry," he whispered. "I won't do anything except copy a file." He offered his hand. "You have my word."

He was the only person she'd met since her arrest whom she could tolerate, let alone trust. Plus, he'd gone to bat for her, summoning the director from Chicago. If she owed anyone latitude, it was him.

"Fine," she whispered, shaking his hand and plugging in the cable. "But if you stab me in the back, I'll..."

Her words faded as Director Williams spun around. "Go! Do it!"

Alex shook her head. "Do... what?" she stammered, confused by the sudden interruption.

But Agent Reed was already steps ahead. He tapped his computer, and she glanced down at her screen.

There on her desktop was a new target drive she could mount. Somehow, his device had created a virtual drive her laptop instantly recognized.

When she double-clicked the icon, a lone file appeared in the Finder.

```
OpenSaysMe.dat
```

"What is it?" she asked, resisting the urge to view it in her binary editor. At least for now.

"It doesn't matter," Agent Reed said, leaning over to point at her screen. "Copy it to your site. The one your Trojan loads from." He squinted at her scrawled notes on the glass. "You never did say what URL your Trojan was using."

She smirked and copied the file, opening another terminal window to start the transfer.

```
> scp -P 3323 /tmp/OpenSaysMe.dat
root@friendsDontLetFriendsUseEmacs.-
com:/var/www/html/header.jpg
```

Agent Reed watched as she hit enter. "Nice," he chuckled, shaking his head. "You need that URL on a shirt or something."

She lowered her laptop lid, pointing to a sticker on the back with the same URL in camelcase. It was probably a waste of ten dollars a year, but worth it to her. Emacs made her cringe.

"Now what?" Director Williams asked from behind them.

Alex startled, not having heard the woman approach.

"Now we delete my proxy hack and let the loader do its job," she replied, flipping through the terminal windows she'd prepared. She connected to the reverse proxy hosts, pasting in her sequence of commands to clean up her man-in-the-middle process.

She'd prepared this cleanup process for emergencies, but

never imagined executing it in a police station interrogation room during a sanctioned hack for the US government.

"What's that?" Director Williams pointed to scrolling text in the bottom-right terminal.

Alex maximized the window, increasing the font. "That, Director Williams, is the Trojan downloading and executing your payload."

The log repeated, scrolling faster than expected. Whatever the hackers in North Korea were doing, they were opening a lot of terminals.

She made a mental note: next time, load from the URL only once per hour. It was only a matter of time before someone competent noticed the unexpected network traffic.

"Can we tell what they're doing on the other end?" Director Williams asked.

"It doesn't work that way, ma'am," Agent Reed replied. "We only know the payload is being loaded on their machines. After that, we wait."

"For what?" Alex spun around, eyeing the director. "What does your payload do?"

For the first time since her arrival, the director smiled, eyes sparkling mischievously. "That, my dear, is classified."

Classified... that was some shit. After all her sacrifices, after giving them her hack and nearly losing everything, the least they could do was give her a hint. *Am I helping people or hurting them?* The question would gnaw at her.

Alex shook it off and returned to finishing her cleanup. Her priority needed to be deleting her backdoor before they caught wind of it.

At the second-to-last terminal, she did a double take.

There, waiting in the window, was a message.

She'd been hacking since she was eight, yet she'd never seen someone actually use the *write* command. While she'd played with it herself a few times, she'd never imagined a practical use —until now.

Glancing at Agent Reed, she saw him absorbed in his own computer, oblivious to her discovery.

She returned to her screen and read the message:

```
root@redwood2>
Message from root@redwood2.local on ttys000
at 03:58 ...
I see you're still mucking around where you
don't belong N3tN1nja. Wasn't there enough
bloodshed in New York for one night? -
Cipher o
```

The implications of the words swirled in her mind, at first incomprehensible. But then it clicked.

This Cipher person thought she was N3tN1nja, and stranger still, they were accusing her of actions she had no part in. Of killing someone. Of taking a life.

Could the government payload I installed be what they meant? But they said New York, not North Korea.

She recalled the message the other night from N3tN1nja. They'd said they were being hunted, but never said where.

As she reread it, another message appeared:

```
What's wrong? The cat got your tongue? You
know this proxy has been shut down, right?
You won't be gleaning anything useful from
it. Not today. o
```

She puzzled over the "o" at the end until Agent Reed spoke up. He must've noticed her being too quiet and seen her holding her cursor over the misplaced character.

"It means 'over.' He's signaling he's done and waiting for you to reply."

"He?" She glanced at him. "You know who Cipher is?"

Agent Reed shrugged. "It's classified."

She shook her head, frustration bubbling over. "Fuck you and your classified bullshit. This guy said N3tN1nja killed someone. That can't be good."

He studied her closely. "Do you know someone named N3tN1nja?"

She bit her lip, blinking rapidly. "N3tN1nja? No, of course not." Her voice wavered. "I just... Wait, you still didn't answer me. Who is this guy? Who is Cipher?"

He stared into her eyes, his expression unreadable. She couldn't tell if he believed her, but it didn't matter. He wasn't about to answer her question any more than she was ready to tell him the truth.

When she looked back to her screen, another message waited:

```
I'm going to make you and Byt3Linguist pay
for messing with my virus. If it's the last
thing I do. o
```

She didn't wait for Agent Reed to ask again. The heat on her face told her his eyes were still boring into her. He knew she was lying. The question was, what would he do about it?

She typed a reply, as if she were N3tN1nja:

```
> write root@redwood2.local
Go fuck yourself, Cipher! You got what was
coming to you for butchering Nari. If you
know what's good for you, you'll stop
stealing from innocent people.
```

She hit enter before Agent Reed could stop her.

"Who's Nari?" Agent Reed asked, glancing between her and the screen. "What are you not telling us, Alex?"

She shoved him. "What am I not telling you? You're fucking kidding me!" She jabbed him again. "You agents are all alike. Who's N3tN1nja, Agent Reed? You tell me. And what the hell are you having me install? Is that why people are dying?"

He groaned as Director Williams whirled around, eyes wide with alarm. "What happened?"

Not waiting for a reply, she rushed to read Alex's screen. "Shit," she muttered. "Shut it down! Get out of there! Now!"

Alex didn't budge. She wanted answers and was tired of doing their dirty work.

Agent Reed, however, did as he was ordered. He reached past Alex and took over her terminals, typing the commands to wipe her backdoor and reboot the host.

As she watched him enter the final command, she caught Cipher's last message before the connection dropped.

```
There are no innocent people in this world,
N3tN1nja, only pawns in an epic game of
chess. I've got your little Raspberry Pi
toy from the cabinet, and I can't wait to
see what secrets it contains. Something
tells me it'll be a fun side project to
crack. If I were you, I'd sleep with one
eye open, because the reaper is looming in
the darkness, waiting for the perfect
moment to snuff out your pathetic exis-
tence. Until then, it's your move. o

Connection lost...
```

She gasped as the implications hit her. If he meant one of the Raspberry Pis she'd spread about Fremont, then he was back home. Hunting not just her, but possibly her entire family.

Her heart pounded as fear gripped her, squeezing the air from her lungs. Once again, she'd painted a target on her family's back. But this time, they weren't being pursued by a politician, they were being hunted by a predator, hungry for blood.

Without a word, she bolted to the corner of the room, her mind reeling with worst-case scenarios.

She turned, back against the wall, and slid down, watching Agent Reed clean the last machine from afar.

It was all she could do to keep from screaming, to keep the panic at bay.

After he finished, Agent Reed pointed at the screen. He and Director Williams exchanged glances before turning to face her.

Alex spoke first, desperate. "I need my family protected," she blurted out, barely holding it together. "If they found my hardware in California, then my family is right there. He said you've got people dying over this in New York—they're killing people trying to find me."

She pointed at her computer, words failing. "I need to know my family is safe. Please." She slid forward on her knees. "Will you move them? I'm literally begging you."

Director Williams paused, eyes fixed on Alex. After a moment of hesitation, she replied firmly, "No."

"No?" Alex leaned forward. "Seriously? No? I hand you the hack of the century on a golden goddamn platter and you—"

"Hold on, young lady," Director Williams interrupted, reaching toward her.

"Fuck holding on!" Alex blurted out, ready to lash out again.

But she caught Agent Reed's eye behind the director. He was shaking his head, warning her to watch herself.

If she pissed off the director, she might lose her deal.

Alex couldn't take this crap anymore. Any of it.

She'd only hacked the proxy machines to get back at the people who'd stolen from her family. The only family she had. The only thing that mattered.

She didn't ask for any of this espionage shit.

As pent-up emotions overwhelmed her, her body hit a breaking point and her limbs gave way, a wave of exhaustion washing over her.

She couldn't fight anymore; the ache behind her eyes was too much. With no strength left to resist, she did the only thing she could. Curling up into a ball, she tipped over on her side and broke down in tears, her sobs echoing in the stuffy room.

Director Williams stood in shock, staring at Alex for a moment before silently sliding down on the ground beside her. She allowed Alex to cry it out, offering a quiet presence as the emotions flowed freely.

When the sobs subsided, the director spoke. "I said no, not out of malice, but caution. If they're really watching your family, they'd likely move on them as soon as they see us coming. We don't need a sniper or a bomb taking them out. Do we?"

Alex looked up through tear-blurred eyes. "No, ma'am... we don't."

"Based on that message," Director Williams continued, "I don't think they even know who you are. It's probably better if we keep it that way." She nodded. "I'll tell you what I'll do, but first you need to sit up." She gestured upward. "Come on. You can do it."

Alex shuddered as another wave of exhaustion passed

through her. But instead of giving in, she pushed herself up, wiping her eyes with her sleeve.

"There we go." Director Williams smiled and turned to Agent Reed. "Why don't you get us another coffee? You know how I like it."

"Yes, ma'am," he said, exiting the room.

As the door clicked shut, she looked back toward Alex, her eyes serious and strong. "I promise I'll keep an eye on your parents and your aunt. But," she held up a finger.

There was always a but.

"My original rules still stand," the director continued. "If you step out of line, even for a second, my offer is null and void. I'll come down on you with the full power of the US government if you screw me. Not only will your parents be deported, your aunt will do time in the cell next to yours. Is that understood?"

Alex swallowed hard. "That sounds like a threat."

Director Williams shook her head. "It's not a threat, my dear. It's a promise. Now what do you say? Can you keep your mouth shut and your nose out of trouble?"

She bit her lip, realizing she had no other option. "I can," she muttered. "I mean, I will. You know, keep my mouth shut."

Director Williams raised an eyebrow. "And the trouble part?"

"And the trouble part," Alex echoed, her throat catching.

"Good." Director Williams smiled, patting her leg. "Good..."

As they sat in silence, one thing still gnawed at Alex.

"Did I..." Her gaze shifted to her machine. "Did I help you kill someone today?"

"No!" Director Williams blurted out. "Not at all. And while I shouldn't tell you this, I will." She eyed Alex, seemingly weighing her words. "The US government doesn't move fast. When I tell you that today's action was an anomaly, I mean it. We usually play the long game. It's how we work. So no, you didn't kill anyone today. What we have in store for North Korea will take months, maybe years to come to fruition. All you did was help us get a foothold inside that godforsaken country. That's it."

Alex nodded, absorbing the information, but something didn't add up. "What about New York? Cipher mentioned something about bloodshed there."

She studied the woman's response, but her face remained an emotionless mask.

Director Williams looked down at her hands. "All I know is that the situation in Alfred is still developing. Whatever lives Cipher was talking about weren't people on our side, I can promise you that. Anything else I can say is—"

"Classified," Alex interrupted, shaking her head. She was getting tired of that goddamn answer.

"Exactly." Director Willams reached out, resting her hand on Alex's leg. "You did your country a great service today, Ms. Mercer. We won't forget it."

"I hope not," she muttered. "For my family's sake."

Her eyes glazed over as her thoughts shifted to her loved ones. She hoped the director was right, that they were indeed safe. She couldn't bear to imagine the alternative; even the thought made her queasy.

The director had given her one new tidbit of information, though. She'd mentioned Alfred.

While Alex had never heard the name before, she assumed it was a town in New York. Perhaps that's where the elusive N3tN1nja was holed up.

THE FIRST LIGHT of morning crept across campus as streetlamps flickered off one by one, surrendering to the new day. A crisp autumn breeze kicked up, carrying the earthy scent of fallen leaves, a reminder of the changing seasons and the relentless march of time.

As the police cruiser pulled up in front of Mosher-Jordan, Alex's dorm, its brakes screeched into the dawn like a rooster heralding her arrival.

A group of students, likely returning from all-night study sessions or guilt-ridden parties, gathered nearby, their curiosity piqued by the unusual sight of the cruiser. They pointed and stared, their whispers muted by the glass between them.

Alex shuddered, covering her face as she felt their questioning eyes. It wasn't every day a student was dropped off by a cop at dawn. The mundane sounds of campus life seemed to amplify the extraordinary nature of her arrival, a stark contrast to the night's events.

"Here we are," Agent Reed said, putting the cruiser in park. He glanced at her. They'd driven in silence since leaving the station. "Director Williams and I appreciate your help with our bluebird pie."

She smirked. "Great... now I won't be able to use my computer without thinking about baking."

"Speaking of that." He reached into his jacket and pulled out a business card, handing it to her.

It bore a nondescript email and phone number in a monospaced font, reminiscent of an old-school computer terminal.

"What's this?" She glanced at him, then back at the odd offering.

There was no reference to his title or anything related to the government or FBI.

"It's my card. Next time you run into a baking problem, or maybe someday you'll want to become a professional chef"—

he smiled, pointing at the card—"give me a call. We can talk about a job, or at least a referral."

She flipped over the crisp white business card. On the back was a maze-like logo: a simple all black design resembling a labyrinth of sorts. But instead of paths through a maze, intricately arranged circuits formed a microchip, shaped like a shield. There were no superfluous gradients or fonts, just pure geometric precision.

"That number will go right to me." He smiled, eyeing the logo.

She turned the card over again, her fingers tracing the embossed phone number. "Is... this your card for US Cyber Command?"

He shook his head, his gaze fixed on the card. "Not exactly."

Something in his face made her pause. This level of secrecy was weird, even after everything they'd been through.

"What is it then?" she asked, tapping the card against her hand.

"It's... complicated."

"Complicated? It has a name, right? What is it?"

He hesitated, his voice barely above a whisper. "Aegis."

"Aegis," she echoed, the word heavy on her tongue.

"Just do me a favor, will ya? Keep it somewhere safe. And don't share that name with anyone else."

Without waiting for her reply, his attention shifted to the windshield, silence settling between them.

"Sure," she muttered, tucking the card into her pocket. Her eyes lingered on her laptop bag, her mind racing with unasked questions.

In the past forty-eight hours, the simple device cradled inside had both saved and nearly ruined her life many times over. Without it, there was no telling where she'd be now.

Computers were all she knew. They were the one thing

that made her different from everyone else. For once, she was a teacher rather than a student. It felt good to make a difference using the device, even if the legality of her actions was questionable.

"What happens next with our... deal?" She swallowed hard, her mind drifting to the immunity document she'd signed.

"Well..." He glanced in the rearview mirror as the hiss of air brakes from a campus bus echoed in the distance. "While the smoke clears with Director Williams, I'll be liaising on your behalf with the university and Ann Arbor PD. I wasn't entirely honest with you, though."

The knot in her stomach tightened. This was it. They were reneging.

"We actually do have some pull inside your school." He winked. "The director might take another route, but it wouldn't surprise me if she sprinkles some government grants around to make your incident on North Campus disappear. If I were you, I'd keep your nose clean for a while."

She chuckled, fidgeting with her hands. "A long while, I think."

As her pulse returned to normal, she stared out the window. A small gathering of older people lingered nearby, staring and whispering among themselves.

It was unusual seeing middle-aged adults on campus, except during move-in and move-out weeks. These adults were all wearing maize and blue sweaters, like walking billboards for the university.

What was going on? And then it hit her as a smaller group of students walked up beside the adults, matching their gaze and stance.

It was Parents' Weekend, and apparently, she was a surprise feature with her police chaperone.

She fought the urge to flip them off, deciding against it.

Rumors about why she was in this car would be rampant for weeks.

"What about our friend?" she asked, returning her attention to Agent Reed.

"Which one?"

"Sanchez?" She eyed him, searching for any indication they might not respect that part of the deal. She'd helped with the hack, but this loose end remained untied back at the station. Even a hint of her involvement in voter fraud could ruin her life and her family's.

Agent Reed shook his head. "He's got a bigger mess than voter fraud to deal with. The list of charges against him and his daughter is a mile long." He chuckled. "Something tells me he won't be bothering you for a long, long time."

She recoiled. "What the hell else was he into?"

When he glanced back, he simply raised a silent eyebrow.

"Let me guess"—she smirked—"it's classified?"

"Exactly." He hit the unlock button on his door. "You should get going. Just make sure you don't up and attack any more police officers. Alright?"

"I promise." She slid out of the car and spun around, bending over to lean back inside.

"Thank you," she said, kicking at the ground. "You know, for giving me a chance to explain myself, and not being an asshole like Agent Gregor."

"You're welcome." He smiled, a dimple forming on his cheek.

For a split second, his soft gaze reminded her of her father; the warm, comforting look she missed so dearly.

And then he waved her away. "Go! Go get some food and sleep. We'll be in touch."

She nodded and swung the door shut.

As she turned to leave, he rolled the window down and leaned forward. "And, Alex."

She twisted around and bent down. "Yeah."

"N3tN1nja wanted me to thank you for not selling them out to the director." He winked, a knowing glance passing between them. "They also wanted you to know they were safe. They'll be lying low for a while, but they said they'd reach out... in time."

His cryptic smile revealed volumes as he slowly drove away.

She bolted upright, frozen in place, watching him disappear around the corner. Her mind raced. *How'd he know N3tN1nja? When had he contacted them?*

Lost in thought, she missed the footsteps approaching behind her.

"Do I have to ask why my niece is getting out of a cop car?" Aunt Min asked.

Alex spun around, nearly flinging her bag off her shoulder. "What the... how'd you...?"

She lurched forward, throwing her arms around her aunt, almost bowling her over.

Until that moment, she hadn't realized the weight of not calling her family from the station. The uncertainty of their safety had pressed heavier on her psyche than she'd imagined.

Seeing her aunt unleashed a flood of emotions. Her pent-up feelings overwhelmed her senses as she broke down into a sniveling mess of choking sobs, trembling limbs, and unbridled joy.

24 / SECRETS IN THE PI
CIPHER

Ever since his message to N3tN1nja had failed to elicit a response, Cipher and his team had been on the move. He'd hoped to provoke the hacker, to goad them into revealing something, anything, that could lead to their location. But N3tN1nja had proven too clever, too cautious to take the bait.

Now they found themselves navigating nearly a thousand miles of poorly maintained backcountry roads that made even North Korea's infrastructure seem modern. And they'd done it all in the name of avoiding detection, knowing full well that capture wasn't an option.

But based on the gastrointestinal rebellion currently raging in his gut, Cipher wasn't so sure it was worth it. Any of the three questionable rest stops they'd visited along the way could've done him in. Then there was the fat man's phone he'd swiped; he hadn't exactly had time to sterilize it before messaging Rajesh about their change in plans.

His stomach gurgled as sweat trickled down his back. He shifted uncomfortably in the unpadded backseat. The Memphis heat combined with unrelenting humidity was practically boiling the car, especially with the AC off. The thought of another eighteen hours to Miami was excruciating.

Glancing around the trash-strewn backseat, he hoped to find some water. Instead, all he came up with was a half-empty case of warm soda. The last thing his roiling stomach could handle was more sugar. They'd eaten enough questionable roadside cuisine for a lifetime. If he had to choke down one more overcooked gas station snack, he'd hurl. He still didn't understand why they called them hot dogs when they tasted like rat—a noxious dish he'd had the misfortune of sampling many times over the years.

He adjusted the laptop, his lower back screaming in protest. After three days crammed in a rolling trashcan, even a freighter back to North Korea seemed appealing. The salty ocean air couldn't be worse than the miasma of body odor he'd endured for the past four days.

As the spotty Wi-Fi reconnected, he watched a stream of lemmings flow into the coffee shop. Maybe it was his stench, his bloodshot eyes, or the fact that he hadn't slept in days, but he couldn't fathom living in a place like this. Day in and day out, nothing but mindless consumerism. Their lives had no meaning beyond drowning out their pain with an endless stream of social media.

When his connection finally stabilized, he averted his gaze from a trio of chipper cheerleaders sipping overpriced pink drinks. Refreshing his open web pages, he smirked. While their situation in New York was still being suppressed by the mainstream American news outlets, splinter blogs and chat rooms buzzed with activity.

Some claimed a serial killer was on the loose, striking as recently as that morning. Others simply shared facts, letting readers craft their own headlines. One piece of footage was particularly haunting: a video of the burning bell tower, framed against the backdrop of a hazy full moon.

Crowds swarmed around the ancient tower, transforming the somber scene into a macabre carnival. The antique structure had burned for nearly twenty-four hours. The superheated bells collapsed in on the structure, leaving nothing but ash for analysis after the blaze ran its course.

The same night, police were dispatched to a nearby petrol station where a woman's body was discovered. Though acid had obliterated her face and hands, he felt a chill of recognition when he saw the picture. The shape, the hair; they reminded him of Choe.

He glanced at his hands, recalling the sensation of her mouth enveloping his fingers as he took her from behind. A grin played on his lips as he replayed the memory, imagining her there again. She may have been planted in his life to manipulate him into doing Pyongyang's bidding, but that didn't mean they hadn't enjoyed themselves. It was an emotion he hadn't experienced since Bosnia.

Lost in reverie, he almost missed the flash of the cell phone under the seat. Its screen flickered to life as a call came through. Though he couldn't risk answering, he palmed the device, confirming the caller.

Rajesh's number appeared, then vanished. One missed call.

That was the signal. He was ready. The transfer was complete.

Just as Cipher was about to crack the device in half, his computer chimed with an incoming message.

He opened the window and read:

> **KI-SUNG**
>
> Mission compromised. N3tN1nja knew we were coming. Barely escaped. Need extraction.

He stared at the text, his mind reeling. He had no idea

who Ki-Sung was, but if they had indeed escaped the attack out east, she might have seen N3tN1nja. The prospect of finally putting a face to the name was enough to push him to break protocol.

He typed out a response:

ANONYMOUS

Prove it. I don't even know who you are.

Ki-Sung's reply was swift:

KI-SUNG

I know what you have planned in Florida. Want to keep it that way? Then get your ass up here.

Something in her tone, that sharp edge, it sparked a memory of Choe. But he shoved the thought aside. He had no idea how she'd found out about Rajesh, but he couldn't risk her talking to his handlers.

As he considered the extraction, something nagged at him:

ANONYMOUS

How do we know N3tN1nja didn't let you go? Picking you up could be a trap.

This time, her reply lagged. The typing indicator flickered on and off several times before her message appeared:

KI-SUNG

Saw them send a message after burning Eun-kyung's face off. They weren't sticking around. Besides, I've been heading south on foot for the past day. I would've spotted a tail.

Ki-Sung's mention of the message sparked a sudden realization. The Raspberry Pi he'd swiped in Fremont was still unexamined—it might hold the key to unraveling this mystery. Of finding N3tN1nja.

He rapped his hand on the glass, making Tae-Woo jump at the unexpected sound.

Yanking the car door open, Tae-Woo snapped, "What?"

Cipher glared at him. "Where's that Raspberry Pi? The one I stole from the old lady's house."

Tae-Woo's brow furrowed as he tried to recall. He nodded toward the rear of the car. "I think it's in the trunk with the gear. If not, then it's back in Oakland."

"Get it. Now!" Cipher growled, his patience wearing thin.

They better not have fucking left it in Cali. Every wasted second gave N3tN1nja and Byt3Linguist more time to vanish.

Tae-Woo scrambled to comply, moving to the trunk with muttered curses. Moments later, he tossed a fragile plastic enclosure through the open window.

"That it?"

Cipher snatched the device, turning it over in his hand.

"Yes," he breathed, his heart racing with anticipation.

If the little box held what he hoped, it could be the key to tracking down the elusive hackers who'd caused him so much grief.

With renewed purpose, he clutched the Raspberry Pi. His mind buzzed with possibilities. It was the break he'd been waiting for. He could feel it.

He wouldn't rest until he'd extracted every last byte of data hidden within the tiny device.

25 / TRUST FALL
ALEX

They made their way from the coffee shop toward the Diag, the heart of Central Campus. On any other day, it would be bustling with students between classes, playing frisbee, or lounging with books, but today it was dotted with an unusual number of over-thirty-year-olds in maize and blue.

For a November afternoon in Michigan, the weather was surprisingly balmy. She could hardly believe that just twelve hours earlier, Director Williams had been drenched in a wintry mix of sleet and snow.

The sky was a crisp, clear blue, with wispy clouds drifting lazily overhead. Even with the breeze whipping the last remains of the fall leaves through the Diag, Alex found herself enjoying the unexpected warmth.

Maybe it was the coffee, or the occasional uncomfortable glances from her fellow students, but she was sweating in her jacket. She shrugged it off, draping it over her arm as they strolled down the sidewalk.

"Why don't we sit?" Aunt Min gestured toward a cement bench near the Diag's bronze Block M.

Alex nodded, words failing her. The last thirty minutes

had been overwhelming; she'd barely spoken since her breakdown in front of the residence hall.

Sipping her Americano, her thoughts drifted to the legend of The Block M emblazoned on the ground before them. Lore said that if a freshman stepped on the M before their first bluebook exam, they'd fail said exam.

She was pretty sure every campus had crazy legends, but she couldn't help wondering if this one held some truth. While she hadn't taken her first bluebook yet, things weren't exactly going her way. And unlike most students who avoided the aging emblem, she'd stepped on that spot many times.

The legend continued, saying that if a student ran naked at the stroke of midnight from Burton Memorial Tower to the stone pumas at the U of M Natural History Museum, the curse would be lifted. But they had to do it before the tower bells stopped ringing.

Alex shook her head, imagining the run. She could barely picture herself in a swimsuit outdoors, let alone streaking.

Besides, the only tower that still rang bells was on North Campus. Burton Tower had long been silenced.

Aunt Min leaned forward, meeting Alex's eyes still fixed on The Block M. "Where are you right now? You haven't said a word since we started walking."

She stared at her cup, cheeks burning. "Running naked... through the Diag," she muttered.

Aunt Min eased back, a mischievous grin spreading. "That's not even *close* to what I thought you'd say."

They both burst into laughter, the sound ringing out in the crisp autumn air.

The laughter felt good. She couldn't remember when she'd last let go like this, her worries temporarily lifted.

"I miss this," she smiled at her aunt. "Just sitting and talking with you."

"Me too." Aunt Min squeezed her knee.

As Alex sipped her coffee, her aunt watched silently, studying her. She knew something was bothering Alex. She was just waiting for her to speak first.

A family member doesn't simply exit a cop car without a story to tell.

"You're probably still wondering about that police drop-off." Alex bit her lip.

"Ya think?"

Alex raised an eyebrow. "Well, the thing is, he wasn't actually a cop."

"Are you sure?" Aunt Min screwed up her face. "Did he know his car had a *Michigan Police* emblem on the side?"

"He was FBI." Alex lowered her gaze, bracing for the reaction.

But it never came.

She looked up to find her aunt staring in stunned silence, eyes wide with disbelief.

"FBI?" Aunt Min whispered, her voice trembling. "What have you gotten yourself into?"

She saw the worry etched in her aunt's features, the fear for her niece's safety. Guilt panged through her, but she knew she had to explain. She owed her as much for all she'd done for her.

"It's fine." She reached out, this time squeezing her aunt's hand reassuringly. "They originally arrested me for attempted voter fraud. And... assaulting an officer. Oh, and I may have stolen his gun." She cringed, seeing the alarm flash across her aunt's face. "But the cop wasn't my fault. I was freaked out, and he cornered me."

Aunt Min's free hand flew to her mouth, eyes glistening with worry.

"Oh, Alex," she breathed. "I can't imagine what you went through."

Alex took a deep breath, recalling the overwhelming fear

that had gripped her at the station. She'd almost forgotten why she'd done what she'd done.

"They tried to break me during the interrogation. Made me question everything. To be honest, I almost gave in, but then I realized I had something they needed. Something irresistible." She swallowed hard, eyes locking on her aunt. "I offered them the virus. The one I'd cracked here at school. I knew it was a gamble, but... it paid off."

Her aunt simply stared, her face a mask of concern.

Alex knew her story sounded far-fetched. She could only imagine what her aunt must be thinking.

"Alex, honey," her aunt began softly. "I'm sure you did what you had to. But... I'm not following. I'm sorry. Can you just... start from the beginning?"

Alex nodded, swallowing down the lump in her throat. "I... I can do that."

Over the next hour, she recounted her hunt for the Reveton hackers, how she'd convinced the professor to let her take the networking class, and how she'd figured out how the virus phoned home using the reverse proxy. She held nothing back.

As the words tumbled out, she became increasingly aware of her aunt's keen understanding. She nodded along with technical details as if they were second nature. At one point, Alex swore she even heard her mutter "*Red Star*," the name of the North Korean operating system.

It was a side of her aunt she'd never seen, a depth of knowledge hinting at an unknown past. One kept hidden. Alex wondered exactly what her aunt did for a living.

Having brought her aunt up to speed on Reveton, Alex paused, gathering her thoughts before delving into the recent events that had upended her world.

Finally, she switched to the Sanchez debacle. She recounted how his daughter had reached out the other day, asking her to hack into a voting machine, and how N3tN1nja had helped her crack it open.

She explained her motivations: the overwhelming fear of not being able to pay for college, of abandoning her dreams. The Sanchezes' ability to harm her family had forced her hand. They'd worked too hard to let that evil family take them down.

Throughout her story, Alex teetered on the edge of breaking down. Tears choked her words, but she didn't falter. She pushed past the tremor in her voice, letting it all out.

She finished with the incident at the school lab.

"I... I messed up. I was terrified. I thought they were the North Korean hackers coming for me. That's when I struck the cop." Alex swallowed hard, staring at a family posing near The Block M. Even the parents skirted the mystical object, as if it might somehow transfer a curse to their child.

"What made you think they were from North Korea?" Aunt Min asked, her eyes hinting at something more. Something guarded.

"It's the only country that uses *Red Star*," Alex replied, now questioning what she thought she'd heard earlier. Maybe her aunt hadn't whispered those words after all.

But then something changed. Her aunt stiffened. The tears she'd been holding back suddenly evaporated, replaced by steely resolve. A hardness settled over her features, a look Alex had never seen before.

"I promised your mother long ago that I'd protect you." Aunt Min stared at her, fierce determination burning in her eyes. "I told her I'd keep you safe... no matter what. That you'd be taken care of, even if it meant dealing with the likes of Sanchez." She looked down, her hands trembling slightly, the only hint of suppressed emotions.

"Wait..." Alex drew in a sharp breath. "My mom knows? About Sanchez?"

She glanced around, half expecting her mother to materialize from the crowd.

The idea of her parents learning about the Sanchez incident had never occurred to her. *What must they think of me now, especially after I told them about nearly killing my first adoptive father?*

Her world was rapidly unraveling.

"Shit," she muttered, hand over her mouth. "Why did you tell—"

"No, no." Aunt Min set her coffee down and slid closer, their knees touching. "Not Soo-yeon, not my sister." She hesitated, then met Alex's gaze. With a shaky breath, she spoke softly. "I'm talking about your biological mother, Evelyn. Evelyn Rose Donovan."

The air rushed from Alex's lungs, her mind reeling. She'd never heard her biological mother's name before, had never even imagined that someone knew it.

She always assumed the Mercers knew nothing of her birth parents, but she'd never asked. They'd given her up for a reason, so to her, there was no point in opening that door.

But the fact that her aunt knew her mother's name, that she'd concealed it all these years, felt like a betrayal. A secret kept, a piece of her identity withheld.

But something was off about her aunt's words. Something didn't make sense.

"You said you told her you'd take care of me." Alex slid back, clenching her trembling hands in her lap. "What did you mean?"

Aunt Min wrestled with her response, caught between having revealed too much and now being compelled to divulge even more. Alex braced for a retreat. Instead, her aunt sighed heavily and spoke, her voice low and measured.

"When I was young, I was a bit of a troublemaker." Aunt Min smirked and closed her eyes, as if recounting a tale she'd long ago suppressed. "My family thought I'd never amount to much. That I'd never be as successful as my sister. And for a while, they weren't wrong."

She opened her eyes, staring at her hands. "I've certainly done my share of bad things to good people over the years, and I regret every minute. But it made me who I am. In my late twenties, I changed. I turned over a new leaf. In '94, I joined CARE International and headed to Bosnia and Herzegovina."

Her eyes glistened, sadness etching her face. "It was the first time in my life I truly felt like I was making a difference. There was so much bloodshed over there, so many displaced women and girls. We were their lifeline, their hope in a world torn apart by war. Every day was a battle, but we cherished every small win."

"That was when I crossed paths with your mother." Aunt Min smiled, and a warmth blossomed in Alex's chest. "Evelyn came to Bosnia with the International Rescue Committee, the IRC."

Alex leaned forward, eyes wide. "The... IRC," she muttered, realization suddenly dawning. "I knew I remembered those letters from somewhere. When I found that chat app on my first adoptive father's computer, it reminded me of something I'd seen when I was little. I just... never knew where."

An uncomfortable silence passed before Alex spoke again. "How... did you meet?" she asked, words fighting through the knot in her throat.

Aunt Min's eyes grew distant. "We met after the Tuzla bombings in '95. She was there within an hour of the attack." Her aunt trembled. "There was so much death. Kids. Entire families, ravaged by the senseless violence. The attacks scarred the city, the people. But your mom, she was a force of nature. She brought light to the darkest places. Watching her in action was like witnessing courage personified. After that, she and I became inseparable. I followed her everywhere, no matter how dangerous. And trust me, she got us into some seriously fucked up situations."

She wiped her eyes, smiling through bittersweet memories. "But everything we did was for hope. For healing the wounds that humans inflict on one another. One moment, we can be evil incarnate, in another, the very embodiment of compassion. But not your mother. She was a constant beacon of light, unwavering in her dedication to helping others."

Aunt Min's voice softened, filled with admiration and longing. "And then she met your father. That's when everything changed. I don't know how he did it, but he squelched that fire within her. He drew her into a darker world. A place where fear and revenge ruled. He nearly extinguished her light. He consumed her, body and soul, almost killing the woman I knew. The woman I loved."

Alex reached out, but she gently pushed her hand away. "No. I need... I need to finish this." She went to wipe her eyes but decided against it, letting the tears flow freely, as if purging herself of the pain and memories.

"What happened to her?" Alex asked. "To my mother."

"You happened." Aunt Min smiled through her tears. "When you were born, she found her strength again. You reignited the woman she used to be, the fierce, compassionate soul I'd always known. She fought to shield you from the darkness, and she almost won. But after three years, she realized she was in too deep with your father. His hold was too strong, and he wouldn't let her go. That's when she asked me to protect you. To take you away from him, to keep you safe. No matter the cost."

Alex found herself crying, sliding closer to her aunt. But this time, she didn't push her away. She let Alex ease up and wrap an arm around her.

They sat in silence amidst hundreds of strangers, an island

of stillness in the bustling current of passing families, each lost in their own thoughts.

Minutes passed, the weight of the revelations hanging thick in the air.

"May I ask you another question?" Alex asked, hoping her aunt wouldn't object.

She silently nodded.

Alex bit her lip, gathering her courage. The question had been fighting to break free since her aunt finished talking.

"If my mom wanted you to keep me safe, then... what happened? How did I end up in an orphanage?"

"My life caught up with me," Aunt Min began, frustration tinging her voice. "Like I said, I was an epic screwup before leaving South Korea. When I got back, no one believed I'd changed. In fact, some of my family even thought I'd kidnapped you. But not my sister. She always believed in me, even when others didn't."

She shook her head, hands trembling. "A month after I returned home, the police raided my flat. Not only did they find all sorts of illicit shit from before I'd found myself, they took you. Shipped you right back to America—your mother's homeland—like some twisted form of justice."

Aunt Min stood abruptly, taking a few steps away. When she turned, tears streamed down her cheeks, and she could hardly hold eye contact. "I tried to fight, I swear I did! I begged them to let you stay in Korea, to place you with Soo-yeon. But no one would listen. You have to believe me. I never wanted you to get hurt. I'm so sorry, Alex."

Her voice cracked, guilt and regret threatening to crush her. She buried her face in her hands, her shoulders shaking with silent sobs.

Alex slid off the bench and stepped in front of her, pulling her aunt's hands down to meet her gaze. "I believe you. I do."

She wrapped her arms around her aunt, squeezing tight, pouring all her love and forgiveness into the embrace.

Aunt Min squeezed back. "I've done some bad things in my life," she whispered. "I hurt a lot of people before I changed. Before your mom. She showed me a different path, a better way to live."

She pulled back slightly, meeting Alex's eyes. "But there's something else you should know. Your mom—Soo-yeon—she never gave up on me. Even when I was at my lowest, she believed in my innocence. She knew about you, about everything. When they took you away..." Her voice caught. "She made it her mission to find you."

Alex's heart stuttered. "What do you mean?"

"She and Jin-woo, they'd always dreamed of coming to America. But after learning what happened to you, that dream became an obsession. They spent years fighting for work visas and citizenship, jumping through every hoop, taking any job they could find." Aunt Min's lips quivered into a smile. "All so they could find you, keep you in our family. They knew how losing you had broken me."

Tears welled in Alex's eyes as pieces of her past clicked into place. "They never told me..."

"They wouldn't. They're too humble." Aunt Min brushed a tear from Alex's cheek. "But they moved heaven and earth to adopt you. They knew how special you were, not just to me, but to all of us. And you, Alex..." She squeezed Alex's shoulders. "You gave me a reason to keep following that better path, to become someone worthy of the faith my sister always had in me."

"Why don't we go back to your hotel?" Alex suggested, suddenly aware of the curious glances from passersby. Their looks felt like intrusions on this intimate moment.

It wasn't every day people saw two women crying in the

Diag of a major university. Even less often during Parents Weekend.

Fifteen minutes later, they were resting in Aunt Min's freshly cleaned room at the Bell Tower Hotel. A fitting name, considering how her aunt had bared her soul, exposing the raw truth of her past like a naked run through the Diag.

In a way, it was like stepping on The Block M, a mistake needing rectification. But instead of a superstitious ritual, her aunt's confession had been a cathartic release, a bell ringing to signal a new beginning for both of them.

Alex lay on the couch, staring at the intricate fretwork on the ceiling while her aunt faced away on the bed. Neither had spoken since leaving the Diag.

Though there was no tension between them, Alex couldn't help but feel confused. So much about how she defined herself was tied to her adoptions and the Mercers. Her bottled-up feelings, her worldview, even her trust issues—all traced back to her troubled past.

But now, Aunt Min had thrown another log on the fire, this one doused with kerosene. Her mother hadn't simply abandoned her like she thought; she'd sent her away for protection.

The idea of giving up a child was hard enough, but sending away your baby, the tiny human you loved more than anything, all because of your situation—that was a sacrifice beyond comprehension. It spoke of a love so deep, so selfless, that it would endure the pain of separation for the safety of the child.

She ran her hands over her face, trying to comprehend the bombshells that had upended everything she thought she knew. Her mother's love, her father's darkness, and her aunt's unwavering commitment swirled in her head.

But after forty-eight sleepless hours, her mind reeled, unable to process the emotional upheaval.

When she closed her eyes, she heard the freshly laundered sheets rustle as her aunt rolled to face her.

"Once I got out, I tried to find you," Aunt Min began. "It consumed me. I spent everything I had and countless days and nights. Every waking moment I wasn't fixing myself, I was searching for you. I even... resorted to reaching out to some of my seedier contacts from my past. It wasn't pretty, but they helped more than the system did."

Alex turned. Aunt Min's face was framed perfectly in the afternoon sunlight coming in through the window. She was a picture of serenity. The lines of worry and guilt had smoothed away, as if the catharsis of confession had brought her peace.

A smile tugged at Aunt Min's mouth. "Sometimes the doors you need opened most need a swift kick rather than a key."

Alex smirked, letting the words sink in. Their meaning resonated with her approach to life's problems. Better a sledgehammer than a lock pick, indeed.

"How'd you find me?" Alex asked, the question bubbling up.

As Aunt Min began to answer, her phone rang on the bedside table. At first, Alex thought it might be her parents, but when her aunt checked the screen, her face darkened. Whoever it was, she wasn't happy to see their name.

She stood abruptly, heading for the door. "I need to take this," she muttered, stepping into the hall.

When the door clicked shut, Alex sat up, listening to her aunt's voice fade down the corridor.

Part of her wanted to know who it was, but another part held back. She'd built a life in America; for all she knew, it could be her aunt's boss. No one likes an unexpected work call, especially on vacation.

Rather than risk snooping, she pulled out her laptop. She hadn't checked her email in over a day. The last time she was on her machine, she'd been focused on Reveton.

She was surprised the FBI had let her keep her computer. Agent Reed probably could have confiscated it as evidence, but didn't. Her phone, though, he'd locked up tight. She wondered if his alluding to knowing N3tN1nja had anything to do with not seizing her laptop.

After logging in and connecting to the hotel Wi-Fi, her emails and messages flooded in. There were so many, she didn't know where to start.

Messages from classmates, professors, and complete strangers, all curious about recent events. Someone had filmed her being hauled away in handcuffs outside the Francois-Xavier Building, her face a mask of confusion.

"My God I look like shit," she muttered, running her hands through her hair. A shower suddenly seemed imperative.

She opened Michelle's emails next and started scrolling through them. There were nearly two dozen, each more dire than the last. Michelle was freaking out.

Popping open the last message, Alex typed a reply, assuring Michelle she was alright and would swing by for clothes soon. Just as she was about to hit send, a new message notification slid in.

It would have been lost among hundreds had she not caught the sender's name: N3tN1nja.

She clicked off the email filter and selected the message. The content appeared:

To: Little Bird
From: N3tN1nja
Subject: RED ALERT - CIPHER IS COMING FOR YOU!

L3x1c0n, you're in grave danger. Cipher has discovered your location through means I can't fathom. He's on his way to your school right now, and he'll stop at nothing to get you. Contact Agent Reed IMMEDIATELY! He's the only one who can keep you safe. Anyone else could be compromised. This is a matter of life or death. Drop everything and RUN!

Her heart raced as she read the message again and again. This couldn't be happening. Not here. Not now.

She'd been so careful covering her tracks. The only explanation was betrayal. Someone close had been feeding information to Cipher.

The list of suspects was short: Agent Reed, Michelle, and Aunt Min. They were the only ones who knew anything about her situation, though Michelle only knew surface details about the virus. Either she played dumb exceptionally well, or she was innocent.

That left her aunt and Agent Reed. But N3tN1nja had pushed her toward him, saying he was the only one she could trust.

While that made sense initially, what if N3tN1nja wasn't actually N3tN1nja? Or worse, what if they were part of Cipher's team?

"Shit, shit, shit," she muttered, standing up and pacing around the room.

She was lost, unsure who to trust. There were too many unknowns and not enough facts.

Glancing back at her half-composed email to Michelle, she second-guessed sending it at all.

Just as she clicked cancel, the door swung open and Aunt Min walked in, smiling, then faltering as she saw Alex hunched over the laptop.

"Is... everything alright?" Aunt Min asked, eyeing her curiously.

Alex stood frozen, trying to make sense of the situation, deciding who she could trust. The weight of the decision pressed down, making it hard to breathe.

N3tN1nja's warning echoed in her mind: trust no one. But her heart pulled her in a different direction.

"Alex, what is it?"

As Aunt Min stepped closer, Alex flinched, quickly slapping the lid on her laptop closed.

This was too much. The fear of choosing, of putting her life in the wrong hands, paralyzed her. She felt like she was on the edge of a cliff, one misstep from the abyss.

But in that moment of desperation, clarity washed over her like a gentle breeze clearing away the fog.

After everything they'd shared, after all the bonds they'd forged, there was one person she could count on. One person who'd always been there, even in the darkest of times.

Her Aunt Min.

Taking a deep breath, Alex met her aunt's concerned gaze. "I can't do this alone," she said, her voice shaking but determined. "I need you to trust me, and I need to trust you. Because right now, you're the only person I know I can rely on."

"Absolutely!" her aunt replied. "What is it? What do you need?"

Alex hesitated for a split second, but knew she couldn't face this alone. Not again. Not after last time.

She flipped open her laptop, entered her password, and spun the screen around.

Aunt Min scanned the message, her eyes pausing. It was subtle, but it was there. She recognized something.

"What is it?" Alex asked, glancing between the screen and her aunt. "What did you see?"

Aunt Min sank onto the bed, pointing at the screen. "Cipher, is that... the person who made the virus?"

Alex stared, confusion clouding her thoughts. It took her a few seconds to replay everything she'd told her aunt. But then it hit her. In all her storytelling, she'd only spoken about hackers from North Korea. She'd never once mentioned Cipher. Hell, she'd only recently learned the name herself from N3tN1nja's message.

"That's the name they used," Alex said. "Lots of hackers use strange handles."

Aunt Min stared at the screen, her face draining of color. "In all the places in all the world, I've only met one person who used the handle Cipher." She glanced at Alex, fear etched into her features. "And that was a bad person. A very bad person."

"You know Cipher?" Alex whispered. "How?"

"How, doesn't matter." Aunt Min shot up and slammed the laptop closed. "Do you have that business card? The one Agent Reed gave you?"

A chill ran down Alex's spine. "Yeah, right here." She reached into her pocket and pulled it out.

"Call him. Now!"

Her aunt nudged her toward the bedside phone, her eyes darting toward the window as if expecting danger to materialize at any moment.

As Alex picked up the phone, she knew she'd made the

right choice. If her aunt had been working against her, she wouldn't urge her to contact the FBI.

When she typed the last digit of the number, the phone made a strange clicking sound and a voice came on immediately, without ringing.

"Hello," Agent Reed said, sounding shocked. "Who is this?"

"It's Alex. I need your help."

"Alex? How did you...? Never mind, I was just trying to call you when I realized I still had your phone. You need to get somewhere safe."

"I know," she muttered. "Cipher... he's coming for me."

Saying it aloud sent a shiver down her spine, making the threat feel all too real.

"Wait, how did you—"

"It doesn't matter," she interrupted. "Where should I go?"

There was a brief pause on the other end of the line, and Alex could almost hear the gears turning in Agent Reed's head as he formulated a plan.

26 / SOCIAL ENGINEERING
CIPHER

After finally getting his hands on the Raspberry Pi he'd stolen in Fremont, Cipher uncovered a goldmine of information. It revealed not just the name of one of his hacker targets, but their location: Ann Arbor, Michigan.

It took several painstaking hours, but the device proved invaluable. While his hacker adversaries had cleaned up most of their tracks, they'd missed some key configuration files and local data caches. The sheer volume of breadcrumbs littering most computers was astonishing, and the average user was blind to them. After his discovery, it only took a few minutes to extract the identity of his target.

Once he informed General Tau of his find, Tae-Woo and his partner sped toward their new destination, abandoning earlier speed constraints. The general even mobilized their other covert assets on the ground to aid in the hunt and to help retrieve Ki-Sung.

Their first encounter with her had left Cipher reeling, she was Choe's twin sister, a detail the nomenklatura had carefully hidden from him. Seeing her had awakened something he thought long dead: an urge to embrace her, to feel a connection he hadn't realized he'd developed with Choe. But Ki-Sung was ice to her sister's fire. Where Choe had played her role as his secret lover perfectly, Ki-Sung remained coldly professional, every inch the trained assassin. The general had hidden more than just their relationship; the sisters had been molded into killers together, another secret kept from him by his puppetmasters.

Now, eight hours later, Cipher stood in a dusty hallway of the University of Michigan College of Engineering. He waited patiently for one of the IT offices to open, preparing to social engineer his way to the target. A skill he hadn't used in quite some time—and one that felt almost foreign now.

The torture and ruthless leadership required in Pyongyang was a far cry from the subtle manipulation needed to extract information from unsuspecting college students.

Entering the lobby of the short, squat building, Cipher noted how the aged structure seemed out of place among its modern glass neighbors. But its style hardly mattered; computer nerds rarely saw daylight anyway.

He'd pinpointed this location using the VPN configurations he'd recovered from the Raspberry Pi. A reverse lookup on the DNS records with the registrar had led him here, to this address.

While N3tN1nja had wiped most of the logs, they'd neglected to delete the device's remote allow-list, which kept track of which hosts they could login from. Either they were getting soft or had made a crucial mistake. Their loss, his gain.

They'd set up several inbound machines on the college network and a few others around town, similar to what they'd done in Fremont. But this time, he didn't expect to find a Raspberry Pi in a cabinet. He wanted a real, breathing person.

The prospect of ending his arch-enemy in this scholarly atmosphere made his heart sing. Schools like this were the epitome of American conceit. The sprawling campuses, ivy-covered walls, and grand buildings—all monuments to the country's self-proclaimed intellectual superiority. But they were nothing more than a facade hiding rot and decay. And he was here to rip that disguise off.

He felt his vision coalescing. Every moment had led to this: the subway bombing, his attack in South Korea, the fortuitous meeting with the general. His virus had guided him to this citadel of American ego, where he'd finally confront those who dared challenge him.

With his mind deep in thought, strategizing his next moves, he almost missed the group of twenty-somethings approaching to unlock the office.

"Excuse me," he said, raising a hand. "Do you work here?" He gestured toward the door labeled CAEN, Computer Aided Engineering Network.

The pimple-faced student leading the bunch spoke first. "We do." He eyed Cipher, looking him up and down. "Are you a... professor?"

"Oh my, no. I could never muster the confidence to teach, let alone here." Cipher gestured around. "This college is well out of *my* league. No, I'm just looking for a student." He flipped opened his laptop to a picture of Alex.

The student leaned in, studying the image. "We're not equipped to do visual lookups."

"That's fine, I have her name. I was hoping you could tell me where she might be." Cipher scrolled down, revealing her name.

"Is she your daughter?" a girl asked, stepping out from behind the boy.

"No, but—"

"Her uncle?" she interrupted, eyeing him suspiciously.

He paused, slowly shaking his head. "Nope."

"Police?" the boy asked.

Cipher reached into his pocket, pulling out a stack of hundred-dollar bills. Enough for each of them to have several.

As he offered them to the girl, she recoiled. "I don't know what sick game you're playing, mister, but you have twenty seconds to hit the road before I call the cops."

The boy, however, didn't hesitate. He reached for his phone. By the time he launched the camera app, Cipher was already exiting stage left.

He couldn't risk drawing attention, not now, not when he was so close. While normally he would have drawn his gun, it was too soon for that. This was only his first attempt to locate his prey.

He wasn't worried about a dead end; they had other ways to find her. They were nothing if not adaptable, and he'd come too far to let a couple of self-righteous college kids stand in his way.

Slipping out the side door, he sprinted across the street, his mind racing, calculating his next move. Hopefully, Ki-Sung was making better progress.

One way or another, he'd get what he came for. And when he did, N3tN1nja and Byt3Linguist would finally learn the true meaning of consequences.

27 / SEOUL SEARCHING
ALEX

When they arrived at the nondescript building on the outskirts of North Campus, Alex thought the driver of the unmarked SUV had made a mistake.

Peering out the tinted windows, she couldn't help but see the building for what it was, a newly-constructed warehouse with loading bays on the side. There was no sign of federal or local law enforcement vehicles, no signage, nor anything that made it stand out.

The building was downright ordinary, its only hint of character an artistic blue and black glass facade covering most of the front. The abstract design rippled with the changing light, adding a touch of modern flair to the otherwise utilitarian structure.

The effect was clearly just glass layered over brick, giving the building a sleek, contemporary feel. Gone were the days of gaudy construction in an upscale town like Ann Arbor. Even warehouses needed to be presentable.

She tried calling Agent Reed from the SUV, but his phone went straight to voicemail. Rather than sit outside and wait, she and Aunt Min headed in. Worst case, they'd call a taxi if the driver left.

Stepping through the front doors and into the waiting area, she knew right away they were in the right place. Tucked up in two of the four corners were strange-looking camera turrets covered with other peculiar sensors. They made you question the apparent lack of security on the outside of the building.

But that wasn't what caught her eye. There, etched into the surface of the inner door, was the microchip shield logo from Agent Reed's business card. The logo for Aegis.

They'd walked into a secret US Cyber Command facility.

At first, she was unsure how to proceed. There was no receptionist or call button to get someone's attention. But within seconds of their arrival, the inner door swung open.

Standing in the entryway was a woman in a simple blue business suit with short, cropped hair. She was the type of person you'd have a hard time recollecting if asked. And continuing with the mystique of the encounter, she didn't say a word. She simply motioned for them to follow, escorting them down a blindingly sterile white hallway.

After a few turns, she directed them to an open door. Alex hesitated, but Aunt Min urged her forward.

They were well past the point of return now.

Inside was another stark white room, as featureless as the halls they'd passed through.

The far wall was covered in mirrored glass, flanked by four black, curvy lounge chairs that looked oddly comfortable.

The room was unnerving. When the door clicked shut, Alex spun around, a shudder passing through her. The agent had vanished, and for all she knew, they were locked in.

Alex's mind raced with possibilities, each more terrifying than the last.

What if this was all a ruse, a trap set by Cipher to lure us in? What if we were just pawns, sacrificial pieces in a larger game?

"Is it me, or does this place smell like lemon Febreze?" Aunt Min pressed her finger against the reflective wall, confirming it was two-way glass.

Alex eyed the ventilation overhead. "They probably pump it through the ducts. I read that lemon's supposed to increase concentration and have calming effects."

Her aunt chuckled, crossing her arms. "I could use some of that right now."

That made two of them.

A sudden wave of exhaustion washed over her, sending Alex collapsing down into an awaiting lounge chair. Her body slowly sank into the plush leather, and she sighed. The stress of the last day melted away like ice in the summer sun.

Not only was the chair the most comfortable thing she'd ever sat in, the room was the antithesis of Ann Arbor PD's cramped interrogation space. They could fit four of those tiny rooms in here, and their chairs? Bloody torture devices. She could still feel the phantom numbness in her buttocks.

If she'd had this chair last night, she'd have been asleep instantly.

As she sank deeper into the cushion, she closed her eyes, remembering the events of the past few hours. Agent Reed had caught them up during the phone call she'd placed from her aunt's hotel room.

After Alex's Trojan installed the US Cyber Command payload, it uncovered a goldmine of leads. Agent Reed had been dealing with the fallout since.

Rather than sit on the intel, Director Williams moved fast, mobilizing her secret arm of US Cyber Command.

According to Reed, there were dozens of ops underway around college campuses in the US and Europe.

Their findings were startling: The North Koreans were using college students as money mules for their virus.

The US government had always wondered how hackers laundered stolen currency. Now they knew; minorities and foreign exchange students on student visas.

It turned out that when you added the stress of school to mountains of student debt and resentment toward the system, you end up with the perfect mule, willing to do just about anything for a few bucks.

The entire time Agent Reed was spilling the beans on the covert op, Alex wondered why he was telling her the details. Then he dropped the bombshell.

They'd recovered several SMS messages from a money mule student in Florida. The logs showed he'd been working with Cipher.

Not only had the international hacker instructed the student to convert a huge sum of stolen cash to crypto, be he also asked him to bring it to Ann Arbor. He didn't say why, other than he had 'loose ends' to tie up.

Cyber Command and local law enforcement apprehended the student at Miami airport en route to Detroit Metro.

That detail hit Alex like a ton of bricks. Cipher was closer than she'd imagined.

First, he'd been near her parents in Fremont, and now he was heading to Ann Arbor, probably to kill her, just as his colleagues had tried to do to N3tN1nja in New York.

Her naivety had endangered her loved ones, and no amount of consoling from Aunt Min could change that. To make matters worse, her aunt hadn't explained how she knew Cipher, and her strange behavior after the phone call added to Alex's unease.

She was beginning to wonder if her aunt was actually N3tN1nja. The timelines were suspect, but not impossible.

Her aunt would've needed to dial in from the plane when she arrived in California all those months ago.

If Alex could determine where her aunt had been before Ann Arbor, she'd know for sure. If she'd traveled anywhere near New York, she'd have some explaining to do. But only the FBI or her parents could provide that information. She wasn't about to ask the first, and the second involved a series of carefully crafted questions so as not to raise any parental alarms.

"What are you thinking about?" Aunt Min asked.

She stood with her back to the glass, a steely resolve in her eyes, the same look she'd worn since receiving the mysterious call.

"Who called you at the hotel?" Alex asked bluntly, opting for directness over subtlety. Even if it hurt.

Aunt Min glanced sideways at the glass. "Not here, not now," she whispered.

"Then when?" Alex rose abruptly, her body protesting. "We've had hours, and you haven't said shit since that call. I want to know who it was."

They glared at each other, the room engulfed in an icy standoff.

Alex didn't hear the door open, but caught the reflection on the wall.

"Alex, Ms. Myeong, please come with me," a familiar voice said.

Alex turned to see Agent Gregor standing in the doorway, her least favorite person in the world after Cipher. He still wore yesterday's overpriced suit, the pit stains even more pronounced.

"I'm not going anywhere with you," she snapped.

"Alex!" her aunt scolded, spinning around. "Don't talk to him that way."

"You don't know how this asshole treated me last night," Alex stepped forward, fists clenched at her sides.

Her aunt gasped, pivoting toward the man. "Is that so?"

Agent Gregor retreated into the hall, eyes bouncing between them. "I'm sorry, alright?" He raised his hands. "Seriously. It was good cop, bad cop, and I think you can guess which straw I pulled."

Alex searched his face for his previous arrogance, but found none.

"Fine," she muttered, unclenching her fists. "But if you fuck with me again, I'll show you how dangerous a sleep-deprived hacker can be. I haven't slept in two days."

Her threats were hollow, but she didn't care. She was done with people yanking her chain.

Her aunt stared wide-eyed, having never seen this side of her niece. She hadn't witnessed Alex's confrontations in the alley or with the police.

Alex was no longer a timid child, and the sooner people realized that, the better. If they kept poking her with a stick, they shouldn't be surprised if they lost a hand.

She was done exchanging pleasantries, especially with this guy. So instead, she stormed out, turning left and marching deeper into the heart of the building. She had no idea where she was going, but anger fueled her forward.

FOUR MINUTES and countless turns later, Agent Gregor unlocked a seemingly ordinary door. As it opened, Alex knew it was anything but.

The room beyond was massive, easily seventy feet square, and it sank into the ground. Floor-to-ceiling computer panels lined the walls, buzzing with activity. Every screen displayed a map, video, or some other visualization. It was a masterpiece of computing, and she couldn't tear her eyes away.

Concentric rings of desks were tiered inward toward the

center, where a trio of screens stood on movable stands. The setup screamed Mission Control. And near the middle, Agent Reed guided what she assumed were the ops he'd mentioned earlier.

As her gaze flitted from screen to screen, she froze. Half the panels to her left displayed a familiar sight: Ann Arbor's Central Campus.

On one panel was the Diag, the same place she and Aunt Min had sat earlier. Crowds of students and parents milled around, taking tours and doting on their children, oblivious to the electronic eyes watching them.

The realization hit her like a punch to the gut: Not only were their lives under constant surveillance, but they were terrifyingly vulnerable. If Cipher attacked in broad daylight, the fallout would be catastrophic. Dozens, if not hundreds, of innocent lives could be destroyed.

And all for what, one lone hacker?

"No way," she shouted at Agent Reed. "I won't be a pawn in your game." She jabbed a finger at the screen. "Too many lives are at risk."

Agent Reed looked up. "Alex, Ms. Jung, I'm glad you made it safely. I was beginning to—"

"You heard her!" Aunt Min interjected. "We won't be your collateral damage or bait. Now, either let us go, or take us somewhere safe."

Agent Reed glanced at the other agents, then sighed. "It's not that simple." His gaze locked onto Alex. "Cipher's activated several North Korean sleepers in Detroit. Suspected DPRK sympathizers."

Alex shook her head. "The what?"

"The Democratic People's Republic of Korea," he continued. "We've been watching these people for years, and they've never so much as sneezed until today. But now, they're headed here. And they're not alone."

He strode up the ramp, gesturing at shipping invoices on one of the massive screens. "We've got a half dozen suspicious vehicles driving toward Ann Arbor from neighboring states. Any one of them could contain a terrorist, or worse, a bomb."

"So you're right," he said, stopping in front of her. "There *are* a lot of lives at risk. But *you're* the only one he wants. The sooner we take control of this situation without letting it get out of hand, the better."

He turned to Aunt Min, his gaze hardening. "I need your niece to help make this problem go away, and I need you to talk to her, Min-Seo. *You* of all people know how badly this can go."

Alex whirled toward her aunt. "What does he mean?" she asked, her voice trembling. "Aunt Min, what is he talking about?"

Min froze, glaring at Agent Reed. Her normally personable exterior vanished, replaced by a hard, unyielding expression of cold determination.

Alex's mind reeled; she'd never seen her aunt like this.

When Aunt Min's stare shifted to Alex, her eyes softened. "It's a long story."

Agent Reed leaned in, glancing between them. "Then I suggest you tell it fast. We don't have much time."

He spun away, sending the agents behind him scattering like startled mice as he made his way back to the center of the room.

Alex's attention snapped back to her aunt, who was already reaching for her hand.

"What—" Alex began.

"No," Aunt Min interrupted, eyeing nearby agents. "Not here. Come. Let's talk in the hall." She gently tugged Alex's hand, leading her out.

They walked silently, retracing their steps down the corridor. At the first intersection, she turned to face Alex, her hands trembling. Alex had never seen her aunt this nervous; it was unsettling.

Her heart raced, a sense of foreboding settling in her gut.

"Remember how I said I was a problem child?" her aunt began. "Yeah... well, I started young. At thirteen, I committed my first hack. I started out phone phreaking for fun, and by fifteen, I was making spare cash doing side jobs for the crime bosses in Seoul. It wasn't too bad. Just using phone networks to hide from surveillance. That, and helping control the dark side of the city. You know, gambling, drugs, and shit like that." She glanced over Alex's shoulder. "Toward the end of the 90s, I got into computer hacking. Cybercrime was taking off back then. It was the Wild West, as you Americans say. That's when *they* took me in."

"Who?" Alex whispered.

"The government. The NIS." Her aunt eyed someone exiting the room behind them, pausing until their footsteps faded.

She continued, her voice low. "They flipped me. The assholes used my past indiscretions to coerce me into doing their bidding. It was that or prison." She shook her head. "They had me working in the gray. They called it 'protecting national security interests,' when all they were really doing was using me to keep the heat off them. I was putting my neck on the line to get them intel so they wouldn't have to break their laws."

Aunt Min swallowed hard. "Not long after that, shit went sideways. Somehow, my crime bosses found out I'd been playing both sides, working for the Angibu—that's what they called the NIS." She turned, pressing her back to the wall. "That's when I went into hiding, and when I met your mother."

Alex listened intently, piecing together fragments of her

aunt's past to understand their family history. But she sensed there was still more. The other shoe had yet to drop.

"When I met your mom, when I met Evelyn, I turned over a new leaf. I was done doing bad things to good people." Her voice cracked. "I honestly thought I'd turned a corner. But after she met your father, Damir, everything changed. She changed."

Alex mouthed the name, *Damir*. The blinders of her past crumbled away. She'd never imagined knowing anything about her real parents, let alone their names.

"It's strange," Aunt Min whispered, gazing intensely at Alex. "You have his eyes, and yet... you're nothing like him."

Alex gasped, her mind reeling. She'd never met anyone else with heterochromia.

Oblivious to Alex's epiphany, Aunt Min continued. "When your mother met him, she turned my world upside down." She drew a shuddering breath. "Evelyn... tore out my heart, choosing him over me, over us. Staying by her side was the hardest thing I'd ever done, especially knowing my love would never be reciprocated. But I did, until his evil became too much. He pushed us over the edge, made us do things neither of us could handle. That's when she asked me to take you away, to keep you safe. I truly thought I could protect you. That she'd find her way back to me if I did."

She paused, wiping at her tears. "After I got back to Seoul, my family turned on me and I lost you. My entire life unraveled. I went to a dark place after that, a really dark place. I got mixed up with some bad people in prison. The kind you pray you never have to meet. It was a nightmare, a hell I thought I'd never escape. And when I got out, that's when Cipher found me."

"Wait, you knew Cipher?" Alex's eyes widened in disbelief.

Her aunt's gaze turned haunted. "He found me after my

release from Cheongju Prison. I don't know how. But he knew things about me, things no one else knew. The state I was in, what I'd... endured." Her eyes darted away from Alex, hiding something. "It was as if he had a window into my soul, like he'd been watching me for years, waiting for the perfect moment to strike."

Alex rubbed her forehead. "Why didn't you mention knowing him before?"

"I'm not proud of that chapter of my life," Aunt Min began, her voice thick with regret. "I was a different person back then. These past few years, I've worked hard to put that darkness behind me, to become someone worthy of... love."

Her eyes darkened. "Cipher has a way of bringing out the worst in people. Of bending the world and those around him to his will. I don't know how he does it, but it's like he reaches inside you and twists your very soul until you're unrecognizable. That's what Agent Reed was referring to."

She glanced at Alex, her expression heavy. "When he said I knew how bad it could get, that's what he meant. I've witnessed firsthand the depths of depravity Cipher can drive people to. He masterminded a subway station fire back in '03. I... I could have stopped him. I should have, but"—her hands trembled—"I didn't. I underestimated him. It happened so fast. One second, we had him, and the next, two hundred people were dead. Two hundred lives and families destroyed in an instant, all because of my negligence, my arrogance." Tears welled up in her eyes. "What I didn't know then was that my Eomma and Appa were on that train. They were coming to see me that day. To ask me to come home. To forgive me and welcome me back, despite everything I'd done."

She slid down the wall, pulling her knees to her chest and curling into a ball. Her body shook violently, each gasping breath a testament to the depth of her regret.

Alex, however, didn't cry. She didn't console her. She just

stared at her aunt, transfixed, her thoughts spiraling with the implications of her confession.

As she stood there in the sterile hallway, a steely determination settled over her, a resolve born from the ashes of her aunt's tragedy.

When Aunt Min failed to act in Seoul, she failed to protect her family. But worse than that, she let Cipher slip away. And now he was back for seconds, except this time he wasn't targeting strangers—he was after Alex and her family.

Alex, however, was not her aunt. She refused to let fear or guilt paralyze her into inaction. She wouldn't make the mistake of underestimating the monster.

If the past year, hell, the past few days, had taught her anything, it was to use her mistakes as stepping stones. To take action. To fight back against those who threatened her and the people she loved.

And that meant only one thing: she had to stop Cipher, no matter the cost.

With a deep breath, she offered a hand to her aunt. She hesitated at first, but gave a small nod, accepting the offer. Alex supported her as she rose, and together, they walked back toward the command center.

Agent Reed emerged as they neared the entrance. "Are you ready?" he asked, his eyes boring into Alex's.

She nodded, jaw clenched. "I am."

"Good." Agent Reed motioned inside. "Why don't you head in? The team will brief you on the plan." He turned to Min. "I'd like a word in private with Min-Seo."

Aunt Min's gaze flicked to Alex, concern flashing across her features before vanishing.

"Of course."

Alex strode into the command center, her mind already shifting gears. She barely registered Agent Reed's voice fading as the door swung shut and the other agents ushered her forward.

They guided her down the ramp toward the hub where they had maps and documents sprawled across a sea of displays.

Alex squared her shoulders, eyeing the array of computers. Whatever lay ahead, she was prepared to face it.

Two hours later, Agent Reed had unveiled his strategy. They were aiming to leverage the events around Parents' Weekend, parading Alex and Min around campus with a busload of disguised agents.

Alex was the proverbial bait to lure Cipher into the open.

The hitch? They had no clue when or where Cipher would strike. Hell, they weren't even certain he knew who Alex was. All he had on her was her Raspberry Pi. Agent Reed had confirmed as much.

When Agent Reed dispatched an agent to California to check on Alex's hidden trove of hacking devices, they uncovered a twist: Mrs. Myeong had reported a break-in days earlier. Apparently, her kitchen cabinet was torn apart, her Wi-Fi destroyed, and her back window and door smashed to bits.

Fortunately, Mrs. Myeong wasn't home during the break-in, but she still ended up in the hospital that night. The agent said that she'd had a panic attack upon finding her home in shambles.

Alex stared at the laptop, racking her brain to remember what she'd done on that Raspberry Pi. What digital footprints she'd left behind.

She couldn't remember if she'd wiped it clean before installing it downstairs. Even then, she'd connected to it constantly from her room. While she'd set up remote wiping tools, they were only programmed to purge the VPN and network logs, not the entire system.

That Raspberry Pi was her first tiny computer purchase. She hadn't fully grasped its potential at the time, loading it with all manner of software, some legal, some not. Retro gaming simulators, an email server, a web proxy, even a print server.

For all she knew, that device could contain every email and document she'd touched during her entire junior and senior years.

"And you're certain that's everything he has?" Agent Reed asked, scanning the list of installed software.

"Everything?" Alex scoffed, leaning back to stare at the ceiling. "I haven't slept in two days and can barely recall last week. You expect me to remember every piece of software I installed last year?"

"Besides," she jabbed at the list, "if he has all this, he knows everything about me. Every friend, every hope, every dream. My entire life before college."

Regret washed over her as she stared at the screen. At the time, the device had seemed clever. A safe place to hone her craft. She'd left it behind to use as a secure jump-off point. A helpful tool, hidden where no one would look.

Until they did.

"Alright." Agent Reed nodded to one of his people who whisked her laptop away.

Once they were gone, he moved beside her. "Let's review the plan one more time. I want you comfortable with how this will work." He swung the movable display to face them.

Alex sighed. They'd already gone over it three times; the last thing she needed was another review.

As Agent Reed's voice faded into the background, her attention drifted to her cell phone perched on a table a few tiers up. She'd watched a field agent fiddling with it earlier.

Her eyelids grew heavy. *Had N3tN1nja messaged again?* She could use an outside opinion right about now. That, and a bed. Without some shut-eye soon, she'd never last five minutes on that campus bus tour.

She could almost hear the low, steady rumble of the diesel engine lulling her to sleep...

"Let's head back to your dorm." Aunt Min's hand gently touched her shoulder.

Alex jerked her head up, eyes snapping open. Heat rushed to her cheeks as she realized she'd dozed off during Agent Reed's briefing.

Embarrassment washed over her as she met the room's collective gaze.

"Sorry," she mumbled, rubbing her eyes. A sharp pain throbbed behind them.

Exhaustion fogged her mind, making focus nearly impossible.

Agent Reed glowered, his brow furrowed. "If you can't stay awake for a simple briefing, how do you expect to handle what's coming? This is serious, Alex."

"Ignore him," Aunt Min murmured, her eyes locked on the agent. "It's okay. You're exhausted." Her hand remained steady on Alex's shoulder.

"Someone get Ms. Mercer some coffee!" Agent Reed shouted, spinning around, searching for a grunt.

"No!" Aunt Min's voice cracked like a whip. "I'm taking my niece back to her dorm. She needs some rest. She's useless if she can't think straight." She gently helped Alex up.

It was the most Aunt Min had said since her confession in the hall. Since admitting her love for Alex's biological mother and her unwitting role in her parents' deaths.

The intervening hours had crackled with unspoken tension, until now. Until she'd leapt to Alex's defense, just like always. Her eternal guardian angel, even when no one else wanted her.

"We're not done." Agent Reed reached for Alex, but Aunt Min swatted his hand away.

"The fuck?" He nursed his wrist.

"Don't touch her!" Aunt Min planted herself between them.

"What's gotten into you?" Agent Reed glared at Alex. "You two are acting like we don't have a stone-cold killer heading our way. Like thousands of lives aren't at stake." He eyed Min warily. "You're not leaving until this plan is drilled into your brain. Every. Goddamn. Step. Perfect." He spun around. "Where's that fucking coffee?"

"Stop," Alex said, her voice catching. "Please... stop screaming." She massaged her temples, head throbbing.

Agent Reed glanced back. "I'll stop when your aunt plays ball. This isn't Daegu. We don't abandon our citizens."

Before Alex could respond, Aunt Min pounced on Agent Reed like a lioness on her prey.

She tackled him into the computer display, sending their bodies crashing to the ground. Crunching plastic and shattering glass pierced the air as her aunt's fists hammered his face.

Her hands were a blur, each blow landing with a sickening thud. Blood spattered across the pristine white floor.

The vivid crimson jolted Alex back to a painful memory—her first adoptive father, his fists raining down on his wife's defenseless form, a young Alex watching in horror.

She sat paralyzed, her mind reeling from the sudden violence and the implications of the memory.

Was this a sign? A warning of what's to come if I don't act? Or a reminder of the brutality that shadows me?

Suddenly, it all became too much. The secrets, the lies, the endless cycle of pain and betrayal.

She had to get away, to clear her head, to make sense of the chaos swirling inside.

Without a word, she rose and walked out, pocketing her cell phone, deaf to the shouts behind her. Her destination was unclear, but staying was impossible. Not now. Not with the ghosts of her past bleeding into her present.

As she walked, her mind whirled.

What does it all mean?

Am I doomed to follow their path, trapped in an endless cycle of violence and deceit? Or can I break free, forge my own way, and end Cipher's reign of terror?

The answers eluded her, but one thing was certain. She wouldn't find them here, amid blinking screens and ceaseless chatter. She needed space, time to think, to strategize.

And so, heart heavy and mind churning, she set off toward her dorm. Alone and uncertain, yet resolved to face whatever lay ahead on her own terms.

28 / CROSSING THE THRESHOLD
CIPHER

They parked in a lot near the hospital, and Cipher left Tae-Woo to watch the car. The town was blanketed in cameras; the last thing they needed was police attention before they struck.

The challenge of the stakeout was twofold: finding and capturing the target amidst the swarms of students.

The American youths scurried like squirrels forever chasing a nut. They rushed from classes to meetings, labs to parties—never having a second to themselves. No wonder they were such easy targets, perpetually distracted, oblivious of their surroundings. And with their parents flooding the town this weekend, chaos reigned supreme.

In a society drowning in noise and endless stimuli, Americans had lost touch with their primal instincts—that innate ability to sense danger lurking in the shadows.

Cipher observed them, a predator eyeing its prey. Their naivety both disgusted and fascinated him, a stark reminder of the weakness he'd long ago purged from himself.

His world had no room for such frivolities, no time for carefree laughter.

He saw their true nature: soft, complacent, and utterly

unprepared for the harsh realities beyond their sheltered collegiate bubble. They were lambs being led to the slaughter, blissfully ignorant of the circling wolves.

But soon, they'd learn the true meaning of fear. They'd grasp the price of ignorance, the cost of their carefree lives. When that veil lifted, revealing the harsh truth of the world, he'd savor in their terror and despair.

For now, he'd wait and watch, biding time until the perfect moment to strike. Let them have their fleeting joy. It would only sweeten their inevitable suffering.

He glanced toward the curb, spotting Ki-Sung walking down the street.

She'd messaged him after his botched bribery attempt. Not only had she found their target's dorm, she'd also secured a keycard to the building from a residential adviser.

Where he'd failed with money, she'd triumphed with her feminine charm. Some well-placed flirtation, a strategic display of fresh wounds, and a promised late-night rendezvous were all it took.

Cipher observed Ki-Sung from across the street behind a bus shelter. She paused at the corner, feigning interest in her phone. But he knew better; she was surveilling their target.

In the second-floor window, he glimpsed a young woman, likely their mark. She was bent backward against the window casing, her lithe form silhouetted against the light. Judging by the way she contorted herself, she was doing some type of yoga, which was surprising considering the window was open.

Any self-respecting woman would close the shades, knowing the kind of vile opportunists that could be lurking about, watching from the shadows. In a just world, she wouldn't have to fear prying eyes violating her privacy. But Cipher knew better. He knew the depths of depravity that men like him were capable of.

A dark thrill ran through him as she bent precariously, her

back curving like a pretzel. As she twisted in impossible ways, he suddenly felt himself getting aroused. Imagining her youthful body deforming around a knife as it dug into her flesh. The sheer number of things he could make her do with even the slightest amount of pain was astounding.

Americans didn't know what real anguish felt like until they had a razor blade slicing through their flesh. His father had taught him the harsh reality of suffering from a young age, shattering his illusions of safety and innocence.

Those brutal lessons had forged him into the man he was today: Cold, ruthless, and unbreakable. He knew that the soft, coddled masses could never understand the dark truths that shaped him. And that knowledge filled him with a sense of superiority.

He licked his lips, imagining what the woman's sweat would taste like as she screamed for mercy.

"Does she turn you on?" Ki-Sung asked, her voice a whisper from behind him.

He turned, glaring at her. "I'm imagining what it would be like to break her, to make her talk."

"What makes you think she knows anything?"

"They live together, her and Byt3Linguist." He turned back to the window. "Surely, she knows a few details about her roommate." He narrowed his gaze, studying the girl as she shifted into yet another mind-numbing pose. "If not, she might still prove useful."

"And what of N3tN1nja?"

He smirked. Her purpose here was driven by one singular goal. Revenge.

"Patience," he murmured. "They'll surface." A smile played on his lips, savoring the efficiency of his plan. "If your intel from New York is accurate, then these two thorns are bound by an invisible tether. They're partners in crime, and their time has run out."

Ki-Sung stepped beside him. "How do you suppose we extract her? We aren't exactly short on witnesses." She gestured toward the throngs of students milling about.

"We wait," he said, leaning against the shelter. The cold facade steadied him. "I'm nothing if not patient. I waited years to unleash this virus, to plan the perfect unveiling. What's a few more minutes if it means destroying my enemies? We're on the precipice of a digital revolution that could reshape the very foundations of society."

Ki-Sung's eyes flickered with doubt. "You don't actually think your virus will change the world, do you?"

"It could have." He chuckled, a mirthless laugh that held no warmth. "But that was before N3tN1nja and Byt3Linguist severed one of my hydra's heads. While they celebrated their supposed victory, my creation was evolving, adapting. It's become more complex than they could fathom. What they didn't realize was that I'm not just another nameless hacker who wields electronic barbs. I can manifest true pain, agony they can't begin to fathom. I will break them down, piece by piece, until they beg for mercy. Just like my father did to me."

Ki-Sung stepped back, leaning against the shelter. "Where does it stop?" she whispered. "When is enough enough?"

His eyes flashed with manic intensity, a mix of emotions passing through him.

He spun around, facing her with a speed that made her flinch. "Stop? It stops when I say it fucking stops. It stops when they've paid the price for what they stole. When they're broken beyond repair and have suffered as I have suffered. Only then will the scales be balanced. Only then will I be whole again." His voice lowered, taking on a dangerous edge. "I'd expect no less from you, given what they took. What they did to Choe."

She whirled around, her eyes blazing with fury, her face mere inches from his. "Don't you dare speak her name, you pathetic excuse for a man. You don't get to use her death as a prop in your twisted revenge fantasy. She meant nothing to you."

He stepped backward, but she advanced, closing the gap. "Her death is on *my* hands, and that's a burden I'll carry for the rest of my life. I will avenge her, but I'll do it with precision and purpose, not by lashing out at everyone in my path like a rabid dog. Unlike you, I still have a shred of humanity left. Unlike you, I understand the value of discipline and restraint."

She jabbed a finger into his chest, her voice low. "Now man the fuck up and get control of your goddamn demons. If you let your personal bullshit jeopardize this mission, I'll put you down myself. I don't need a liability like you screwing things up. So, either get your shit together, or get out of my way. Because if you interfere with my objective, I'll end you just as swiftly as I'll end N3tN1nja. And trust me, I won't lose sleep over it."

Staring into her eyes, he saw straight through to her soul, to the rot festering within. She was a frail shell of a person, a pale imitation of the sister she claimed to avenge. He wasn't sure whether Choe's death had broken her, or if she'd always been this pathetic. But one thing was certain: She was nothing like her twin. Where Choe had been fierce, passionate, and alive, Ki-Sung was a hollow husk, a walking corpse pretending to be an assassin.

He let out a derisive snort, his lips curling into a sneer. "Whenever you think you can put me down, *bring it*." He leaned in, his voice a whisper. "But until then, let me tell you something. You don't have what it takes. You're nothing more than a broken little doll playing at being a killer. You don't have the fire, the hunger, the sheer force of will to do what needs to be done. Not like Choe did, and certainly not like I do."

He pulled back, his eyes cold and dismissive. "So go ahead, whenever you're ready. Try to end me. But know this; I've stared into the abyss and come out the other side. I've embraced the darkness that you're so afraid of. And that makes me stronger than you'll ever be."

As he stared into her hollow eyes, one thing became clear: He would need to end her before the mission was over. Not only had she said too much, but she didn't deserve to be part of his grand plan.

"Now, how about we go introduce ourselves to our new friend?" He tilted his head, a cold, predatory smile spreading across his face as his attention shifted back to the girl in the window.

Ki-Sung rapped her scarred knuckles against the door, a hollow echo reverberating within.

Cipher stood confidently beside her, forcing the friendliest expression he could muster. He noted the razor-thin separation between them and the young woman inside, realizing they couldn't take her here; it could get too noisy.

The girl's music drifted through the door, its soothing tones befitting the erotic oscillations her body had performed moments earlier.

When the door swung open, a musky aroma wafted out, tinged with lavender. He inhaled deeply, trying to lock in her scent before it was tarnished by the stench of fear.

"We're looking for Al—ex," Ki-Sung said, her voice adopting a stilted, deliberate cadence. "Al—ex Mer—cer." She smiled, gesturing toward Cipher. "We surprise her. We come from Cali-fornia."

The girl stared blankly, momentarily confused by the strangers at her door. Her gaze flicked between them.

When Ki-Sung bowed, the girl smiled and returned the gesture.

"You must be..." the girl paused, eyeing Cipher with uncertainty.

"Her aunt and uncle," he grinned, "originally from Seoul."

She tilted her head, squinting. "You don't look like you're from Seoul."

"You're right." He smirked, a wave of arousal passing through him. "That's because I'm a transplant. I moved there over a decade ago."

He glanced past her, taking in the room. Two distinctly different personalities crammed into a confined space.

On one side, a colorful explosion of mass-produced culture covered every surface. There were magazine cutouts and strange abstract renderings of computer panels hanging from trees, emblazoned with billboards of American brand names. It was eye-watering.

The other side was a stark contrast, a simple black and white canvas filled with hand-drawn pictures and iconography of hacker culture. Cartoon daemons, burning houses, ASCII art, and computer graffiti.

It was obvious whose was whose—one side spoke of commercial conformity, the other screamed hacker rebellion.

His gaze returned to the young woman, glistening with sweat. Their eyes met, and once again, he felt a dark hunger stirring, a twisted anticipation of what was to come.

"I'm so sorry," the girl said, shaking her head. "My name is Michelle. Why don't you come in?" She stepped back, gesturing into the room.

Cipher smiled. "Michelle," he purred, letting the name roll off his tongue like honey. "What a lovely name."

He gently pressed his hand against the small of Ki-Sung's back, urging her forward. As he crossed the threshold behind her, he felt a shift in the air, a palpable tension, like the world itself was holding its breath.

The door swung shut with a soft, ominous click, sealing them inside.

In the silence, Cipher heard only his pounding heart and the echoes of Michelle's unwitting invitation ringing in his ears.

She had no idea what she had just let into her life. But she would learn. Oh yes, she would learn.

And he would be her teacher.

29 / A DEADLY VOW
ALEX

As Alex stepped off the bus, her stomach clenched as the familiar scent of diesel fumes filled her nostrils. She stifled a cough and scanned the sidewalk, half expecting a contingent of police to appear out of nowhere and shove her into an unmarked vehicle. But the street remained eerily calm.

The journey took hours. She'd considered finding somewhere secluded to think, but her mind and body yearned for only one destination: Her own bed.

Relief washed over her as she gazed up at the gothic stone lettering etched into the entrance of *Eliza M. Mosher Hall*. Despite the chaos engulfing her life, her dormitory stood as a comforting constant, a reminder of the future she'd fought so hard to build.

For a moment, the weight of recent events lifted from her shoulders, replaced by a sense of belonging. Of being home. Within these walls, she wasn't a pawn in some grand government scheme or a target for shadowy foreign entities. She was just Alex, part-time hacker, full-time student, with classes to attend and friends to laugh with.

She inhaled deeply, savoring this brief glimpse of

normalcy. Thoughts of final exams and roommate squabbles felt like a luxury, a fleeting reprieve, but one she desperately needed. At least until she could rest and face the storm once more.

With a newfound determination, she focused on the promising warmth of her comforter and the squish of her favorite pillow against her cheek. As she reached for the door, her phone vibrated in her pocket.

Her heart raced. She wasn't expecting any calls, and the last people she wanted to hear from were her aunt or Agent Reed. But when she flipped the device open, a name she longed to see flashed across the screen.

She grinned from ear to ear and pressed talk. "Mom!"

She retreated down the sideway and made her way to an empty bench, knowing the thick brick walls of her dorm would interfere with the signal.

"Lexy!" Her mother's voice was warm and comforting, like being wrapped in a blanket.

A lump formed in her throat. "It's so good to hear you, Mom. I feel like... it's been forever. How've you been?"

She brushed leaves off the bench and sat, closing her eyes, letting her mother's familiar tones wash over her.

"It has been too long," her mother replied, her voice clear and lucid. Alex's tension eased slightly; from the sounds of it, her mother was having a good day.

"How are you and your aunt getting along?" Mom asked. "Are you having fun? She's been gone quite a while, and for some reason her phone keeps going to voicemail. I was starting to worry, but I didn't want to call you and ruin her surprise."

Alex sat up straight, her eyes darting around. *What did Mom mean? Had Aunt Min really been away for a while, or was Mom's dementia playing tricks again?*

"Aunt Min's great," she said, her voice strained. "She's

taking a nap right now. Too much walking and sitting around in the airport, I think. Where did she fly into again?"

She held her breath, hoping her mom might reveal something to confirm her suspicions.

"I bet you're right," her mom chuckled. "She mentioned something about being stuck in layovers for a few days. I think she said there was weather in Denver or Chicago... I don't know." She sighed. "I couldn't imagine spending two days in airport hotels. But I guess if I got to see you, it would be worth it."

Alex's eyes welled up, torn between curiosity and a deep, aching sadness.

Her parents had been her lighthouse in the storm of her childhood. They'd spent years building the trust that only adoptive parents would understand. Especially ones with a child from a storied past.

Alex cupped the phone close to her mouth. "I miss you, Mom. I wish you..." Her words trailed away as the weight of what she was about to say hit her.

Having her mother here would only amplify her anxiety and fear. It was best if she wasn't underfoot.

"I know, sweetie," her mom whispered, voice cracking. "I... wish I could be there. Maybe we can drop you off for your next school year at the end of summer. Your father and I could both go. We could make a vacation of it. You could show us around campus."

"That sounds really nice," Alex said, her mind instantly leaping to whether she could afford school next year.

She pushed the thought aside. At least for now, her parents were far away.

They were safe.

She couldn't fathom explaining her current predicament to either of them, especially after what happened with the

Sanchez family. They were clueless about technology, let alone politics. She was just lucky her aunt understood.

Her aunt.

If what her mother said was true, Aunt Min could've easily detoured to New York before coming to Ann Arbor. She might not have had much time, but she could've pulled it off.

The question was, if she was N3tN1nja or not.

"Shit," her mom growled. A crackle sounded over the line, like she was covering the phone.

Alex tensed, hearing faint voices on the other end. Her senses sharpened, suddenly alert to her surroundings.

A car lingered in the distance at the corner, its nose barely visible. It had been there for a few minutes now.

Just as she considered moving, a student dashed in front of the vehicle, blowing a kiss and waving it away. The car pulled forward and turned, vanishing into the distance.

"It's my boss," her mom whispered, uncovering the phone. "I'm at work. He needs me to clean some rooms. VIP guests, my ass," she muttered. "I bet he's bringing his fling in again. Someone should tell his wife what he's up to."

A pause hung heavy on the line. "I'm... sorry," her mom stuttered. "You don't need to hear this. I wish I was there, sweetie. Have fun with your aunt, okay?"

Alex swallowed hard. "I will," she whispered. "And, Mom?"

"Yes?"

"I love you." She covered her mouth, fighting back a flood of tears.

"I love you too, sweetheart. To the moon and back."

As the line clicked dead, Alex sniffled, her mother's words echoing in the silence.

She stared into the distance, her mind racing through the

implications of what she'd just learned while fighting to suppress a surge of familial emotions.

Packing her feelings into a mental box was a skill she'd honed since childhood. It had been essential during her time with her first adoptive father, when he beat his wife. But compartmentalizing only worked for so long, and she could feel the edges of those boxes fraying as she tried to stow away her family concerns.

Her gaze drifted to a group of parents and students milling around the distant bus stop when her phone vibrated again.

Half hoping it was her mom, she instead saw Michelle's name flash on the screen. She'd sent a message. Alex perked up, glancing toward their dorm window, wondering if her roommate was inside.

Flipping open the phone, she typed in her password and hit OK.

As the message loaded, she gasped, her heart seizing. A cold wave of horror washed over her, the phone nearly slipping from her suddenly numb fingers.

There, on the tiny, pixelated screen, was Michelle—bruised, bloodied, and bound. She lay curled in a fetal position, frayed ropes digging cruelly into her skin.

Michelle was lying on her side in what appeared to be a battered old blue van, its metal walls scratched and rusted—a scene ripped from a horror movie.

But it was Michelle's face that sent Alex reeling.

Bloody wrappings covered her eyes, the dressings oozing crimson. Fresh, untreated gashes marred her cheeks and chin. Her once flawless complexion was a canvas of cuts and bruises.

This wasn't a simple beating to make a point. The attacker had taken joy in their assault, each strike carving out a fresh spot on her body, elevating Michelle's pain to new heights.

She looked away, doubling over as nausea surged through her.

Her body convulsed as she imagined each blow landing on her friend. And it was all because of her.

"This can't be happening," she muttered, putting her head between her knees. "Not again."

She clutched her phone, her mind flashing back to her adoptive mother lying in pools of blood all those years ago. That image was etched in her memory forever.

But this wasn't a decade-old nightmare. This horror was new.

And this time, it was *her* fault.

With the image branded into her mind, she forced herself upright, lifting the phone to read the accompanying text.

> **MICHELLE**
>
> Byt3Linguist — or should I say, Alex? By now, you've seen what I'm capable of. Michelle is just the beginning. If you don't surrender in the next hour, she won't be the only one suffering. Thousands of innocent lives hang in the balance, all because of your meddling. Their blood will be on your hands if you try anything. Come to the parking lot at the end of Nichols Drive, near the Huron River. Bring N3tN1nja. And, Alex, don't keep me waiting. If you do, the consequences will be more than either of you can bear. The choice is yours. — Cipher

This was too real. Terrifyingly, gut-wrenchingly real.

Her mind fractured into razor-sharp shards of panic and dread as she grappled with Cipher's message.

Why me? Why Michelle? And where the hell am I supposed to find N3tN1nja?

The ultimatum was clear: Surrender herself and N3tN1nja, or bear the guilt of countless deaths. Cipher had backed her into an impossible corner, weaponizing her own compassion against her.

Now the clock was ticking, each second an eternity of agonizing indecision.

Surrendering meant placing herself at the mercy of a sadistic monster. Worse, there was no guarantee he'd spare Michelle or the nameless thousands he threatened.

Her mind flashed to Michelle's wounds. She could almost see Cipher inflicting similar horrors on countless others, forcing her to watch.

But refusing to comply... The thought alone made her stomach heave with horror and self-loathing.

She shook her head. She couldn't live with herself knowing her inaction had condemned innocent people to unimaginable suffering.

It was the same battle her aunt had fought and lost a decade earlier, and now it was repeating with her.

Except this time was different.

She wouldn't make the same mistake as her aunt.

To Alex, there was really only one choice. Only one way to be true to herself, to the person she aspired to be.

Tears blurred her vision as she struggled to think, to hack her way out of the problem. He'd asked her to meet near a parking lot not far from the hospital.

She knew the spot well, having passed it countless times on the bus to North Campus. It was just off the main loop around the hospital.

"Think, Alex. Think!" She leapt up, pacing around the bench, her phone clenched in her hand.

Suddenly, a thought struck. She quickly scrolled to N3tN1nja's last message and fired off a reply:

L3X1C0N

I need your help NOW. Where are you?

The response was instant, but not what she hoped:

Message Failed to Send
The message to Unknown Caller failed to send. This person isn't receiving messages at this time.

"Shit!" She kicked a nearby pile of leaves, sending them exploding into the air. Passing parents eyed her with disapproval.

"Sorry," she muttered, ducking her head in embarrassment.

That plan wouldn't work. She needed something simpler. Something closer. Somewhere Cipher wouldn't balk at, even if she didn't bring N3tN1nja.

But it had to be a place she knew better than anyone. A place where she could gain an advantage.

As she spun around, her eyes locked on the distant forest, and inspiration struck. The running trails through Nichols Arboretum. Not only did they connect to that same lot, they weren't far from her dorm.

It was her sanctuary, her favorite place to clear her head outside of a computer lab. She'd spent countless mornings exploring those winding paths, memorizing every twist and turn, every hidden nook and cranny.

In those quiet moments, surrounded by nothing but trees and her own thoughts, she'd found a sense of peace, of control, something she hadn't felt in over a year. Now, that intimate knowledge could be the key to turning the tables on Cipher.

A plan began to form in her mind, the pieces clicking into place like lines of code.

She'd lead Cipher into the woods, using her familiarity

with the terrain to her advantage. The art exhibit and influx of parents in town added another layer. Once inside, she could alert the police and create some distractions to slow him down.

It fit together perfectly.

Her only hope was that Michelle could still walk.

She knew it was a desperate gamble. Cipher was no fool; he'd be expecting her to try something. But running? That likely wasn't on his list.

It was her only play, the only way to save Michelle and possibly thousands of innocent lives.

As she turned the plan over in her mind, she realized what was missing: A failsafe. A last-ditch move if things went sideways. Something devious and destructive, utterly unlike her usual self.

In that moment, she knew what she might need to do to end Cipher's reign of terror once and for all. Something her aunt had never managed, something Alex only hoped she had the strength to pull off.

With a deep breath, she steadied her shaking hands and began to type, fingers flying over the keypad on her phone.

ALEX

> Change of plans. Meet me at Nichols Arboretum off Geddes Road, near the Scenic Overlook. Bring Michelle, or the deal's off.

She hit send before doubt could creep in, her heart hammering in her chest.

The die was cast, the stage set for a final, fateful confrontation.

In the bright midday sun, Alex squared her shoulders and set off; not toward the trails. Not yet.

She had another destination in mind. Somewhere she could acquire a weapon to turn the tide. She only hoped her interrogators hadn't yet collected the firearm she'd lifted from the police officer.

It felt strange hoping for such an oversight, especially when it came to a deadly weapon. But without it, her task would be far more daunting.

Her mind raced with contingencies, but there weren't many left. Each step brought her closer to the aerospace engineering building, to the computer lab where she'd stashed the pistol in a moment of panic.

She pictured the cluttered room. Under the desk, near the back wall, tucked into a tangle of cords behind the computer. That's where she'd hidden it.

It was a long shot. The chances the weapon remained undiscovered were slim. But it was a chance she had to take. Without that gun, her odds of overpowering Cipher and surviving his deadly game were even slimmer.

She quickened her pace, her sneakers pounding the pavement with purpose. The fastest bus to North Campus was just around the block, and time was running out. Each minute ticked away like the countdown on a bomb.

She may have been backed into a corner, but she wasn't going down without a fight. The gun would level the playing field.

Cipher wanted a showdown, and that's exactly what she'd give him—but on her terms. With a weapon in hand and a silent vow steadying her resolve, she'd end this once and for all.

30 / MACHINATIONS OF A MADMAN

CIPHER

He reread the message, anger simmering beneath his skin like molten lava. His fists clenched, the burner phone creaking under his grip.

"Is everything alright?" Tae-Woo asked from the passenger seat.

Cipher glanced at Jin-Soo in the rear of the van, sitting beside Michelle's frail, curled form. "It's fine," he grumbled, returning his attention to the laptop on the console.

When he entered the location Alex had sent into his map app, he sneered. The arboretum was down the street from her dormitory. Not surprising. Probably a place she knew well, where she felt safe and in control.

He'd have chosen the same spot if he'd been in her position. Familiar territory, ample hiding places, and plenty of opportunities for traps or ambushes.

What surprised him, however, was that she hadn't chosen a public place. This was far from it—a wooded area near his current parking spot.

The woman's audacity was astounding. She thought she could dictate terms, as if she had any power in this game. He was calling the shots, not her.

A cruel smile twisted his lips as he contemplated the source of her naïve courage. Even after seeing the picture, she still doubted him. She had no idea who she was dealing with.

He would show her the price of her arrogance, teaching her a brutal lesson in humility.

She would beg for mercy, pleading for death. He would savor every moment of her suffering, drinking in her despair like fine wine.

With a final, dismissive glance at the message, he pocketed his phone and started the engine, the map seared into his memory. It was time to end their game, but not on her terms.

No, he had a far more satisfying plan.

He'd let her think she was in control, that she could reach the arboretum unscathed. But Ki-Sung was already shadowing her every move, waiting for the perfect moment to strike.

Alex would never make it to their supposed meeting spot; at least not without a few broken bones and bruises to match. She'd be his puppet by the time she arrived, a testament to the futility of defying him.

With Alex neutralized, he'd use her to get to his true target: N3tN1nja. The elusive hacker had been a thorn in his side for too long, always one step ahead, always undermining him from the shadows.

But not this time. This time, he'd use Alex as bait, luring N3tN1nja into a trap. And at the perfect moment, he'd spring it, watching with malevolent joy as his nemesis finally fell.

Anticipation coursed through him as he envisioned the scene. The look of horror on N3tN1nja's face as they realized they'd been outsmarted, their screams as he exacted revenge for every humiliation, every setback.

A vicious grin spread across his face. Today he'd triumph over those who dared defy him, who had the audacity to obstruct his grand vision.

Cipher glanced at Tae-Woo. "Tell our assets to meet us

here in ten minutes." He pointed to an intersection on the map. "And tell them to come armed."

He turned the key, and the engine roared to life, echoing the savage joy in his heart.

It was time to set the stage for the final act.

And what a glorious finale it would be.

31 / PARANOIA PURSUED
ALEX

The last time Alex had seen the bus this crowded was during midterms. It was standing room only, her least favorite time to ride. She hated gripping the overhead bar, but today it was especially aggravating. Each jostle reminded her of her exhaustion and the unpredictability of her situation.

Her hastily planned forest meetup now seemed less brilliant. Adrenaline had fueled her response to Cipher, but the wait for the bus had given her time to think, to second-guess herself.

Maybe it was the elderly adults doting over their grandkids, a bittersweet reminder of the fragility of life. Or perhaps it was the Asian woman limping through the crowd with a cane, avoiding eye contact, a living embodiment of the wounds people carry. Either way, uncertainties flooded her mind.

Standing behind the woman in her tattered clothes, Alex saw her plan to lure Cipher into the arboretum for what it was —riddled with holes, fraying under the harsh glare of reality.

What if Cipher saw through my ruse? What if he anticipated my traps and turned them against me? What if my desperate bid to save Michelle and others only ended up endangering more innocent lives?

Questions swirled, a dizzying maelstrom of fear and self-doubt. She gripped the bar tighter, knuckles whitening as anxiety threatened to overwhelm her.

She had to focus. She couldn't let her nerves derail her, not with so much at stake.

Even as she tried to summon her earlier resolve, she couldn't shake the sinking feeling in her gut. The nagging sense that she was in over her head, playing a game whose rules she barely understood.

The bus lurched to a stop, jolting her from her thoughts. They'd arrived at the Commons.

It was time. Time to see if she'd be entering the woods with the upper hand or scrambling to cover her back.

"Excuse me," she muttered, easing past the woman and pushing through the crowd toward the exit.

She could only hope her hastily woven net would hold against the monster she'd soon face.

Before it was too late for them all.

Off the bus, she skirted the Commons. There was no point going inside and risking an encounter with someone she knew; that was the last thing she needed now.

As she turned toward the distant EECS building, she glanced over her shoulder, unease prickling down her spine.

The woman from the bus wasn't far behind, oddly close given how unresponsive she'd been to the bus stopping. She'd just stood there, staring at her shoes.

Alex forced her gaze forward, fighting the urge to look back again.

"You're going crazy," she muttered, chiding her paranoia.

There could be countless reasons for the woman to head this way. She wasn't necessarily following her.

But as Alex fought to rationalize the action, her instincts screamed that something was off.

Quickening her pace, she glanced at the reflective glass of the Duderstadt building. There, in the mirrored surface, she saw the woman speed-walking closer, her earlier limp all but vanished.

"Shit," Alex breathed, realization hitting hard.

She was being tailed, and this woman was no random passerby. Her movement, the focused intensity of her stride—it all pointed to one chilling conclusion.

She was a professional. Trained. Deadly. Nothing like the cops from days earlier.

And Alex was her target.

Adrenaline surged as her fight-or-flight instincts kicked in. She had to lose her pursuer before checking if the weapon was still there.

Without hesitation, Alex took off into a sprint, cutting across the grass toward the computer engineering building.

If she could make it inside, she might lose the woman in a crowded lecture hall or the maze of hallways.

Even as she plotted her escape, a sinking feeling settled in her gut. This woman wasn't about to give up easily. She was a pro, and if she caught up to Alex before she could lose her…

"Alex!" a distant male voice called out.

Her heart leapt with desperate hope as she searched for the source, praying it was a cop like before.

But no. She quickly realized it was Professor Newton, standing near the entrance to the chemical engineering building.

"Professor!" She waved, veering toward him.

She jogged up, glancing back. The woman's gaze locked on hers, cold and calculating.

A shiver of fear shot through her, leaving her nerves on edge.

"I didn't see you in class today, and you never turned in your assignment. What happened?" Professor Newton waved his hand in front of her face.

She shook her head, struggling to focus on him instead of the woman staring at her from the neighboring building.

"I... I got..." She froze, realizing she couldn't tell him anything. Not about attacking a police officer, getting pulled into a government hacking op, or being chased by an assassin.

Professor Newton must've noticed her distress. He leaned in, lowering his voice. "Is everything okay?" He glanced over his shoulder, following her gaze.

The woman, observing the shift in his body language, turned and entered the building. All he saw was her backside.

"I have to go," Alex stammered, stepping backward. "I... I'll send the assignment in. I promise."

He shook his head, concern etched across his features. "Alex, what's going on?"

"Nothing." She forced a smile, the lie bitter on her tongue. "I'm just running late." She couldn't risk involving him. She'd already hurt too many people with her mistakes.

Without another word, she dashed toward the entrance to the H. H. Dow building. Once inside, she mentally mapped her path through the maze of connected buildings.

As a student, she had an advantage. She knew these halls like the back of her hand. If there was anywhere she could lose the woman, it was in the labyrinth of these aging structures.

Her mind raced as she navigated the familiar corridors, her breathing harsh and ragged.

She didn't have to look back to know she wasn't being followed. The eerie quiet told her she was alone.

And that simple fact was the only thing driving her forward. She had to keep her lead, to buy herself enough time to retrieve the gun from the lab.

As she wove through labyrinthine passages, she couldn't

shake the memory of the woman's gaze from outside. It was as if she were still watching, anticipating Alex's every move.

Her time and options were running out, the net closing with every passing second.

Bursting through the exterior doors, she emerged at the back of the building, just a few hundred feet from the Francois-Xavier Building.

Her target was well within reach. She prayed she wasn't too late, that her pursuer hadn't somehow outmaneuvered her.

With a final burst of speed, she sprinted across open ground, her heart pounding like a countdown to oblivion. Each step brought her closer to her goal and the inescapable confrontation ahead.

She knew, with grim certainty, this was only a temporary reprieve. No matter how fast she ran or how cleverly she hid, she couldn't evade her fate forever.

Sooner or later, she'd have to face the consequences of her actions, to stand and fight against the encroaching darkness that sought to consume her.

But now, all that mattered was reaching that lab, arming herself for the battles to come.

The rest would wait.

Until she was ready.

Until there was no other choice.

With a final, desperate lunge, she grasped the door handle and wrenched it open, plunging into the cool dimness of the Francois-Xavier Building.

Praying it wasn't already too late.

32 / CORNERED
KI-SUNG

She watched from the shadows as Alex burst through the doors of the aging aerospace building, her desperate sprint ending abruptly.

A cold, mirthless smile tugged at Ki-Sung's mouth.

She had to admit, the little hacker was clever, using the campus's maze-like layout to shake her tail.

But Ki-Sung was no ordinary pursuer. She was a ghost, a whisper of death in the wind. And she had come prepared.

Upon arriving in the overpriced college town, she made it her mission to study every detail, familiarizing herself with every nook and cranny her prey might use. Especially where Alex took classes.

The police blotter had been particularly enlightening. A few hours of digging uncovered an unnamed woman's recent run-in with the law.

Right here, at this very spot.

It didn't take a genius to deduce it was Alex from the description. Why she'd fled here, of all places, was another story.

The building was more than a convenient escape route. It

must hold something the girl needed. Something she thought would give her an edge.

Ki-Sung knew better. It was her job to anticipate such erratic moves, plotting every possible scenario.

There was no path, no option that ended with Alex walking away alive.

The girl's fate had been sealed the moment N3tN1nja killed her sister Choe. She didn't care if Cipher needed her or if the general hunted her down for breaking protocol.

Alex's path would end here.

With fluid grace, Ki-Sung moved from behind the evergreen shrubs, gliding across the street and into the shadows like a wraith.

She'd give the girl a moment to catch her breath, to believe she'd found safety.

Then, she would strike.

Swiftly. Silently. Deadly.

Just as she'd been trained to do.

The hunt was nearing its end.

And her prey had nowhere left to run.

33 / DESPERATE MEASURES
ALEX

The vestibule held only a few students with their parents, poring over maps of the campus. When Alex burst through the front door, they jumped, falling into one another. She mumbled a hasty apology, her words lost in her pounding feet, as she rushed down the hall toward the lower levels.

Reaching the stairwell, she descended quickly, her footsteps echoing in the seldom-used space. At the bottom, she pushed through a fire door and lunged for the lab entrance, grasping the handle. It didn't budge.

"Crap," she muttered, realizing she'd forgotten her student ID.

Peering through the narrow window, she scanned the lab, hoping for a miracle, that someone was working inside. To her dismay, it was empty.

"Damn it!"

She spun around, searching for another way in. There were four doors to the left and one to the right near the stairs, the janitor's closet she'd noticed the other day.

Her mind flashed back to the students upstairs, a flicker of hope igniting. Maybe one of them could help.

As she turned toward the stairwell, a shift in light caught her eye. Someone was coming down.

Her blood ran cold, a sickening certainty settling in her gut. It had to be her pursuer, the relentless assassin dogging her every step. There was no other explanation. The students wouldn't drag their parents down here.

Panic seized her as she weighed her dwindling options. She couldn't go back up, not without risking a confrontation. And she couldn't stay here, trapped like a rat in a maze.

Without thinking, she shot forward, trying the handle on the janitor's closet. To her surprise, it was unlocked.

Barely daring to breathe, she slipped inside, easing the door shut with a soft click.

Darkness enveloped her. The acrid smell of cleaning supplies filled her nostrils as she strained to hear over her thundering heart.

Footsteps echoed in the hallway, drawing closer with each second.

Alex stood perfectly still, hardly daring to breathe.

This was it. If her pursuer found her here, trapped and unarmed, it would all be over. Everything she'd fought for, everything she'd sacrificed, would be for nothing.

Please! Just let them pass by. Let me have this one chance.

When the footsteps didn't pause at her door, relief flickered briefly.

A faint scraping sound made her flinch, her arm brushing a storage shelf. It made the softest of squeaks, and she held her breath, praying no supplies fell. Fortunately, nothing did.

The metallic grating sounded like it was coming from her door, but it wasn't. It was close, though.

She eased forward, feeling in the dark until her fingertips found the doorknob. She gripped it, holding the door in place.

If she felt even the slightest tug, she'd shove outward with all her might. Exhausted as she was, the sudden move might just catch her pursuer off guard.

The tug never came. Instead, a faint click sounded, followed by the squeal of an underused door easing open.

'Fuck,' she mouthed.

Someone was entering the lab. The same lab she needed to reach.

She couldn't hide forever. Every second she delayed, her pursuer either gained ground or an edge. Surely, they didn't know why she was heading to the lab. The longer she kept that advantage, the better.

Steeling herself, she took a deep breath and gently turned the doorknob, easing the door open a crack.

Light from the hallway spilled in, briefly blinding her and illuminating her tense face.

Slowly, she peered out, straining to see the lab.

The door was ajar, a sliver of darkness beckoning her forward. Someone had propped it open with the doorstop.

She had no choice. She had to go in, to face whatever awaited her. It was the only way to get the gun, to even the odds in this insane game of cat and mouse.

With her heart in her throat, she eased the closet door open, wincing at the faint creak of the hinges.

Step by painstaking step, she crept into the hallway, her muscles coiled for action.

The short distance to the lab felt like miles, each footfall an agonizing test of her nerves.

Her heartbeat pounded in her ears, threatening to drown out all other sounds.

At last, she reached the threshold. Her trembling hand pulled the door open. The darkness seemed to draw her in, promising either salvation or damnation.

She hesitated, the weight of the unknown pressing down on her.

But she couldn't turn back now. Not when she was so close, not when everything hinged on what happened next.

With a final, steadying breath, she yanked the door open and stepped into the inky darkness. Instinctively, she flipped the lights on, only to find Professor Newton bent down near the second row of computers.

He looked like he was searching for something.

"Alex!" His eyes widened with shock. "I thought I might find you here."

"What..."—she tilted her head, confusion clouding her thoughts—"what are you doing here?"

"I figured you might show up here," he began. "I heard about your arrest the other day. In the lobby." He gestured upward.

Alex's mind raced. He might have known about her arrest, but the police report wouldn't include details about this lab. At least, not the public one. And they certainly wouldn't have mentioned the gun. *So what was he searching for then? Unless...*

A sickening realization dawned, making her skin crawl.

What if Professor Newton wasn't here by chance? What if he was involved in all of this, a piece of the evil puzzle I'd never considered?

She recalled their earlier encounter... how he'd appeared just as she was being pursued. At the time, she'd been too grateful to question it, but now...

Now, it all seemed too convenient, too perfectly timed.

"You're working with her, aren't you?" she asked, her voice trembling. "The woman chasing me. You're part of this twisted nightmare."

His face contorted, but she couldn't tell if it was confusion or deception. "Alex, I don't know what you're talking about. I was just worried about you, that's all."

He stepped toward her, hands raised in a placating gesture.

But she wasn't buying it. Too many people had already taken advantage of her.

Not anymore.

"Stay back!" she warned, her eyes darting around the room, searching for a weapon.

There was nothing there. Nothing but computer equipment.

"I don't know your angle," she continued, "but Cipher isn't getting away with this. I won't let it happen."

"Alex, please, just listen," Professor Newton pleaded, his words only fueling her paranoia.

She lunged forward, shoving him hard in the chest. He stumbled backward into the row of computers.

Monitors crashed to the floor. Keyboards and mice skittered across tiles as he flipped headfirst into the next row, equipment raining down on him.

He groaned as she shot toward the back row, recalling vividly which desk she'd hidden under nights earlier.

As she ducked down, she eyed his moaning form struggling under the pile of machines.

"I trusted you," she muttered, hot tears streaming down her face.

She swiped her hand over the machine, searching blindly for the gun—her salvation. "I thought you were on my side!"

Her hands came up empty.

"No," she whispered. "No, please." She yanked the computer off its mount, peering into the space behind.

There was nothing but dusty candy wrappers and a few cords. No gun, no clip. Only emptiness.

She collapsed, staring vacantly at the remains of computers splayed across the floor.

With her attention focused on finding the weapon, she hadn't heard the professor rise. Her world had narrowed to a single, desperate task.

She didn't register his presence until his shadow loomed over her, making her heart skip.

She looked up. He stood there, eyes filled with sadness, his hand outstretched.

He opened his mouth, but before he could speak, a gunshot rang out, deafening in the enclosed lab.

Professor Newton's eyes widened, his mouth hanging open in a silent gasp as a dark stain bloomed across his chest.

He crumpled to the ground, his life's blood pooling beneath him in a spreading crimson tide.

Alex flinched, her ears ringing from the sudden blast. The deafening crack reverberated in her skull, leaving a sharp, metallic taste on her tongue. Her breath came in ragged gasps as she peered over the desk.

There, in the doorway, stood the woman from the bus, a smoking gun in hand and a cold, impassive expression on her face.

"Hello, Alex," she said, her voice as sharp as a razor. "I believe we have unfinished business."

Alex's mind raced, fear and adrenaline surging through her veins, her body trembling in the aftershock of the blast.

"Was that them?" the assassin demanded, stepping into the room and training her gun on Alex's chest.

"Them who?" Alex asked, eyeing the weapon. The woman's cane was nowhere in sight.

"N3tN1nja!" the assassin snarled. "We have a fucking score to settle. A bloody goddamn score." Her gaze flitted between Alex and the professor. "They killed my sister, and I won't rest until I've painted the walls with their blood. Now, tell me, you little bitch, was that them?"

Alex's heart pounded. She hesitated, confused by the question. *Was the professor N3tN1nja?*

She opened her mouth, then closed it, eyes darting away. She didn't know.

"So it wasn't them," the assassin hissed, narrowing her gaze. "Too bad. That would have made this next part easier on you." She raised the gun to Alex's head. "Tell me where they are, and I might just let you live long enough to watch me gut Michelle like a fish."

The mention of Michelle's name jolted Alex with anger, burning away the last vestiges of her paralysis.

She couldn't let that happen, couldn't let this monster use her friends as pawns in her twisted game.

She had to fight, had to turn the tables, even if it meant risking everything.

In that moment, Alex knew with sickening certainty that the assassin wasn't here to kill her. Not yet. If she wanted her dead, she'd have pulled the trigger already.

No, this woman wanted N3tN1nja. And that meant she still had a chance, however slim, of making it out alive.

In a burst of desperate speed, Alex lunged sideways, snatching a hard drive from inside one of the cracked-open machines. She hurled it at the woman with all her might.

The assassin reacted with inhuman swiftness, ducking as the device sailed over her head and slammed into the wall behind her.

But that momentary distraction was all Alex needed.

She charged forward, a wordless cry tearing from her throat as she crashed into the assassin. They tumbled to the ground in a tangle of flailing limbs and flying fists.

The gun skittered away, lost in the chaos of their struggle, but Alex barely noticed. All she could think about was survival, doing whatever it took to survive.

With the gun gone and the woman reeling, Alex twisted her body in a whirlwind motion, landing an elbow strike to the assassin's throat.

It was a move she'd learned in taekwondo, but never delivered to anything but a practice dummy.

Until today.

The woman clutched her neck with both hands, kicking and clawing wildly, struggling to breathe through her swelling windpipe.

Now was Alex's chance to run, but instead, she did the only thing she could think to do.

She snatched up a heavy-duty power cable from the mangled mess of machines and wrapped it around the woman's neck.

Without pausing, she knelt on the woman's chest, twisting the cable and yanking with all her might.

Her muscles screamed. Her heart raced. Every cell in her body laser-focused on one primal goal: survival.

The woman's arm shot upward, waving frantically, desperate to land a blow.

But her motions were telegraphed, her eyes betraying her next move.

Alex twisted away, yanking harder, the cable biting into her palms, drawing blood. But she didn't stop.

Gritting her teeth, she channeled every ounce of her rage, her terror, into this one savage act.

She braced for a final, furious assault. A last stand worthy of a professional killer. But it never came. The woman's body betrayed her, surrendering to the stranglehold.

There was no more fight. No resistance.

The assassin's eyes, once ablaze with fury, now stared blankly. Lifeless. Their fire snuffed out.

As Alex watched, the flush drained from her attacker's face, leaving behind death's ashen mask.

Her lips took on a bluish hue, the telltale sign of a soul slipping away.

The body beneath Alex grew heavy. The weight of a life ended.

She'd witnessed it—the last flicker of awareness in her

attacker's eyes. The realization of their end. And then, nothing. Just an empty shell, a life extinguished.

Alex's breath came in ragged bursts, adrenaline still surging through her veins.

As seconds crawled by, the rush ebbed, replaced by a chilling void. The weight of her actions crashed down. The irrevocable act of taking a life.

A mix of emotions washed over her.

Relief—at the threat neutralized.

Anger—at the cruel twist of fate that brought her here.

Sorrow—for a life lost, however corrupted.

Guilt—for the blood staining her hands, her very essence.

"I think... she's... dead," Professor Newton sputtered.

Alex spun around, her eyes locking onto the pale-faced man propped against the wall, his shirt soaked in blood.

"Shit," she hissed, releasing the cord and crawling to his side. She examined him carefully, her movements slow and deliberate.

The bullet had pierced his left shoulder, missing his heart by inches. A good sign, she thought. He might survive this.

His eyes fluttered closed as he caught his breath, then reopened to glance past her. "I'm... not them," he wheezed.

Alex looked back at the motionless woman on the ground. "Them who?"

"N3t... N1nja," he muttered, the name barely a whisper on his lips.

When she turned back, she spotted a blood-smeared phone in his hand, its screen aglow. He'd already dialed.

She snatched it up, pressing it to her ear. Agent Reed's voice crackled through, frantic screams filling the background.

Realization hit her like a thunderbolt. Professor Newton wasn't just another academic, he was a government asset, like the woman. But a good guy. A Cyber Command agent embedded in the university, likely monitoring the student body for terrorists or other threats.

It all clicked into place. His presence here, his thorough search of the room, he must have expected to find something she'd left behind. But like her, he'd come up empty-handed.

Alex slumped against the wall, the phone pressed to her ear.

"John?" A man's voice crackled over the line. "Are you alright? Help is on the way. They should be there shortly."

"He's fine," Alex said, her voice hoarse. "He'll be fine."

"Who—" The man's voice caught. "Alex? Is that... you?"

Aunt Min's scream pierced the background. "Is she there? Is she alive?"

Alex didn't reply. Her gaze locked onto an object against the far wall.

The assassin's pistol.

Without hesitation, she tossed the phone aside and lunged for the gun. Snatching it up, she checked the magazine. Full, minus one bullet.

As she turned to sprint out, a faint vibration reached her ears. It was coming from the assassin's body.

Heart thundering, Alex tucked the gun into her waistband and rifled through the woman's pockets until her fingers closed around the buzzing device.

The screen flashed an incoming call from a name she knew well: Cipher.

With trembling hands, she accepted it and raised the phone. An eerie silence greeted her, stretching on for several agonizing seconds.

Then, a voice: "Ki-Sung?"

Her eyes locked onto the lifeless body, a chill snaking down her spine. The assassin had a name.

Emotions crashed over her: Fear, anger, grief, a searing thirst for justice. This faceless monster, this architect of so much suffering, was now within reach. His voice made her blood boil.

She thought of Michelle, held captive by a psychopath. Of Professor Newton, wounded on the floor, victim of Cipher's ruthless game. Of her family, of countless lives shattered in his twisted power play.

And in that moment, something inside Alex snapped. A dam of pent-up rage, built over months of fear and helplessness, burst.

She couldn't stay silent. Couldn't let this opportunity slip away. Cipher needed to know she was coming, that his reign of terror was ending.

Reckless? Perhaps. Foolish? Maybe. But in that instant, she didn't care.

All that mattered was making Cipher understand. His reckoning was at hand.

He'd underestimated her for the last time. Now, she was primed to strike back with every fiber of her being.

"Ki-Sung is dead," Alex said, her voice arctic. "And, Cipher, you're next."

She killed the call and pocketed the phone. There was no time for fear. No room for hesitation.

Michelle's life hung by a thread. Every heartbeat counted.

With a final glance at Professor Newton's unconscious form, Alex turned and sprinted out, the gun, a reassuring weight at her side.

She had a friend to save. A score to settle.

And God help anyone who dared stand in her way.

34 / CONTINGENCIES AND CONSEQUENCES
CIPHER

He slammed his fist against the ceiling of the van, unleashing a bloodcurdling scream that reverberated inside and out. Raw, primal fury coursed through his veins, threatening to consume him whole.

A woman getting into her car a few spaces down yelped and spun around, nearly throwing her coffee as she glared at the source of the disturbance.

But Cipher didn't flinch. His world narrowed to a pinprick of blinding rage, a singular thirst for vengeance.

In a fit of uncontrolled rage, he smashed the burner phone against the console, sending plastic shrapnel flying in all directions.

"What the fuck, man?" Tae-Woo recoiled, swiping blood from his cheek.

Cipher continued, pummeling the steering wheel with his fists. Pain barely registering through his haze of fury. He turned on Tae-Woo, eyes ablaze with manic intensity.

"What the fuck? You want to know what the fuck?" His voice, a raw, guttural snarl. "I'll tell you. Our little bitch trailing Alex just—"

"Chill out, dude," Tae-Woo cut in, ducking his head and motioning to the elderly woman still gawking from her car.

Cipher's gaze snapped to the unwelcome observer, eyes narrowing to predatory slits.

Rather than wave her away, he rolled down his window. His face contorted into a grotesque mask of contempt.

"Go back to your crocheting, you nosy bitch!" He flipped her off.

The woman gasped, scrambling into her car. As she pulled away, she slowed, eyes locked on the menacing van and its occupants.

But Cipher had already dismissed her. His attention snapped to the back of the van, settling on the canisters in the corner—his backup plan, a last resort if all else failed.

His gaze drifted past the ominous containers landing on their captive.

Michelle's eyes, wide with terror, met his. She writhed against her bindings, desperate to escape the madman before her.

He drank in her fear like a fine wine. A fleeting taste of power in a world conspiring against him.

He savored the memory of her muffled screams from hours earlier, when he'd carved his mark into her flesh. Her wounds were a bloody reminder of who held the power here. Him.

Her fear, intoxicating as it was, was merely a sideshow. A fleeting distraction from his true objective, the endgame he'd orchestrated for the past year.

Byt3Linguist and N3tN1nja. The real targets. Thorns to be ripped out and incinerated. They'd wounded him, severing one head of his hydra. But the second lay dormant, primed to strike.

And strike it would. With a vengeance that promised to shake the world to its foundations.

His eyes raked over the woman's battered form. A flicker of satisfaction coursed through him, not from her suffering, but from Byt3Linguist eliminating Ki-Sung. That was one less loose end he had to sever.

Grudging respect stirred within him. The hacker's cold efficiency in dispatching Ki-Sung mirrored his own ruthlessness.

Yet even as he acknowledged her skill, a darker emotion writhed in his gut. The notion that anyone else had power over him, over his carefully laid plans, made his blood boil. Rage surged anew, threatening to consume him.

He was the architect, the puppet master. He couldn't afford any more interferences, no matter how convenient.

With a growl of frustration, he snatched up the radio. His eyes swept the entrance to the park, lingering on a distant tree line as he keyed the mic.

"Maverick, Raven here. What's the weather update?"

The reply crackled back instantly. "Clear skies, Raven. Crystal clear."

He nodded and switched channels, his gaze dropping to the circle on the map. "Hey, Neo, any status on the game?"

"It's still pre-game, Raven," came the second reply. "But I'm watching, chilling on my couch, waiting for the kickoff."

A grin of satisfaction spread across his face. He could picture exactly where the man was lying in wait—the same corner where Ki-Sung had watched Alex disembark earlier.

The general's assets were his insurance policy, his failsafe against fate's cruel whims.

If Byt3Linguist thought she could outmaneuver him, she was in for a rude awakening. He had contingencies upon contingencies, ready to ensnare her no matter which path she chose.

She might be clever, but he was the grand architect of this game.

A cold smile sliced across Cipher's face, devoid of mercy.

With a curt nod to Tae-Woo, they slid out of the van, striding across the street toward the park.

The hour had come to collect his due, a debt to be paid in blood and anguish.

35 / THE BLEEDING EDGE
ALEX

The bus was surprisingly empty given its earlier overcrowding. Alex had expected a sea of hovering parents to hide within, not this stark exposure.

The last thing she needed was someone noticing the gun bulging in her jacket. It was bad enough it poked her side.

Even as she fixed her gaze on passing cars, she felt their eyes. Three students up front, their glances like needles on her skin. The first time she turned and met their gaze, they scattered like startled birds.

Their whispers grew, eyes darting between her and each other, stoking the unease in her gut.

She couldn't make out their words, but their tone was unmistakable. They were mocking her for some reason.

She tried to focus on the task at hand, preparing for the encounter with Cipher. But their constant stares and muffled voices wormed their way under her skin.

After countless glances and far too many hushes, something inside her snapped. The day's horrors, the gun's burden, the constant dread—it all erupted in a molten surge of fury.

She leaned forward, locking eyes with the nearest guy, a meathead wearing a muscle shirt in November. "Got a problem?" The words exploded, echoing through the bus like a gunshot, bursting from her lips before she could stop them.

She knew it was reckless, knew she should keep a low profile. But at that moment, she didn't care.

She was done being a passive observer. Done letting others talk behind her back.

If these assholes wanted a fight, she'd oblige. Gladly.

The meathead's reaction blindsided her. He rose, navigating the swaying bus with surprising grace, closing the distance between them.

"Shit," she hissed. *Why can't he take a damn hint?* She had no time for this, not with the world hanging by a thread.

He paused before her, his eyes holding something unexpected. Not anger, but...

Alex tightened her grip on the gun, rechecking the safety. She'd already touched it countless times in the last ten minutes, a nervous tic betraying her inner turmoil.

He leaned in, his gaze fixed on her forehead. "Are you... okay?" His whisper cracked. "I mean... do you need help?"

She shook her head, confused. This wasn't the bravado she'd braced for.

Her eyes narrowed to slits. "And why would I need *your* help?"

The man glanced over his shoulder before turning and pointing at her forehead. "You're... bleeding."

"What?" The word slipped out as her trembling fingers touched her forehead, coming away slick with blood.

A jolt of pain seared through her skull. The sight of crimson on her fingers, glistening in the harsh bus light, sent her world spinning.

Ki-Sung must've hit her during their tussle. Alex hadn't felt the wound, hadn't registered the pain through the haze of adrenaline and fear. But now, staring at the bloody stain on her fingers, reality crashed down with nauseating force.

The man crouched down, eyes level with hers. "I can flag the driver if you want? The hospital... it's right there." He gestured out the window.

Alex squeezed her eyes shut, fighting a sudden surge of vertigo. She then forced herself to look out the window, taking in her surroundings.

Only then did she realize where she was. There, across the street, was the parking lot where Cipher had wanted to meet. It was jammed with cars, a sea of metal and glass capable of hiding anyone or anything. Michelle could be in any of them, bound, gagged, her life hanging by a thread.

The thought made Alex's blood run cold, fear and desperation coiling in her gut. She couldn't falter now, couldn't waste a heartbeat. Michelle's fate hinged on her resolve, her ability to push through hell itself.

"Thank you, but no," Alex said, barely above a whisper.

Her eyes lingered on the hospital as it disappeared behind buildings, a fleeting mirage of safety. "I'll manage. My dorm has a nurse."

The lie slipped out as she met his gaze. She had no intention of returning to her dorm. "Really, I appreciate your concern. But I'll be okay." She offered a tight, unconvincing smile.

The guy hesitated, clearly not buying her act. But something in her expression stopped him from pushing further.

With a terse nod, he retreated, leaving Alex alone with her demons and the weight of the gun at her side.

She was done running. Done hiding. Done being afraid.

It was time to face her demons head-on. Blood be damned.

She leaned her uninjured side against the cool window, watching the world outside pass in a hazy blur of colors and shapes. Her mind raced through dozens of possible encounters with Cipher, each more terrifying than the last.

Her plan would work. It had to. It was all about timing.

Beneath the fear and doubt, a steely resolve took hold. She'd come too far, sacrificed too much, to turn back now. No matter what horrors lay ahead, she'd see this through to the end.

For Michelle. For herself. For redemption.

The hiss of pneumatic doors jolted her back to reality.

Her eyes refocused. The park materialized outside. This stop was actually closer than walking from her dorm, and getting off here meant avoiding the cemetery.

"Wait!" she shouted, "Hold the door!"

She launched from her seat, squeezing between the closing doors. The threshold alarm buzzed as the door slammed into her, knocking her off balance.

She winced, her head throbbing both from the impact and the cut. But she needed to get out.

Once she stumbled to the sidewalk, she checked the gun in her pocket and scanned her surroundings. She'd never used this stop before; it felt oddly unfamiliar despite its proximity to her dorm.

"Get your shit together, girl," she whispered, mentally reviewing her plan.

If she was going to pull this off, she needed to set up her phone. Something she should've done on the bus.

Walking slowly to the nearby park entrance, she reached for her device, but realized quickly it wasn't hers. It was Ki-Sung's.

Her heart stuttered at the thought of losing her lifeline. Then, relief flooded back as her fingers found the burner in her other pocket. Checking it, she saw a dozen missed calls, all from the same two numbers. Aunt Min and Agent Reed.

Scrolling through the wall of messages, she felt a rising tension in each one.

Her aunt was losing it, every word searching for a sign Alex was alive.

But that was a concern for another time. Right now, she needed to check her signal and make sure she could connect to the exhibit.

She exited the emotional stream of messages and opened the crude web browser, refreshing the open page. The last time she'd used the app was nearly a month ago when she'd helped her roommate test her equipment.

She remembered that day in their dorm fondly. It had been chaotic, filled with playful arguments and stressful barbs. They'd had countless heated debates that afternoon, but emerged closer, cementing their bond as not just roommates but best friends.

Lost in the bittersweet haze, Alex missed the telltale crunch of gravel behind her.

Reality slammed back as something hard bit into her side —the unmistakable kiss of a gun barrel.

"Hand it over, Barbie," a voice hissed, hot breath invading her space. "And the gun, too. Slow like," he purred, "or your guts paint the sidewalk."

Alex quickly pocketed her phone and froze, her blood turning to ice.

How could I have been so careless?

Her focus on the plan, on her perceived advantage, had left her exposed. They weren't just prepared, they were ten steps ahead.

"Just so you know, this baby's got a silencer," the man breathed. "I could drop you right here. No one would hear a thing. I'd be in those woods before anyone even noticed you were down."

His threat slithered down her spine, reminding her how vulnerable she was out here alone. She'd chosen this spot for its isolation, not as her potential gravesite.

As her eyes darted around, a chilling realization dawned.

The expected throng of students and parents, the bustling energy of the art exhibition... they were all missing.

Horror crashed over her. She must've gotten the date wrong in her head. The show, it was tomorrow, not today.

In her frantic chess game with Cipher, she'd fumbled a crucial move. And now, she was cornered.

The area was deserted; no oblivious bystanders to use for cover, no one to call for help.

If she screamed or fought back, no one would come to her rescue.

"The gun!" the man snarled. "Now!"

She slowly reached into her pocket, pulling out the assassin's weapon. Her one advantage, now a cold, dead weight in her hand. A grim reminder of the lethal game she'd entered.

The second it came into view, he snatched it away, sliding it into his jacket before jabbing her even harder.

She winced, her mind racing as she weighed her odds. *Can I twist away? Land a blow? Create an opening?* But the cold steel against her ribs reminded her how little control she had.

"The phone," he breathed. "Nice and easy."

Suddenly, his demeanor shifted and the pressure on her side all but vanished.

Alex followed his gaze. He was eyeing an approaching couple. They were fast-walking toward them, lost in their exercise bubble, earbuds blocking out the world.

As they strode past, the woman abruptly looked up, her gaze falling on Alex. Her eyes widened in concern. "You're bleeding," she said, gesturing at Alex's head.

"It's fake," her attacker replied, not missing a beat. "We're LARPing." He smeared Alex's forehead, then licked his finger with a grotesque smirk. "Mmm. Ketchup."

The woman cringed, studying the wound. "It looks so... real."

Alex's eyes widened, a silent scream for help.

But the woman's gaze remained fixed on the gory spectacle, blind to her desperate plea.

For a heartbeat, hope flickered in Alex's chest. Maybe this woman would see through the charade. Maybe she'd sense Alex was in danger.

But the hope vanished as quickly as it came. The woman's attention snapped away. "Bob!" she shrieked. "Wait the hell up!" She tore off, chasing her partner, who was now a distant silhouette.

Alex watched her lifeline vanish, despair settling like lead in her gut. Her one chance at rescue, gone in an instant.

A low, menacing chuckle slithered from her captor. "Looks like it's just you and me, Barbie."

Without warning, he plunged his hand into her pocket, his fingers grazing her hip as he fished out the phone.

She recoiled at the unwanted contact, revulsion clawing up her throat.

"Move," he snarled, shoving her forward. "Someone's itching to meet you. You'll be fast friends, I'm sure."

Alex stumbled, barely catching herself as she was propelled into the park.

The trees seemed to close in, their shadows writhing like grasping tendrils, eager to swallow her whole.

In that moment, she knew with icy certainty that whatever horrors Cipher had planned...

Escape would not come easily.

Yet, as despair threatened to overwhelm her, a spark of defiance kindled in her chest. She'd be damned if she'd go down without a fight.

Her mind raced, seeking any advantage, any way to turn the tables. Then, like a sledgehammer, it hit her.

She stumbled again, intentionally this time, a sharp hiss escaping her lips as she clutched her leg. She slowed to a painful crawl, each step a performance of agony.

"Pick up the pace," he snarled, steel biting into her side.

Alex whirled on him. "I can't, you sadistic prick. In case you hadn't noticed, your assassin friend did a number on me before I put her down."

She gestured to her leg, to an imaginary wound hidden beneath her jeans. "Want me moving faster? Tell your boss to carry me himself. Otherwise, this is the speed you get."

The man's face twisted with anger. She could almost feel his trigger finger twitch, death a hairsbreadth away.

But her grimace of pain gave him pause. Perhaps he realized a corpse was more trouble than it was worth. Or maybe, deep down, he was just a coward.

"Fine," he spat, shoving her again. "But if this is some game..."

He let the threat hang in the air, unspoken but crystal clear.

Alex just smiled, a bitter, humorless twist of her lips. "I wouldn't dream of it," she said, her voice dripping with sarcasm.

She turned back to the path, faking a limp while biting back imaginary groans. All the while, her fingers worked in her pocket.

The moment she'd conceived her ruse, her hand had grazed an unexpected treasure in her jacket.

It was her phone.

The fool had snatched Ki-Sung's device, not hers.

Hope stirred in her chest, a defiant spark in the suffocating darkness. She strained to recall the intricacies of the crude web page she and Michelle had written months ago. If she could trigger her plan, even without seeing the display, she might just have a chance. It was a desperate gamble, but it was all she had.

Perhaps she wasn't merely Cipher's pawn after all. Maybe, just maybe, she could still be a player in this twisted game.

As she hobbled deeper into the trees, each step reminded

her of the reckoning ahead. She clung to that knowledge like a lifeline.

In her mind, a plan was forming, a way to use Cipher's arrogance against him.

She would face the monster, the demon who had shattered her life.

She would look into his eyes and see the depths of his cruelty.

And somehow, she would make him pay for every moment of suffering, every shattered dream, every life he'd destroyed.

This was her fight, her chance to reclaim her destiny.

And *she* would not let it slip through her fingers.

Not this time.

36 / THE BEST LAID PLANS
CIPHER

It had been fifteen minutes since Maverick missed his check-in, and Cipher was getting pissed. No, scratch that. He was well past pissed. He was fucking furious.

Was this General Tau's idea of professionalism? Radio silence now, of all times? It was unacceptable. A goddamn disgrace.

Twice he'd squawked the moron's radio. Twice, silence mocked him. Even with civilians around, the protocol was clear. Turn your radio down and chirp back over the open channel. It was simple enough for a child, let alone a supposed professional.

America. Land of the free, home of the soft. It had neutered these so-called operatives, dulled their edge to uselessness.

His eyes scanned the tree line, hungry for movement. Nothing. Just an endless stream of parents and students flooding the sidewalk from the dorm. Like lemmings to a cliff.

What was this, some twisted field trip?

He shifted uneasily under the canopy of trees. That damn art installation loomed overhead, only adding to his agitation. Computer panels dangled from wires like broken promises, dark and lifeless. Like a network abruptly shut down. It felt like a bad omen, a glitch in his carefully laid plans.

"I don't like this," he snarled, his voice barely carrying over the swelling crowd. "It's getting too crowded in here. Too many variables to track. Too many ways this can all go to shit."

"Over there!" Tae-Woo pointed toward the hospital, beyond the garish parade of sculptures.

Beyond the orange-painted Greek pillars and the pyramid of stacked cows was Maverick, and he wasn't alone. He was escorting someone.

It took Cipher a moment to recognize Alex—Byt3Linguist—limping beside him. Her head of blonde hair was unmistakable, even at this distance.

But N3tN1nja was nowhere in sight. The bitch came solo. Either that, or...

He whirled around, cursing his tunnel vision. A second wave of people flooded in from the south parking lot, unnoticed in his rage-fueled fixation.

The park was suddenly crawling with people, parents and students alike, oblivious to the deadly game unfolding in their midst.

It was time to bring in his insurance policy.

Cipher leaned close to Tae-Woo. "Call your brother," he whispered. "Tell him to bring the canisters."

"The canisters?" Tae-Woo's face drained of color. "We're not even sure they're legit."

"Do it!" Cipher hissed. "And make sure he remembers the goddamn masks. I'm not choking on that shit-storm."

Tae-Woo eyed him. "What about the girl in the van?"

Cipher shrugged. "I don't give a shit about that twat. Just get those fucking canisters here. Now!" He pivoted, eyes locked on Alex's approach, his heart pounding with anticipation.

Tae-Woo didn't hesitate. He dialed his phone, walking away and whispering urgently to his brother.

As the pair closed in, now a stone's throw away, Cipher's gaze sharpened. He blinked, his focus narrowing on Byt3Linguist.

Something... was off. A strange sense of familiarity washed over him.

There was something about the way she moved, the set of her shoulders, the defiant tilt of her chin. It reminded him of someone—a ghost from his past that he couldn't quite place.

He shook off the eerie sensation. Sentiment was a luxury he couldn't afford. Not now. Not with this bitch, this perpetual thorn, finally within reach.

As Alex limped into range, Cipher advanced. A predator's smile carved his features. "Well, well, well," he purred, savoring each syllable. "The elusive Byt3Linguist graces us with her presence." His eyes raked over her, disappointment twisting his mouth. "I expected more from the hacker who brought my virus to its knees."

He paused, waiting. She didn't bite.

"Speechless, are we?" He circled her, pausing behind to look her up and down like a piece of meat. Even beneath the baggy clothes, her potential was... intriguing.

"The nights I've spent, dreaming of this moment. Imagining the look on your face when I finally—"

A distant commotion cut him off. Shouts and laughter echoed through the trees, the approaching crowd growing louder by the second.

Cipher spun around, eyes widening as a second wave of parents spilled into the clearing. Their faces glowed with excitement, as if headed to some demented frat party.

Worst of all, they were heading straight at them—a sea of potential witnesses and a nightmare in the making.

With a sinking feeling in his gut, Cipher realized his carefully laid plans, his long-awaited revenge...

Was about to get a lot more complicated.

37 / THE ART OF DECEPTION
ALEX

Cipher's head snapped around, eyes locking on the surge of parents behind him. Alex's heart leapt, a dizzying cocktail of relief and dread flooding her system.

She'd been counting on the art exhibit to provide cover, to give her an edge in their deadly game of cat and mouse. But when she feared she'd gotten the dates wrong, her world had threatened to implode.

In the chaos of the past few days, her usually razor-sharp mind had blurred. Now, each misstep could mean the difference between breath and death. She prayed her blunders were fewer than his.

The maniac's glare swung back to her, and she cringed. His eyes blazed with unholy fire, promising to consume anything in his path. The swelling crowd clearly rattled him; they were wrenches in his meticulous machinations, obstacles to be obliterated.

Watching his composure crack, she knew she had to push harder. To break him, to shatter his desperate veneer of control.

"Where's Michelle?" Alex reached forward, boldly nudging his shoulder. Terror and exhilaration jolted through her like lightning. "We had a deal. Where is she?"

His nostrils flared, eyes boring into the crowd like laser beams. "What fucking deal? I made no such promise." His gaze met hers. "I said one hour, and not to come alone. N3tN1nja's absence means you've failed." His jaw clenched, gaze sweeping the crowd. "And now these people pay the price." He gestured grandly, a twisted showman. "Thank you, by the way, for bringing me here. You've simplified my task considerably."

Alex swallowed hard, struggling to hold herself together. If she was going to survive this, she had to stay strong, to keep her wits about her.

"What makes you think N3tN1nja isn't here?" she asked, her voice steady despite her inner turmoil.

She inched closer, eyes locked on his. "What if I told you they're already here? That Byt3Linguist and N3tN1nja are one and the same?"

The words hung between them, a challenge and a revelation all in one. She caught it—that flicker of doubt in his eyes, a hairline fracture in his certainty.

But his doubt vanished quickly, replaced by a cold, calculating glint. He wasn't buying it.

He knew she wasn't N3tN1nja, not at her age.

She needed to keep him off balance. To deepen that doubt, to make him question everything.

"Or perhaps," she mused softly, "I'm just smoke and mirrors. A decoy to blind you to the real threat. Much like your virus, actually."

Her eyes drifted to the tree line, lingering just long enough to draw his gaze. "N3tN1nja could be breathing down your neck. Someone you've already crossed paths with. Maybe even..."—her voice dropped lower—"someone you think you've caged."

Uncertainty flickered in his eyes, his brow furrowing as he struggled to process her words.

She could almost hear the gears of paranoia grinding in his mind, each thought a new seed of doubt taking root.

"Or," she whispered menacingly, "they're out there right now. Watching. Waiting. A sniper's crosshairs dancing on your carotid, ready to paint the trees red at my command."

Her eyes bored into his, letting the poison of her words seep deep. His gaze flicked to the trees, fingers twitching involuntarily toward his throat.

"You're... bluffing," he croaked, certainty crumbling in his voice.

"Am I?" Her lips curled, a predator's smile. "Ki-Sung and her sister shared your same conviction. Look where it got them. Care to wager your life on being right, when they were so fatally wrong?"

For a split second, genuine fear crossed his features. In that instant, she knew she'd cracked his armor.

Now, it was a game of seconds. Keep him off balance while she made her play.

Her finger hovered over her phone, a hair's breadth from action, as Cipher's gaze darted to her escort.

They exchanged a knowing look and a nod. Cipher's eyes flickered as he spun around, his gaze locking onto a figure weaving through the crowd. The newcomer had a bulky duffel bag slung over his shoulder and another clutched tightly in his hand.

Alex's heart raced as she studied the man's approach. His purposeful stride, the grim set of his jaw, the way his eyes scanned for threats... it all pointed to one chilling conclusion.

Time was running out.

She had to act fast, to set her plan in motion before it was too late. But just as she moved to press the button, Cipher's laughter cut through the air.

"Time's up, little hacker." He turned to face her, triumph twisting his features. "Your precious friend... Michelle, is it?" He sneered. "If she's N3tN1nja, then my job was laughably simple. Because she's either dead or dancing on death's doorstep as we speak."

The words slammed into Alex like a freight train, shattering her world. Pain exploded in her chest, a supernova of agony obliterating every last shred of hope.

But she didn't falter.

Instead, something primal awakened within her. Rage, pure and unfiltered, erupted from her core, a volcanic fury incinerating reason, obliterating restraint.

With a battle cry that tore from the depths of her soul, she slammed her finger down, unleashing digital hellfire.

The silent displays hanging overhead burst to life, displaying a rainbow of images and blaring music at full volume.

The sudden explosion of sound and light sent the crowd into a frenzied panic. People screamed and ran in all directions, their cries blending with the deafening roar from the trees.

Alex hurled herself at Cipher, every instinct screaming to make him pay, to wipe that smug grin off his face.

But he was too fast. In a blur of motion, a gun materialized from his waistband, his eyes wild with desperation.

Before she knew it, a single shot rang out, cutting through the chaos like a thunderclap.

Searing pain exploded in her side, white-hot agony driving the breath from her lungs.

She crumpled, knees slamming into unforgiving earth, fingers clutching her side, coming away crimson.

As the world tilted on its axis, as screams and gunfire faded into a distant, muffled roar...

The bitter truth crystallized in her fading consciousness.

She'd failed.

38 / THE TWISTED MIRROR
CIPHER

"No!" A woman's shriek pierced the cacophony. "God, no!" Her voice trembled, a counterpoint to the deafening chaos.

She collapsed to the ground, just beyond Alex's reach. The raw anguish in her face made Cipher whirl around, surveying the carnage from Alex's little trick.

A wall of people hemmed him in, gun barrels leveled from every angle.

Tae-Woo sprawled motionless, blood seeping from his temple. Maverick—or whatever the fuck his real name was—lay crumpled behind a tree, his leg a mangled mess, his weapon mockingly out of reach.

In a fluid motion, Cipher dropped to one knee, snaking his arm around Alex's throat. He jammed his pistol against her temple, feeling her pulse flutter beneath his grip.

The girl was out cold, but still breathing. Good enough.

Using her as a human shield wasn't his finest hour. But survival trumped pride. Better her skin than his.

When all hell broke loose, his finger had twitched on reflex, blasting a hole into her flesh.

It was an accident. A knee-jerk response to that goddamn sonic ambush.

Yet, looking back, it felt like fate.

The instant he told her Michelle was dead, the life drained from her face, replaced by pure, unfiltered anger.

It reminded him of Evelyn, his wife, his love, his betrayer.

Memories flooded his mind, painful and raw.

Evelyn's face, twisted in anguish, clutching their baby to her chest, screaming at him to stop, to let her go.

Gunshots.

The smell of blood.

The weight of the smoking gun in his hand.

She'd taken everything from him: his progeny, his future, his hope. And in that moment of blind rage, he'd taken it all back with the squeeze of a trigger and the shattering of his soul.

That day, he truly embraced the darkness, and let hatred consume him.

Hatred for her homeland of false promises, for the system that chewed him up and spat him out, for the people who watched him suffer and did nothing.

What struck him most about seeing Alex's face up close wasn't the emotions it stirred within him, it was her eyes. They were like his: one green, one blue, a mirrored opposite. Heterochromia was rare, especially in these colors.

It was like staring into a mirror, but backward. Where she was light, he was darkness. Where she was hope, he was despair.

As he gazed into those mismatched eyes, so hauntingly familiar yet alien, something stirred within him. A flicker of recognition, a glimmer of a long-buried truth.

Could it be? After all these years, after all the blood and pain and loss...

Was this girl—this hacker who'd crippled my empire—

somehow my daughter? Part of the family I'd destroyed, the life I'd shattered with my own two hands?

The thought was too much to bear, too painful to contemplate. And so he pushed it down, burying it deep in the recesses of his shattered psyche.

He couldn't be distracted, not now, not with his world crumbling and his enemies closing in.

He had to focus on survival, on escape, on the next move in this deadly game of chess.

But even as he tightened his grip on Alex's throat, pressing the cold barrel harder against her temple...

He couldn't shake the feeling that somehow, in some twisted, cosmic way...

This was all meant to be.

Then his focus shifted to the woman still sobbing on the ground. He realized only then that he recognized her face from somewhere.

"Min-Seo?" he stammered, leaning forward.

Impossible. She'd died in Seoul. Before his subway attack. He'd made sure of it.

"You're a goddamn monster!" she growled, clawing to her feet, her eyes locked on him with pure hatred.

"Min!" a man shouted from the crowd. "Get down!"

"Impossible," Cipher muttered, confusion and disbelief warring in his mind.

He hadn't seen her in nearly a decade. She was a specter from his past, returning to haunt him and dredge up his darkest, most painful memories.

Seeing Min-Seo was a gut punch, a visceral reminder of the day his world shattered. The day he lost everything... and here she was, robbing him yet again of his last chance at redemption, his last hope for a future beyond pain.

With his mind battling between reality and ghosts, he almost missed the agents closing in.

He yanked Alex closer, his heart pounding like a bass drum in his ears, a deafening soundtrack to his own personal hell.

"You fucking killed her, Damir." Min-Seo eased closer, her face streaked with tears. "You killed your own flesh and blood," she spat, each word dripping venom. "*Your own daughter.*"

The words hit him like a sledgehammer, driving the air from his lungs and sending his mind reeling.

No. It couldn't be. It wasn't possible.

His daughter was dead, lost forever, a casualty of his blind rage and despair.

Yet even as he tried to deny it, even as he fought against the truth with every fiber of his being...

Deep down, he knew.

He remembered that first glimpse of Alex. The flicker of recognition, the familiarity beyond coincidence.

Her skills, her strength, the fire in her eyes...

It was like looking in a mirror, reflecting his own twisted soul.

As the pieces fell into place with sickening clarity, he realized the true depth of his folly, the magnitude of his sins.

He hadn't been chasing his enemy all this time. He had been hunting his own child, his own blood.

The same blood now staining his hands, dripping from the wound he'd inflicted, the life he'd tried to snuff out.

A choked sob tore from his throat, a sound of pure anguish. The gun clattered to the ground as he released Alex, letting her slip from his grasp.

He stumbled back, eyes wide and haunted, his face a mask of horror and despair.

What have I done?
What kind of monster had I become, bringing such pain

and suffering to the one person I should have cherished above all others?

He stared at Alex, at his daughter, the daughter he'd never known. The child he'd betrayed in the most unforgivable way.

Like his father had done to him, he too had done to her.

And in that moment, staring into her eyes, he saw his own damnation, the inescapable judgment of his twisted soul.

39 / WAYFARING STRANGER
ALEX

She faded in and out of consciousness several times, and in each moment she came to, all Alex could hear was the music blaring overhead. The words of Michelle's favorite song blasted throughout the arboretum.

> *I know dark clouds will gather*
>   *'round me*
> *I know my way is hard and steep*

Someone who looked and sounded like Aunt Min screamed from behind Cipher, her sobs raw and gut-wrenching.

And then everything faded as Alex fell to her knees. Light passed in and out of her vision.

> *But beauteous fields arise before me*
> *Where God's redeemed, their*
>   *vigils keep*

A silhouette stumbled toward her. It *was* her aunt.

"You fucking killed her, Damir!" Aunt Min screamed, her voice cracking with anguish.

Damir? That name rang a bell. She'd heard it before.

She wanted to reach out, to call to her aunt, but she couldn't. Her body wouldn't respond, her limbs heavy and numb.

"You killed your own flesh and blood." Aunt Min paused, mere feet away, her voice fading in and out. "Your... own... daughter."

I'm going there to see my mother
She said she'd meet me when I come

The words of her aunt replayed over and over again in Alex's mind, a sickening loop of revelation and disbelief.

Your own daughter.

Your own daughter.

What did she mean by that?

Was it really possible? Could this monster, this demon who'd torn my life apart, be... my father?

She felt herself falling again, except this time, instead of someone squeezing her neck, she gasped for air as an image formed in front of her.

Cipher stared back, his face a mask of shock and horror. Like he'd seen a ghost, a specter of his twisted past come to haunt him.

"I'm sorry," he whispered, his words a broken, pitiful apology. "I'm so sorry."

As he spoke, hatred coursed through her veins. A black, venomous rage that consumed every other emotion.

She didn't want his apologies, his pathetic attempts at atonement.

She wanted him to suffer, to feel every ounce of the pain and despair he'd inflicted on her, on everyone he'd ever known.

It was too late for forgiveness, too late for redemption.

The only thing left for him...

Was the reckoning he so richly deserved.

And then the hailstorm of bullets rang out, a staccato of gunfire that pierced the air like the wrath of an angry god.

The sound was deafening, a roar that drowned out everything else.

Alex screamed silently, a primal, wordless cry of rage and despair.

And then the chorus of the song kicked in, a haunting, ethereal melody that seemed to mock the chaos and the carnage.

> *So I'm just going over Jordan*
> *I'm just going over home*

She could feel her blood seeping out of her body as desperate hands grabbed at her.

But it was Aunt Min whose voice she heard the clearest, a lifeline in the darkness that threatened to swallow her whole.

"Hang on, Lex... please, God... let her hold on."

Her voice repeated again and again as Alex lay there, her aunt's tears falling on her cheeks, mingling with her own.

In that moment, as the life drained from her body and the world faded to black, Alex felt a profound sense of emptiness, a hollow ache that had nothing to do with her wounds.

She'd finally learned the truth about her past, about the man who gave her life only to try and take it away.

But instead of closure, instead of peace... all she felt was a yawning void, a black hole of unanswered questions and unresolved pain.

She wished she'd been the one to end him, to put a bullet between his eyes. To watch the light fade from his mismatched gaze.

She wished she could've made him pay for every moment of suffering, every shattered dream and broken life.

But most of all, she wished she could've looked into his face and told him the truth.

That he meant nothing to her. That he was no father, and he certainly wasn't family. Not like her aunt, or her Appa and Eomma.

He was a monster, a twisted shell of a man who deserved nothing but hatred and scorn.

As the darkness closed in and the music faded to a distant echo, Alex clung to that truth, that final, bitter reality.

And with her last breath, she whispered the words she would never get to say to his face.

"Fuck you, Dad. Fuck you."

40 / THE AWAKENING
ALEX

Laughter tugged at the tendrils of Alex's consciousness, pulling her from her dream state. She'd relived that last moment countless times, wishing she'd been the one to kill him, not the one who died.

Her eyes opened to a stabbing light, sending pain coursing through her head.

"The lights," she muttered. "Turn... off... the lights."

She wasn't sure who was in the room, but judging by the commotion caused by her words, she wasn't alone.

"She's awake!" someone said, followed by shuffling feet.

Seconds later, she felt shadows surround her bed and the light dim, relieving the shooting pain behind her eyes.

"Thank you," she said, her voice gravelly. She sounded like she was talking with a mouth full of rocks.

"Get her some water," her mother said. "She needs to drink."

"E—omma?" Alex struggled to open her eyes.

When she did, she saw her parents' silhouettes standing beside her. Her mother's hand brushed her cheek before tenderly pressing a cup to her lips.

Alex swallowed the cool, refreshing liquid, the sensation

both soothing and startling. She hadn't realized how parched she was until then. The water seemed to breathe new life into her exhausted body.

"What... what happened?" she asked, struggling to rise. "Where am I?"

Her mother gently pressed against her chest. "Lie down."

"You're in the hospital," a familiar voice said. It sounded like...

Alex looked left and met the gaze of Michelle standing beside her.

Tears suddenly flooded Alex's eyes as her heart burst, a surge of emotion overwhelming her. She reached a shaking hand out toward her friend, desperate for the physical reassurance that this was real, that Michelle was truly standing there, alive.

Michelle stepped closer and met her halfway, interlocking her fingers with Alex's and giving them a gentle, comforting squeeze.

"I'm so sorry," Alex said, her voice quivering with the weight of her guilt. "I didn't know he—"

"Shhh," Michelle interrupted, her eyes soft with understanding. "I know. He was a fucking maniac. But he's gone now. He won't bother us again. Any of us."

Alex smiled and glanced down, meeting Aunt Min's gaze at the foot of her bed.

Suddenly, the door to her room flung open, and Agent Reed entered, wearing a wry grin.

"Well, well. Sleeping Beauty finally graces us with her presence." He chuckled, shaking his head. "You know, if you wanted to skip finals, there are easier ways to go about it than getting shot and falling into a coma."

Despite his light tone, Alex saw genuine relief in his eyes.

"But seriously," he continued. "You had us all worried.

The doctors weren't sure if... well, let's just say we're glad you decided to wake up."

He paused, clearing his throat. "I have to say, that was some quick thinking out there in the field."

She shook her head. "What... do you mean?"

"How you dragged your feet after getting off the bus. We were watching you from the arboretum cameras. I don't know what came over you, but that stunt gave us the time we needed to mobilize our forces. We wouldn't have gotten all those buses there in time if you hadn't slowed them down. Hell, without you, we could be knee-deep in an anthrax nightmare right now."

He nodded and crossed his arms. "Oh yeah, in case you were wondering, we neutralized that nasty shit in Cipher's bag. The brass in Cyber Command are calling the op a success. No one got hurt who didn't deserve it. Well, no one except you and Michelle, that is." He winced.

"Anthrax," Alex mouthed, a pang of guilt shooting through her. Not only had she nearly killed Michelle, but hundreds more could have died due to her mistakes.

"It's not your fault," Aunt Min said, brushing her foot and pulling her eyes to hers. "He was pure evil. He would have hurt anyone who got in his way."

Alex nodded, staring back at her aunt. While she was right, she couldn't help but wonder if some part of that evil lived inside her too. If the darkness that consumed Cipher was a hereditary curse, a ticking time bomb in her own genetic code.

The thought sent a shiver down her spine, a cold, creeping fear that she might one day lose herself to the very thing she'd fought so hard to destroy.

"Next time"—her father's voice drew her from her thoughts—"don't make such a fuss because we missed Parents' Day."

Alex chuckled, meeting his gaze. He seemed to have aged

years since she'd been gone. The worry she'd caused was etched in every line of his face.

Yet he still smiled at her.

"Do me a favor?" he asked.

"Anything," she whispered, her heart clenching at the raw vulnerability in his eyes.

"Stop trying to take on the world by yourself." His words were both a plea and a command. "You're not alone, and you never will be." He glanced over at Michelle and Agent Reed, smiles tugging at their lips. "Something tells me you have more people looking out for you than you realize."

A warmth bloomed in Alex's chest, a sense of love and gratitude that brought fresh tears to her eyes. She smiled back at her father, at her family and friends. A profound peace settled over her for the first time in longer than she could remember.

"I promise... I'll try," she said softly, meaning every word.

And as she lay there, surrounded by the people she loved most in the world, a glimmer of hope stirred in her heart.

Maybe, just maybe, everything *would* be alright.

Even in a world filled with evil, she wasn't alone. Her destiny wasn't set in stone, determined by blood or circumstance. It was a choice, one she made daily.

She had the power to shape her future, to be a force for good. And with her family by her side, she knew she could face any challenge.

Alex was ready to heal, to grow, to become who she was meant to be. On her own terms, with her own strength.

She was never, ever alone.

THE MALE NURSE finished Alex's vitals. As he prepped to

change her bandages, she spotted her aunt approaching and asked to postpone it.

"Hey, Lex," her aunt said, eyeing the nurse. "Should I come back?"

"I'm just finishing up," he said, glancing at Alex. "I'll be back to change that dressing after I finish my rounds. Should be about thirty minutes."

"Thank you," Alex smiled and nodded.

Her voice was much clearer now that she'd sat up and got some fluids and rest.

The past week had taken its toll on her body. With the gunshot wound added to the mix, it wasn't surprising she'd been out for almost two days before waking up that morning.

Aunt Min stepped up beside her, futzing with her pillow.

Alex smirked, gently touching her arm. "They're fine. Really. Why don't you sit down?"

As she went to sit, Alex shifted to face her. "Is everything okay? I thought you were all heading back to the hotel to get some rest."

Aunt Min nodded. "We got about halfway there and I had to turn around. I just..." She glanced down at her hands. "I realized we never had a chance to talk, you know, alone."

Alex stared into her aunt's eyes, overwhelmed with unasked questions.

She didn't know where to start.

"The answer's no," Aunt Min said, her eyes hardening.

"No?" Alex mouthed. "And what was the question?"

"Your mom said she told you about my trip, about my being caught up in layovers."

Alex squinted and shook her head, still not putting together the answer with a question.

"I'm not N3tN1nja," Aunt Min whispered. "But I know who they are. Well, now I do. I had my suspicions, though. My layover confirmed them to be true. It's not every day an online stranger asks you to meet in a nondescript hotel with precise directions on how to lose a tail. When I met them in New York, they told me everything."

She stared down again, fiddling with a golden ring on her thumb, one Alex had never noticed before.

"So, they're fine then? N3tN1nja?" Alex swallowed hard.

Aunt Min's face softened, a smile tugging at her lips. "They're good. Some minor breathing issues from smoke inhalation, but yeah, they'll be fine. Nothing a little rest and relaxation won't fix."

"It's not Professor Newton, is it?"

Aunt Min shook her head, laughing. "No, it's not him. He's with Agent Reed and US Cyber Command. He's doing well, though. Should be out of the hospital today."

Their eyes met, and relief washed over Alex. Knowing the professor and her hacker friend were alright filled her with a renewed peace.

As Aunt Min's words settled, questions bubbled to the surface. She wanted to know more about N3tN1nja, their connection to her aunt, their role in the chaos that had upended her life.

Curiosity burned within her, a desperate need to make sense of it all.

But as she opened her mouth, something stopped her. A quiet voice in the back of her mind urged patience.

There would be time for answers later, when wounds weren't so fresh and scars had begun to heal. For now, she had enough to process.

She reflected on the chaos that led her here. The virus, the North Koreans, the government's role—a tangled web of secrets and lies she was only beginning to unravel.

Suddenly, a thought struck her. "Aunt Min, what about the virus? What's happening with it now?"

Her aunt sighed, weariness creeping into her features.

"Last I heard, it slowed down, but it's still out there, mutating and taking on new forms. Cipher was always good at changing personas; his virus is the same. Plus, the government won't shut it down completely. They're getting too much intel from the North Koreans to pull the plug."

Alex frowned, suspicion nagging at her. "I think there's more to the virus," she murmured. "More that it was doing. I just couldn't figure it out on my own. Not yet, anyway."

Aunt Min raised an eyebrow, a flicker of intrigue crossing her face. But as quickly as it appeared, it vanished. "I'm sure the government has it under control. Cyber Command has experts monitoring the situation."

But Alex wasn't convinced. She'd seen the virus's devastation firsthand, the lives it could destroy. And she suspected the government's priorities weren't always apparent when it came to the greater good.

She shook her head, pushing the thought aside. There'd be time to investigate later, to unravel the virus's mysteries. For now, she needed to focus on recovery, on rebuilding her shattered life.

"Yeah," she said, forcing a smile. "I'm sure you're right. The government knows what they're doing."

But even as the words left her mouth, she couldn't quite believe them.

Instead, her mind grappled with the week's revelations. She found herself thinking back to her admissions essay and the speech she'd given to her high school teachers. Her words about hate being a call to action took on a new meaning now.

She had believed the road to a brighter future lay in reaching out with an open heart, in building a world of love and understanding. But recent events had shown her the complexity of human experience, the shades of gray that existed between right and wrong.

She reflected on the path she'd taken, the anger that fueled her actions, and the revelations about her past. She thought of the virus, the destruction it had caused, and the mysteries still surrounding it.

Her outlook had definitely changed, shaped by the trials she'd faced and the choices she'd made. She'd seen the depths of human darkness, but also the resilience and strength of the human spirit.

Perhaps her speech had been idealistic, envisioning a world not easily attained. But that didn't mean it wasn't worth fighting for.

She'd been forever changed by her experiences, but she refused to let them define her. She'd continue seeking truth, standing up for what was right, and building that world of love and understanding she talked about. She'd just have to do it one small act at a time.

"Tell me," her aunt said, interrupting her thoughts. "Have you considered their offer?"

"Offer?" Alex muttered, her brow furrowed. "What offer?"

Aunt Min looked at her expectantly, then picked up a paper from the end table and passed it to Alex.

As she scanned the document, her eyes widened in shock. Agent Reed must've dropped it off in all the commotion earlier.

It was a letter from Director Williams, offering her a substantial sum of money from funds recovered during the virus op. They were to be used for her education and to ensure her silence on the matter.

"Is this for real?" Alex whispered. "They're just giving me this? No strings attached?"

Aunt Min nodded, smiling slightly. "I think they want to make sure you have the means to pursue your dreams. That, and you agree to keep this ordeal under wraps."

Alex let out a snort, shaking her head in disbelief. "Well, I guess crime does pay," she quipped.

Her aunt chuckled, gently squeezing her hand. "Just don't make a habit of it, okay?"

Alex grinned, feeling a weight lift from her shoulders. The future suddenly seemed a little brighter.

With this money, she could focus on her studies, on building a life beyond the chaos and trauma of the past few weeks.

As she looked up at her aunt, a sense of gratitude washed over her. "Thank you," she said softly. "For everything."

Aunt Min smiled, her eyes twinkling. "I've always got your back, Lex. Always."

With that, Alex settled into her pillows, clutching the letter in her hand. The road ahead wouldn't be easy, but for the first time in ages, she felt a glimmer of hope. And that, she knew, was priceless.

EPILOGUE
ALEX

Alex glanced around the dorm room, taking in the emptiness that once held the chaos of her college life. The walls, now bare, echoed memories of late-night study sessions, laughter-filled movies, and the occasional tear-stained heart-to-heart.

"That's the last of it," Aunt Min said, hefting the final box into her arms. "You sure you don't need any more help?"

Alex shook her head. "I can get the rest. Thanks for helping us move."

Her aunt nodded, a proud gleam in her eye as she made her way out the door.

Michelle stepped forward, pulling Alex into a tight hug. "I can't believe it's over," she muttered.

Alex squeezed back. "It's not over, girlfriend. We're just getting started. Besides, we'll see each other in Cabo this summer, remember?"

Michelle laughed, forcing back a grin. "You better not bail on me, Mercer."

"Wouldn't dream of it," Alex winked.

With a final wave, Michelle followed Aunt Min out, leaving Alex alone in the empty room.

She sighed, running a hand through her hair as she contemplated her offers. Chicago or California? Bank or tech? The future stretched out before her in a dizzying array of possibilities, leaving her unsure which path to choose.

A knock at the door startled her.

Turning, she saw a female messenger dressed in brown from head to toe, envelope in hand. They were staring at her. But that wasn't what caught her off guard. The woman had a strange glimmer in her eye. Almost like she'd been crying.

"Alex... Mercer?" the messenger asked, her voice wavering.

Alex furrowed her brow. "That's me."

The messenger handed her the envelope, their fingers briefly touching.

And then, without a word, she hurried away, leaving Alex staring after them.

"That was weird," she muttered.

Glancing down at the pristine white envelope, she noticed her name printed in a simple font on the front. But there was no indication of who it was from. No return address.

Curiosity got the better of her, and she tore it open, her eyes widening as she retrieved the contents.

It was an acceptance letter, welcoming her to the US Cyber Command Special Operations School—a program she'd never heard of, let alone applied to. And there, listed as her references, were none other than Agent Reed and Director Williams.

Her eyes fell on the logo in the corner of the letterhead—a shield with a microchip etching. The same emblem from the card Agent Reed had given her three years ago, after their hacking incident nearly got her killed and expelled. *Aegis*, she remembered. That was the name he'd whispered to her, a secret not meant for paper.

As she recalled that pivotal event, she noticed a sticky note at the bottom. It was short and written in perfect handwriting:

> *Best of luck, Little Bird*
> *— N3tN1nja*

Alex grinned, a surge of excitement and purpose coursing through her veins.

Maybe, just maybe, her future wasn't limited to two paths.

Maybe it was a journey, a mission, a calling.

And with the support of those who believed in her, she was ready to answer it.

AUTHOR'S NOTE

While the story of Alex, Cipher, and her family is entirely fictional, the virus and all the hacking approaches and technologies used in this book are entirely real. Each of the tools I used are actual Unix commands you can run on your own machine to track network routes, investigate local binaries, and even chat with each other. From the Reveton virus to reverse proxy attacks and the ongoing battles in cyberspace, the topics covered are all legitimate.

Throughout this narrative, I referenced organizations such as the US Cyber Command and technologies like North Korea's Red Star OS. Those aren't figments of my imagination, they're actual entities and software that shape the geopolitical tech landscape. The freedom to choose our operating systems in the United States is a privilege not afforded everywhere in the world. While speculative in nature, the cyber espionage tactics described in this story offer a glimpse into potential real-world digital incursions and defenses.

Cybersecurity is not just the domain of fictional characters or clandestine organizations; it's a critical aspect of our daily lives. One of the simplest yet most effective ways to safeguard your data is to maintain robust backups with multiple copies, both onsite and offsite. Disasters can strike unexpectedly, and the better prepared you are, the more secure you'll be.

In addition to backups, having an antivirus installed and knowing your way around your computer are a must. Awareness of what links to click, which attachments to open, and where to enter sensitive information can significantly reduce your vulnerability to cyber threats. All too often, people are caught off guard, clicking innocuous pop-ups and entering their credentials where they shouldn't. Bad actors are everywhere, and it's important to familiarize yourself with the digital environments we live in every day.

No, I'm really not the best person to teach you these details, but familiarizing yourself with your computer is one of the most crucial skills you can learn.

If you're interested in the topics covered in this book, or just want to learn how to protect yourself, I suggest some extended reading:

- *The Art of Invisibility* by Kevin Mitnick — A guide to protecting your online privacy and security by a world renowned hacker.
- *Ghost in the Wires* by Kevin Mitnick — The true story of a real hacker's adventures.
- *Dark Wire: The Incredible True Story of the Largest Sting Operation Ever* by Joseph Cox — Another great book about hacking and the lengths the FBI went to wiretap the world.
- *Cybersecurity and Cyberwar: What Everyone Needs to Know* by P.W. Singer and Allan Friedman — An accessible overview of cybersecurity issues
- *The Lazarus Heist: From Hollywood to High Finance: Inside North Korea's Global Cyber War* by Geoff White — The jaw-dropping story behind North Korea's dangerous cyber-criminals, the Lazarus Group, who hacked Hollywood and the world.
- *Countdown to Zero Day: Stuxnet and the Launch of the World's First Digital Weapon* by Kim Zetter — The story of Stuxnet, the virus that sabotaged

Iran's nuclear efforts, and its implications for cyber warfare.
- *Permanent Record* by Edward Snowden — The man who risked everything to expose the US government's system of mass surveillance.
- *This Is How They Tell Me the World Ends: The Cyberweapons Arms Race* by Nicole Perlroth — A story about how the US government collected and lost its hoard of zero-day attacks.
- *Ethical Hacking: A Hands-on Introduction to Breaking* by Daniel G. Graham — A hands-on guide to hacking computer systems from the ground up, from capturing traffic to crafting sneaky, successful trojans.
- Official website of US Cyber Command : https://www.cybercom.mil/ — For information about the real-life US Cyber Command and its mission.

THANK YOU FOR READING!

Thank you for joining Alex and her family on this thrilling journey of discovery. I hope you were captivated by the twists, suspense, and the unbreakable bonds of family that carried them through the darkest times.

As this chapter closes, you might wonder what lies ahead for Alex. While I can't reveal too much yet, know that her journey is far from over—she will play a central role in the Aegis series, with the rest of the books promising to be just as thrilling and emotionally charged.

To follow Alex's story and to stay updated on future releases, subscribe to my newsletter at:

swmichaels.com/subscribe

By signing up, you'll be the first to know about new books, exclusive content, and behind-the-scenes insights into my writing process.

If you have any thoughts, questions, or just want to connect, feel free to reach out at:

author@swmichaels.com

I'd love to hear from you. Your support means the world to me.

Once again, thank you for reading this story. I hope it has left you entertained and eager for more. Until next time, happy reading!

ALSO BY S.W. MICHAELS

The Aegis Series
Proxy War (This book)
Prompt Execution

More coming soon...

Books by Other WideAsleep Publishing Authors

SEAN WILLSON
The Portalverse Elemental Origins Series
Drowning Earth
Martian Tide (Novella)
Dead in the Water
Gasping for Air
Trial by Fire

The Dark Nebula Series
Isolation
Discovery
Generations
Beacon
Graveyard
Nursery

ABOUT THE AUTHOR

Even at a young age, I wanted to write, but I never imagined I could actually do it. To say I had self-doubt would be an understatement. While my early forays into the craft began with cutting my teeth on genres like science fiction, the allure of thrillers always called to me like a siren song.

Perhaps it was the result of my early years filled with ups and downs, challenges, and hardships—experiences that taught me the most compelling stories often lurk in the shadows. I learned that even the most dysfunctional people, those who seem hell-bent on self-destruction or pushing away the people who love them, can have a story worth learning from. There's something undeniably fascinating about watching a train wreck unfold, witnessing the slow-motion collapse of a life spiraling out of control.

In crafting my thrillers, I aim to explore the depths of human nature, delving into the psyches of characters who are flawed, broken, and sometimes downright unlikable. Yet, it's their very imperfections that make them so compelling, drawing you in and forcing you to confront the darker aspects of the human experience. It's through the struggles of those characters, their poor choices, and their moments of redemption, that we hold up a mirror to our own lives, reminding us that even in our darkest moments, there is always the potential for growth and change.

While crafting tales in other genres has its own unique challenges, there's something special about writing a thriller that's another level of artistry. It's the thrill of weaving a narrative filled with twists and turns that keep you on the edge of your seat, immersed in the heart-pounding excitement of each story. It's the rush of emotions, the quickening of the heartbeat, the sense that anything can happen at any moment.

As I embark on this new chapter of my writing journey, I'm thrilled to delve deeper into the world of thrillers. My goal is to build a universe of books and standalone novels that will be an experience, one that leaves you breathless and eager for more.

This debut novel marks the beginning of an exciting adventure, and I cannot wait to share more stories that will captivate, thrill, and keep you reading long into the night. Thank you for joining me on this journey, and I hope you enjoy the ride as much as I've enjoyed crafting it.

ACKNOWLEDGMENTS

First and foremost, I want to thank my incredible wife and our three amazing children. You are my rocks, my unwavering support system, and the bright lights that guide me through every day. Your love, patience, and encouragement have been the driving force behind my pursuit of this dream. I dedicate this book to you, as a testament to the power of following your passion and never giving up. I hope that my journey inspires you to chase your own dreams, knowing that you can achieve anything you set your minds to.

To my mother, thank you for instilling in me a love for reading from a young age. Your constant presence with a book in hand during my childhood ignited my imagination and laid the foundation for my own storytelling. Your influence has been instrumental in shaping me into the writer I am today.

I'm grateful to my friends, beta readers, and editors for their support and invaluable feedback. Your insights have refined my craft and kept my creativity flowing. This book wouldn't exist without you.

Finally, to my readers, thank you for taking a chance on me as an author and for joining me on this thrilling adventure. Your support means everything, and I hope my stories continue to captivate you for years to come.

As you embark on your own journeys, always remember that your dreams are within reach. Embrace the challenges, learn from the setbacks, and keep pushing forward. Your perseverance and dedication will lead you to extraordinary places.

www.ingramcontent.com/pod-product-compliance
Lightning Source LLC
LaVergne TN
LVHW090714120525
811014LV00006B/31